D0765322

Bones

# Bones

Franklin Fisher

University of Utah Press
Salt Lake City
1990

Copyright © 1990 University of Utah Press
All right reserved

⊗ The paper in this book meets the standards for perma-
nence and durability established by the Committee on
Production Guidelines for Book Longevity of the Council
on Library Resources

Portions of the novel published previously and subsequently revised are:
"Bones," *South Dakota Review*, Vol. 15, No. 2, Summer 1977, 27–46.
"Flying Things," *Carolina Quarterly*, Vol. 32, No. 3, Fall 1980, 25–43.
"Martyr," *Western Humanities Review*, Vol. 38, No. 3, Autumn 1984,
227–42.

Library of Congress Cataloging-in-Publication Data

Fisher, Franklin, 1939-
     Bones / by Franklin Fisher.
          p.     cm.
     ISBN 0-87480-348-9
     I. Title.
PS3556.I7615B6 1990                                          89-21542
813'.54—dc20                                                 CIP

For my kids

Bones

# 1

Lorin slipped through the hedge in his back yard into the
neighbors' Victory garden, where hidden among vines he slit
open two pea pods with his thumbnail and scooped the peas into
his cupped palm, leaving the shells hanging. In his haste back
through the hedge, his grip loosened and a pea escaped, bouncing across his knuckles and into the wilderness of dead leaves
under the hedge.

He pawed through the leaves but it had vanished, and he
sat paralyzed by complexities. He could return to the vine and
supply his loss, but he knew the thought would nag him that
he might have gone back anyway and thus possessed one more
pea than he had initially. He could of course take two more peas
and accomplish that hypothetical advantage, but how could he
be sure he would not have taken two if he had gone back without losing one, in which case he would still have been one ahead
of the best he could hope for now. The image of that spectral self
dancing just one step ahead of him, better than himself by one
pea that he would be unable to supply though he stripped the
neighbors' pea patch to the roots, was a torture. Worse, to get
even one pea he would have to slit open a new pod, and having
slit a pod, he would have to take all the peas in it because he
could not leave the pod short by one. But taking them all would
leave him no better than he was now, because though he opened
countless pods and removed countless multiples of peas, he
would never have as many as he would have had if he hadn't
lost one.

His mother found him sitting on wet grass under the hedge,
turning over brown thready leaves, sniveling, his mouth full of
chewed peas, unable to explain his tears, which she ascribed to
fear of punishment, which was also true.

He drifted to sleep and felt his bed shaken by something small and old that scuttled away, laughing like a hinge. He drew a picture of it the next day and hid it under a pile of dirty clothes in his bottom drawer. When he came home from school in the afternoon, he found the drawing on top of his bed, pinned to the coverlet, and felt his stomach turn cold. That night his mother came into his room after he was in bed and asked him if he ever played with his penis. He said no. She told him about a boy she had known in school who had gone insane and had to be locked up in the hospital in Provo for the rest of his life, with his arms strapped down. He didn't do it at all, Lorin said. Everyone at school knew why he had gone insane, his mother said. Even the girls. Lorin assured her he never did. Some people went blind, she said. He never would do it either, he promised. She sat crying on the edge of his bed. He lay there with the covers pulled up to his chin, blinking back tears as the ceiling grew dark.

———

His father baptized him in the tiled font next to the recreation hall, triggering a primal memory. He wore white pajamas and his father wore a white suit. The bishop talked with one of the mothers in the front row of folding chairs set up by the font, and there were other parents sitting in other rows with their kids who were getting baptized that night. As he was lowered into the water, the voices suddenly shut off, and he was alone with blue tile and the burn of something chemical in his sinuses, then a distant memory of once wandering out of a door into someone's back yard, down a brick pathway that led past a garage wall with a white trellis, rounding a corner into a garden dense with boysenberries and green vines draped over wires, and startling something that was standing by a hollyhock. It was gone the next instant as he stood there, his feet burning from the bees in the clover, shrieking until people burst into the garden and scooped him off the grass. His father rocked him back and forth and sang "Pony Boy" into his ear. Two women stood laughing by the trellis. It had been taller than he was and had had eyes like spoons. The wet pajamas clung to his body when he came up, and water ran from his nose. His father helped him climb out of the font and patted him on the bottom. He decided he would not mention this memory.

# 2
---

$H$e came home from college in the summer, knowing coming home was a mistake. The bishop called him into his office
and asked him if he'd thought about a mission. He had more than
thought about it; he got attacks of the runs every time the subject came up at home. He did not, however, tell the bishop that.
He told the bishop he had been thinking very seriously about a
mission and had decided that he wasn't entirely sure he was exactly ready yet in every respect altogether.

Would he like to talk about it, the bishop asked.

It was hard to put into words, Lorin said, feeling sweat gleam
on his forehead. It wasn't that his testimony was in trouble or
anything. It was just that he'd begun to realize that testimonies
were more complicated than he'd thought they were when he
was young and innocent, ha ha. He suspected if he went on a
mission right now he would just be going through motions. There
were one or two wrinkles he still needed to iron out in his own
mind. You needed to have a firm grasp on all the implications
of the gospel before you could do a decent job converting other
people. He wouldn't feel intellectually honest if he went right
now, actually.

The bishop asked him if he'd had sexual intercourse.

Well, that was the other thing, Lorin explained, feeling his
body suddenly hollow out. He had, but only once or twice, and
not recently. Once was with a girl last fall after they'd gone to
a movie in Hollywood and afterward gone for a drive in the
mountains in her car and gotten lost and run out of gas and finally ended up at her apartment at dawn because a police car
had picked them up on a private canyon road they had tried to
walk down and she had thought he was mad at her.

The bishop looked at him sadly.

The other time was with a girl he'd met at a party for some foreign students. Actually he'd met her before, but they hadn't come to the party together. There was some folk singing and things had gotten a little rowdy and after everyone had gone they'd found themselves alone in the house and didn't want to leave it unguarded before the owner came back because there were valuable carpets and things in it. They hadn't been drinking or anything.

The bishop took out his pen and played with the clip.

There was actually a third time, Lorin said, if you wanted to count that one, but it was equivocal since they'd heard someone coming up the stairs and stopped before he was finished.

It wouldn't be necessary to explain all this to his parents, the bishop said. They would just say that, after talking about it, they had decided Lorin didn't feel ready for a mission yet. They could talk again when he came home for Christmas. The bishop spread his elbows on the desk, rested his chin on his clasped hands, and gazed at him mildly. Unless Lorin were saying he wasn't interested in going on a mission.

No, no, he wasn't saying that at all, Lorin said, his wool pants itching through the sweat on his legs. He *wanted* to go. He was looking forward to talking about it at Christmas. Christmas would definitely be perfect.

He was so grateful to the bishop for not destroying his parents' peace that his nose ran when they stood up to shake hands, and he left the office making wild promises to himself that he would not get close to a girl who even looked horny between now and Christmas. He would date only Mormon girls for the time being. There were plenty of Mormon girls in Los Angeles.

Explaining the delay in his mission plans to his parents was harder, and Lorin was disappointed that they couldn't be nicer to him, especially in view of the concern he'd had for their peace of mind. His mother cried quietly in her sewing room most of the time, and his father found it convenient not to talk to him except at the dinner table with his sisters and his brother present. The girls wanted to know how come Lorrie wasn't going on his mission like they'd said he was, and Stephen, who was getting to be a mouthy teenager, kept asking why he wasn't going out with chicks while he was home, was he getting queer? It was hard to think of facetious answers with his father staring at him and his mother trying not to cry. His digestion quietly deteriorated through July and August, and he left for school a week early hoping to regain weight before classes started.

Guilt made him reckless, and he got laid by a Mormon girl from the San Fernando Valley, whose fiance was on a mission in France. When he went home to Salt Lake for Christmas, he went skiing both Sundays and alluded vaguely, when anyone asked him, to telephone conversations he had either had or was going to have with the bishop. They would talk for certain at Easter, he said. At Easter, however, he came down with a raging flu in Los Angeles that lasted all week. He described the symptoms to his parents over the telephone, with long pauses to gasp for strength. A friend, he explained, had put off going home herself to nurse him in the apartment she shared with another girl. He did not explain that the other girl had gone home to San Diego. He felt sordid and corrupt afterward, because he had never done it for an entire week before without leaving the house.

——

The last summer he was home his mother cried every time he came in late, and his father bitched that he never talked to them, never bothered telling them what he was doing now, what his plans were when he finished school, acted like a damned distant relative. He realized there wasn't anything he could tell them that wouldn't give them pain. When he began cautiously mentioning Yvonne in his letters home, they didn't ask if she were a member of the church, which relieved him but also made him feel shabby because it meant they now took for granted that he would always hurt them.

——

A little guilt was good because it meant you were considerate.

## 3

A chill crept through his bones when Yvonne decided to move for the third time. This time it was to a bungalow on a narrow side street in West Los Angeles, looking onto a cemetery. She made him go with her to look at it. He had been perfectly happy in her studio apartment in Westwood with the freckled walls and moldy tile in the bathroom; he had also liked the Santa Monica triplex with the grapefruit tree in the back yard and someone's dismantled bicycle tilted against the garage. Lorin was indifferent to these moves himself (except that he couldn't work for a week after each uprooting), but he worried about their implications. Yvonne dreaded moving, he knew, and he also knew she only moved when she was unhappy.

She always brought in friends to help. She threw on old clothes and ran from room to room directing the removal of trunks and packing cases. She laughed hysterically when the bottom fell out of a carton Michael was carrying, spilling shoes and cosmetic cases down the front steps. Scott rolled up her wall hangings. Ken wrapped the small plaster statue of a nursing mother into a nest of blankets and tucked it carefully into the back seat of his Volkswagen. Tom boxed up her stones, her shells, her baskets, and Farley carried her broken and stringless lute like a sick child down to the sidewalk, making a separate trip to bring out the large board on which she had glued and shellacked her reproductions of medieval miniatures.

In the new place she spent hours redistributing her treasures. The castanets and wicker-covered wine bottle went next to the radiator; the clear blue jug with the gilded rose leaning out of it went on the bureau in the bedroom. Lorin, who did not approve of most of her collection, always kept off to one side during her moves, interfering only to the extent of reserving—usually by standing in one place and not moving—some small nook for his easel, his paint case, his table, his portfolios and canvases. If he was going to humor her impulses to find peace with her surroundings, she was going to respect his need for continuity. Besides, he didn't like her friends. Scott and Farley stepped around him, carrying boxes, and talked to him as though they were his friends too, and Ken actually asked his advice about where to put the besom broom and the walnut mirror, but he felt tolerated.

When they were gone he came out of the room he had saved (in this case a step-down screened porch crowded with a wheelbarrow, a lawnmower, and a garden hose coiled on a lawn chair with sun-rotted webbing), rubbing his hands, and gave her a peck on the cheek just as she turned her head away, and he knew he had been a bad sport. He avoided her the rest of the day, humming as he puttered around his tubes and brushes, and smiled mysteriously at her when they met in doorways.

———

He didn't mind her new place. It was dingy and the shower faucet hissed, but it was large. From the front room you had a view of weeds ripening along the base of a cyclone fence across the street, and beyond the fence the rolling lawn with tombstones scattered like teeth, and a line of trees on a distant edge, and beyond the trees, on clear days, the gentle blue peaks of the Santa Monica Mountains. Once the newness wore off, he found he could work very well here. He drove her into Westwood Village each morning (he needed to keep the car in case of emergencies) and dropped her off at the bookstore where she worked and from where she would walk up to the dance studio on campus in the late afternoon for her class. He returned to the bungalow and spent the day at the easel, drinking quarts of coffee as the shadows of the pitosporum that grew outside the screen crept across his slab floor. Sometimes he went out to visit friends. At five-thirty he picked her up from the dance studio, and they ate dinner by candlelight on whatever she was able to throw together with leftovers in the refrigerator or what they had picked up from the delicatessen on the way home. After that they went their separate ways again, she back to the university for rehearsal, Lorin to the Blue Couch, which was open only at night.

They had been living together since October, and he had the guilt under control now. The Blue Couch didn't pay much, but with her small salary, supplemented by the pittance sent by her parents to an old address she did not tell them she had moved from (a friend lived there now), they might have been very comfortable in their little nest facing the cemetery.

It was hard to define what was wrong. Lorin prided himself on being understanding and not asking questions. Usually he knew what she was unhappy about. Last time it had been the quarrel with her parents, during a visit to Riverside, that had deepened the estrangement. The time before it had been the reappearance in town of an old lover, who had happened into the bookstore. Lorin had learned about that through a casual remark by Andrea when the three of them were having lunch at the Hamburger Hamlet. Yvonne had cut her off, and Lorin had pretended not to notice her white face or Andrea's embarrassed eyes. This time he couldn't think of anything to blame it on, and he woke each morning sick with dread.

She was becoming strenuously cheerful in his company. She laughed helplessly at his jokes, sometimes leaning against a wall with her arms clasped to her sides. When they made love she no longer bothered with preliminaries. He walked into the living room their second night in the bungalow and found her sitting on the floor looking preoccupied, only to brighten when she saw him and asked him if he were prepared to have all the clothes torn from his body. In bed she bit and clawed. She cried out "Love me! Love me!" at the very moment he was doing the best he could. She screamed when she came and sobbed with pleasure afterward. He surprised her at work the next day and found the ashtray on her desk filled with lipstick-smeared stubs. Normally she smoked only at parties, and then only if there was guitar music on the record player. He could not bring himself to ask her if there were something she wanted to tell him. If she had started to volunteer the information, he would have run from the room with his hands over his ears, singing at the top of his voice.

——

Except that the neighborhood made him nervous, Lorin liked his job at the Blue Couch. A lot of his customers were from UCLA, and though he disliked most of them personally, it pleased him that he was mixing with West Coast intellectuals and that his friends in Utah would not recognize him. He liked it that a half-dozen of his paintings hung on the walls and people looked at them. Malcolm had a low response to the visual arts but had said it was all right when Lorin had asked if he and a few friends could hang their stuff in the Blue Couch. It would give the place the look of a little gallery, Lorin said, maybe bring people back who wouldn't come back just for the capuccinos he made, ha ha.

Malcolm lived over an empty synagogue on a condemned block in Santa Monica. He had quit the doctoral program in anthropology at UCLA and had started a poetry magazine called

Dragon Wyck, for which he wrote most of the copy himself and printed on his own offset press and distributed at irregular intervals at second-hand bookstores near the beach. His father was a patent attorney in White Plains, who sent his son money so he would stay in Los Angeles. Malcolm had rented space formerly occupied by a dry cleaner's and furnished it with tables and chairs from flea markets and a long blue couch from the lobby of a hotel that was being torn down on Wilshire. He'd found a cash register in an antique store in El Segundo. A little carpentry work, which he had done himself, had provided a counter behind which he had fitted a used gas stove and refrigerator. He had also built a fake fireplace that stood like an island in the middle of the room, extending to the ceiling. Lorin had painted used bricks on the sheetrock over the fireplace.

The Blue Couch shared a block with a carburetor shop and a mission with a blue neon cross that flickered and hissed at night. There was always glass in the street. Lorin parked in back beside the dumpster and went in the kitchen door to avoid yoohoos from the bar across the street. He made sandwiches and espresso and carried them to tables, and when it wasn't busy sat and talked with people he knew. When there was a poetry reading he saw that the bolts were tight on the platform the poet stood on. He paid the folk singer out of the till. He changed records on the hi-fi. He looked at his paintings and then looked at everyone else's.

———

It was little things—a furtive look when she lay curled on the bed and opened her eyes and discovered he had been watching her. It was a loose scrap of blue paper that fluttered out of her notebook that she grabbed and put back before he could recover it for her and wasn't there when he leafed through the notebook later after she was asleep. He heard the phone ring one rainy Sunday when he was working on the screened porch, and he heard her feet pounding across the bedroom floor and into the hallway to reach it before he did. When he wandered in a few minutes later, cleaning his brush with a rag, she was reading in the beanbag chair and didn't mention the call, though he stood around cleaning his brush for several minutes. One night in bed he accidentally touched her foot while she was asleep, and she moved it away. The next night he did it on purpose, and she moved it away again. He got out of bed and slept on the couch, and the next morning she did not ask him why.

———

He went around the house collecting objects for the still-life he was going to give to a musician friend if it turned out well. He prowled corners and drawers and closets, stepping over Yvonne, who sat on the bedroom floor changing the bandages on her toes.

"Perhaps I'm in your way," she said.

He carried likely objects to his screened porch and laid them out on the floor in the yellow glare of the overhead light until he thought he had enough, and then stepped back to look at them. The selection of your material was less important than what you did with it, but you didn't want to waste time finding out you were trying to do two different paintings on the same canvas. He discarded a brass doorknob and the bicycle seat he'd found under the steps, and, after thinking about it for a minute, he also took away Yvonne's hair dryer with its pink plastic bonnet and the old pair of wing-tip shoes he had ruined when he had chased a girl named Phyllis into the water during a party at someone's beach house last year and left them in front of the fireplace all night to dry.

What he had in mind, he thought, was a study of imitations of life as metaphors for music. He dragged over the cane-backed chair he had purchased at a discount house on Olympic Boulevard over Yvonne's protests that it was awful as well as badly made. He spread a dark green paisley cloth, spotted with paint, over the chair, exposing part of the curved back with its corkscrew of unraveling straw, and propped the lute upright against one of the arms. He wasn't sure where she'd gotten the lute. It was actually only the corpse of a lute; it had no strings, its rose had been broken out, leaving a wounded mouth in the belly, and it was missing all but three of its tuning pegs. He placed the basket with a doll's head peering over the edge on the table next to the chair. The basket was the varnished hide of an armadillo lying on its back with its tail in its mouth. His father had brought it back from his mission in Venezuela and had given it to Lorin when Lorin became a deacon. He hesitated over the plaster foot because he had taken it from the supply room in the art department a couple of years ago, and someone might recognize it in the painting and ask him to return it. He could think of several people who were self-righteous enough to say something. On the other hand, he would be through with it by then. He heard her come to the doorway behind him and stop.

"Perhaps you're deep in thought," she said.

He put the foot on the chair in front of the lute and tilted the tin rooster against it, then changed his mind and put the foot on the part of the paisley that spilled onto the floor, anchoring a second center of interest. He didn't know what to do with the rooster, so he left it leaning against the basket to decide about later. The rooster was from a weather vane on a barn in Randolph. He had recovered it from a pile of rotted siding the summer his cousin had torn the barn down. After a minute he heard her go away. He carried a low footstool to the right side of the chair and put the stuffed caiman on it, and propped his charcoal self-portrait at an angle beside it. Someone in his life-drawing class had asked him why he'd forgotten the crown of thorns, so he was going to use the self-portrait ironically. He had mounted it on a piece of tagboard and kept it in the back of a closet until now. The lamp that was a girl in a gold dress with a light socket coming out of her head seemed too big to go next to the statue of the nursing mother, but he was running out of spaces, so he left them on the table beside the armadillo basket for now, and wedged the chrome coffee pot between them to reflect the doll's head and create one more level of reality within the composition.

Stepping back to look at it, he had to admit the arrangement looked arbitrary. He tilted the self-portrait against the golden-girl lamp and put the lute on its back on the floor and the plaster foot on the arm of the chair. He heard Yvonne trying to be very quiet in the kitchen. He transposed the coffee pot and the tin rooster and tipped the nursing mother, head and baby down, against the footstool. He wondered what she was doing in the kitchen and why she didn't come back out to see what he was doing. He felt the tight knot of panic that always came when he realized the possible combinations were infinite and he would never see them all and would never know if the next one would have been the right one.

He stood with his hands in his pockets and listened to street noises through the block and a distant conversation in someone's back yard. He reflected that the arrangement in front of him was only a mnemonic anyway. The real organization would occur during the act of painting because art created its own inevitabilities. He pulled the chain on the overhead light and went off to find her. She was still in the kitchen, standing at the sink and eating one of the sandwiches she had made to take for her lunch the next day.

"You probably don't feel like messing around right now," he said.

"I believe I could be talked into it," she said.

"Don't let me interrupt anything you'd rather be doing," he said. She was always embarrassed when he caught her with food in her mouth.

# 4

Simon took them to dinner at his parents' house in West
Hollywood. Lorin tried to appear unimpressed. The house rose
above the trees on a hillside, overlooking a vast basin of lights.
Dinner was served on the terrace. Lorin, who prided himself on
being charming to older women, talked to Simon's mother and
tried to keep her from seeing the bronze fingerprints he had left
in his napkin from the duck, which he had never eaten before.
She was, it turned out, an alarming woman. She shrieked when
he reached for the basket of rolls and then handed it to him herself, laughing merrily at her overreaction. "I didn't tell you about
Simon's sister, did I?" she asked, looking suddenly tragic. "Last
year they picked her up in a knife fight with another girl at her
high school. Two years ago she got pregnant." Simon's mother
began to cry.

"How terrible," said Yvonne, reaching across the table to put
a hand on Simon's mother's fist.

"She was going to give it away for adoption but she had a
miscarriage first. Ever since she's had a great sadness."

"This is very kind of you to have us for dinner," Lorin said.

She lifted her shoulders. "Simon's friends. What can I say?"

"You have a lovely house," Yvonne said.

"I wish you would have seen the Chinese vase before we
got rid of it."

"Instead, tell them about the fruit trees Dad planted," Simon said from the other end of the table, snickering in a cloud
of Turkish smoke.

"Never mind that," Simon's father said.

"I hate those trees," Simon's mother said. "Around the pool
looks like duck shit."

"I don't want to hear about it," Simon's father said.

Simon's father played gangsters and insane scientists. In seventh grade, Lorin had seen him in a jungle movie as a leather-faced white hunter who loses his nerve. He had also played a Jewish chief of detectives whose men don't respect him until the stakeout, during which he's killed covering one of them. After that they know they've been blind. He had also been a newspaper editor whose office gets smashed and whose head is beaten bloody—Lorin still remembered the clots in his white hair—by a mob enraged at the paper's call for restraint in the face of something or other. Lorin had not known these people were all the same person until Yvonne told him. They didn't look alike and none of them looked like Simon's father. The first time he had met Simon's father, he was reduced to shuffling wordlessness. He wondered how many other times he had seen the face in front of him and not known he had seen it before.

Simon's mother had played bobby-soxer roles in a few movies before sacrificing her career for her family. She mentioned that several times during the evening.

"Let's go back to my place and role-play my parents," Simon said as they were going out to the cars.

"I thought your parents were charming," Yvonne said.

Lorin thought disrespect of that kind was unbecoming.

———

In bed, Yvonne told him that everyone knew Simon had been seduced when he was thirteen by the girl who came in to clean. "They had this wonderfully sordid intrigue that went on for months," she said. "What stopped it was when Simon's mother burst in on them in Simon's bedroom with a butcher knife and threatened to cut off his penis."

"Good Lord," said Lorin, who was always excited when Yvonne talked about penises.

## 5

*I*t was while sweating naked in a dark room after making love that you wondered how you would feel if the telephone rang and your father told you your mother had just died. You stared at the silhouette of the ripped awning outside the window and the leaves masking the streetlight across the road by the cemetery, and you could hear your mother's voice in your ear. It said, "Oh, Lorin." It was a disappointed voice, weary from having read you stories at bedtime when you were small and wore jammies to bed. You turned on your side and curled up, wishing that Yvonne were not lying there next to you breathing like a percolator and apt to wake up if you twisted around too much. The guilt was more controllable, he had noticed, while you were still horny. The instant you exploded, you knew you had let everybody down. You lay there in the dark with your thoughts, and your hand stole to your dick and closed around it, and you promised yourself it would never rise again.

Trying not to jiggle the bed, he moved as far away from Yvonne as he could, so that if she woke up she would know he was avoiding her, and counted the ways he was not happy. Something terrible was happening to them, and he didn't know what it was. That was one thing. Another was that she seemed not to understand the importance of foreplay. Lorin was too embarrassed to say so, but he could imagine foreplay lasting all night and resuming after breakfast. Another thing was that he was using too much palette knife. He was too preoccupied to concentrate, so he was taking the easy way out. His angel on a motorcycle looked glib, and so did his three grey-haired men looking at a headstone. These were both hanging in the Blue Couch, and his friends had been polite about them. That was another thing. It was all right for Pavel to drip Russian-Jewish weltschmertz all over his pictures. If your work was any good, Pavel said, it came out of the pain of your cultural memory-traces. But when Lorin used motifs out of Mormon folklore, he got patronized.

That was another thing. He hated telling people he was from Utah and waiting for the next question. Sometimes he said no, and then added that he was kind of an ancestral Mormon; but then they looked at him oddly, and he had to explain that what he meant was a cultural Mormon, ha ha. By that time they had lost interest, and he felt stupid.

He turned over, forgetting for the moment that Yvonne was in the way. Their knees bumped and she sat up, her eyes wide and alarmed in the dim light from the street. Then she fell back down and turned over, dragging the covers over her shoulder. He lay on his back and stared at the black mirror on the closet door across the room. You didn't want to forget that you were a cultural Mormon, because your heritage defined you and fed your art. His heritage happened to include survivors and buried records from ancient civilizations. It included transparent rocks used to translate unknown writings and find lost cattle. It included spirit matter that ran along your nervous system like electrical impulses and was transmissible by touch. It included devils and angels walking the earth like people, and visits from the dead. He didn't exactly believe these things, but they provided him with metaphors.

He didn't quite believe, for instance, the family story about his great-grandmother seeing the apparition of her daughter in the kitchen, but he was glad everyone else in his family did. Lorin had admired his great-grandmother when she was alive, even though her wrinkled bristly little face had put him off. She was a tough Yorkshirewoman who had converted in her teens and emigrated to Utah, where she had married her sister's husband and had had lots of children, and had still mowed her own lawn at ninety. Her life had been governed by gritty practicalities. She had scrubbed floors in county schoolhouses and taken in boarders. She was not fanciful and had no patience with people who were, and on a wet spring morning in 1904 she had come out of the bedroom in the house in Randolph that she shared with her husband on alternate weeks and had seen her oldest daughter, dead seven years, standing in the doorway to the kitchen, smiling at her. He would like to see Pavel match that with his cultural memory-traces. He felt Yvonne turn over and waited to see if she was going to put a hand on him in her sleep. Sometimes she did.

His great-grandmother didn't scream or faint when she saw

the kid standing there, but she did drop the thundermug she was carrying out to empty. When Lorin's great-grandfather came by a few minutes later from the adjacent house, he found her on her knees scrubbing the carpet while a half-circle of night-shirted children stood watching her. She told him about the thunder-mug, and then—after sending the children back upstairs—about the visitation.

He thought about it for a minute then went outside, where he examined the spongy ground on both sides of the boardwalk leading from the kitchen door to the coalhouse. There were, of course, footprints. There were always footprints. He had gotten twelve children on her body and was to get two more before dying of a pleurisy in 1910, and footprints were everywhere, criss-crossing each other like strings of ants from the kitchen door to the gate, from the pump to the coalhouse, crowding and mashing each other along the edge of the boardwalk, stamped into wet leafmold under the cottonwood. He peered into the lilacs, inspected the coalhouse and the privy, walked around the house three times, the third time suddenly doubling back and racing across his own footprints, and finally went back inside, where Lorin's great-grandmother was sponging up the last of her mop water.

It was time, he said, to exercise his priesthood and call on the Lord for an explanation. They gathered the children, who had crowded at two windows to watch, and knelt in a circle in the front room for family prayer, into which he worked ambiguous language that wouldn't scare them. He thanked the Lord for the many and divers blessings they all enjoyed, for the strength to walk in the ways of righteousness, for their health, for the gospel. Then he asked that their spiritual eyes be opened to know the meaning of the blessed visit that had just been vouchsafed them. After a long silence he looked at his wife and said the Lord chose to keep his own counsel. The children were disappointed. So was Lorin.

They never did find out what she had come for, and Lorin's great-grandmother never forgave herself for losing control and dropping the thundermug and breaking the connection. One minute the girl—she had died at fourteen, during a diphtheria epidemic in Randolph—had been standing there, her thin little hands folded across the front of her dress, smiling, showing gums, and the next minute only shadows and dapples of sunlight moved in the doorway.

He was starting to stir from looking at Yvonne's exposed back and turned over so she wouldn't think he wanted to make love again. He also didn't believe, except in spirit, that his black-sheep great-uncle, now dead, had been visited in 1919 by a mysterious person who had dictated a melody to him and vanished without a trace, even though the alternative was to believe that the great-uncle, who could not read music, had composed a hymn out of thin air in the Phrygian mode. This great-uncle had owned the barber shop and soda fountain in Randolph and was the family embarrassment. He drank, it seemed, and was said to visit brothels in Evanston. He had lived in a peeling house next door to the barber shop with a wife whose eyes were always red and a number of children who turned out poorly. He had a fine voice within a narrow middle range, A-flat to E above middle C, and he played by ear a small melodeon that he kept in a corner of the living room and forbade his wife or children to touch. He had been one of the night-shirted children who watched their mother mop up the thundermug spill, had gone to hell in his teens, and by his middle years had become a fixture in Randolph, smoking his pipe in his undershirt and swearing at the neighbors who passed his front porch on Sunday mornings on their way to church. He abused his wife, who complained to the bishop. The bishop spoke gently to the uncle; the uncle slapped the wife around, dared the bishop to excommunicate him, and told his old mother that everything they told her about him was lies. It broke his mother's heart, but in the end he was, like her, to know a prodigy.

He was asleep one night, the story went, and woke to the sound of something creeping through the trash on the floor. His wife slept in a different room, so he was alone. He opened one eye and felt his heart stop. A man had just come out of the wall, carrying a brass horn. It was a young man, with reddish hair, frayed around the ears, and a thick lower lip. He was picking his steps through the litter of newspapers, rags, bottles, and plates of dried food toward the bed. Lorin's great-uncle curled into a tight ball and yelled, "I won't stop you! Take everything!"

The man kicked aside a bottle and sat down in the chair next to the bed. Without looking at Lorin's great-uncle, he put the horn to his lips, puffed his cheeks once or twice, took a deep breath, and began to play. The horn was curled into an oblong spiral with four valves and a wide bell, which he held between his knees. His face was scarlet except around the lips, where it was white. Lorin's great-uncle was terrified to be in the same room with a lunatic housebreaker, but had the presence of mind to realize that this melody bought him time, and began to listen very closely. The tune was in a minor key, whose second scale degree was flatted—that much he recognized at once. It was melancholy, but with a lilt that carried you over rises and around sharp corners where the time signature changed, across grassy meadows where the heart broke. It was stepwise and singable, except for an ugly passage of consecutive fourths that it escaped by chromatically altering the last note and recovering the dominant by surprise.

Quivering under his blanket, Lorin's great-uncle followed every dip, pursued every melodic inversion, hummed in his mind the top note of a steep climb that the player, his face dark with the strain, could not reach, followed as it tumbled down metallic stairs to a vestibule where the color changed briefly, turned dark, and at last tiptoed three whole steps up and stopped. The man lowered the horn, sank back into his chair and contemplated the far wall. "Please don't kill me," said Lorin's great-uncle.

The man stood up, cast him a pale glance, and began to dissolve. Lorin's great-uncle didn't want to watch this, but he was too frightened to close his eyes. The man's fingertips began to run and presently resolved themselves into the strings of goo that had hardened months ago on the wall after dripping from the impact. The partitioned quarters of his face separated into the corner of a picture frame, a torn edge of wallpaper, the wrinkled flue of a heating stove where it bent to enter the ceiling, and a pale blue eye that burned cold against the top panel of the door. His high collar and frock coat hardened into moonlight etched with shadows of spattered mud on the window, and the coat's buttons flitted back and forth over the garbage, droning frantically. The horn had uncurled and now proceeded smoothly down the wall ahead of a silvery trail, its soft little valves veering gently left and right.

Lorin turned over to see if Yvonne was by any chance awake. Sometimes her sleep cycles were uneven, and she would wake in the middle of the night and want to make love and would not remember it the next day. Her eyelids, however, did not twitch in the gray light. He turned over again, his back to her. His great-uncle did not open his confectionery or his barber shop the next day. He remained in his house with the doors locked while his wife crept from room to room, wringing her hands and listening to the melodeon as he picked out notes and discarded them until an angular little tune she had never heard before gradually evolved; whereupon he would shake his head, get up and pound his fist into the wall, sit down, and start again. By midnight, having eaten nothing all day but drunk an alarming amount, he had reconstructed the melody and was ready for vindication.

He burst from his house, stumbling down the broken porch, and careened down the town's main street toward the bishop's house, where he beat on the door. The bishop received him mildly despite the hour but Lorin's great-uncle had come not to submit but to gloat. Pushing past the bishop he entered the small dining room and sat down at the upright piano, on which, with two unsteady fingers, he picked through the melody that by now was burned onto his brain. "Ever heard it before?" he asked. The bishop shook his head. "All right, listen again," said Lorin's great-uncle, and played it again, this time adding tentative harmonies with his left hand. "Sure you've never heard it before?" he asked. The bishop was sure. "It's pretty, though, Earl," he said. "You make it up yourself?" "No I did *not* make it up myself!" said Lorin's great-uncle, reeling on the piano bench, hugging himself. *"Now* listen."

In a voice hoarse with the day's abuse he sang the words to "Though Deepening Trials Throng Your Way," following not the melody in the Deseret Hymn Book but the melody revealed to him in the night. When he had finished he stood up and jabbed a finger into the bishop's chest. "What do you think of that, you sanctimonious tit-wringer?" he said. The bishop, who ran a hard-scrabble dairy farm at the edge of the county, did not have much use for music—that is, he had no strong opinion one way or another (the battered upright in his house was played by his twelve-year-old daughter who had never gotten past "The Happy Farmer" and who now stood with her grim and curlered mother at the door to the dining room)—but he was uncomfortable hearing a hymn sung to the wrong tune. "I said it was pretty, Earl," he said. "Where did you hear it?" "An angel gave it to me," said Lorin's great-uncle, and pushed past him and went out the door.

The story and its implications—angels appeared to scoffers—spread through the town like a stain. Lorin's great-uncle, his affable self once again, returned to his normal patterns of life, humming his strange tune as he clipped hair or measured out jellybeans, the thick veins on his nose bright with the complacency of a secret he would share if you asked him nicely. Drink finally rotted his brain, and Lorin remembered him as a very old man, drooling in a nursing home in Ogden before he died, his one touch with the other world the last light to fade. He hummed bits and pieces of his little tune to the very end to anyone who would listen, and he always asked you if you wanted him to tell you where he'd gotten it.

Lorin pulled back the sheet and looked at Yvonne, who groped for it without waking. The tune existed. Someone in Randolph had written it down, and the transcription, yellow and cracked, lay in the genealogy files of Lorin's great-uncle's youngest daughter, who had never married and who rarely showed it to anyone because she thought it was not very good.

As an artist, you liked having stories like that as part of your heritage. They told you it could be true even if you didn't believe it.

# 6

Normally it gave him pleasure, at the beginning of a working day, to look at his tubes lodged away in their compartments
inside his case, the newer ones plump and dimpled, the old ones
curled like scorpions. Ordinarily he liked to run his collection of
brushes through his fingers, sort out the wide ones from the narrow ones, and rummage through the stumps of charcoal, dis-
colored fragments of chalk, the roll of packaging tape that had
gotten wet and could not be unrolled, the pencils, the tablespoon
he used to pry open his can of white lead. Today he turned over
his tubes and brushes and put them down like an apple sorter
looking for worms, conscious that he had already missed the
pleasure he always got from the rush of smells when he first
opened his case in the morning. He squeezed burnt orange, virid-
ian emeraud, cerulean, Chinese red onto the hospital tray he used
for a palette, without caring whether he would use them or not.
He dashed out sullen shapes at scattered intervals across the
canvas—an orange caiman, a blue lute, a nursing mother thrust
head first under the arm of the wicker chair. He brushed in a back-
drop of flaming red around the negative space he was saving for
the rooster. He sketched an ugly girl in green, with a light bulb
floating out of her mouth.

He couldn't stand it and left his brushes to soak while he
drove back to the Village. In the bookstore he browsed the re-
maindered table, examined the coffee-table books, eased over to
the racks of calendars, then began a systematic inspection of the
biography shelves. He had not seen her at her desk when he had
passed the office. She was not on the floor helping customers.
He thought about asking a clerk to check the ladies' room for him
but decided not to call attention to himself. He edged to the iron
staircase and when no one was looking slipped behind the cur-

tain into the stockroom, where only employees were allowed. She
was sitting at a long wooden table, studying her check register.
Unopened cartons of books lay on the floor beside her. He cleared
his throat, and she stared at him as though trying to think where
she knew him from.

"I was in the neighborhood," he said.

"I worked two jobs all last summer, and I'm working this
one now, and I only have two hundred and sixteen dollars," she
said. She looked on the edge of tears. She had not said she was
happy to see him.

"I didn't mean to barge in," he said. "I just wanted to say
hello."

"Lorin, what am I going to do?"

"Can you ask for a raise?"

She folded her arms on the table and put her head down on
them.

"Maybe I can ask Malcolm for more hours," he said.

"Why am I doing this?" she asked. "Why am I killing
myself?"

He thought about telling her he was not in such good shape
himself, but that would sound competitive.

"Maybe we can talk about it at dinner," he suggested. "Think
about alternatives." He wasn't sure what he meant.

"Food," she said. She sat up and looked at him. "I haven't
eaten lunch."

"You'll feel better after you've eaten," he agreed.

He stood looking at her earlobe. She turned the pages of her
check register. She was obviously waiting for him to leave.

"Um," he said.

"How can I have only two hundred and sixteen dollars after
last summer?" she said.

"Maybe there's something else on your mind," he said.

"What?"

"I mean I understand about buyer's remorse."

She put her hands in her lap and looked at him for a long
time.

"If you follow what I'm saying, of course," he added.

"Perhaps you're being mysterious," she said.

"I'm talking about buyer's remorse. You know what buyer's
remorse is."

"Perhaps we can discuss this another time," she said. "Alan
is going to come looking for me."

"You do know what I'm talking about, don't you?"

"Perhaps if I think about it all afternoon it will come to me,"
she said.

"I just want you to know I'm open to discussion," he said.

Back home, he drifted around the house looking at studies he had done of her. A profile in leotard and white leg-warmers, sitting on the floor with her back to the wall, hung over the radiator. A charcoal rendering of her face asleep hung over the sink in the bathroom. A pencil drawing of her sitting in the bathtub, shy and vulnerable, hung in the kitchen. A sequence of fast pen-and-ink sketches he had made when he had gone with her to a rehearsal lined the hallway. He had done those while sitting in a corner of the studio in a black depression from seeing her handled by men in tights. He untied his portfolio and sat in the beanbag chair in the living room turning over drawings on the floor, admiring his way with an elbow, a knee, the hollow of a groin. He imagined her improvising in one of the rehearsal rooms at the university, naked as a sunbeam, alone except for the shadowy man who sat at the piano controlling her moods by chromatic shifts and changes of tempo. He imagined her bathing with the shadowy man afterward, the two of them face to face in a claw-footed tub like the one in the triplex, sharing private jokes while she soaped his rigid prick where it broke through the water between them.

His stomach was burning by the time he went to pick her up. Instead of going into the women's gym and waiting in the lobby in front of the dance studio he sat outside on a bench under a eucalyptus and a few minutes later watched her come out and stand on the steps, looking around her. She descended two more steps and bent to look across the tennis courts at the narrow road that led down from the lot he always parked in. He was in plain sight, but she couldn't seem to look in the right place. That made him angry. She set her basket down and pulled back a sleeve to examine her watch. She stared into the distance between the men's gym and the grassy slope, as if trying to remember if there were something different about today that she had forgotten. A man came down the steps behind her, and she turned and said something to him. He evidently said something funny because she put a hand on his wrist, and they both laughed. She would suffer for that. The man continued down the steps and she ran back up them and disappeared inside, returning a few minutes later to stand on the step second from the top, a hand on her hip. She turned and paced to the end of the step, swinging her basket at her side, spun around and paced back the other way, and stopped short when she saw him. She tilted her head, paused, and then ran down the steps and across the lawn toward him. She ran clumsily. That pleased him.

"Blending into the old shrubbery, are we?" she said.

"Just checking how noticeable I am," he said.

"Ready to go?" she asked. She knew she had been seen. You could tell when they ignored your innuendos. He stared past her at the steps she had come down, where she had trifled with somebody else's wrist. She turned to see what he was looking at, and he stood up and started walking across the lawn.

"Wait!" she said.

He kept slightly ahead of her all the way to the car. At the delicatessen he stood off to one side while she paced back and forth in front of the glass case. He answered her questions about preferences with grunts. He didn't say anything when the cashier, looking innocently over her head while spilling change into her hand, shorted her and she didn't notice. Back in the car she looked at him quizzically, but he put his head out the window to watch for a clear space in the traffic before pulling out. At the house he ate his corned-beef sandwich and pickle in silence, looking at her earlobe when he had to look at her at all. She had not once asked him why he had waited outside the gym instead of coming in as he always did.

"Some more wine, perhaps?" she said.

"Why not?" he said, looking at his glass.

"Why not indeed?" she said, and poured it.

He drank it and stared at the stem of his glass. If she wasn't going to ask him what was wrong, that was going to be her problem, he had decided.

Was he planning to romp down to the old Blue Couch tonight? she wondered.

Grunt.

She begged his pardon?

Yes. Yes, he was planning to romp down to the old Blue Couch tonight. He romped there most nights. In fact it was sort of expected of him. It was not much of a place, in fact you wouldn't want your sister to go there, but his employer, not to mention his customers, would be disappointed if he didn't put in an appearance, so yes he was going to romp right on down.

She had left the room during the part about not wanting your sister to go there and now returned carrying a fresh leotard which she folded up very small and placed in the bottom of a large woven bag with handles and a drawstring. "I wonder," she said, "if while you're getting ready to romp down you might perhaps drive me back to school. Andrea can bring me home. I'll probably be late."

"Why not?" he said. Andrea usually drove her out, too. Exactly what Andrea's problem tonight was he would not ask, not if he were standing on hot coals.

He drove her back to the university at breakneck speed, speaking only to swear at every red light. He let her out at the parking circle without a word, and she ran away across the lighted grass toward the gym without looking back. To punish her he did not go directly to the Blue Couch but drove to the beach and sat on cold sand for an hour watching green breakers. He left when three Mexican teenagers in leather jackets came up and asked him if he was a beatnik.

———

While delivering a club sandwich and two orders of onion rings, he saw the girl who had come in with Simon and Harry get up and go to the row of paintings on the far wall, where the booths were, and pay close attention to his study of Yvonne. He went back to the kitchen, his heart pounding, and returned carrying two capuccinos and a mocha parfait which he delivered to the booth she had been standing beside, but she had moved on and was inspecting one of Pavel's acrylics. He stalled for a minute, talking to the couple who had ordered the capuccinos, while he watched to see what she thought of it. He was too polite to say so, but he had always thought Pavel's work had too much second-hand Kokoschka in it. This one was an interior of a room, and everything flickered and twitched and suggested swirls of spiritual forces. She didn't spend much time on that one, he noticed. She moved to one of Noel's double self-portraits and studied it with her mouth open. Noel was clever, you had to give him that. He was pushing himself in a baby pram in this one. The figures were carefully modeled, and there was hardly a visible brush stroke. The pram was on a tennis court, which was an arbitrary and slightly dishonest fillip since it implied a dramatic context that wasn't compositionally necessary. She spent a little longer checking that one out. With Noel's work you were never sure you weren't being tricked.

He was running out of things to say to Helen and Brock, but fortunately she had gone on to the next one. This was another of Noel's, not a bad one, in fact he even liked it, though it was derivative. The boy was delicately rendered to the point of transparency, lying on his elbows on a mottled red carpet. All that was lacking was the harlequin suit. She didn't seem to care for it, and went on to Harry's heap of shimmering dead fish at the edge of a shimmering table. Lorin guessed that everyone had to go through an expressionist phase. You let hundreds of nervous brushstrokes fill up the stretches of canvas you didn't know what to do with, and you had saved yourself the ordeal of choosing between space and form. Harry would probably invent the Blue

Rider school next. She examined that one longer than she needed to, but then he saw by the way her eyes moved that she was counting the fish heads. She paused briefly to look at the potted palm that stood dying in the corner and picked off a brown spear which she rolled between her thumb and fingers while slowly walking the length of the adjoining wall. She passed by Lorin's "Moroni on a Motorcycle," which was just as well—it was smart-ass and the patchy beard on the angel's face showed the worst excesses of palette-knife technique. She stopped in front of an odd little oil sketch by Simon of a black hunched bird perched on a fishnet, with what looked like mussel shells over its eyes. That one amused her, and so did Noel's street scene next to it, consisting of warped skyscrapers floating in a pale amber sky as though in a concave mirror. Another of Lorin's—three bent old men in a churchyard who were Nephites but looked like trolls because no one but himself knew what a Nephite was—got a longer inspection, but he could see by the way she brushed her hand down the back of her hair that she was bored. She stepped as though to look at the next one and discovered she had come to the door of the john. She turned, smiling at her silly mistake, and then after wavering for an instant went back to look at Lorin's Yvonne again, and he couldn't stand it any longer.

This was a study he was especially pleased with, even though Yvonne had hated it. She was naked, stretched on her back across an unmade bed, sunlight from the window glistening on her body like sheets of gold. Her eyes were closed, and a knee was drawn up. Because he had done it as a surprise for her birthday he had had to work from rehearsal photographs. The ecstatic face he wanted had come from the picture snapped at the instant she had jammed her toe against the piano in the rehearsal room at the university. The arched back was from a shot, turned side-ways, of her standing at the edge of the stage curtain, prepared to fling an arm toward the handsome executioner who stood bulging in tights and jerkin and looked like a fairy. Memory and invention had given him the warm skin and the delicate stipple of sunlight on pubic hair. There was a touch of Modigliani in the absence of contour in the thighs and arms, but he didn't mind that.

He made a last pleasantry to Helen and Brock, and then walked up behind her. "It's not for sale but you may touch it."

She turned, startled, and smiled at him. "Who's L. Hood? Is he somebody local?" She had seen his signature in the corner, disguised as wrinkles in the blanket.

He put his thumb against his chest and bowed, holding the tray behind him. A loose napkin fluttered to the floor.

"Oh," she said. Her smile tightened at the corners.

He walked past her to the kitchen, his face burning, and clattered cups and plates and waited for her to follow him and tell him she liked it and ask who the model was. When he looked out she was just going out the door, Simon and Harry behind her. She turned and waved goodbye to someone out of sight behind the fireplace.

He went out of his way to be polite to everyone the rest of the night.

# 7

On the day his life changed he tried to concentrate on

mechanics. He brushed out the tin rooster where it had shared space with the self-portrait and relocated it floating over the arm of the chair. He slapped through a second layer of orange keyed higher toward yellow around the head of the lute and found he had created a slanted exclamation point with a halo. He loaded a palette knife with burnt umber and wiped across the halo, and found he had left a tire track, striated with crumbs of dried yellow caught in the mixture and dragged along. He assaulted the tire track with a thumb coated with white lead and watched sadly as the rich earth color turned to chalk stamped with whorls.

He was too embarrassed to mention it, but he got excited when he imagined Yvonne in bed with other men. With a wide, saturated brush he began moving a heavy blanket of cerulean across the upper third of the canvas, which had formerly been red, enclosing the doll's head and burning through the glass eye that stared over the edge of the basket. That she was seeing someone caused him a great and terrible anguish but also gave him a hard-on that threatened to split his skin. He stared at the cerulean and tried to remember why he had put it there.

He changed brushes and began breaking the stuffed caiman into segments that floated across the face of the lute like footprints. She was trying to pretend everything was normal, but she forgot he knew all her signals. Infidelity made her miserable. He had been the antidote for Max, the harmless divorced law student who had preceded him, and now she needed an antidote for the antidote. In her last days with Max, she had come to Lorin's room and climbed through the window that opened directly over his bed. They would make love and she would weep on his chest in the night and tell him what a dear man Max was and how she couldn't bear to hurt him but also couldn't bear to return to the little apartment where Max was even now wondering where she was and why she didn't love him any more. She showed Lorin a sestina Max had written for her. She showed him pictures of Max's children. She smiled sadly.

His hand shook as he picked up the fleck of bronze on the tail of the caiman and touched it into the cheek of the lamp-girl. Nights she moaned in bed with him she was storing up the things she would tell the next night to *his* antidote. He imagined horrible disclosures on nights he stayed late at the Blue Couch, sweeping out other people's crumbs and sterilizing their cups. She probably felt guilty while she was doing it, but she could handle guilt. She probably thought a little guilt was the price you paid to be happy. She probably smiled sadly. They probably went through his portfolios.

———

In the afternoon he interrupted the still-life, which had developed sticky impastos from having the lamp-girl and the self-portrait relocated so often, to call her at work with a trifling endearment. Cash registers rang in the background and voices blurred close at hand. Why yes, she said; they had ordered it several weeks ago and the shipment had come in only that morning. He had been thinking about her all day, he said. No, it would not be necessary to lay aside a copy, she said; there were plenty on hand. Would she rather he ran his tongue along her swollen clitoris first or kissed the backs of her knees first? He was entirely welcome, she said, her low, polite voice thick with anger. The line went dead, and he was three digits into her number again before deciding to stop.

———

At the Blue Couch, he sat at a table listening to an argument between Harvey Ellingson and a thirtyish woman with heavy eye makeup and a bare midriff, around which hung a thin gold chain. He thought about pressing his swollen member against her midriff, avoiding the chain, and was startled when she turned to him and asked if he didn't agree. He said he agreed. He decided he had said the wrong thing when Harvey turned away, looking pissed, and lit a cigarette. Lorin didn't know the woman, and wondered if wanting to press against the exposed skin of someone you had never seen before meant you were indiscriminate. He wondered if the girl with the bangs would ever come in again. He wondered how she happened to be friends with someone as odious as Simon.

Later he sat at the round table near the fireplace with Pavel and Gail, listening to the playwright from Bakersfield describe his ion-transfer therapy and wondering if he should check around to see if anyone needed refills of anything. The playwright, it seemed, was undergoing treatment in a clinic in Encino for a pain in his left leg. The leg had been quietly throbbing for a year, interfering with sleep, sitting, the act of love, climbing stairs— anything that required a change of position—and then had abruptly worsened, to where even standing in place was excruciating. It felt, he explained, as though a nerve was on fire. A first diagnosis had determined that the medullary sheath cushioning the sciatic nerve had grown thin, and the prescribed treatment had been the ingestion of large doses of yeast, in tablet form, to thicken the deposit of myelin. That having failed, a second diagnosis had determined that the nerve suffered from a lack of potassium, and the curious physiotherapy he was now undergoing was intended to supply it.

Three afternoons a week he was in the basement of the clinic, face down for an hour on an examining table with a sheet draped over his buttocks, concealed by curtains from other patients undergoing other therapies, while he took the ion-transfer cure. A woman in a starched white dress swabbed the back of his left thigh with oil of wintergreen and wrapped the thigh in chemically heated packs. His left hand was immersed in a salt bath through which a mild electric current passed, which she increased by turning a knob in front of him every fifteen minutes. He was to watch the dial and call her if either the current or the hot packs started to hurt. While he lay there, feeling his hand lose sensation and his leg boil soft, a remarkable thing was happening, invisibly. Ions from the oil of wintergreen were kicked by the impulse passing through his body into his sciatic nerve, and the nerve, he reported solemnly, throbbed less and less each week. He could walk now; he could sleep and climb stairs without pain. He expected in time to be able to resume the act of love. He was not cured, but he was better. He did not know how the thing worked; he admitted it sounded like quackery, but he was better. He turned his chair aside and flexed his knee above the table to show them. It sounded plausible to Lorin.

"I always wondered what being turned on meant," Pavel said.

"When Charles was doing his novitiate he said you had to wear a wire chain under your cassock," Gail said. "It went around your thigh and had little barbs, and you weren't supposed to limp or anything to let on when you were wearing it. It's called a catena, and it's what you do for penitential practice. Charles said the first time he put it on he got an erection."

Gail was in theater arts at UCLA and lived with an ex-Jesuit. Lorin had seen her perform in whiteface with a mime troupe at the Unicorn on Sunset Boulevard.

"What was it, wired?" Pavel asked.

"I was just thinking if little prickly barbs can do that, just think what a whole current could do." She closed her eyes and hummed like a current.

"You going to tell us, Farrell?" Pavel asked.

The playwright relit his pipe and looked injured.

Lorin discovered he had business that took him past Simon's table.

"Freshen your cup, Simon?"

Simon looked into his cup. "Oh. Thank you."

"Shannon?"

"That would be very kind, Lorin," Shannon said. Lorin found it difficult to be civil to Shannon.

"Harry?"

"No thanks. I drank a quart at work."

"Um?" He looked at the girl. She smiled and pushed her cup across the table.

He refilled the three mugs in the kitchen and brought them back, trying to remember which one belonged to whom.

"If the music is too loud I can turn it down," he said.

"It *is* rattling the windows just a little," said Shannon.

"Simon?"

"Hm? Perhaps just a hair."

He went to the kitchen and turned the volume down, wondering if she thought he was being servile. Coming back around the counter he saw Pavel approaching the table and hurried to get there ahead of him. He drew a chair up and sat next to the girl, making room on the left for Pavel if he wanted to use it.

"I like to play this one loud just to irritate Pavel," he said, feeling emanations from her warm body.

"What?" said Pavel.

"It's this Jew, see, who converted to Catholicism," said Lorin. He felt her looking at him. "Hi," he said.

She smiled. She had big teeth.

Pavel blinked. "Were you talking about my brother?" Pavel's brother had converted and was now in seminary, breaking his parents' hearts. It was a touchy point with Pavel.

"No. Mahler."

"I think I came in too late," said Pavel, sitting down. "That one went right past me."

"The Resurrection Symphony, Pavel," said Lorin, who hated conversations like this.

"What Resurrection Symphony?" said Pavel.

"Oh Lorin, you're so oblique," said Shannon.

"When you call me oblique, smile," said Lorin, getting up to go back to the kitchen as though he had an order he'd forgotten, though in fact he was going to sulk.

———

In bed he told Yvonne about ion transfer therapy. He mentioned its probable folkloric connection with certain kinds of faith healing involving ritual and consecrated oil. Probably placebo effect, ha ha. He tried to think of ways of getting around to the wire chain on the leg, but she was smiling politely, so he stopped.

# 8

In Rossetti's painting of the Annunciation, the Virgin was a neurasthenic adolescent kneeling on her unmade bed and shrinking into the corner, sick with dread at the angel blazing in front of her. Seeing it represented like that, you could almost believe it had happened. Lorin had never told anyone he liked a Pre-Raphaelite painting.

To imagine Joseph Smith's visit from Moroni he tuned out Yvonne's breathing and pretended the shadow of the ripped awning on the wall opposite the bedroom window was another window, this one looking out onto barns, rail fences, an iron pump in the kitchen yard, and winding country lanes leading past furrowed pastures. He didn't know what upstate New York looked like, but you could invent. He lay in bed and imagined he was Joseph Smith kneeling beside it, engrossed in prayer and therefore unprepared when the room shuddered and lit up.

The angel standing there when he looked up emitted an unsteady pulsating light that sent shadows of the bedpost and the ewer on the nightstand skittering across the walls like spiders. His white robe hung open to the navel, exposing bleached woolly hair on his white chest, and pale iridescent nipples. Lorin stared at him for a long time, feeling a late summer breeze from the open window stiffen the hairs along the back of his neck, reminding him that he was alive and that the apples would be ripening soon, and that in a couple of months the sky would begin to fill with scaly clouds and a sharp wind would cut its way down from Canada, and that soon afterwards the woods on the neighboring farm would fill with snow, and the withered flowers on his grave would be buried and forgotten. He studied the compressed lips and the icy blue eyes of the angel and tried to guess how much trouble he was in, until a thread of drool dropped onto his clasped hands, startling him. Some of the small sins he had been about to mention in his prayers were actually big ones, and he wondered if he could anticipate the worst by saying so now. He wiped his chin with a pajama sleeve and cleared his throat, but the angel had already begun talking.

Lorin felt a measure of relief because the voice was thin and faint, as though coming to him across a great distance; he had been afraid his whole family was going to hear, if not the whole neighborhood. As it was, he knew that anybody seeing the house from the road would think there was a fire in his bedroom and raise the alarm. He envisioned unshaven farmers with gaiters pulled over their underclothes gathering at the kitchen door with buckets in their hands, wives and children running back and forth to the pump, finally bursting through the door and pounding up the stairs, arousing the whole family. He saw them fling open his door and stand there staring like owls as the angel over his bed began a new list of accusations in that distant, metallic voice, and he saw his mother bury her face in her apron in shame.

He couldn't tell if the vaporous light had anything to do with it, but the air currents in his room were definitely disturbed. Dust rising from his quilt gathered in tiny streams just above eye level and floated there like pennants before drifting toward the white figure of the angel and dissipating with a gust from the window. Sounds also seemed affected. He had been conscious of the distant barking of a dog while saying his prayers, and though he could hear it now it seemed muffled, coming to him in erratic bursts and sometimes cutting out altogether. Spatial distortions had not occurred, though. He took a chance on the movement passing unnoticed and darted a glance around the room while the angel was talking, satisfying himself that the crude wooden chair and table that his father had built still occupied the same plane they had before; the walls had not moved, though the drawings he had thumbtacked along the wainscotting fluttered cryptically.

The angel had stopped talking, and Lorin looked up at him and nodded to show that he understood whatever he had been saying, and the angel went on. Lorin wondered if this had anything to do with coming in Yvonne's mouth, because he could explain that. The angel was talking about plates buried in a hill by the time Lorin had composed his explanation—it was an accident and she said she hadn't minded—and Lorin hoped they could just pass on with a warning. He clasped his hands in front of his face to show he was paying attention. He noticed they were a sickly white and that the hairs on the backs of them stood upright. He unclasped them and wiped his palms on the quilt. He touched the back of his left hand with the palm of his right hand and pressed the hairs down and felt them rise again when he lifted his right hand slowly. Visitations created electrical fields.

The angel had passed on to hypothetical threats, and Lorin was relieved to hear that they had to do with inscribed tablets in the ground. If he dug them up prematurely or showed them to anyone else he was in trouble. Beneath the sound of the voice, which had remained acoustically remote but to which he had gradually adapted, Lorin was conscious of a pale green haze shimmering against some inner screen deep in his brain, gradually hardening into a low, grassy hill studded with boulders. This, he understood, was where the plates were buried. He recognized it as a corner of pastureland near the neighbor's woods, a place whose terrain was wrinkled and where cows occasionally wandered and broke their legs and had to be shot. He saw the scars of picnic fires and the line of trees near the summit, and the grey outcropping of rock that marked where the hillside fell away and where his steps would have to be nimble to keep from losing his purchase as he climbed down. Splotches of bright orange and yellow marked the places where the thin soil had nutrients enough to grow wildflowers. He knew he could climb down and back up if he had to. The angel was explaining about the stones and the breastplate, but the light in the room, Lorin noticed, was beginning to change. As he watched, it drew away from the corners of the room and gathered around the angel's body. Lorin saw tiny black eyes squeezed nearly shut in the wrinkled face, and shoulders like coat hangers drawn up to tiny ears, shaking with laughter; and then the light winked out and he was left by himself in a dark room, feeling a thin breeze play over his back from the window. He huddled against Yvonne and she moved her foot. He would paint this some day.

## 9

$T$wice that week, in the Village, he saw the girl who had

come to the Blue Couch with Simon. Once she was sitting at the counter of the drugstore where he had gone after not finding Yvonne at the bookstore. She wore a lab coat and was eating a grilled cheese sandwich and reading a book. A pickle slice lay on her plate with a bite taken out of it. He sat on the stool next to her and reached across her for the napkin container in order to see what she was reading. She watched his hand fumble with the napkins, then looked at him. "I'm meeting someone," she said, and returned to her book. He moved to a different stool. He wasn't sure she had recognized him. He left before whoever she was meeting turned up.

The other time, she was coming out of the bank across the street from the Westwood Fox Theater just as he was going in, and he held the door open for her. She thanked him and did a double-take. He kept going, toward the teller line, and she entered the crosswalk. Through the glass doors they watched each other get smaller.

That night, at the Blue Couch, he induced a half-dozen entrances for her, each with its follow-through. In one she came in with Simon and the two or three friends Lorin most disliked, whom she promptly abandoned at their table to go look for him, finding him at the stove behind the counter. There she undressed, told him he was a fine painter but a poor cook, and busily set to work whipping his parfaits, slicing his sandwiches, frying his hamburgers, from time to time stopping to ask for a kiss where hot droplets of grease had burned her. She was brisk and efficient and told him to stop moaning. When it was time to leave, she put her clothes on, dried her hands on the towel he had optimistically fetched from under the dishwasher, and ran to catch up with Simon and the others who were just going out the door.

In another version, she came in with the same friends but lingered behind after everyone had gone, and stripped to the skin and sat curled in the large black leather armchair next to the fireplace and watched, glowing in the candlelight, as he swept between tables and gathered up stray espresso cups and watered the plants. By the time he was finished, had returned the broom to its corner and the sterilized cups to their rack, flung off his own clothes in the kitchen and come around the fireplace, bobbing, to meet her, she was already dressed and rummaging her purse for her lipstick. She looked up, surprised, and asked if he could give her a ride home, a disappointment she sweetened by carrying his clothes in her lap and holding his brisk member at every stoplight, informing him when the light had changed.

That version ended at her door, but another one (with its kitchen interlude vague but promising) took them both into her warm little dwelling, wherever it was, from which he was not ejected until she had peeled naked and made him rub lotion all over her body, which had chapped from its exposure to the stove and the night air. Another got them as far as the bathroom, where through a transparent curtain he watched her take a warm shower and she left while he took a cold one, and still another lowered them between crisp, clean, freshly ironed sheets which she advised him, correcting his grip before turning over to sleep, were to remain crisp and clean. He was working on the sixth one when Pavel inquired about the fatuous smile on his face.

"A medley, Pavel," he said, masking his surprise. "Don't you ever have medleys?"

"All the time," said Pavel.

They had been listening to the folk singer, and when Lorin looked around he noticed Simon and Shannon at the table by the boarded window, the girl with the bangs between them. He had nearly missed them.

"I see we're wearing our green pointy tonight, Shannon," he said, lifting mugs from his tray and placing them on the table. He gave her the cleanest one.

"Do you like it?" Shannon asked, spreading his fingers to brush a cigarette ash from the front of his poncho. His hands were enormous. "I offered to let Gloriana wear it tonight but she was afraid she would trip over it."

"I like it very much," Lorin said, tucking away the name in a back pocket of his mind.

"Why thank you, Lorin. You're so effusive tonight."

Once, in a three-dimensional design class, Lorin had watched Shannon spend a week carving a block of maple into a baby with a clothespin head. Shannon spent a few days sanding and oiling the baby, then wrapped it in a blanket and carried it around with him everywhere he went. He obviously enjoyed the stares and averted faces on campus, and he serenely ignored comments along the sidewalks of the Village as he carried it into stores and restaurants. Lorin told him he'd heard a gang of mothers was planning to drag him out of his apartment and beat him up. "Marvelous," Shannon said. One day he appeared on campus without it. People asked him where his baby was, and he smiled politely and asked, "What baby?"

"Give me a minute and I'll say something nice to Gloriana too," Lorin said, winking at the girl with the bangs.

"Don't be obvious, Lorin," said Shannon.

"He can say anything nice he wants," she said. She winked back.

His heart sang in the kitchen as he slathered mayonnaise and Dijon mustard on thick slices of sourdough and spread layer after layer of turkey, cheese, pastrami, lettuce, two kinds of sprouts, sweet tomatoes, pinning his creations together with toothpicks. It meant she acknowledged they had met earlier today. By the time he brought their orders out, Malcolm had joined them and was smoking one of Simon's Turkish cigarettes.

"If you don't like your orders you may trade with each other," Lorin said. He returned to the kitchen and poured coffee for himself and brought it to the table, dragging a chair. He wedged the chair into the space between Gloriana and Malcolm.

"Am I in your way or something?" Malcolm asked.

"Yes."

"I'll move over," Gloriana said.

They were talking about woodcuts for Malcolm's next issue of Dragon Wyck. Lorin did not want to listen but had no choice short of leaving the table, and he wasn't through with her yet. She little imagined, as she sat picking at her Denver sandwich, that she had just wakened from untroubled sleep to a bright morning between warm, fragrant sheets, or that inches away they were twisted and sodden; or that she had stretched and yawned, and turned to discover the radiant tool where she had left it, and offered good morning to its glassy-eyed owner; or asked for (and gotten) a chaste kiss to the left of her navel where a grease burn still smarted; or that, prompted by his gritted teeth to suppose his bladder was bursting, she had sprung out of bed and led him by the handle to the bathroom, where she sat on the edge of the tub and waited, finally asking him to leave if he didn't intend to do anything because she needed to.

There was still room for a seventh sequence, but Shannon had joined a conversation at another table and Malcolm had left to do an order of onion rings and Noel had come over and was showing Pavel slides of a children's exhibit at the county museum and Pavel was holding them up to the light and Lorin felt suddenly alone with her and shy. She was picking up the slides Pavel was through with and pretending to be interested in them.

He leaned toward her and said, "Would you like some more coffee? On the house if you're quiet."

"I don't think so," she said. "I'm trying to keep from dancing now."

"The other side of the fireplace. Look for a potted palm and keep going right."

"I remember."

He was composed by the time she returned. She smiled as she sat down, and he saw his chance to presume. He cupped his hand to his mouth, and she leaned over to listen.

"What's a nice girl like you doing in a dump like this?" he asked. When she smiled her face looked round. She cupped her hand to her own mouth and applied to his ear.

"I had a fight with my roommate. It was an escape." The edge of her hand stirred the longer wisps of beard at his cheek.

"Where do you know Simon from?" He could go on like this all night, he thought. He was almost kissing her earlobe.

"We're neighbors. We live in the same building." He felt a spasm of hatred for Simon. "He said some friends of his worked here."

He suspected Simon had not mentioned his name, because she hadn't recognized it when she had seen it on his painting of Yvonne. He wasn't going to say anything, but when he had introduced himself, she'd had the opportunity to say something about his painting.

"Do you think Shannon is strange? I think I offended him by not wearing his poncho when he offered it."

"You two don't have to whisper," Shannon said. "We don't listen to you even when you talk out loud."

The most terrible story Lorin knew was a story about Shannon. Once, it seemed, in high school in San Bernardino, Shannon was grabbed in the locker room by four football players just as he had thrown his last stitch into his locker and closed it to go to the showers. The football players were already dressed and had been waiting for this moment. They pushed and dragged Shannon over benches and between tiers of lockers, where other kids who were not in on the prank watched without saying anything, glad that this was not happening to them. He was pulled screaming through the vestibule between the towel room and the lavatory; one of his tormentors hit the crash bar of the door, and the other three shoved him outside, pulling the door shut and locked behind him. It was the end of a period, and students were coming and going along the asphalt quad between classes. A crowd gathered to watch the spectacle of a tall skinny kid, stark naked, beating with both fists against the steel door and shrieking while small spurts of urine drew horizontal lines across the door and ran in long fingers to the bottom. He was rescued by one of the coaches and taken home hysterical, where he required sedatives. His father was said not to be sympathetic; he felt his son should have given a better account of himself than that. Lorin wished he could tell her that story.

He moved his chair closer so they could hear each other under the music. His expression carefully tempered to look interested, he learned useful things about her. She was not an artist, he learned. She did not dance or write poetry. She was a senior in biology, though this was only her third year. She was part of a special Dean's Test Group for gifted students and had been put on an accelerated schedule. Someone had probably stepped on her IBM card with a hobnail boot, she said (clearly not for the first time). She thought beatniks were interesting but were conformists in their own way. Didn't he? She was from El Centro—that was in the Imperial Valley—but considered San Francisco the only civilized place to live and hoped to relocate there as soon as she had taken her master's.

With a very little effort Lorin wove the loose strands of the seventh sequence together and laced it up snugly before her eyes as she talked on and on, none the wiser. She little suspected her sudden splitting off into a roommate only now yawning awake in the next room (just added) and padding sleepily in to join them in the early-morning shower, the two of them afterwards patting him dry with downy towels and tying a bright blue ribbon around his rosy prick; or their further division into a roomful of girls with bangs, wearing hand-stitched green ponchos and combing their hair in front of mirrors that gave back a profusion of round faces at right, acute, and oblique angles to each other, smiling at the dozen or so beribboned erections that wept with pleasure as their owner lay on the floor, twitching.

"Now that you've seen the dump, don't be a stranger," Lorin said.

"I'm already not," she said.

———

Over breakfast, he asked Yvonne how her evening had gone in the company of Andrea, who had whisked her away to dance like the wind earlier than usual last night. She said, "Very well, thank you," and smiled agreeably.

That was all right, he reflected after driving her to work and returning to his screened porch and laying out his brushes in the fresh morning light; they would see about that. She would have answered differently if she had known the girl with the bangs had turned up at the Blue Couch again for no other reason than that she had seen him in the street in the afternoon. Before setting to work he took off all his clothes and rummaged through her dresser until he found a crisp blue ribbon which he tied into place. It was only a matter now of ignoring the doorbell and keeping one eye on the shrubbery in the back yard, because there were pre-school urchins in the neighborhood.

## 10
---

At Simon's party Yvonne left him to find the bathroom and got lost coming back. Lorin looked for a conversation to join, and not finding one pulled a cushion from the sofa onto the floor and sat down on it, his back to a wall, and nursed his clear-plastic glass of wine in both hands. He made a furtive inventory of the other guests, darting his eyes left and right while pretending to concentrate on his thumbnails. Noel was there, cross-legged on the floor entertaining the three girls sprawled in front of him with an elaborate story that seemed to draw them through fits of helpless laughter. Lorin had never understood Noel's charm. He was small and fine-boned with a pale unblemished face that reminded you of a ventriloquist's dummy, but to Lorin's certain knowledge, at least five girls of their mutual acquaintance had had their way with Noel during the last year. Perhaps there was something in the image of vulnerability he projected. Women wanted to protect those childish limbs, so they took them to bed. Pavel, with his ascetic face, hard black beard, and recently smoldering eyes—until last year his name had been Paul—did not seem to attract women who wanted his body. Lorin watched Pavel for a few minutes. He was sitting on the couch talking to Sharon, who had shared Lorin's locker in the art department one year. Pavel's feet were extended and he stared at the ceiling as he talked, his head tipped back and resting on the back of the couch; now and then he glanced at Sharon to see if she were following him. Sharon sat sideways with her legs under her, nodding and not taking her eyes off Pavel, but you could look at this satisfying picture all night and know that neither would maul the other's body if the lights suddenly went out. Lorin suspected Pavel was lonely but enjoyed being mysterious.

The wall was starting to hurt his backbone and he realized he had been slumping. He sat up and took another sip of wine and looked around. Shannon was sitting on a wooden chair that made him look brittle and angular. He was talking to a black girl whose gleaming hair was piled high and who leaned forward on her ottoman to listen, lifting her chin and stroking her throat with the backs of her curled fingers. Harry was out of sight in the kitchen, arguing with someone who thought Adlai Stevenson was a sissy. Other people whom Lorin knew either from the Blue Couch or the university stood or sat in groups, or drifted, stepping over his feet, trying to talk over the music that pulsed from the massive speakers on the wall across from the couch. He thought he might mention to Simon that the music was rattling the windows just a little, to see what he would do. Besides the glance he had seen exchanged between Noel and Yvonne as she had stepped past him on her way to the bathroom, another canker had begun to glow on his heart. He had hoped to see Gloriana here. He sipped his wine and peered over the rim of his glass at the cluster of people standing by the bookcase, the small knot that had gathered in the doorway to the kitchen, the fawning couple nested buttock to buttock in the slippery black armchair opposite him, the masculine girl with short hair combed back into folded wings and wearing horn-rim glasses, who came out of the bedroom in knee-socks and heavy shoes and plaid bermuda shorts and proved on second glance to be a boy, the thin girl in a short skirt who stood by the iron plant stand near the door and picked dead leaves while waiting for someone to talk to her, the trio with their backs to him being entertained by Noel, but he did not find her.

He had not known he was hoping to see her here, and he looked around for persons or objects to fasten his resentment to. Among the guests he didn't know were a middle-aged man wearing a brown beret who sat tootling a recorder, which was rude when there was music on, a barefoot young man in a three-button suit with a button-down collar on his shirt, someone who looked like a Norwegian fisherman in filthy levis and a striped turtleneck jersey, a girl with a dozen or so thin bracelets jangling on her wrists, another wearing jodhpurs and lace-up boots. A guitar had been stashed in a corner, and Lorin noticed its owner glancing at it occasionally and wishing someone would ask him to play it. Empty wine bottles had been kicked out of the way under the table, gorged ashtrays lay here and there on the floor, and a haze of smoke hung between eye level and the ceiling. It was legal smoke, however. Lorin knew there would be no pot. Simon was terrified of being arrested for having pot in his apartment and absolutely forbade anyone who came to his place to bring it.

Sitting there, his back to the wall in the crowded room hung with paintings better than his own, the woman he lived with circulating happily in the next room to make him miserable, the friend with whom she made him miserable sitting in plain view across from him entertaining three groupies, Lorin concluded it was a mistake to have come. Simon just then stepped over Lorin's feet, carrying a bottle of wine in either hand, and stopped when he saw who it was.

"Lorin. I didn't see you come in."

"I'm sorry we were late," Lorin said. "Yvonne had a rehearsal."

"Did you get any wine?" Simon asked, looking at Lorin's empty glass. "It was in the kitchen."

Lorin put his hand over his glass. "Yes, we did. Thanks."

Simon appeared to remember the bottles he was carrying. "I was just bringing in some more from the bedroom. Could I pour you some?"

"Actually, I think I'm fine," Lorin said, and extended his glass. His hatred of Simon was fed by the fact that he became tongue-tied all over the body whenever he talked with him. He withdrew his glass the next moment and pretended to scratch the inside of his elbow. Simon had withdrawn the bottle but recovered himself when he saw Lorin's glass extended; he held it out again, prepared to pour, just as Lorin caught his error and withdrew his glass.

"Perhaps you'd like white instead?" Simon asked, holding the other bottle up for Lorin to see.

Lorin had extended his glass again, tentatively, his elbow bent in order to be scratched again if necessary. "I didn't see that. I was actually hoping I'd prefer that, yes. Just a touch if possible. No, no, that's all right. Thank you, Simon."

Simon murmured something gracious and went on to the kitchen to spread stories about him. Lorin sipped his white wine to dilute the red that was already dissolving the lining of his stomach and reflected that he would not have asked Simon where Gloriana was even if he hadn't been tongue-tied. Where is your little friend with the bangs and the round face, ha ha? I should think she'd at least be over to complain about the noise (wink). No, there was no way he could ask without seeming interested. It was just possible, of course, that Simon had not invited her, or that she had declined because Shannon would be there and he made her uncomfortable. Perhaps she had not known Lorin would be there. She might have had a prior engagement, for that matter. Just possibly she was taking off her clothes that very minute on some grassy, moon-soaked hillside above one of the canyons and staring coldly at the oaf she was with, who would keep his distance, if he were smart, though his seams burst. Lorin was preparing to continue this sequence when she turned around (Noel had finished the story he was telling) and saw him.

"Hi," she said.

It took him a moment to place her, but by the time she had come over and sat down by him, moving an ashtray and several glasses aside to make room, he had recovered the various pieces and was hastily rewinding the sequence he had just started.

"I didn't see you come in," she said. "I was hoping you'd be here."

"I waited until no one was looking," he said.

That left them without anything more to say. She was wearing a simple light blue dress that buttoned all the way down the front like a lab coat, held at the waist by a white belt. She wore stockings but had left her shoes over where she had been sitting while listening to Noel. A small run had started over one toenail. He had re-invented her too often. That was why he couldn't remember what she looked like.

They were staring past each other. Any minute she was going to discover he was mediocre and get up and leave. "Let me buy you a drink," he said, thrusting his glass at her.

She hesitated, then took it, sipped once and held it out for him to take back. "Keep it," he said. "It's a present."

"Don't you want it?"

"I hate wine," he said.

She looked at him curiously. "Why? I'm that way about beer."

"It gives me heartburn."

"What you should do is eat something first to coat your stomach," she said. "Something with lots of butter on it."

"Sometimes I do. I get heartburn anyway."

She looked concerned and, in a strange way, relieved. In a company of aesthetes who didn't understand the body's processes, the biologist had an edge. Lorin was relieved too, because now she would not have to get up and go away. He had, of course, started the sequence over again, replacing the faceless oaf with himself and changing her cold stare to a bitchy grin.

"Do you have ulcers?" she asked.

"Probably."

"Then you're wise not to drink it."

"I drink it all the time," he said.

"Well, *that's* silly. Don't you know what alcohol does to ulcers? Ulcers are open sores."

She explained ulcers to him, giving him graphic details of the effects of irritants on raw mucous membranes. She reminded him what happened to snails, who were all mucous membrane. Sprinkle salt on a snail and he retreated into his shell, frothing in agony. Sprinkle more and he boiled dry. Could Lorin imagine something like that happening inside his stomach? He could, but fortunately Yvonne had just come up and was standing in front of him. He saw silver buckles on two black shoes that materialized inches away from his crossed shins. One shoe pointed directly at him. The other, its heel positioned at the arch of the first, pointed to the corner of his cushion. It was a graceful position, and probably had a number. He looked up and she was smiling, though the corners of her mouth twitched a little.

"I keep just missing you," she said. She nodded to Gloriana, who nodded back.

"But do you notice how I'm still here?" he said.

He had been conscious while sitting there of Yvonne having a good time with other men for his benefit. She had scrupulously avoided Noel but busied herself laughing at John Drury's jokes for starters, then moved on to feed Keith Meredith olives from a toothpick, and then disappeared with Ron Nash into the kitchen and did not come out for a long time. While disclosing his heartburn to Gloriana he had seen, over by the iron plantstand, a forehead-to-forehead conversation between Yvonne and Perris Jackson, a black pianist (actually yellow, with a ravaged, leather face), who was connected with the dance department. While admitting to the probability of ulcers, he had noticed her attention momentarily leave Perris and center on himself. She placed a hand on Perris's wrist, and he knew he was due for a visit any moment. She would want to see how she was doing.

"Have you by any chance been to the john yet?" she asked. "I don't mean to pry or anything."

"I don't believe I have," said Lorin.

"You'll want to look in the bathtub when you do," she said.

"All right."

"What's in the bathtub?" Gloriana asked.

"It's sort of a painting, actually," said Yvonne, laughing. "It's all crumpled up and soaking under water."

"Why in the world?"

"He wants to scrape the paint off and use the canvas over again," Lorin said.

"Can you do that? I thought you just painted over something you didn't want any more."

"The one underneath always shows through," he said. "This way you can pretend your mistakes never happened." He stared at Yvonne's ankles and hoped she noticed he was talking about her.

"Do see it if you happen by that way. There's something so offhand about barging into the john and finding a painting right there in the bathtub first thing. You expect to find another one under the bed and another back in the refrigerator with the onions."

"Ask me where he takes a bath while it's soaking," Lorin said.

"Oh," said Gloriana.

"I believe I hear the cheese and olives calling me," said Yvonne, laughing happily. "Do excuse me just for a bit. I won't be a moment."

They watched her stumble over a pair of feet on her way to the kitchen and slap her knees when the poor devil (it was Harry, crimson to the ears) scrambled to help her up, knocking over her plate of radishes and sliced cucumbers.

"I've seen her before," Gloriana said. "Who is she?"

He told her, and she looked at him thoughtfully. He knew that look. It was an appraising look. He was turning out to be more interesting than she had thought.

"Do you suppose we'd better go look?" she asked.

"She'll be disappointed if we don't," he said. He was going to add something mysterious about disappointments in general, but she was already on her feet and padding across the carpet toward the bathroom. He made a necessary adjustment before she turned to see where he was, and then got up and followed her, stepping over Pavel's feet and ignoring Noel.

"I'll just leave this door open so people won't think we came in together to fool around," he said, as they stood by the tub. He hoped she might respond by saying something cooperative like, "Evil to him who evil thinks." "That's very circumspect," she said, and looked down at the drowned painting.

It was a large canvas, crumpled and gathered in folds piled on top of each other and still covering most of the bottom of the tub. The folds caused abrupt discontinuities of color and line. A fat angleworm, nestling in folds of grey earth, was severed by a rotting patchwork quilt of mottled greens and reds and oranges in its turn cut off by a sheet of blue sky on which a tiny rose floated. There was more, and he suspected it was useful to see familiar things in unexpected contexts, but he was weak, he realized, and he could not help reliving every brush stroke, including the ones covered by the folds, and he could not see the antic juxtapositions that lay before him because he was seeing the thwarted likeness of a fat nude on a stool, surrounded by jugs of flowers in a darkened room. Only by knowing that was what it was could you recognize the rind of a face highlighted by a tensor lamp placed just outside the frame, the green and blue flowers strewn on the curtained ledge behind her shoulders, the expanse of backlit flesh containing an undefined breast with its soft wrinkled nipple. But knowing this, other things would come together—the pasty toes curled over the rung of a stool (unmistakable but baffling), the scaly banjo of a kneecap, the sparse tumbleweed over which layers of grey sky glowered, tinged with pink. The model was a woman well past seventy, and a great favorite in both the painting and sculpture classes that used the windowless studios in the art department basement. She wore her hair in a prim grey bun and swept off her robe with a flourish before ascending the dais. The flesh on the underside of her arms hung in pleats, her breasts were flattened, her belly was voluminous, her buttocks draped over the edges of the stool. Her name was Grenda, and she was an object of horror to Lorin. He had a hundred or so sketches of her, kneeling, sitting, crouching, standing, reclining, throwing a spear, holding Shannon's maple baby wrapped in a blanket, but he had attempted only one painting, working from two charcoal sketches rather than from the life (she would not sit longer than a few minutes at a time). The result of his labors had so embarrassed him that he had hidden the canvas on the farthest rack he could find in the storage closet, its face to the wall, and stacked in front of it five or six dusty unclaimed canvases that had been kicking around for years. Morbid fascination had driven him back to look at it every few months, late at night, while he was still in school, and then he had forgotten about it. Simon had doubtless browsed through the storage closet, claiming anything that had not been moved for a year and bearing it home to bathe, re-stretch, re-size, and paint lambent flowers and rocks on. It was exemplary thrift, and just possibly Simon did not know whose canvas it was that lay softening in his bathtub.

"Well, now you can tell her we saw it," said Gloriana.

"So we did," said Lorin, whose heart could not help aching a little as he looked at his artifact in its last hours on earth.

They returned to the living room and sat down on the floor next to the bookcase, someone having preempted his sofa cushion. Gloriana still held the plastic glass he had handed her, though now it was empty.

"I didn't think it was very good," she said, dropping her voice. "Did you?"

"That's why he's stripping it to use over again," he said.

His mind was already charred with fantasies, but a new one briefly licked over its surface. In this one, his poor ravaged nude did not scrape clean but survived in patches scrubbed as hard and smooth as glass at different points on the canvas, here a ripple of shadow where a thigh had curved, there a glint of the comb that had held her hair back, elsewhere the marbled white of an eye, a thick yellow toenail, one leg of her stool, a few chips of red flowers behind her. More, the thin wash in which he had laid out parts and proportions before proceeding with the heavy work had seeped into the very threads with which the canvas was woven, staining it with the ghost of his intention. In his fantasy, Simon had to incorporate that ghost, those patches and fragments, had to contain in whatever entity would shortly glow from that canvas the cruder nerves and vessels that Lorin had already put there. The toenail would become the heart of a foreground poppy, the comb the staked fence enclosing an overripe garden, the shadowy underwash of her body the contours of a spectral hillside hazed over with nebulous pulsing flora (Simon would turn the original painting on its side), the damp rose of her nipple a dangerous polyp.

"I guess she's not coming back," Gloriana said, watching the swing of Yvonne's skirt as she came out of the kitchen with a plate of food and joined Noel and John Drury and Simon by the record rack. "You'll have to tell her later."

"Maybe I won't tell her at all. Make her wonder."

"How is your stomach?" she asked.

"I try not to think about it." He put a hand on it. He very much wanted to get back to the subject of disappointments because it was getting late and he was afraid she would leave soon.

"Does milk help?"

"Not always."

"Why don't you ask Simon if he has any? Would you like me to?"

"He probably doesn't."

"Why don't I go look," she said, getting up. "I'll try to find a clean glass."

She padded off to the kitchen, still in her stocking feet, leaving him alone with her on a moonlit hillside hazed over with nebulous pulsing flowers, a handful of which she plucked and wove into a ring that she slipped onto his quivering member, next weaving a chain to attach to the ring the better to lead him through clover fields under a blazing sun past Yvonne who danced naked while smiling at him and being flung back and forth between two male dancers with strong hairy hands that left bruises on her legs. She was back in less than a minute.

"Just goat's milk," she said. "I guess that's no help."

He shook his head and tried to look tragic.

"I have some milk at my place," she said.

He hoped that Yvonne had not seen them leave, though it would only be for a minute. He could still hear the party as he stood with his head pressed against the wall beside Gloriana's door while she looked for her key. The flames in his stomach had reduced to a low persistent smolder, and perhaps milk would put them out. The mild anguish he had felt at seeing his dead canvas in Simon's bathtub had not gone away but had congealed into a lump at the base of his heart and sat there and drained poisons.

"My roommate may not be asleep," said Gloriana, fitting her key into the lock and easing open the door. "Let's be very quiet until I see."

The pressure of the stucco wall against the top of his head felt good. It gave him the sense of stability that the deck under his feet did not as he stood there listening to the voices three doors down and trying to pick out Yvonne's.

Gloriana stuck her head back out the door. "You can come in while I'm looking," she said.

He followed her and stood just inside the door while she tip-toed across the living room and disappeared into the short vesti-bule that led to the bathroom and bedroom. The apartment was identical to Simon's except it was a mirror-reverse and spread with its own assortment of objects. A pink stuffed elephant on the couch, a stack of magazines (Newsweek, Collier's, Esquire, Arizona Highways) on the coffee table along with some scattered sheets of graph paper and a fat ring binder, matted prints of Eu-ropean cathedrals and village churches on the walls, no potted plants in iron plantstands but a vase containing weavable zin-nias on the top shelf of the low bookcase. A puffy white quilt lay heaped in a chair, a pile of books on the floor waited for dis-tribution on the shelves, a small-screen Philco television set shared the top of a cabinet with a stuffed baby alligator. Otherwise the place was featureless.

"It's okay, he's asleep," she said, coming back in.

Lorin followed her into the kitchen, his ears ringing, and sat down at the breakfast bar while she took a glass down from the cabinet over the sink and fetched out a carton of milk from the refrigerator. He didn't mind two percent, she hoped, holding up the carton. No, no, two percent was fine, he said, lost in thought. He was surprised at the number of things he was learning to-night. She filled the glass and returned the carton to the refrig-erator, then sat down across from him. He felt her watching his Adam's apple as he drank.

"Feel any better?" she asked.

"It always takes a few minutes," he said. "Are you sure we're not going to wake your roommate?"

"As long as we're quiet. How long have you had ulcers?"

"I don't know if that's what they are, actually. It may just be indigestion."

"Haven't you been to a doctor? You could at least get them diagnosed. It might be something serious."

"I probably should. Maybe that's what I'll do, actually. Listen, I'd hate to think we were disturbing your roommate."

"He's okay. How long have you been having the symptoms? You looked like you were in real pain."

"I don't know. Four or five years. Maybe six. Sometimes it isn't so bad."

"Four or five years! And you haven't done anything about it all this time?"

"It isn't always there," he said. "Sometimes I don't feel anything for days, then I drink a lot of coffee and it comes back. Milk helps."

"Is that helping?" She nodded toward his empty glass.

"I think it is. Listen, what I really need to do is lie down for a minute somewhere, if that's all right."

"Sure. Come on in the living room." She climbed off her stool and he followed her back through the doorway. "Here," she said, picking up the elephant from the couch. "Would you like a pillow?"

"No, that's all right. You're sure we're not going to wake him up or anything." He glanced at the doorway to the vestibule.

"He's a very heavy sleeper, poor lamb," she said. "If he's just getting to sleep he'll have trouble sometimes if there's noise, but once he's asleep he doesn't even hear the alarm clock." She sat down in the chair across the room after tossing the quilt onto the floor, the elephant on top of it. Lorin sat down on the center cushion of the couch, hesitated which end to put his head at, then decided on the end farthest from the bedroom so he could watch it. His head propped against the armrest, his shoes off and lying under the coffee table, he suddenly felt unprotected.

"He won't mind my being here or anything, will he?"

"I don't think so," she said. She had not stopped smiling. She was enjoying this.

"I mean I won't be here long, but I hate to be an intruder."

"If he comes out to beat you up we can say you were in my half of the apartment."

"I think I'll go back to the party," he said and started to sit up.

She had jumped up from her chair as soon as she saw he was not amused and now stood over him, pushing him back down onto the couch with both hands on his chest and laughing. "I was only teasing," she said. It struck him she was being familiar on very short acquaintance, and he was on the point of telling her he had not come here to play games. "It's okay if you're here," she said. "It really is okay."

"I just hadn't thought that your roommate might be a man," he said. "I can't help it. It just didn't occur to me. I don't want to make things awkward."

She looked interested. "How were you going to do that?" She motioned for him to move over against the backrest and sat down on the edge of the couch. He felt pinned in place.

"He wouldn't be very happy, would he, if he knew somebody had followed you home and was lying here on the couch while he was asleep?" He hoped she was going to tell him they had an understanding.

"He probably wouldn't," she said.

"That's how," he said.

"But I just said he wouldn't like it. I didn't say I had to do only what he likes."

A tiny worm of suspicion had popped its head up through the thin skin of his imagination and sniffed the air before disappearing to resume tunneling.

"For instance, he doesn't like it when I go off with a bunch of beatniks to coffee houses either, but that's his problem."

"Ah," he said.

"Of course I probably wouldn't have gone the first time if we hadn't just had a fight."

"That's too bad," he said.

"Oh, he doesn't say anything about my going. Just like he probably wouldn't say anything if he came out and found you here. He just sulks for a few days and works late and doesn't look at me when he comes home."

"That can be unpleasant," he agreed.

"How is your stomach feeling?" she asked.

He was rubbing it and trying not to notice. "A little better, I think."

"Here, let me," she said. She pulled his hand away and applied her fingertips to the spot just under his rib cage and to the left of his xiphoid process. "Right here?" He nodded and she began to massage in gentle circular motions with both hands, using just the tips of her fingers. Genial warmth rushed in from adjacent tissues. His stomach felt better already.

"I don't know why that should help, but it does," he said.

"Sure you do. It stimulates the blood vessels in the area and increases the circulation."

He didn't know why increased circulation should make it hurt less but he didn't want to ask since she had just told him he did. She was using the palms of her hands now, and he felt his shirt front creep up from beneath his trousers and clear his belt. He hoped there was no lint in his navel.

"Does your roommate have ulcers too?" he asked.

"No. He gets migraines." She was watching her hands. "So it doesn't help to rub his stomach."

"That's a shame, since you do it so well, ha ha."

"You're very kind to say so."

The truth was, he was feeling much better and that worried him. He was not born yesterday, and he knew one or two things about signals. He had come down here to her apartment with no very clear idea of what he expected to happen, but he knew he was not braced for anything important. He knew also that he had felt safe and happy in his fantasies and that the warm pressure of her hands on his stomach interfered with the sequence in which she pushed him, naked and moaning, into the closet and went to play with her roommate while he stood there in the dark between coats and dresses.

"What does he do that he should have migraines?" he asked. "I don't mean to be nosey."

"He works at Rand, but he's always had them. He's a physicist." Lorin watched her face as she kneaded his stomach with one hand. The other one was in her lap. "Let's see. He's tall, thin, and brilliant, and drives a Porsche. And he can be a real pain."

"That's too bad," Lorin said.

"I suppose I can be one too," she said. "Here. Turn over and I'll give you a back rub as long as I'm at it."

"Actually, I'm in pretty good shape right now," he said.

"Over," she said.

With his shirt tail out and his shoes off he felt seedy, but it would be an affectation to resist. He struggled onto an elbow and turned over, feeling his pant legs climb over his socks. He squirmed until all his edges were comfortable against the cushions, then settled his cheek onto a forearm and looked bleakly across the room toward the curtained front window while Gloriana set to work.

"We haven't been roomies all that long, really," she said, squeezing and releasing the ridge of his trapezius on either side of his neck. Goose pimples raced to his scalp. "Just long enough to know we probably wouldn't want to do this permanently. Have you two been living together long?''

''Year,'' he mumbled into his arm.

''Because, oh, I don't know. We like each other all right,'' she went on, the heels of her hands pressing small wavelets of euphoria into his infraspinatus and teres major. ''But if we didn't live together we probably wouldn't even be friends. We don't have all that much in common. We like different people and go different places. That's all right for a while, but pretty soon one of you starts conforming to the other just to keep peace in the family, and then each of you thinks the other is a pill.'' She laughed. Her fingers meantime found magic buttons hidden in his rhomboideus minor and major. He could scarcely breathe for pleasure. She was going to reach his latissimus dorsi soon and he was going to die. ''I guess it sounds like we've had another fight. Actually we haven't. It's just like this all the time now. Did anyone ever tell you that you were awfully bony?''

He groaned as the nerves radiating from his spine lit up like filaments.

''He plays a banjo,'' she said. ''Some of the mathematicians and physicists at work have formed a little folk singing group. They get together during lunch hours with their little guitars and banjos and brown bags in one of the offices and do Kingston Trio songs with equations on the blackboard. It's kind of dreary but he loves it. Here, I can't do this if you keep sinking into the couch. Get down on the floor.''

He demurred once, then got up and followed her around the coffee table and lay down on the carpet, his elbows spread like wings. He rested his chin on his laced fingers to watch the vestibule to the bedroom. She hiked up her dress and knelt, straddling his legs. ''If he comes out we'll tell him I'm giving you artificial respiration,'' she said. With her small, strong hands, she kneaded and brought peace to his weary intercostals. She attacked his shoulder blades again with a good solid foundation under him this time, and they knew the bliss of a thumb pressed into hidden places. She traveled to his neck for the part of his trapezius she had missed the first time, and for good measure his splenius capitis, and then began the mystic descent down the regions of his spine.

''I don't mean to bore you with his life story,'' she said, leaning her whole weight onto his third and fourth thoracic vertebrae and stirring with the ball of her fist. ''But you did ask.'' Streaks of yellow pain flashed at the back of his eyes as he imagined those two vertebrae separating and occluding. Tiny needles danced out from the pressure point, under layers of muscle, and dropped down both sides of his rib cage where they quieted just short of his pectorals and waited for the next wave. Each assault came as a surprise. She moved down the width of a small fist and leaned her whole weight again, one hand on top of the other. This time the pain was a rich magenta, and the needles careened wildly over old pathways and into new ones, traveling up both edges of his back to his armpits and down his triceps to his elbows. He moaned at the next point down while frantic spots of red whirled against a background of white that, an instant later, was really black masquerading as white. He suspected that primal memories lay stored in your spinal column and got released when your receptors were violated. What he was seeing were ancient and terrible battles that he had seen before when he was a wisp floating in the night-world of the pre-existence, with chaos emerging in spasms from principle, light from nothing, the beginning from what had preceded the beginning. He watched as luminous corpuscles shot through dark oceans and were snatched at by luminous cilia. Space unfolded like a cabbage and became time, which curled at the edges and darkened along the veins and became necrosis. She was still talking to him as she worked, but when your body was transformed into an instrument picking up primal signals from a wordless past it couldn't process discursive information. He would have it in a minute; it was something about how they respected each other's Indian village; he would fine-tune it when she was through. She had worked her way to the end of his thoracic vertebrae and started on the lumbar, and the small of his back bristled with vitamins. It embarrassed him to hear the sounds he was making. He wished she would stop talking so he could concentrate on feeling his synapses unhook while sleep crept toward him like a blanket of foam. He held his breath as she moved lower from his second to his third lumbar vertebra. He was surprised at the primal memories that lay coiled between the second and third lumbar vertebrae. Something with silver eyes flashed past in a garden. A dwarf with a head like a prick and arms like coat hangers scuttled under a blue apron. She moved still lower, and light burst from his feet and legs. He knew what was coming. Pleasure and pain were the same in what was coming. Gloriana herself seemed to pause for an instant. She shifted farther back along his legs to re-establish her balance, and then leaned forward again, fist on hand, and with all her strength massaged—oh God, oh God— the sacro-lumbar region itself. Needles spilled onto the soles of his feet. His instep burned as hairs turned in their follicles. He floated upside down through luminous green oceans, and billows of sleep rocked him and nursed him.

He wasn't sure how she had gotten there, but she was lying beside him on the floor with her dress pulled up. Her knees rubbed together, and he hated himself for the idiotic smile he could feel contorting his face. He felt as though he were radiating a nimbus, and he could not remember if they had done it yet or were about to. Her hand was under his shirt and she was stroking the hair on his chest with electric fingers and remarking that his chest was very bony, but that didn't tell him anything. He was dimly aware that a threat lurked in the next room and that Yvonne had probably missed him by now and would want an explanation when he turned up not horny. He tried to think of one while he floated on the edge of sleep and watched a bank of teeth smile at him, but his attention kept drifting off and pulling apart like pictures in smoke. He noticed a cool breeze had settled on his buttocks, and he heard her say, "Now hold very still." He caught a whiff of clean hair and wine on her breath, but otherwise his impressions were private. In one, a strange snake with a head at either end whipped across his field of vision and popped suddenly into a duck's mouth. He would have dismissed this as facile symbolism except that it was not a real snake at all, but a flat, stylized, abstraction of a snake. It was segmented, each segment a different color lit from behind like stained glass, and along its edges were tiny hairs of light. Its heads were not real heads either but disks containing brightly colored spirals. Teeth rimmed the outside edge of the disks as hairs of light rimmed the body. The stream it swam in was real enough, containing boulders and silt, with grass along the bank and dead rooted twigs around which rushing water split. The snake whipped upstream, near the surface of the water, moving by flexing and thrashing its brittle segmented body and moving at a terrifying speed. It had jumped into the duck's open mouth at the very instant Lorin became aware there was a duck there at all. The duck, too, was real enough, at first—white, orange bill, pleasant rictus—but it had just gobbled its death. Its bright black disk of an eye shrank to a pinpoint, its white body turned brown and then grey; and then, as the air was sucked away from inside it, the rubber surface of its body shriveled. The back sank in, the bill and tail retracted, the breast folded in to meet the inside surface of the folded wings.

In another impression, human faces he had never seen before swarmed toward him and receded like blowing feathers. There was the face of a man whose lower lip hung open, exposing spotted teeth and the membrane, layered with bubbles, that connected his gum to his lip. There was the face of a girl, the down on her upper lip bleached white and her cheeks etched with scarlet acne. There was a woman with one eye out, an angry mass of veins supplying its place. There was an unshaved derelict with no teeth, opening and closing his mouth like a grouper. The number of faces grew moment by moment, until he couldn't tell any longer which were the spaces between the foreground heads and which were the heads grown small with distance.

Other impressions came and went. He saw coils of vegetation open and put out leaves that in their turn opened and contained spiders. He saw square doors open in blank skies and disgorge clouds of opaque light in which furtive things crept. He saw broken steps leading to a house in which something wrinkled sat behind the door and waited. He saw men in pantaloons dancing with alligators. As the critical moment approached (she was making strange cries in his ear), he was seeing sailboats at rest along the shore of a lagoon, their empty masts weaving patterns in the sunlight. The hillside over the lagoon was covered with houses and trees, with here and there the steeple and louvered dormer of a church, and in the distance (he discovered he was pulling back and could see farther now) more hills rose and fell, with houses and barns and silos and the bright patchwork of fields, and beyond that steeper hills with mansions. As the moment broke, the landscape slipped from its roots and rushed toward him. For a long time he watched lawns, flower beds, pretty houses with shingled roofs pour down the hillside into the lagoon, pulling after them the trees, the quiet lanes, the distant fields and silos, the mansions on the remote hills. Buildings appeared on the crest of the farthest hill and sank out of view into a valley, only to reappear on the next crest closer and careen once again down into a valley and appear again still closer. Towers, steeples, farmhouses, meadows with rock walls, wooded pastures rose and fell as they approached; the closer landscape was already a blur as tier upon tier of houses and markets swept down the final hillside into the water. The water swallowed them with scarcely a ripple, lapping quietly at the bare shoreline when it was over; and only by paying careful attention was Lorin able to see that the surface was dimpled with small whirlpools.

The sudden quiet made him open his eyes. They had been making a great deal of noise, he realized. An unfamiliar face with four eyes and two noses and a mouth overlapping another mouth was looking at him. "Well," she said. He closed his eyes again and the whirlpools had become pinwheels. He opened them and the parts to her face had fallen back together. She was smiling at him cross-eyed. He tried very hard not to hear footsteps in the bedroom. There were a great many footsteps just outside, going past on the deck, also loud voices, and he wished they would go away. He disliked lying there with his pants down, but every time he mustered the resolution to pull them up he discovered he had been asleep, having wild dreams. At such moments Gloriana put her fingertips on his eyelids and closed them, and he would start again from a different dream to hear a different series of noises from outside. Finally, though, it ended, when she kissed him awake, shook him by the shoulder and told him he mustn't go back to sleep; it was very late, he had better go home.

She had put herself back together and was kneeling beside him with large worried eyes, tugging his pants up over his hips. He had been dreaming he was in a drugstore trying to select a greeting card from a rack that rotated on an axis, and someone kept rotating it before he could make his choice. He took hold of the rack with both hands, but it turned anyway, and he started awake and saw her worried eyes. In a panic he asked what time it was, but whatever she told him didn't register because he was consumed with the problem of getting his belt fastened and his fly zipped. He got up and stumbled to the door. She followed him, her hands clasped anxiously in front of her until she had to unlock and open it for him. He heard her softly call goodnight as he made his way toward Simon's apartment, bumping into the rail at intervals. Simon's window was dark with the curtain pulled closed, and Lorin by now had the presence of mind not to pound on the door with his fist. He put his watch up close to one eye and made out, through layers of gauze, that it said twenty minutes to four. He lurched to the staircase and crept down, holding onto the rail with both hands (the overhead light was burned out), walked into the coke machine in the arcade at the bottom, and ran across the courtyard to the street. He hadn't remembered Gloriana's door close; she was probably still standing there watching his humiliation.

He found his car under a streetlight on the next block and drove home, steering across two or three lanes with one hand while digging the knuckles of the other into his eyes, once nearly ramming a yellow Porsche stopped at the light where Wilshire crossed San Vicente. His breath was short by the time he pulled into his driveway, his hands had grown more fingers before he reached the front door, and he despaired of finding a key that would fit. One did, finally, and he entered, humming bravely. He stopped in the kitchen and poured a small glass of wine which he drank in two long swallows, to steady his nerves. He hummed a little more loudly and went into the bathroom, and even stayed long enough to brush his teeth, which had grown unhygienic with all the wine and the going to sleep and waking up. Coming out of the bathroom he paused to yawn loudly and stretch, clapped a hand to his stomach, hitched once at his belt, straightened his shoulders. He marched into the bedroom, but of course there was no one in it, and got undressed and went straight to bed.

# 11

*T*he next few days were awkward. Yvonne came home briefly the next afternoon while he was daubing at his still-life on the screened porch. He heard her enter the house by the front door and go into the bedroom, and he heard the jangle of hangers in the closet and the shriek of the top drawer of the dresser. A while later he heard the front door close and Andrea's Volkswagen start up and pull away. Yvonne hadn't even come out to the porch to see what he was doing, and she had seen his car in the driveway. He didn't go to the Blue Couch that night, or answer the phone the two or three times it rang, and she didn't come home after rehearsal. He practiced the solitary vice while thinking about her stepping into a mountain pool in a leotard made of shaving cream, and went to bed late. The next day he drove to the university to ask how to remove his name from the records so it would be as if he had never been born at all as far as the university was concerned. He was told that retroactive withdrawals could be used only for a course not completed and only at the discretion of the professor, whom he would have to consult personally.

Yvonne was at the house when he returned, Andrea with her. They were sitting at the breakfast table eating saffron rolls with slices of roast beef and cheese. Yvonne looked at him with grave, sincere eyes. She had to get right back to work, but Andy had wanted to see the place that day if possible and had offered to drive her home for lunch. She didn't know quite how to put this, but she and Andy had been talking for some time about moving in someplace together, and it was sort of coming to a head since the lease on Andy's apartment ran out at the end of the month, and actually they had hoped she would just be able to move in here rather than both of them picking out an entirely new place, and all things considered (a pause here while Yvonne looked down at the table top and then back up) this seemed perhaps a good time to begin making the necessary arrangements, if those could be done in a day or two. Andrea sat smiling at Lorin, her hands folded on the table among the saffron crumbs. He rather liked Andrea. She was unprincipled and would be party to any program of lies required of her, just to see how it turned out. She wore electric blue contact lenses and her hair hung in two long black braids down the front of her shoulders. Her chin was weak, but in a black leotard and tights she looked elastic and as strong as a whip. Her fiance had been killed a year ago in a motorcycle accident near Palmdale, and Yvonne had worried aloud to Lorin that she seemed not to have had a sex life since, nor wanted one. She had given him a pleasant jolt once; the three of them had been walking to her apartment building along a sidewalk covered with crushed St. John's breadfruit pods, and she had remarked that they smelled like sperm, much to Yvonne's embarrassment. Yvonne thought they smelled like earwax.

Lorin said he would see what he could do and went back to his screened porch. He heard them leave a short time later. He spent the afternoon carrying his boxes of clothes and books, his portfolios, his paint cases and canvases and other effects out to his car, where he stuffed what he could into the trunk and piled everything else in the back seat. Tears burned in his throat when he saw how little difference the removal of his belongings made on the appearance of the rooms. He pulled the madras spread off the bed because it was his, and that helped. He dismantled the still-life he had set up what seemed a long time ago, when their troubles were fresh, and carried each part to its respective shelf or drawer or cabinet or nook, except the wicker chair itself, which was his, and which he carried to the back yard and turned upside down on the grass to be rained on and mold to death. He folded up his easel and laid it on the floor behind the driver's seat, and laid the painting face up on top of everything, gumming the upholstery and the headliner with wet paint. He had to admit the picture was starting to come together. It was a pity to stop now. He used the bathroom one last time and took the mouthwash with him, not because it was his but because he didn't want her to have it. As a final gesture he removed the front-door key from his chain and dropped it where she would find it if she stopped to look before flushing, and then went out and got in his car.

———

He slept in the car that night, all four doors locked, in a parking lot at Will Rogers State Beach, his knees bent under the steering wheel, his head on a rolled-up army blanket placed against the passenger's door. Strangers were looking at him through the windows when he woke up the next morning, so he slept the next night parked on the shoulder of a wooded side road in the hills east of Malibu, only to find when it was light that he was in a driveway leading to an enormous iron gate behind which two doberman pinschers paced. He spent the third night parked in the lot behind an abandoned movie theater in Venice and heard things scuttle over broken glass until dawn. The fourth night was spent in a cul-de-sac between two rows of beach houses, within sight of the carousel on the Santa Monica pier, until he was wakened by a flashlight and two belligerent men in uniforms told him to move his ass out.

He decided she had been punished enough, and at noon—it was Sunday—went to visit Shannon and Harry for lunch and arranged to sleep at their place for a night or two. They were not happy to have him there, and Shannon was rude. Something in the way Shannon sat on a kitchen stool was an affront. He sat with his legs crossed, a hand cradling an elbow, his palm open to the ceiling, the cigarette between his fingers nearly touching the back of his wrist. He tilted his head to one side and looked at you quizzically when you were talking to him. Shannon towered over Lorin when they both were standing, and he wore his hair in bangs because he wanted to look like a little English schoolboy. Harry was easier to take, and of all his friends Lorin disliked Harry the least.

Harry had a benevolent disposition and was hard-working; his greatest fault was that he was naive. Lorin didn't care for his paintings at all. Seven or eight or them hung on the walls of the apartment, including the bathroom walls. An obsession haunted Harry's work. He worked without models or references, pursuing a private vision that Lorin thought indicated trouble somewhere up the road. It was a woman, in the same violent portrait revised endlessly. She took form through slashes of whites and pinks separating out from slashes of blacks and browns and greens. Where several slashes terminated, an upper lip curled, exposing slashes of teeth. Where shorter slashes of white and brown cohered, muddy eyes glared out over red lids. Nostrils, sometimes more than two, were torn into whatever space remained below, sometimes pulling the lip, as though by fishhooks, to join the scar of a septum between them. Harry's brush strokes were not always on the mark, and strings of flesh flew past the body's limits and tangled with slashes of costume and vine at the edges of the composition. Sometimes fingers emerged from these over-reaches, gripping rags, their knuckles scarred white. The movement of the strokes always returned your eye to the ruined face, the lip pulled up or torn away to expose teeth, the eyes spread wide to expose black irises surrounded by white, the ragged buds of ears pulling outward from the jaw, straining the sutures of the skull. The skull was hairless.

Lorin was glad to have the floor space and the sleeping bag borrowed from one of the girls next door, and tried to be comfortable with what he had. He took the sleeping bag with him when, a few days later, he gave in to an impulse to drive to the Bay Area and see an old girl friend from Salt Lake who was teaching at an experimental open school in Berkeley. He spent the weekend trying to find her, but her listing in the telephone directory led him to a block of soiled row houses that were being demolished and the school was not listed. He slept across the Bay in a park where people wandered in pairs all night and carried his sleeping bag under his arm when he went for breakfast at a place in the Cannery. He left late Sunday night and drove back to Los Angeles, exiting 101 just in time to catch the heaviest part of commuter-hour traffic. He was back in the Village by ten o'clock, his head grainy from lack of sleep and the long drive. He climbed the stairs to the apartment, ripe for a quarrel, and pushed open the door just in time to hear Shannon shriek and see the covers yanked over two heads and two quivering bodies. He tiptoed past and closed the door to the two halves of the apartment. He crawled into Harry's bed and drifted to sleep, listening to nervous whispers on the other side of the door.

Late in the afternoon he returned the sleeping bag to the girls in the next apartment and thanked them so effusively and described his disappointed trip with it over the weekend so beguilingly that pretty soon it was supper time, and afterward they offered to let him use it on their floor that night. They made jokes about which one was going to slip into it with him while he was asleep, but as neither did he stayed awake a long time to no purpose. During the week he was there he used the typewriter belonging to the one who taught high school to write a formal letter to the owner of the Blue Couch, announcing his resignation and his relief to be through with all the fraudulent intellectuals, bad artists, creeps, hypocrites, junkies, and friends who stabbed you in the back while they were pretending they liked you, and the dirty floors and the greasy stove. It looked intemperate when he read it over, and he worried that Malcolm might balk at sending him his last check, so he wrote it again, substituting rapier ironies for the invective, and personally delivered it one morning when he found Malcolm curled like a shrimp under the long table made from a door at the Blue Couch.

"Where the fuck have you been and what the fuck is this?" Malcolm held the envelope close to his nose, trying to read the name.

"It explains everything," said Lorin, and stalked out.

———

Over the next few days he was transient and irritable, and kept leaving things behind at the places he stayed. He forgot to take his electric alarm clock when he left the girls in the apartment next door to Shannon and Harry's, and never went back for it because he hated warmed-over goodbyes. He left a bag of dirty laundry at Dennis and Angela's, a pair of tennis shoes and an umbrella at John Drury's, a carton of books at Lisa and Mark Telford's, where he also broke a cup while carrying it on a saucer between the breakfast table and the sink after Mark had gone to work, leaving him alone with Lisa. At the last place he stayed, a redwood bungalow up a canyon rented by the girl who had shared his locker and whose husband was in the army in Germany and where regrettably he took advantage of his host's absence, he forgot his toothbrush and mouthwash on the day he finally left for Utah. A man's disintegration began with his possessions, and he was getting away just in time.

———

This period of wandering was freshened, of course, by trips to the well. You could savor your misery by visiting old haunts still vibrant with mirages of Yvonne, but at the same time to turn away from water on principle made you look like a martyr, and he did not want to give her that satisfaction. Accordingly, when he was not busy making himself miserable by visiting old haunts or looking for a place to spend the night he played happy games with Gloriana, and those made him miserable too. In fact this was how he met her roommate finally. They were eating sandwiches and drinking French onion soup from coffee mugs on her couch one afternoon while he was still living in his car, when they heard a key in the lock and the door suddenly opened. Nothing stopped your heart like the sound of a key in a lock when you were on the other side of a door where you shouldn't be. Lorin felt pale but forced himself to look up. The roommate stopped when he saw them, then came in and closed the door while Lorin stared.

It was, incidentally, the merest chance that they had not been handling each other at that instant, in fact that they were seated at opposite ends of the couch, Lorin with his feet on the coffee table and Gloriana with hers tucked under her and her skirt pulled over her knees. A few minutes earlier while the soup was still too hot to drink he had been browsing the inside of her thigh while she had held her skirt up and had sat with her head thrown back, her breath coming in catches. A narrow miss like that triggered good intentions, and for the length of time it took Gloriana to manage introductions and Lorin to lay his soup on the table and rise to shake hands he made wild promises to himself never to come here again. She seemed flustered herself, but the introductions went smoothly enough—Floyd, Lorin; Lorin, Floyd—and by the time Lorin had finished shaking hands and realized he was staring he was satisfied there would be no rudeness or violence.

He could not, however, forbear staring during the brief conversation that followed. Floyd wore a checked yellow shirt open at the throat and a green golf sweater. He had worn a cloth cap when he came in, which now hung on a feeler of the television set. He was about Lorin's height, could not have been more than a year or two older, and was if anything thinner. The wrinkled forehead and flared nostrils were the accidental stresses on a man who doesn't like what he finds when he comes home, but it was the fixed units of his person that most arrested Lorin—the pale eyes, the thin nose, the long bony face, the heavy lower lip and receding chin, the unstable adam's apple. No one but himself knew what Lorin looked like from the cheekbones down, but the other correspondences were stark and merely waited for somebody to notice them. Lighten Floyd's hair, force him to grow a beard that looked too heavy for his skinny body and accentuated the forward thrust of his head, dress him in baggy denims and a fatigue shirt whose collar was frayed nearly off, and it might have been himself that Lorin stared at and felt disliked by. As it was, they might have shared the same gene pool.

"There's some soup left if you're interested," Gloriana was saying. She hadn't moved. She still sat at her end of the couch with her legs under her, her elbow on the armrest, her soup mug held over the napkin on her lap lest the gentle swirling she gave it spill some.

"I've eaten," Floyd said. "Harold took us all to the Nickelodeon."

"That was nice."

"I've been there," said Lorin.

"After the third martini we decided lunch could wait and after lunch nobody felt like going back to work, so here I am."

"That's a lot of martinis," said Gloriana.

"I've never had their martinis," said Lorin.

"Mail come yet?"

"The Newsweek came, and a letter from your mother. Otherwise just throwaways."

"She say anything I need to know, or should I have another martini first?"

"No new crises. Jim has already been to New York and back and you didn't write to him and isn't it about time all this funny business in Los Angeles stopped. And your father has quit playing tennis because of his knee. You can read it."

"Oh shit."

"I get letters like that," said Lorin.

"I think I'll get clearance for the tunnels and go sulk there a few days."

Lorin mentioned the resemblance to her the next day over lunch at Clifton's Cafeteria, and alluded to it again jestingly during a walk through Pershing Square. She hadn't noticed, she said. "You were right, though," she added. "He didn't like you."

"That's funny. I thought the world of him."

"After you left he didn't mention you once."

To avoid the chance of other unpleasant encounters, Lorin didn't go to her apartment any more but snatched her from corridors between classes on campus or arranged closely timed rendezvous in the drugstore across the street from the bank on Westwood and Le Conte, and they would drive off to a secluded spot in the mountains where among the dead leaves, concealed by scrub oak and the brow of a hill from either riders on the bridle trail below them or the grounds keeper in the walnut orchard above them, she would nervously be all things to his passion. Once or twice, late at night, she consented to be all things to his passion in the front seat of his car while parked in a dark lot at the beach, but only once or twice.

She was not aware of half the happy games she took part in. She was also unaware of the doubling she was party to when they drove along certain roads, stopped at certain beaches, ate at certain booths at the Farmers' Market, browsed at certain basket shops. She did of course know his arrangement with Yvonne had come apart, and professed the barest twinge of regret that her luring him away for milk to feed his ulcer had contributed, but just because two adults slipped off together for a minute and on an impulse ended up in bed it didn't mean there was a commitment, for heaven's sake, did it? "I mean, she didn't have to go home with somebody else just to prove something. It's not as though we were suddenly in love with each other. I'm not. Are you?"

He murmured of course not. He wished she would be quiet. They were on wet grass on a hill overlooking the San Diego Freeway, under a clouded moon, and something cold had just run over his leg, and he was imagining her pink and warm from the shower, nestled into downy sheets after locking him out on his screened porch with a sleeping bag and a towel.

"I mean we may have been wrong to do it in the first place," she said, "but if that's all it took to cause a breakup it couldn't have been much of a relationship. She didn't *have* to break it off, and I certainly don't feel guilty about what we've been doing since, even if I do feel a tiny bit guilty about the first time." She was smiling affectionately. Lorin grunted of course not. After a minute she said, "I don't know how much longer Floyd and I will be living together, for that matter. No, it's not because of you, and no you don't look like him."

———

Most of the time during those last weeks, though, he made his sentimental pilgrimages by himself because you fondled sores to more purpose alone. He never drove by the Blue Couch, never went to recover his few paintings from the walls—they may have been stacked in the john now for all he knew—but he very often, late at night, took the narrow side street that wound along the perimeter of the cemetery and drove slowly past the small house without looking at it. By concentrating on the sound of blood roaring in his ears he could darken his peripheral vision on that side as he went past and not have to see if there were lights on or if Noel's car were parked in the driveway. He was embarrassed to be hanging around the sites of his wretchedness this long, like an unhappy ghost, but Lorin never acted in haste, and you didn't punish someone while there was still a chance she was sorry.

# 12

You wore a funny kind of underwear after going through the endowment ceremonies in the temple. They were in one piece; the legs came down to your knees, the back split open to accommodate bodily functions, the sleeves hung loose, exposing your armpits, the neck was scooped low. They offered no support. They had symbolic marks in the stitching over your nipples and belly button. They were called temple garments, or garments for short, and Lorin had dreaded the day when he would have to wear them. They made it especially important, he reflected one morning after he and his companion had been nearly run down by a fat lady in curlers while crossing a busy intersection in Ypsilanti, that you not be in an accident that would send you to the hospital where strangers would undress you. They were one of the things that, thirteen months into his new life, he had not gotten used to. Another was wearing a dark suit that itched every day. Another was opening someone's gate, walking through someone's front yard up to a door, feeling watched from behind the curtains, and knocking. Another was not drinking coffee, the lack of which had given him blinding headaches for the first several weeks. The sweaty dreams were a nuisance too, but those might have been from living in a part of the country he wasn't used to. The first night in a strange bed did that to him too.

They would not know him now, those enemies and betrayers in Los Angeles. If he appeared in their midst, they would not blink at his transformation, because they would not recognize him. He had no beard. He wore dark suits and neckties. He carried an attache case heavy with tracts and softbound copies of a book with an angel blowing a trumpet stamped in gold on the cover. He kept an appointment book in his inside coat pocket. He was never seen except in the company of a companion a couple of years younger than himself, also wearing a dark suit and carrying an attache case. He pounded cold pavements with this companion in a distant northern city, whipped by winds off the lake, breathing industrial grit. He knocked on doors that opened a crack to disclose a nose and further back, cast in shadow, an eye, which he informed that he was Elder Hood and his companion was Elder Sorenson, and what church they represented, and had the eye and nose heard of it and would they like to know more, whereupon the nose withdrew and the crack closed. He sat up late poring over texts and supplements and reference guides until his eyes hurt, the better to have at his fingers' ends the riposte to every challenge. He knew the passage in Amos that foretold the closing of the heavens and the suspension of revelation, and he knew the passage in Joel that promised revelation would be restored in the latter days. He could locate a rhapsodic verse in Zechariah that clearly showed Zion was not to be confused with Jerusalem, and if someone looked at him askance he could flip to a little-known passage in Isaiah that implied the same thing and said furthermore that Zion would be mountainous, and a passage in Micah that said the same thing, only better. With his eyes closed he could pick out sections of Numbers, Ecclesiastes, Jeremiah, Ephesians, John, and Hebrews that described a premortal existence; references in Ezekiel, Isaiah, Daniel, and Hosea to a postmortal one, reinforced by passages scattered all through the Gospels, Acts, Epistles, and Revelation. There were sobering accounts in Luke, Hebrews, and Second Peter of the consequences of apostasy, and harrowing accounts of the misery, in Jude and Revelation, of the ugly third of heaven cast into hell and never privileged to be born.

The head swam, but there was more. He had committed to memory the location, chapter and verse, of every detail, every fugitive utterance in the Old and New Testaments (indexed, for convenience, in his missionaries' guide) referring to modern-day revelation, in order to soften up his listeners to the realization that they must have believed in such a thing all along if they accepted the Bible. While they looked confused, he could gradually introduce the possibility that the modern-day revelation they were talking about just might possibly already exist, and he and his companion just happened to have something in their attache cases that he would like to show them. He had become fairly proficient at dramatically riffling the pages of his Book of Mormon in their presence, looking at them sideways to whet their interest. He had learned the right combination of confidence and modest bemusement to lend his voice when he read aloud, from his Doctrine and Covenants, Joseph Smith's 1832 prophecy of

the Civil War and where it would break out, the better to enflame
their desire to know more, because the nose did not always with-
draw and the crack close. No, more than once he and his companion were let past the door by a worried housewife in curlers
from whom they extracted an invitation to return in the evening
when her husband would be there.

He had also learned not to expect too much from such an invitation. The same housewife was a different person when they
came back in the evening. She no longer wore curlers and the
worry-lines around her eyes had hardened. Behind her they could
see her husband reading the paper in his cracked naugahyde
recliner and the children lying on the floor in the blue glare of
the television screen. She had told her husband they were coming and he had told her to tell them to get lost when they did.
She was sorry, but that was that. Sometimes they did get let in,
and even met the husband, who either scowled and left the room
or slouched at the far end of the sofa, looking bored, or—on the
very rare occasion when he chose to be polite—shook their hands,
smiled, and tolerated them. Sometimes they got as far as the second or third visit before they were stopped. "Sure, sonny. Gold
plates. Heh, heh." He lay awake nights wondering if he were
being punished for waiting so long to go on a mission.

———

Sorenson was his third companion, and the most congenial
one. His first one, Elder Cobb, had been a fat, happy country
boy from Georgia, with spaces between his teeth and too much
Brylcreem on his hair. Lorin had made the mistake once of calling him by his first name, so startling him that for the remaining
two months they were together Cobb never seemed quite at ease
with him and never went to sleep before Lorin did. His second
companion Lorin frankly disliked. This was Elder Beech, whose
father was a bishop and also an expensive attorney in Phoenix.
Elder Beech wore a crew cut, preached eloquently, had a peculiar, frozen smile and found stories about people breaking bones
unbearably funny. (He was fond, for instance, of reliving a football game he had played the year before as a sophomore in college, in which, as a running end, he had carried the ball across
a stack of teammates and opponents and had landed heavily,
cleats and all, on the back of a hand stuck out of the pile. He even
supplied the sound when he told the story.) Elder Cobb had finished his mission and gone home to marry the girl he had left
behind (the joke among missionaries was that you lost either your
hair or your girl while you were in the field; Cobb had kept both
and gained forty pounds). Beech had been made a district leader

and was given for his junior companion a young elder from California, whose family had coerced him into serving a mission and who was having emotional problems.

Lorin had been transferred to a different district and assigned Sorenson as his senior companion, with whom he got on very well. Sorenson had just previously worked with a muscular zealot from Sacramento, and was now a senior companion himself for the first time. He was from Dallas, was short and pudgy and looked like a frog with thinning hair, and he wore glasses with heavy black rims. He admired Lorin's sense of humor but thought that Lorin swore a little too much. He had been given a two-week leave just after being assigned to Lorin and had flown back to Dallas where his father was dying of bowel cancer. He had returned a few days after the funeral, shaken not only by the death but by the close brush he and his girl friend experienced several times before and after, and Lorin had to spend some time keeping him in spirits on both counts. The pleasures of the flesh got you in big trouble if you were a missionary.

———

This fact was of some consequence to Lorin, because he missed such pleasures very much. Most missionaries were between the ages of nineteen and twenty-two; most were fresh-faced and pure in body if not in mind. Lorin was already well past the normal age for missionaries when he had turned up in the bishop's office the Sunday after returning to Salt Lake from Yvonne's warm bed, and if he was not as scarlet with sin as he might have been he nevertheless had much to omit during that first humiliating interview. The bishop was the same apple-cheeked bald ad man he had avoided three years ago, and he was still nobody's fool, and he had as reasonable a fix on Lorin's past few years as anyone could have from knowing Lorin's family and hearing Lorin's parents speak sadly of the way their oldest had turned out. His questions were tactful but direct, as before, and Lorin lied as little as possible, feeling wretched the whole time. He gave Yvonne and himself separate residences and mentioned the unhappiness of the relationship and its definitive end several times. He reduced the number of encounters with Gloriana to one or two, and transposed the girl in the canyon back a year, stressing her separation from her husband as much as the letter of truth would permit. When the bishop, with a grave expression, asked him if he had trouble with masturbation he said no, and afterward felt bad about that too.

During the weeks and months that followed, up until he received the letter from Church Headquarters calling him to the

Great Lakes, he worried that he had made an important mistake. His mother's tears of joy, his father's quiet pleasure, Sonia and Katy's excitement, Stephen's guarded admiration (disguised as sullenness), all these filled him with an unaccountable self-loathing. The night of his missionary farewell in sacrament meeting, he looked down from the pulpit and saw shiny snakes squirming through the congregation, getting into people's hair, crawling over laps and entering sleeves. In the mission home, a large old mansion on North State, he shared a room with five other elders for the four days of indoctrination classes and woke up each night certain that he had wet the bed, relieved to find he had only sweated through to the blanket.

In the temple he sat shivering in a tiled booth wearing only a white shin-length poncho, open at the sides, while an elderly man dressed in white touched him on the face and under the poncho with fingers dipped in a bowl of water, and another did the same in another booth with fingers dipped in oil, and whispered Lorin's secret name into his ear. Later, dressed in white trousers, shirt, tie, and shoes, he sat with two hundred or so other nervous elders in an immense room whose walls and ceiling were covered with planets and stellar things, and listened to a re-enactment of the Creation; in another room, decorated with giraffes and jungle plants and reached through double doors concealed by a curtain, he watched a dramatization of the Fall. His mind was numb during most of the four hours the endowment ceremony took; his stomach made unpleasant sounds and developed, before he was through with the second covenant, a painful and embarrassing bubble of air because you fasted on the day you went to the temple. Sometime during the long morning, he put on the white robe with the knot on one side and the gather on the other, the apron with its stitching of leaves, the white sash over the apron, the strange cap that resembled a baker's hat. He remembered extending his hand, as the elders left and right of him did, and receiving the hand grips called the Sign of the Nail and the Patriarchal Grip, given by a temple worker in white who passed along the rows of seats, a kindly smile on his face. He remembered raising his right hand and bowing his head with his eyes closed to affirm dreadful oaths of chastity, fidelity, and honesty, and placing his thumb under his left ear and drawing it across his throat to his right ear and later cupping his palms onto the left side of his abdomen and drawing them across to the right. In a pastel green room without murals he was one of ten elders selected for the Circle of Prayer, and stood with his left hand on the right shoulder of a red-faced sweaty elder named Crumb who shared his room at the mission home, and felt the left hand of a thin pimply elder he hadn't seen before on his right shoulder. Later still he stood at a veil with holes in it, the inside of his right knee pressed against the inside of the right knee of the temple worker on the other side of it, the instep of his right foot pressed against the temple worker's right instep, the temple worker's hand thrust through one of the holes to rest on Lorin's right shoulder. Their cheeks were also pressed together, the veil rumpled between them, and Lorin responded to the whispers in his ear by whispering back into the temple worker's ear. The veil was pushed aside, the Patriarchal Grip was exchanged, and Lorin passed through into a corridor behind several elders who had just finished ahead of him. He entered a room filled with pastel yellow chairs and couches, glittering chandeliers, elaborate molding with gold leaf, and a great variety of mirrors on the walls.

He was startled to see himself for the first time in his white clothes with the strange hat. To hide his nervousness he looked around for somebody he knew among the milling elders, who had nothing more to do now than wait for everyone behind them to finish so they could all leave. He saw Elder Norton, another of his roommates, standing by a lamp with a carved wooden base. Lorin had noticed that everyone seemed under the kind of tension that caused fits of hysterical giggles among grown men, and he was grateful to see a friendly face. He approached Norton, extending a hand. "Guess what they told me my name is," he said. "David. Just David." He was about to josh about being disappointed it wasn't something like Mahonri Moriancumer but was stopped by the look on Norton's face.

"You're not supposed to tell anybody that, you dumb ass!"

Lorin looked around, hoping nobody else had heard. One or two elders on the other side of a couch were looking at him curiously, but they were too far away to have heard. They were probably looking at him because he was older than anybody else in the room.

———

He was not sure, then, when at last he found himself in that distant northern vineyard to pluck heathens from the vine, that something funny had not happened deep in his brain. It worried him that though he hated what he was doing he nevertheless did not miss painting. Sometimes he would unbend to Sorenson, who seemed to have fewer anxieties than his earlier companions, and tell him as much about Yvonne as he thought would not make him uncomfortable, always leaving out the hardcore fact of their living together. Sorenson always seemed pleasantly interested, and now and then even a trifle envious.

Sorenson was majoring in chemistry at Southern Methodist University—he would be a senior when he returned there from his mission—and was thinking seriously about chemical engineering as a career. He had a beautiful but bitchy girl friend (Lorin had seen her picture and heard Sorenson's stories) who was waiting for him back in Dallas and wrote him madcap letters twice a week which he read to Lorin. Lorin found them mildly salacious, but as Sorenson and the girl had somehow remained technical virgins despite breathing heavily in each other's laps since high school, they would probably make it through inviolate to a temple wedding as soon as Sorenson was released, and tell their hundreds of randy children and grandchildren that they had saved themselves from the worst until they were safely under the wire. Lorin wished only the best for his companion. He envied people who had so little to hide.

The large frame house whose back bedroom they lived in belonged to a Presbyterian family named Green. The husband and wife were in their late forties, and had an indeterminate number of children and grandchildren whom Lorin never managed to sort out. Some of the children still lived at home. Apart from the one or two times he or Sorenson had jokingly tried to interest the couple in talking about the church, the Greens remained on the periphery of their life. They approved of these young men for their clean lives and dedication to values, and they enjoyed telling their friends they had rented the back room to a pair of Mormon missionaries, but otherwise they kept at a friendly distance. The room didn't have its own access to the outside, but the family had tacitly agreed not to notice the two of them as they came and went through the back door and vanished through a corridor leading off from the TV room to their own room which did, blessedly, have its own bathroom and its own hot plate, and in which Lorin and Sorenson were able to install their own telephone.

They were rarely in the house during the day in any case, because the business of door-to-door tracting, conducting cottage meetings, returning to the homes of investigators, weekly meetings with their district leader, and the other nuts and bolts of life as proselytizers consumed most of the day, and the one day a week that was theirs for diversion usually saw them as far away as they could get in the limited time they had, floundering through meadows on cross-country skis or ice skating on one of the small lakes that dotted the state. Their day started early; they took turns frying bacon and eggs for breakfast, and Lorin counted the days until he could drink coffee again, the one vice he planned to resume when he was released. On days when they had no appointments, they selected a quadrant of the suburb they were currently working, drove Sorenson's car to the nearest shopping center and parked it for the day, and then began knocking on doors up one street and down the next, pausing for lunch at a Woolworth's counter or a delicatessen, and resuming an hour later, Lorin's heartburn making him irritable. This continued until nightfall, when they would treat themselves to dinner at some place a cut or two above Woolworth's, sometimes with another pair of elders from their district, and afterwards knocked on a few more doors just to round out the day before returning home to write letters, update their instant-preparation books (you were often called on to give a sermon without advance warning, and needed an indexed source of topics), look up scriptural references to have an answer next time for some conundrum a hostile contact had flung at them, or write their respective weekly report for the mission president, accounting for one hundred sixty-eight hours since the last report, or simply unwind.

Lorin liked days when they had appointments for follow-up visits. There was always trauma in that first meeting—the nightmare walk through somebody's front yard to a strange door, the deep breath before knocking, the silent prayer that no one would answer, the multiple versions of resistance to their opening line when someone did—but a follow-up visit could almost be a pleasure. It meant, for one thing, they had been liked. Nothing quite compared, for Lorin, to knocking on the door of a house where last time they had been liked, and where this time they were expected. The smile of recognition, however guarded, fired his courage, and he could follow his hosts and his companion to the living room or kitchen and sit down charged with the confidence that he had piqued their interest once and could pique it again. For another thing, a return visit meant questions, and questions were someone else's initiative. They revealed the slits in the armor, and Lorin, spared the horror of wondering where to begin, could penetrate those slits and know he was touching a useful nerve. Let someone ask them about, say, miracles, and he could expound for an hour on the constancy of natural law and explain how its apparent violation consisted merely in a visible effect proceeding from an invisible cause, for instance the horse brushing an electric wire and dying without knowing the cause of its death. This provided a way into the discussion of the physical nature of spirits versus the physical nature of angels, an important doctrinal distinction, and it was as though the investigator rather than the proselytizers had brought it up.

Or let someone ask about original sin, and Lorin, after a disarming pleasantry (not many sins were very original, ha ha), explained that no, we made our own beds and slept with our own lumps, not with Adam's. This led naturally enough to the discussion of Adam's complicity in the whole plan, because (and only Mormons knew this) Adam was none other than the Archangel Michael himself, who, as Michael, had been party to the Creation, and as Adam, held the priesthood, partook of the fruit knowingly in order to bring mortality on himself and Eve and consequently their descendants (whom otherwise they would not have had), and thus set in motion the chain of events that made it both necessary and possible that the Redeemer be born to salvage the wreckage of sin and mortality. (Dead silence usually followed this disclosure. It was one of the make-or-break points in the series of lessons.)

Did Mormons believe in the Trinity, like other Christians? a middle-aged housewife with hymns on the piano asked. Of course, they told her blandly, understanding that the burden of the question lay in its anxious last clause. Were they asking her to enter something wholly alien, or were there points of congruity with order as she had always known it? Of course, they said reassuringly. This led handily to an elaboration of one of the first principles, that God was physical and so was Jesus Christ and they weren't the same person at all, except in purpose, and that the Holy Ghost was someone else again, and was not physical. From there it was easy to move to the disclosure that God himself was once mortal, and that mortal human beings, locked into a continuum of eternal progression of which this life was only a part, might themselves aspire to godhood, each with his own universe to create and embellish. How did they reconcile eternal progression with perfectibility? asked an unpleasant man whom they didn't see again. A quiet reference to relativity and an allusion to Zeno's Paradox settled him handily, though he did not look as crestfallen as Lorin suspected he should when they left his house for the last time.

As the junior companion, Lorin tended to let Sorenson do most of the talking, though they took turns, as the custom was, giving the first discussion, or the second discussion, and so on. Lorin's powers of improvisation ran thinner in some places than in others, which meant that at times it was best to let him fade into silence. He was not particularly good, for instance, in discussions about covenants and faith, so Sorenson usually took over there, but he could be luminous on the subjects of revelation or inspired translation, or devils or angels. It was a fruitful marriage of temperaments, and in just a few months' time the two of them had conjured belief in three or four investigators, and had baptized two of these already, in the swimming pool of the local YMCA, with several elders from their zone, as well as the zone and district leaders and the mission president himself and one of his counselors in attendance.

Lorin was interested to see which aspect of church doctrine or arcanum had turned the tide for which new convert, because everybody had a different point where resistance fell. With Mr. Atherton it had been the promised reunion with his wife, who had died a dozen years ago. With the Streatleys it had been the presence of authority in the restored priesthood, which Methodism made no claim to and which the Streatleys had found a serious omission. With Virginia Morris, a graduate student in linguistics at the Catholic university in Detroit, it had been as much as anything else a reference in the Book of Mormon to elephants on the American continents when no elephant fossils had been discovered at the time Joseph Smith had produced the book. It was a good record, and he was ripe for catastrophe.

# 13

*T*hey were tracting late one night through a raw suburb

whose streets were still unpaved and whose houses—Korean War
vintage—had been built on a landfill and had started to settle
crookedly. Their amusement, when tracting was going badly, was
to re-invent the people who had closed the door in their faces.
Tonight they had been turned away by a pharmaceutical sales-
man with a nose like a potato, who had been accompanied by
a German shepherd that slunk away when it saw them standing
in the doorway holding attache cases; by a crew-cut, pipe-
smoking architect whose wife made her own dentures at the
kitchen table; a plump divorcee with sprayed-gold hair, who
worked days as a chiropractor's receptionist and played the organ at night in a cocktail lounge; a physicist who had mistakenly
bought a twenty-thousand-dollar house in a neighborhood of
eleven-thousand-dollar ones and whose wife gave him stomach
aches; the manager of a local Baskin-Robbins, where business was
slack during the cold weather; an elderly widow who did her own
yard work wearing heavy gloves and drank beer in the kitchen
with the curtains drawn; a jeweler with a grey unhealthy face
and a southern accent, who painted his own murals on his walls
and didn't drink at parties because it would not look right for
a watchmaker's hands to shake in the mornings. Somewhere in
that cross-section, there should have been the combination of at-
tributes that would have let them get past their first sentence.
The law of averages should have seen to that.

They were by now weary, heartsore and discouraged. The
night was cold, streetlights hadn't been installed in this suburb
yet, hard grainy snow whipped around their ankles, and the
lights of the houses they had left and those that still lay ahead
glowed in warm mockery on both sides of the quiet street. They

were about to trudge back to Sorenson's car and go home, when they noticed a single light burning in a back window of a house they had given up for dark. It was a small, homely brick-and-frame bungalow with a sad little privet hedge, lacking foliage, lining the edge of the lawn where the mailbox stood. Two cast-iron trestles, framing iron leaves, supported the porch-eave and tried to hide behind a pair of matched arborvitae bushes on either side of the stoop. Lorin and Sorenson looked at each other's red noses and wet eyes, and trudged across the street and rang the bell. It was obviously not promising, but they had heard too many accounts of success opening like a sunburst behind the one door that had been nearly passed by in despair. They stood on the stoop, facing each other and saying nothing, and Lorin rang the bell again. A moment later they heard a shuffle, and the inside door opened on a young wife with freckles and bad teeth, who peered at them angrily through the storm glass.

"We're missionaries for the Mormon church," said Sorenson. "Do you know about the Mormon church?" His lips were stiff from the cold and Lorin wasn't sure she could understand him.

"Just a minute," she said, and flipped on the porch light. "Now, what?" Her voice was faint behind the glass.

"Missionaries," said Sorenson. "Mormon church. Heard of it?"

"No," she said, and was about to close the door when her glance fell on Lorin, and she stopped. "Missionaries?" she said. Lorin was trying very hard to look cold and tragic and harmless. "You mean *Christian* missionaries?"

He nodded, catching the runoff from his nose with the back of a finger. Sorenson said, raising his voice, "I wonder if we might talk to you and your husband for just a few minutes. This is Elder Hood. I'm Elder Sorenson."

"You must be kidding," she said. "You're really missionaries?" She had opened the storm door a crack to hear better. The two rubber-banded tassels of her hair flipped back and forth behind her head as she looked from Lorin to Sorenson. "I thought they went places like Africa. Are you selling Bibles?" She looked at Lorin, who shook his head, watching his white breath gather on the storm glass. "Listen," she said, "I don't like to be rude but I don't know you, see, and it's late. We were just going to bed." Lorin nodded, watching the collar of her bathrobe ice over and disappear.

"We wouldn't want to keep you long," Sorenson said. "Elder Hood and I just wanted to tell you one or two things about the church we represent and leave you some reading matter and ask you to give us a call if you had any questions." Lorin nodded, watching hairline crystals form in the hardened cloud he had left on the glass. There were Golden Questions you were supposed to ask—what do you know about the Mormon church, would you like to know more—but when the first one drew a blank, you let the dynamics of the situation dictate your next move. Sorenson was good at the soft sell. Though you needed to get on the other side of that door, there were times when the best tactic was one of restraint, briskness, even an amiable indifference. You had come to deliver information and then you had to hurry off because you had other places to be. They could accept the information or not, as they chose. This way you didn't threaten their composure. Sometimes it worked.

"You really are missionaries," she said. "Isn't that funny."

"Funny?" said Sorenson pleasantly.

She opened the crack wider. "My horoscope today said to avoid financial agreements. When you rang the bell I thought it was somebody selling life insurance or something."

"That's a good one all right," said Sorenson. Lorin rumbled with laughter.

"But it *is* late," she said. Sorenson glanced at his watch and looked startled. "Good grief, so it is." He smiled ruefully at Lorin. "Well, we've done it again, Elder." He turned back to the girl behind the storm door. "I'm sorry, Mrs.—" He glanced at the nameplate under the doorbell, but the name was behind a clear plastic strip that had frosted over. Lorin looked at it too. "Well, we won't keep you any longer," said Sorenson, turning again to the girl, the corners of whose mouth twitched slightly. "Let me just leave you a little brochure if I may, a pamphlet really, and you can—well, I seem to have run out." He stood on one foot, balancing his open attache case on his knee, and fumbled between two of the dividers, while Lorin watched a few granules of snow drop past him from the porch eave and eddy onto a mantled rosebush. "Well, I'll have to leave you this one instead," said Sorenson, snapping the case shut, holding a tract between his teeth. "My card is stapled inside, and if you think you'd like to see the other pamphlet, just give me a call. Or for that matter," he said quickly, "we could just stop by tomorrow and leave it with you. We have time to come by in the morning don't we, Elder?"

Lorin glanced at his watch. "Yes, I think so."

"No, I think I'd better call you," she said, her eyes hard and suspicious again. She opened the crack a little further to accept the tract that Sorenson handed in. She looked at the cover and burst out laughing.

"I'm afraid it's not a very good picture," admitted Sorenson. The tract was the one called "Joseph Smith Tells His Own Story," and the picture on the cover was a portrait of the prophet wearing a high Victorian collar and ascot, staring icily at the viewer and looking like an outraged hawk.

She covered her mouth. "He has beady eyes," she said.

"He sort of does in that picture," Sorenson said. "I wish they'd used a different one."

"He saw through his fingertips once," said Lorin.

She looked up. "What?"

"During a vision," said Lorin. "His whole body was filled with light, and he could see out at the ends of his fingers and toes."

She stared at him while Sorenson stood in pained silence. Then she tittered once. "Vision," she said.

"I'm afraid so," he said.

There was complete silence for a few moments, except for the patter of snow that blew against the front window, while she stared at them each in turn. Her lips were pressed tightly together and her face was white behind its sprinkling of freckles.

"Did you guys come directly here? I mean did you stop somewhere first before you got here?"

"We almost didn't come at all," said Sorenson. "We thought nobody was home."

"No, but I mean why right now? Why not five minutes ago?"

"We were across the street and saw the light on. We didn't see it before."

She put a hand over her mouth. Her eyes were bright and wet as she darted them back and forth, now at Lorin who stood there staring back, his fingers numb around the handle of his attache case, now at Sorenson, owlish and confused. Still covering her mouth, she pushed open the storm door with the hand that still held the tract with its beady-eyed author on the cover. "Maybe you'd better come in," she said.

Trying not to seem surprised, because God worked in mysterious ways, they entered, Lorin first and then his companion, and stood uncertainly in the middle of the living room, leaving half-circles of snow on the carpet. She pointed them to a small tweedy sofa and turned on a table lamp that stood next to it. "Wait till I get my husband," she said and disappeared down the hallway toward the room where they had seen the light. Left to themselves, they looked around them.

"Nice house," said Sorenson.

"Yes," said Lorin.

The house was warm and tidy and smelled of tuna fish and

fresh bread and chicken noodle soup. From where they sat they could take in most of it, from the grained cabinets hung over the sink to the breakfast bar separating the kitchen from the dining area, which lacked a table, to the asphalt tile running from beneath the carpet down the hallway to the bedrooms, to the low table in front of the curtained window they had trudged past to reach the door. On the table smiled a porcelain mandarin bought with green stamps. On the other side of the wall behind them was the garage, in which there doubtless stood a shiny new Volkswagen. Lorin suspected he could have invented them. Mutters floated up the dark hallway, followed by the creak of bedsprings, and a moment later the girl came out, briskly, as though she had just won an argument. She flopped into an armchair across from them and folded her arms while an embarrassed young man in pajamas and wool socks and bathrobe followed her into the room.

"This is Richard," she said. "Tell him what you just told me about the fingers."

They stood up to shake hands with their host, who tried very hard to look in charge. "I see we've come at a bad time," Sorenson said. There was no remaining chair in the room, so Richard, after thrusting out his lower lip to appear thoughtful, sat down next to Lorin on the couch.

"I understand you're missionaries," he said, and cleared his throat.

"Tell him what you told me," said the girl.

"I'm not sure that's a good place to begin," said Lorin.

"Hey, come on."

He had impulsively shot the wrong bolt first, but it had gotten them into the house. The worst that could happen now was that more of the same might crack his listeners' credulity or expose them as sensation-seekers. While Sorenson rummaged nervously through his attaché case Lorin faced the brave eyes of his host and said, "I don't remember just how this came up, but what I was saying to your wife—"

"We're the Klings," she said. "He's Richard. I'm Alice."

"Yes," said Lorin, feeling off balance. "We're very happy to know you. I'm Elder Hood, and this is Elder Sorenson." They shook hands again. "What I was saying to your wife may have sounded a little funny, so maybe I should explain—"

"No, just tell him what you told me about this guy." She waved the tract. "He was having this vision, right? Now, go on."

The worst had happened. They had been let in for the wrong reason. "Well, I won't say anything about the vision itself," said Lorin, glancing at Sorenson. "I mean not that it isn't interesting, but that's a whole story by itself. Actually it's pretty central.

We can tell you later if you probably have any questions." Sorenson was taking things out and putting them back. Lorin cleared his throat. "What it was, actually, was that he said, this was afterward of course, that while he was having this vision it seemed like his body was filled with light and he could see out at the ends of his fingers and toes."

"See?" she said to her husband, her chin thrust out.

"Wasn't he wearing shoes?" he said into his hand.

"Oh no, don't try to get out of it by making jokes!"

"I never said it couldn't happen," he said.

"You did too! You said I was fantasizing!"

"Well isn't it the same thing?"

"God, you're dumb." She turned to Lorin and rattled the tract at arm's length. "Was this guy fantasizing?"

"I don't believe so," said Lorin, and exchanged a glance with Sorenson, who had stopped rummaging.

"What we believe it was," said Sorenson, "was a temporary increase in the faculties of his mind. You know—certain cells in your body, the ones in your eye, are sensitive to light, that's how you can see. Probably all that happened here was that a lot of different kinds of other cells got suddenly sensitized too. It isn't necessarily as mysterious as it sounds."

"See?" she said, glaring in triumph at her husband.

"It will happen to everybody sooner or later," said Lorin.

"What Elder Hood means is that our church believes in a physical afterlife where these increased faculties will be normal," said Sorenson, who clearly wished Lorin would shut up. "What Joseph Smith had was just sort of a preview."

"We'll all go around heaven seeing with our toes?" asked their host.

"God, Richard," said his wife.

"I'd like to begin at the beginning," said Sorenson, glancing at his attache case. "I mean, I think this would make more sense if we started there."

"Do you believe in visions?" Lorin asked his host, whom he had decided he did not much like.

"No, not really," said Richard. "But I don't think that's something you can pronounce on positively. I think you have to think about semantics."

"Do you believe in God?" Lorin pursued.

Richard drew himself up. "I believe in a cosmic spirit."

"That's a good starting place," Sorenson said, as Alice burst into laughter. She had a squeaky laugh.

"He just read that somewhere," she said.

"I did not. Besides, what difference does it make, if that's what I believe."

Lorin decided to adjust his terminology and go in for the kill. "Do you believe in a sixth sense?"

Alice laughed and clapped her hands. "Do you guys know what we were doing just before you came?"

"Alice," said Richard.

"No, this is weird," she said. "I mean at just exactly that second you rang the bell. It was like you were waiting until we were through."

"I'm awfully sorry," said Sorenson, pink to the ears.

"We rang as soon as we got here," said Lorin.

"That's what's weird," she said.

"It might interest you to know that our church believes in eternal marriage," said Sorenson, pulling chestnuts from fires.

"What's that mean? No divorces?"

"No, it means you keep on being married in this afterlife I mentioned. That is, if you're married in the temple. I think I'm getting a little ahead of myself."

She looked interested. "Does that mean—" She waved her hand in rapid circles. "—you know?"

"Yes it does," said Sorenson, pink again.

"Fantastic." She had taken off her slippers and now curled her legs under her, nestling back in the chair.

"It also means the family remains intact," Sorenson went on. "Your children and everything, I mean."

"We haven't decided about children yet. Have we, Richie?" She wriggled prettily against the back of her chair.

"I'm sure you will soon," said Sorenson. "And when you do, I'm sure you won't want to lose them."

Richard cleared his throat. "My wife and I believe that children aren't necessarily mandatory in a marriage. I realize that's an unpopular view."

"But we are thinking about it," she said.

"It might interest you to know that our church teaches that we existed in a spirit form before we were born," said Sorenson. "There's even some idea that we have a say in who our parents are going to be."

"Boy, did you pick wrong, Richard!" Her husband sniffed and folded his arms.

"I mentioned this because we were talking about children," Sorenson said. "The church teaches that there are a certain number of spirits needing to be born. Mortal life is just a step along the way, see, but an essential step."

"Hey, but can we go back to that vision?" asked Alice. She had shifted her position in the chair in which she sat curled, and Lorin watched her exposed toes flex against the tweedy arm.

Sorenson was clearly flustered, and Lorin was sorry to have gotten things started on the wrong foot. She shifted again and her toes disappeared under a fold of bathrobe, but he imagined them still there, pink, flexing, little white flocks of fresh lint between them. He turned his attention to the white freckled knee just as she noticed it herself and tugged her robe over it. "I mean don't take too long because Richard has to go to work tomorrow, but he doesn't believe me about how that's happened to me and I want him to hear."

"Happened to you?" asked Sorenson, fearfully.

"About the fingers, I mean. Only it was all over." She pointed at Richard. "Only he doesn't believe me, he said I was fantasizing. Listen, I don't fantasize about *that*."

"Alice," he said. "Look, it's only happened once—"

"How do you know? Maybe it happens every time and I just don't tell you any more! Maybe it happened tonight!"

"Did it happen tonight?" he asked, sitting forward.

"No, but if it did I wouldn't tell you."

"My wife sees things she's not looking at," Richard explained.

"I'm not going to talk to you any more, Richard!" she said. "First you say it's only happened once and then you make it sound like I go *around* that way!"

"Is there anything we can do?" asked Sorenson, and Lorin thought very hard to discover whether something here needed the laying on of hands.

"About what?" she asked.

"Well, if this thing has been bothering you maybe you'd like to talk about it," said Sorenson, the soul of tact.

"It didn't bother me. I liked it."

Lorin earnestly hoped nothing required the laying on of hands. He and Sorenson had participated in a laying on of hands the week before and he wasn't anxious to do it again. It might not work with only the two of them. What had happened was this. There was a phone call late at night from the local branch president summoning them ten miles out of town along icy roads to the home of one of the members, whose wife had been seized by something. They arrived within the hour, their fingers numb, their mouths foul with sleep, and found the branch president, one of his counselors, and two other missionaries assigned to that district sitting in the front room, talking quietly. The branch president had his arm around the shoulders of a man who sat staring at the floor. "Here are the other elders," the branch president said, looking up. "Glad you could come."

Brother Heinmiller had been in the kitchen, the branch president explained, putting things away and preparing to let in the dog and go around locking doors, when he heard a crash from the bedroom, followed by a violent pounding. Guessing that his wife had fallen he rushed in and found her lying on the floor, next to the open closet. The bureau had been pulled over and its mirror lay shattered across the floor. She lay on her side, her ankles caught between the mirror frame and the wall. The pounding noise was her heels against the wall. His first impulse was to pull her away from the bureau before she broke her shins, which were already bleeding, but her arms pressed into her sides as if pulled there by a rope and her body was too rigid to give him a firm grip on anything. Her lips were pulled back from her teeth, one of which had cracked. Her eyes were locked into a wild stare, the irises surrounded by white.

It occurred to him to pull the bureau away, and when he did she screamed and rolled onto her back. She lay glaring at the ceiling, the spittle flying from her lips, her chest heaving. He knelt beside her and took her hand, which she pulled away. He passed his hand over her forehead and she turned her face away. He spoke to her gently as she struggled to get up, and held her by the shoulders, the elbow, the back, in an effort to help her, and she said, "It's all right. Please go away." She fended him off with her elbows and got to her feet, gazing hotly around her as though she hated everything she saw.

She tried to walk and bumped first into the edge of the closet door and then into the wall, all the while making a strange sizzling sound with her mouth. He hurried in front of her and saw she was laughing. She turned and knocked her shin against a leg of the overturned bureau. "I knew it," she mumbled, and laughed her disturbing little laugh again, which sounded like bacon frying. He held up his hands to prevent her from walking across the fragments of mirror, and she whirled away from him and stumbled against the foot of the bed. She gave a shriek of laughter and said, "I knew it." She reached the window and stood leaning her hands on the sill with her forehead pressed against the glass, breathing in great heaves, and finally turned and made for the bed. She shrank coldly from his touch as he helped her to lie down; she didn't answer him as he sat by her side and asked if he could get her anything, and wouldn't she like to close her eyes, and how was she feeling now. She merely looked at him. As he backed out of the room, her eyes followed him all the way to the door.

Lorin listened with all his ears, and wondered if menopause or epilepsy had symptoms like that. It sounded a little like what he had read of religious ecstasies, except that she hadn't appeared to be enjoying it, and he was not sure there really were ecstasies. In any case Lorin knew the family and didn't think they were the kind to have mystical experiences. Heinmiller was the circulation manager of a local newspaper and worked nights clerking at Safeway. His wife, a fat but pleasant woman, played the organ at the branch. One of their sons sold auto parts in the next township; the other had wanted to be a doctor but had ended as a pharmacist in Toledo.

Lorin hoped it wasn't possession by a demon, but there weren't many alternatives left. He watched the high beaded forehead and the bony nose as Heinmiller, in a shaky voice, supplemented or corrected the branch president's review of the incident. He was obviously comforted by the small arm around his shoulder. The branch president was a diminutive man, with red hair and pale blue eyes. He taught sociology at one of the state colleges and was accustomed to taking charge.

"I'm going to ask you, Russ, to stay out here while we go in. Can you do that for me?" He patted the shoulder and stood up, darting a glance at his counselor, who nodded. "Brethren?" said the branch president, smiling tightly at the others. They rose and followed him down the hallway, leaving Heinmiller alone, first the branch president, followed by his counselor, a tall man with heavy dark-rimmed glasses, named Oakley, followed in turn by Elders Burton and Zaret, who were both in their first year in the mission field, followed in their turn by Sorenson, and finally Lorin himself, who had seen that glance pass between the branch president and Oakley, and thought he was going to have the runs. They stopped at the doorway to the bedroom, where they made a considerable crowd, and the branch president, dropping his voice, said, "I don't need to tell you brethren what I think this is, or why I didn't want Russ to come." Lorin narrowed his eyes and nodded, though he did not know what the branch president thought it was, and would have given a great deal to know. "I don't think we need to alarm Dorothy if we can help it," the branch president added. "Hi, Dorothy," he said as they filed in.

She still lay on the bed, where her husband had drawn a quilt over her, reaching to her chin. Her head was propped against a pillow and she watched them come in. Her eyes darted from face to face. Lorin entered last, stepping over the rubble of keys, coins, hair curlers, a wallet, cuff links, perfume bottles, and shards of a mirror, and joined Sorenson and Zaret on one side of the bed, facing Burton, Oakley, and the branch president.

"What are you going to do?" she asked, slurring her words.

"Now don't worry about a thing, Dorothy," said the branch

president. "You gave us a little scare is all, and I've asked the elders to come give me a hand."

"I knew it," she said and made a strange sound in the back of her throat that Lorin with a spasm of fear recognized as laughter.

"What I want you to do is close your eyes and try to relax. Can you do that for me? Now, brethren, if you'll just try to fit in—"

It was awkward at best. This was done most often using a chair, and as a rule no more than three or four holders of the priesthood took part. Lorin suspected that the heavy-duty numbers this time meant something and he felt his scalp creep. She lay in the center of the bed, and the mattress was unluckily soft. The branch president had to lean one knee against it in order to place his hands on her forehead. To keep from losing his balance he was forced to lean his elbow against the headboard. Elder Zaret, directly across from him, hesitated but at last reached out and placed his hands on her crisp grey-flecked hair. Zaret was an uncommonly big man, at least six and a half feet tall and well over two hundred pounds. He wore thick glasses and had an irritating habit, on occasions less worrisome than this, of giggling in a high voice. A convert himself, Zaret tended to sit by reflectively while his companion did most of the talking, as though trying to remember at which point in which discussion he had himself turned the corner and could he have held out longer. Brother Oakley was next. He had a long reach, and placed his hands just to the left of the branch president's hands on her forehead. Sorenson, who was the shortest, had to kneel on the bed to reach across Oakley's and the branch president's hands and place his own hands on her hair to the left of the part. There was no longer an unoccupied quadrant of her head. Lorin and Elder Burton looked at each other across the bed. "Go ahead," said Burton. "No, no, go ahead," said Lorin. Burton climbed onto the bed, tilting against Oakley, and laid his hands gingerly across Oakley's and the branch president's hands, and Lorin, after wiping his palms against the sleeves of his jacket, placed them across Burton's, the heels of his hands resting clear, however, over her eyes. He was able to keep his balance with only one knee on the bed.

"I don't need anything," she said. Her voice was whiny. There was the barest hint of an ugly slyness at the corners of her mouth, and she was in obvious discomfort at the hands placed on her head. She squirmed once under the quilt as the branch president cleared his throat.

Lorin felt the sweat drip down the leg of his pants as the

branch president began the blessing. The very phrase "We the Elders of Israel"—though spoken by a small man in a rumpled suit without a tie—savored of mysterious ancient powers to bless and curse. It hooked the present into a dim sepia past filled with bearded men in tents and brassy cities on the desert through whose streets roamed harlots and lepers. He imagined stone passageways and labyrinthine staircases leading to veiled rooms with incense burning in shallow vessels, and domes rising in the distance, and beyond them, rustling against a hot sky, groves of olive trees with cool dark branches weighted with clusters of whimpering doves.

Lorin listened intently to the words spoken in a quiet voice by the branch president, punctuated by moans from Sister Heinmiller, whose head tossed back and forth on the pillow under their twelve priestly hands, because he might have to do this himself some time. He was familiar with the language of invocations, benedictions, baptisms, confirmations, grave dedications, ordinations, patriarchal blessings, blessings on the sacrament, anointing the sick with oil, but he was hearing things now that he hadn't heard before, just as he had during the endowment ceremony in the temple. He had never been to a dedication of a new temple, but he knew that the dedicatory prayer was exhaustive. Walls were blessed against earthquakes, electrical circuits against malfunction or brownouts. Heating and plumbing systems were consigned to God's protection, likewise staircases, that they might not fall, and windows, that they might not shiver. At the end, he had heard, came the bone-chilling Hosanna Shout, repeated three times by the selected congregation in the temple, followed by dead silence.

What Lorin was hearing now had this same kind of thoroughness. He was hearing names of enemies, pronounced one after another. It was eerie to feel you had control over something you couldn't see. Something was in the poor woman that wasn't going to come out if it didn't have to, and the branch president was going to get it by naming it and telling it it had to. Lorin wished he didn't feel fraudulent about being here. For all he knew, his endowment ceremony in the temple hadn't taken because he'd lied to the bishop about his sex life, and if the demon didn't come out of Sister Heinmiller it would be his fault. He had weakened the authority of the priesthood just by being in the circle with the other priesthood holders. He was like a corroded battery that had passed inspection. Lorin suspected that casting out devils was something like conduction by touching wires. He suspected that a lot of healing was done by conduction, like the transfer of potassium ions from oil of wintergreen into a nerve that was low in potassium. He had meant to ask Sorenson about that. The woman with the hemorrhage had reached through the crowd to touch Jesus's clothes and Jesus had felt virtue drain out of him and had stopped and looked around to see who had siphoned it off, and the woman was cured. The Gadarene swine had attracted the spark of a legion of devils when they had been expelled from the man foaming among the tombs. Lorin wondered, while the branch president continued steadily naming, where the devils had gone after the pigs had run squealing into the sea and drowned themselves. Just possibly salt water was a grounding medium, and they had been discharged into the murk of the ocean floor. He would try to remember to ask Sorenson if salt water could do that. The branch president, meanwhile, seemed to have found a bare wire. His voice went on as before, businesslike and unexcited, but Sister Heinmiller's body had gone rigid, and her breath came in short, quick gasps, as though she were breathing off the top of her lungs. Between his wrists Lorin saw the corners of her mouth drawn down. She raised her body, straining against the quilt, and the branch president, raising his voice for the first time and with his eyes still closed, pronounced a terrible command in the name of Jesus Christ and by the power of the holy Melchizedek Priesthood in them vested.

Several things happened simultaneously. She whinnied, and her cracked tooth started to bleed again. Lorin felt a jolt in both arms, from his elbows up to his armpits, as though he had touched an electric barbed-wire fence. He noticed that every hair on the back of his hands was standing up, and while listening to the sound of an ocean washing through his head reflected with some embarrassment that he could not be absolutely certain that he hadn't, at the critical moment, said "Jesus H. Christ" very loudly.

When at last he looked up hoping to read faces he was surprised to find himself clear across the room from the bed and the others already milling around the room, talking quietly and straightening things up. Elders Burton and Zaret had put the dresser back on its feet and were picking up the scattered objects and putting them back on top. Sorenson carefully gathered the mirror shards, using his handkerchief, and dropped them in the wastebasket. Brother Heinmiller was in the room, still pale but smiling now as he stood talking with Oakley and the branch president and his wife. She was weak but appeared to be in good spirits. She had gathered the strength to reach out from beneath the quilt and take her husband's hand, and the flesh on her arm hung reassuringly soft. The branch president made a joke and patted the clasped hands of the couple, who laughed weakly, and then he left the room. Lorin knelt to help his companion with the pieces of glass. "All in a night's work," he said under the buzz of sounds, to make sure he had a voice.

"Sort of takes it out of you, doesn't it?" said Sorenson.

"I was thinking just the opposite," said Lorin, and wild horses would not have made him say more.

Back in the living room, they pulled on overshoes and buttoned coats and patted pockets for gloves and stared out windows until Heinmiller appeared from the bedroom, escorting his bundled wife by the elbow. She walked unsteadily and sat down on the nearest chair, darting glances at the room full of people. The branch president had called the hospital and she was to spend the night there for observation.

Lorin had, later on, only a confused recollection of the events that followed, because his mind was on other things. They entered the night from that blighted house, and for a distance traveled the same icy roads past the same glittering highway markers and the same darkened shopping plazas, until the last car in the procession, Zaret's, a green Studebaker with a stepped-up idle, fell back and swung onto the viaduct at the edge of town. Lorin watched it vanish into the stream of headlights along the freeway. The patient was delivered; the rest was a haze of hospital waiting-rooms with potted trees, and nurses in crisp hats, a matron at the check-in counter, banked snow in a parking lot, an injured dog along a road that he was not sure he really saw, and finally a large elm tree looming dark against the pearl-grey dawn framed by a window which Lorin, lying in bed with aching thighs, caused to flit left and right by opening and closing alternate eyes, while Sorenson slept on the other side of the room, snorting through asthma. By squinting, Lorin could break the faint light into particles and watch them drift along the sill, crowding closer together as they moved faster and faster, until pain stabbed at the root of his eye and he brought them back to the starting place, clustered and jumping excitedly and already beginning to drift again. He watched them until the elm cast a shadow. It was only another hour or so.

———

His fingertips had stayed numb for a day or two, and the insides of both arms were still a little sore. He hadn't mentioned this to Sorenson, but he reflected on it now while he sat in a warm house that smelled of food, listening to symptoms he hoped he would not have to act on.

"No," said Alice, "Richard gets all upset if I talk about it. Besides, it's only happened once, if you want to know."

"That's what I thought," said Richard.
"You didn't know!" she said, her eyes flashing.
They would not, thank God, have to act.

## 14

Driving home, Sorenson asked Lorin, casually, meaning no criticism or reproach, if Lorin were very sure that hitting a pair of new contacts with the spooky stuff were the best way to begin. Lorin, still feeling guilty at having made a shambles of the first discussion and therefore still prickly and defensive, replied that it probably didn't matter which leg you put in your pants first as long as your fly got zipped. Secretly he had to admit, however, that he had lost his head. Excited by Alice's response to the story of Joseph Smith seeing through his fingertips, he had skipped over the contents of the vision and told the story of the Mormon family in Cache Valley who were wakened one night in 1915 by the sound of hoofbeats outside their door and went out to find a stranger on a white horse who handed the father an envelope and galloped off into the night. The envelope contained a slip of paper on which was written, in a handwriting they had never seen before, the news that their son had been killed in France. Months later the family received an official communication from Washington saying their son had been killed, and that he had died on the very day and at precisely the hour that the father on the other side of the globe had been handed the envelope by the stranger on horseback.

Then Lorin had told the story of the farm wife in the early days of settlement in Payson, south of the Salt Lake Valley, who was visited one Christmas Eve by a white-haired stranger asking for food. Her husband was in Germany on a mission for the church and there was not much food in the house, but she wrapped part of a fresh loaf of bread in a piece of old calico and gave it to him. He thanked her and went away; when she looked out the window he had vanished, and when she stepped outside to see where he had gone, there were no tracks in the snow.

Alice had said that part gave her goose bumps, but it had gotten better. Several years later, after the woman's husband came back from his mission, she found the piece of calico in his trunk and asked him where he had gotten it. He told her a stranger with white hair had handed it to him, wrapped around half a loaf of warm bread, one Christmas Eve while he was standing hungry and demoralized on a street corner in Karlsruhe.

Sorenson had sat blinking miserably behind his glasses on one side of Lorin, while on the other side their host had slouched, yawned, smiled ironically, scowled, pulled at his wool socks and chewed at a hangnail. Alice, directly across the room from Lorin, had sat upright and attentive, her arms locked around her knees, her eyes shining. Thus encouraged, he had told the story of his great-grandmother and the visitation from her dead daughter, and was about to tell the story of his own encounter with one of the Three Nephites a few summers ago but remembered in time that she didn't know what a Nephite was. He did manage to work in one anecdote about a seer stone before Alice, responding to a gesture from Richard, reminded everybody that it was late and they had better stop all this and go to bed.

They had been invited back, though. That was the important thing. Sorenson could not criticize if they had been invited back. Lorin had made the usual sounds as they were getting ready to leave, and Alice, ignoring her husband's pained expression, had said she guessed it would be all right if they came back as long as they didn't stay too long. She hadn't had a talk like this with anybody for months. There had been less promising foot-in-the-door starts, in other words, whatever the unusual character of this one. Lorin was, he couldn't deny it, pleased, so pleased that he let Sorenson have all the credit for the other return invitations they got that week, and never once disrupted a first discussion with something that belonged in a later one. He even promised himself he would be quiet and let Sorenson do the talking on their second visit to the Klings, which he was looking forward to with more pleasure than usual.

———

He was relieved that something could give him pleasure at all just now, because he was not otherwise in good spirits. He had never felt quite well since the night at Sister Heinmiller's bedside. He knew about suggestibility, and for this reason when he awoke each morning with hollow knees and a feeling in his stomach that there was a bridge somewhere that he would have to throw himself from before night, he told himself it would go away when he stopped thinking about it. It did not go away, but at least it got no worse. He also knew about devils entering your body through apertures you had carelessly left open, and changing your whole chemistry. His symptoms were unstable, which made the malaise hard to pin down. Sometimes it was a chill that began in his kidneys and spread upward the length of his back to his shoulders and down his chest. Sometimes it was the feeling, when he was trying to sleep, that worms were crawling up and down the bones of his legs. Sometimes it was a foul taste through his whole body, as though an organ had broken loose and lay rotting somewhere between folds in his viscera. Sometimes breathlessness so tightened his diaphragm that he could hardly utter an articulate sentence, as though adrenalin had rushed into his system and would not drain off. Sometimes it was shakiness in all his limbs as he climbed stairs or walked from one end of a room to another.

Other times, when he felt all right physically, he found he disliked everybody who touched his life at any point. This included Sorenson, who was unusually naive at such times and therefore exasperating. It included Elder Zaret, who giggled like an idiot; Elder Beyer, the district leader, who was self-righteous and smug; the mission president, who was a Utah politician out mending fences. It included Brigham Young, who had been a power-grabber and empire-builder and very probably a cunning old reprobate, and Joseph Smith, who was a strange man even if you admired him. It included Heavenly Father and Jesus Christ, both of whom had been responsible for a lot of grief in the world, and Noel and Yvonne and his old bishop and the fat model he had painted to give Simon something to put in his bathtub. He was almost glad when the malaise returned to distract him.

———

The second visit to the Klings was on a cold blustery evening later the same week. No new snow had fallen, and what was already on the ground had hardened to a dirty polished crust that broke under your feet and filled your shoes with cold particles. Sorenson politely declined the brandy and then the coffee that Alice offered them and then proceeded to business, laying out charts and folders on the floor by his feet. Alice was dressed for receiving visitors this time, complete with stockings and shoes, though low-heeled ones that she kicked off anyway in order to sit in the same chair with her legs curled under her. Richard wore a baggy grey pullover and old pants with a hole in the back pocket. He had stayed in the bedroom while they were taking off their coats and getting settled, but had finally come out to the living room with his lower lip stuck out thoughtfully and had pretended to be surprised at seeing them there already. He sat on the couch with his hands in his pockets and for the first fifteen minutes or so kept a cool smile on his face that suggested he had the question to confound them if he chose to unleash it.

The tract they had given her was an extract from Joseph Smith's autobiography. It described his first vision at the age of thirteen, his series of visits from the Angel Moroni, his recovery of a set of engraved gold plates in a hillside containing the records of an ancient civilization in America and an account of the ministry of the resurrected Jesus among the people of that civilization, his translation of these records by means of a pair of transparent stones buried with them, his years of persecution by people who didn't believe him, the appearance of John the Baptist in a forest one morning to confer the priesthood on him and a friend named Oliver Cowdery, and the formal organizing of the church.

Alice was disappointed. "Do you guys believe all that?" she asked.

Sorenson smiled. "It asks a lot, doesn't it?"

"I thought it was kind of boring, if you want to know," she said.

Sorenson's smile turned a shade cold. "I'm sorry to hear that," he said. "Which parts did you find boring?"

"I don't know," she said, turning over several rumpled pages on which Lorin could see heavy underlining and an occasional scribble in the margin. "This thing that happens to him—you know where I mean? He's praying in the woods and something happens to him before he has the vision. Something is holding him down so he can't move, and it starts to get dark?"

"Yes," said Sorenson.

"What is that?"

Sorenson lifted his shoulders. "Joseph Smith thought it was something that didn't want him to have the vision. Call it whatever you like."

"I don't *know* what to call it."

The correct answer, of course, was the devil but Sorenson knew when restraint was advisable, and Lorin was keeping his mouth shut on this visit, having promised himself he wouldn't interfere. Anyway he was busy noticing a run that had started in the toe of one of Alice's stockings and remembering a mannerism of Gloriana's that had always interested him. When Gloriana was feeling especially prim, perhaps the tiniest bit irritated with him, a change would sometimes come over her vowels, as though she were trying to sound British. "That's not necess'ry," she had said once when he had timidly suggested an interesting improvisation in the front seat of his car. And once during a complicated arrangement of knees and elbows involving a pillow among dry leaves on a hillside behind Malibu, she had said, ''You cawn't be comfortable.'' He had been in a facetious mood, unluckily, and had replied, ''Yes I cawn,'' and that had been the end of that for the afternoon. He suspected Alice had little mannerisms of her own. Richard had the look of someone used to giving in.

''About all I can think of to compare it to is a clinical depression,'' Sorenson said, still treading softly. ''Only worse, of course, because it was violent. Does that make any sense? I don't mean that's what it was.''

''I guess so,'' she said. She continued to look down at the page in her lap, as if hoping something better would turn up.

''I don't mean it *was* a depression,'' Sorenson said. ''Just that the symptoms were sort of like that. We think it was something outside of him, not just a state of mind. I guess I didn't make that clear.''

''We think it was the devil,'' Lorin said.

''That's what I thought he meant,'' she said as Richard snorted. ''Shut up, Richard. Only he doesn't say so. And then he gets into this glorious personage bit and all the beholds and spake unto me's and everything. And when the angel comes in later, it's the same thing. The angel even starts quoting the Bible to him. I sort of skipped those parts, actually.''

''Well, maybe we should look at some of those parts more closely,'' said Sorenson, reaching into his attache case that lay open on the floor.

''I mean I like the *idea* and everything,'' she said. ''I really liked this angel standing in the air in the bedroom like that. But if that had happened to me, I wouldn't talk about it the way he does.'' She ran her finger down the margin and read stray sentences. ''His robe was exceedingly white. His whole person was glorious beyond description. The room was exceedingly light. I mean, what is *that*?''

''You probably wouldn't use the same language,'' Sorenson suggested.

She looked up and grinned. ''No. For one thing I'd be scared shitless.''

''I think the problem is maybe that we're just getting bogged down in the language,'' said Sorenson. ''You have to remember he was a farm boy without much education. But he read the Bible a lot.''

''I did kind of like the part about how the angel is surrounded by light and how it gathers around him just before he floats away and disappears through the ceiling.''

"We think resurrected beings can radiate light," said Sorenson, uncertain if he were being twitted. "We don't know what the principle is, but it's probably a form of energy."

She was frowning at the page open on her lap. "What I can't figure out is how come nobody else sees him the next day when he's out in the field talking to Smith. I mean if he's still wearing that white robe he's got to be conspicuous. Especially with all the light."

"I don't know why nobody else saw him," said Sorenson. "It doesn't say there was anybody else close by. Maybe nobody else was there *to* see him, or maybe he was only visible to Joseph Smith just then."

"That's what I think," said Richard into his hand.

"Of course other people did see him later on," Sorenson continued. "Or at least another one like him. Remember the three witnesses."

"I was going to ask you about them," she said, turning pages until she came to a place near the end of the tract. "It looks to me like only two of them saw the angel. This third guy, Harris. I don't buy him. He's trying too hard."

"Martin Harris might be a problem, you're right," said Sorenson, unruffled. "The other two seem pretty positive, though, don't they?"

She looked doubtful.

"It might interest you to know," Sorenson went on, placidly preparing his bombshell, "that all three of them broke with Joseph Smith later on and left the church, but they all swore to the end of their lives that they saw the angel."

She looked interested. "Yeah?"

Lorin meantime having already said more than he had intended to, had been amusing himself by studying Richard, who grew fidgety and pretended not to notice. When he got tired of that he allowed his attention to wander over to what looked like a heel print on the wall next to the light switch, and from there to the porch light that shone orange and blurred through the front window curtain, and from there to the ceramic mandarin on the round table in front of the window; then to a painting on the wall above Alice's head that appeared to be of stemless daisies flung across a background of yellow paste; then finally to Alice herself, just as the discussion turned to the angel hovering in the air in Joseph Smith's bedroom.

Until that moment he had not connected her with the wispy creature of his borderline dream last night, who had stroked him through his temple garments and breathed gently into his ear, and then had floated away against a cloud-flecked ceiling, her mouth covered by a hand, her eyes brimming mirth. The interlude had been neither very imaginative nor very long; he had vaguely supposed it was a lingering warm shadow of Gloriana and had gone to sleep mildly tumescent, planning to save up for a detailed fantasy later on. Realizing now that he had been mistaken, he received a small, pleasant jolt. It put her in a different light to find her drifting into his subconscious already. For the next several minutes he paid close attention to her out of the corner of his eye. She chewed her nails, he noticed. He hadn't noticed that before. He didn't like that, because her hands otherwise were pretty. They were pale and lightly freckled, and she waved them when she talked. They were perhaps too fragile. The bones in her wrists stood out, and her fingers were so thin that the diamond ring above her wedding band kept slipping back and forth, the stone sometimes getting between them. But he didn't mind fragility. There was something trusting about it. It was something you enjoyed being gentle with. He wished, though, that she wouldn't chew her nails. When she covered her mouth with a hand they were all you could see.

Sorenson was anxious to get off the subject of angels, preferring to leave that for a later exploration, such as when they would discuss the three degrees of glory in detail, which was the subject, incidentally, of that vision that Elder Hood had mentioned last time. He'd like, he said, if no one minded, to sketch in a little background right now, and come back to the other thing later. He wanted to say a little about the history of the Christian church following the death of the original disciples and mention one or two things about the Great Apostasy.

"No, wait a minute," she said. "This angel used to be alive? I mean really a person? I want to get this straight."

Yes, he was really a person, Sorenson assured her. His name was Moroni—accent on the second syllable, and the last syllable pronounced like the organ in your head—and he had been a military leader of some people called Nephites. He had compiled their history on gold plates that he had then buried in what is now Upper New York State and then died it was thought sometime in the fifth century A.D. But they'd get to that later.

"Yeah. What are Nephites?"

While Sorenson explained about Nephites, Lorin let his attention wander back to Richard, then quickly over to the daisies on the wall when he discovered Richard was looking at him. They were one of two ancient Semitic civilizations, Sorenson explained, who inhabited the American continents roughly from 600 B.C. to 420 A.D., when they were wiped out by the rival civilization called Lamanites, who incidentally were the ancestors of the American

Indians. It was believed that Jesus Christ, after his resurrection, appeared among the Nephites and established a branch of his church there, corresponding to the one he had established with Peter, and selected twelve disciples from among them. The Aztec god Quetzalcoatl was probably a corruption of the symbol representing Christ. "Actually I'd like to lead up to this by a different way if that's all right."

Richard cleared his throat. "Do Mormons believe God can do anything?" he asked, laying his trap.

Sorenson smiled. "I'm not sure what you mean."

"Can he make a rock suddenly become too heavy to pick up?"

"Actually, I don't know how to answer that," said Sorenson. "We believe God is subject to natural law. I guess if making a rock too heavy to pick up is consistent with natural law he could. We do know that if you bombard certain metals with electrons you change their molecular structure."

"Wait a minute," said Alice, waving her hand. "Be quiet, Richard. You mean these whatever they're called are Aztecs?"

"No. The Aztecs and Mayans and Incas all came later. They're descendants of the Lamanites. I'm not too clear on dates, actually."

"If God is limited by natural law," said Richard, who had been brooding, "how come this angel was standing in the air?"

"I don't know," Sorenson said. "It wouldn't have to be a violation of natural law, any more than aerodynamics is. I'd actually like to go back to the beginning."

"Jesus, Richard," Alice said. "You know about reversing magnetic poles and everything and how it makes things weightless."

"Some people think there's a man who's really an angel living in one of the upstairs rooms in the temple in Salt Lake," Lorin said.

She smiled gratefully, and Lorin saw a pale rash of goose pimples sweep over her arms.

"Maybe we could start by going over some of the material you've already looked at in that pamphlet," said Sorenson. "You remember it talks about a kind of religious revival going on in the early nineteenth century in the part of the country Joseph Smith lived in."

"A real angel," she said, her hand covering her mouth.

"Actually, I hadn't heard about that," Sorenson said.

Lorin didn't want to make trouble, and he was afraid he just had. "Just a rumor," he said. "I wouldn't want to vouch for its authenticity."

Richard cleared his throat again. "Kind of a silly one," he muttered.

Lorin did not want to let that go by. "Not that it isn't possible," he said.

"Anyway," Sorenson resumed, "this revival movement—it involved the Shakers and the Hard-Shell Baptists and a lot of others—had raised a lot of questions in Joseph Smith's mind that were really the same questions that were being asked since the time of the Reformation. Now, do you know what the Reformation was?"

"I mean has anyone actually seen him?" she asked.

"Nobody I know," said Lorin, wishing he hadn't brought it up. "It's just one of those things you hear about when you're growing up."

"He could get out if he wanted to, couldn't he?" she asked.

"If he was really there, yes," Lorin said.

"How?" asked Richard, who had been keeping track of the implications of his questions. "Walking through walls?"

"The same way he got in, I guess," said Lorin, preferring to answer a heckler with curtness. He would have answered differently if he hadn't felt he was being baited.

"Anyway, the main question people had been asking about was authority," Sorenson said. "You know. If you reject the authority of the Catholic Church where does that leave you? A lot of these revivalist ministers were claiming they had authority themselves direct from God. Some of them even thought they were Jesus Christ themselves."

"We knew somebody like that in college," she said. "Remember Mickey Bailey, Richie?"

Suddenly Richard unleashed his question.

"Are Mormons the ones with all the wives?"

"What?" said Alice.

Sorenson smiled. "We'll be coming to that too."

———

As follow-up visits went, this one could have been much worse. It left a bad taste in Sorenson's mouth, largely because he had found it difficult to introduce anything substantive into the discussion, and he wished out loud, on the way home, that Lorin would try not to say quite so much about angels next time since they seemed to deflect Alice. Lorin was in good spirits over the evening's work, and would have agreed to anything. He promised he wouldn't say another word, but in his bones he was confident. The job was as good as accomplished, or he was no judge of turning points.

———

Some day he was going to paint the Three Witnesses. It went without saying that you would be terrified if you saw an angel, and they had signed an affidavit swearing that they had seen one. If you could visualize the confusion ripping their minds like a chainsaw, you could almost persuade yourself they had. He would use Shannon as his model for Martin Harris, not because they resembled each other but because he wanted Shannon, who was immune to insults, to look foolish. For Oliver Cowdery he would use Simon, because he wanted to teach Simon humility. Harry would be the perfect model for David Whitmer. He was well meaning and friendly. Lorin would be his own model, of course, for Joseph Smith.

While Sorenson discussed the difference between Holy Spirit and the Holy Ghost with a Lutheran family in Dexter one evening and explained how the Light of Christ differed from either, Lorin imagined his scenario. He imagined his three friends—who had, after all, been loyal and had helped him while he was translating the gold plates—asking him if they could see the plates now. Not that they doubted or anything, but could they just sort of, you know, see them? He told them he didn't have the gold plates any more. When he was through with them, an angel had come and taken them back. Harry looked hurt. Shannon said he was quite sure Lorin could find a way of showing them the plates if he really wanted to. Even Simon looked disappointed. So now he was going to show them. It meant he had to show them the angel too, but that would be their problem.

He buttoned his vest and pulled on his morning coat, aware that they were watching him nervously from the kitchen table, wondering what he was going to do. He gestured toward the door by a tilt of the head and walked out. He heard them scrambling to get their coats. He was already past the barn when he heard them burst out the pantry door and call for him to wait. He slowed enough to let them catch up, but he was irritated and didn't feel like talking to them. He continued along the rutted wagon road that ran past the smokehouse, hearing the three of them behind him whispering excitedly. He climbed through a barbed wire fence, carefully watching his thumbs and the cuffs of his trousers, and cut across a field waist-high with ripe grass. He hadn't thought to worry about stepping on a snake until he realized he couldn't see his feet, but it was too late to turn back and go around. The others had gotten through the fence by now—predictably, Shannon had snagged something and bellowed—and he heard them swishing along the pathway he had flattened. He led them over a small crest and down a gully into the woods, where, finding a spot near the spring where the grass was cropped short, he stopped, kicked aside a few spongy branches, and cleared a space where they could kneel down in a circle.

This was the only time he was going to do this, he explained, so it would be just as well if they paid attention. Simon found a dry place where the ground formed a little depression and knelt first before someone else got it. Harry and Shannon knelt close to him, but Harry got up again immediately and went to the other side of Simon, where the ground looked softer. Lorin waited patiently while they jostled against each other and re-positioned their knees and feet. Shannon noticed that one of his knees was wet and dragged a handful of dead leaves over to kneel on. Finally they seemed to be settled, and Lorin knelt in front of them. The three of them bowed their heads and clasped their hands in front of them. Simon's eyes, grey and serious, focused on a tuft of weeds in front of him that was bound together like a te-pee by a sheet of spider web and apparently had a spider inside it. Harry's eyes were closed and the veins stood out in his fore-head. Shannon pretended to close his eyes but it was obvious he was squinting. He glanced back and forth at the other two and then tried to see what Simon was looking at. He ventured to glance up and saw that Lorin was looking at him and quickly closed his eyes and dropped his head. Harry cleared his throat.

Lorin closed his eyes and concentrated very hard, but he could tell it was not going to work. He opened his eyes, brushed a spot of dirt from his pant leg, took a deep breath, let it out. He looked at the other three, kneeling with their eyes closed. Harry brushed away a fly but didn't open his eyes. Lorin wished he liked them better. They followed him like ducklings every-where he went, asking if it was time to show them the plates yet, wishing he would talk to them, offering to hold the plates for him while he looked in the hat. Once this was all sorted out, he would do something for them—let them be deacons or bishops or something. Simon would probably like that; he had not been teaching school long, and the idea of authority would appeal to him and perhaps give him a psychological edge over the sullen adolescents he taught reading and ciphering to, and whom he was still afraid of. Shannon's bald head and gray lambchop whiskers Lorin had always found embarrassing, just because the man was too old to be spending so much time with young people. Harry, he suspected, would not amount to anything. The grey look of failure had already touched his face, and he moved his lips when he thought no one was looking, as though he were thinking of things he could have said in a conversation he'd had yesterday.

Still, the three of them deserved kindness and couldn't help it if they drove him wild. Shannon, he noticed, was becoming fidgety and kept opening his eyes to glance left and right at the other two and closing them again. He stretched his upper lip over his teeth and reached into a nostril with his little finger and brushed something out, then opened his eyes again and saw that Lorin was watching him. Lorin tried to keep his face expressionless but Shannon turned red and struggled to his feet, leaning on Simon's shoulder to get up. Simon opened his eyes, startled. Shannon brushed the leaves from his wet knees, mumbled an apology, and limped away. The others watched him disappear over a low hill into some trees farther away from the spring, and suddenly the air turned bright.

Lorin nodded to the angel who stood between him and Harry, holding a set of plates open against his white robe. The angel nodded back, then passed in front of Simon and then Harry, holding the plates open to let them see, then balancing them on one knee to turn the page and let them see that one too. Harry and Simon stared at the angel with their mouths open, and only looked down at the plates he was holding when he tapped with his fingers to get their attention. Lorin had to smile when Harry moved closer to Simon and Simon put an arm around his shoulders, not only because he could relate to their alarm but also because he could see, as they could not, that another angel was standing just outside the small circle they had formed, with several sets of plates on the ground beside him, and he knew what they would think when they turned and saw him. There was another one further off, stacking plates on a table, and two more on the other side of the spring setting up a display among the broken limbs scattered across the ground. Not all of the plates were bound together by rings, and some of them looked more battered than others. Most of them, Lorin realized, were plates he had not seen. More angels were coming out of the woods, carrying plates.

Simon was looking around him with frightened eyes; his lips were white. Harry pawed his shoulder with both hands. The angel continued to turn pages patiently, thrusting the engraved surface under their noses and running his finger along a line from time to time. Lorin excused himself and got up to look for Shannon. He found him behind a dead log in a stand of maples, kneeling and tugging at his side whiskers. He cleared his throat and Shannon looked up with hot, frantic eyes. Lorin patted him on the shoulder and knelt down next to him. They'd start from the beginning again, he said; just take it slowly and be methodical and sincere. He felt Shannon's shoulders quiver under his supporting arm, but nothing happened.

"Are you sure you're concentrating?" he asked.

Shannon nodded furiously.

It took several tries, but on the third or fourth Lorin noticed, to his relief, that the air had started to turn bright again. He looked at the bare feet on the ground in front of him, waited a moment to gather his breath, then looked up and nodded at the angel who was holding a bulky set of plates that kept falling closed. Lorin looked over at Shannon, who stared back, his face white and his upper lip shiny with sweat. There was no point in rushing, Lorin decided; they would take their time. Shannon gripped his hands together under his chin, closed his eyes tightly until the tears seeped out, and concentrated. Lorin idly watched the pages being turned in front of him, nodding to indicate it was time to turn another one, remembering this or that character he had seen floating in the stone in the hat, musing over others that looked unfamiliar to him, wondering if they were familiar figures carved by a different hand or if they were unknown runes that he was yet to be introduced to. He was aware that for all of his familiarity with this sort of thing there were dimensions and planes that he had not seen and that would take a lifetime to imagine.

He glanced past the pocked sheet of gold in front of him and saw an angel disappear behind a scaling maple tree about forty yards away and slowly peer around it from the other side. He caught a white flicker in the corner of his eye and looked to his left in time to see another one moving across a short clearing and disappearing behind a boulder. Looking back in the direction he had left Harry and Simon he could see the flit of white fabric lighting up the tangled darkness of the copse and realized there was an angel behind every tree. He was so absorbed in this discovery that it was several seconds before it registered on his hearing that Shannon was grunting and breathing heavily. He looked at his friend and was alarmed to see him staring at the angel, his eyes bulging like eggs and his tongue loosely floating in a pool of bubbles on the floor of his mouth. Shannon's hands drew little clawing gestures in the air. Lorin reached to put a hand on his arm but Shannon suddenly started to his feet, stood there swaying for a moment, his arms dangling, staring at the imperturbable face of the angel. Then with a wild burst of laughter he broke and ran off into the trees, passing several angels who came out of their hiding places and gathered to watch him disappear. Lorin heard him crashing through the underbrush for several minutes afterward.

He was not sure who he would use as models for the angels. There were more than he had planned.

———

Sorenson asked him if he would like to offer a word of prayer before they left Mr. and Mrs. Kling until next week. Lorin said, "What?"

# 15

In the weeks that followed, even Sorenson had to temper
his doubts because they kept getting invited back, and little by
little the structure of the discussions was pulled into recogniz-
able shape. They got invited back even following discussions that
Alice had not appeared to find interesting, and that was a good
sign. They talked about the pre-existence one night while she
listened narrow-eyed and skeptical and Richard looked desper-
ately for a way to get past his wife and down the hall to the bathroom without making her angry. Another time they talked about
the nature of revelations, and how they were different from visions. Alice liked them less once the difference was made clear.
Richard finally excused himself to go to the bathroom, and stayed.
On still another evening—it was during a spongy thaw, and they
had tracked brown sodden leaves all the way to the couch—they
discussed the Great Apostasy, drawing from writers such as
Hegesippus, Eusebius, Mosheim, and John Wesley, all contained
in useful extracts in the Ready References sections of their missionary Bibles. Sorenson did most of the talking this time. He
explained, while Alice listened politely and Richard stared in
resentful silence at the porch light through the window and Lorin kept quiet, how the early church had begun to fall away even
during the time of the apostles, and how within a century the
priesthood and thus all claim to authority had been lifted from
the earth, not to be restored until the nineteenth century, by the
resurrected John the Baptist and Peter, James, and John, who con-
ferred it on the heads of Joseph Smith and selected converts to
the restored church.

On an evening fragrant with the breath of the coming spring
they finally talked about angels. Alice noticeably picked up during this discussion. Lorin explained that angels were solid flesh

and bone, muscle and sinew and vital fluids, like the rest of us. The difference was that they had died, and their bodies had undergone chemical and morphological changes that were not very well understood. They could appear charged with lambent energies or looking like ordinary people. They could be present but invisible. They could pass back and forth between the physical world and the spirit world, and exploit natural resistances like gravity or wind in order to move between extreme points on the surface of the earth almost instantaneously. It was even possible, he said, starting to talk faster lest Sorenson cut him off with a worried look, that they could move, like electrons, from one space to another without traversing the distance in between. He told the story of a man who had been seen entering an elevator on the ground floor of the Continental Bank Building in Salt Lake and was not there when the door opened on the second floor, and the story a friend had told him about picking up a hitchhiker in the desert south of Fish Springs, who had warned him about an approaching sandstorm and vanished from the car when Lorin's friend turned his head to look. He mentioned the angel who had stepped out from behind a barn one night and shown the gold plates to David Whitmer's mother, who up until then had not believed they existed, and the angel who had been seen on the road between Harmony, Pennsylvania and Fayette, New York, carrying the plates in a knapsack.

The weeks passed. They called on her sometimes in the afternoon, once finding her doing the laundry in the small kitchen, the moisture from her clothes dryer humidifying the air and making the pages of their tracts and Bibles limp in their fingers, once finding her out of sorts from having gotten the car stuck in a bank of fresh snow on the way home from grocery shopping. They found her once in a thready pink housecoat recovering from a cold, and Lorin's pulse tripped as he noticed the soft puffiness of her mouth and eyes; he was pleased every time she blew her nose and then groped for the brown grocery sack in which she had stuffed the day's used Kleenexes. They had more or less written Richard off and no longer tried very hard to arrange an evening appointment when he would be home, instead concentrating their heavy guns on Alice alone.

Little by little it was happening. The big problem was getting her through the Book of Mormon. She liked the idea of a mysterious vanished civilization, with its cities and highways and temples, its catastrophes and earthquakes, its inhabitants receiving strange messages from supernatural visitors, but she kept getting stalled on the wherefores and it came to passes. The long stretches of straight doctrinal writing by Alma, Mosiah, one Nephi or another, Samuel the Lamanite, Mormon himself or his son Moroni, were more than she could handle with any kind of attention. It was necessary to mention from time to time, as a way of keeping the spark lit, that the city of Zarahemla, for instance, had been found and dug up by archaeologists, exactly where the Book of Mormon had said it would be; that other cities, roads, great walls, fortifications and so forth, the very ones she was reading about, were periodically discovered tucked into high valleys and clinging to concealed mountain walls in South and Central America, and that explorers constantly reported finding tiny squalid tribes of white Indians living in isolated settlements in the jungles, presumably descendants of the few survivors of the destroyed Nephite nation.

While she struggled through the book, they pressed on. They talked about the Urim and Thummim, the transparent stones buried with the plates and used by Joseph Smith to translate the hieroglyphs, using a process that she unfortunately found funny. They talked about Kolob, an astronomical body of some kind mentioned in the Book of Abraham, that was located in the center of the galaxy and from which time, as we understood time, was calibrated. They talked about the physical properties of holy spirit, which was actually a substance composed of highly refined particles and could be transferred from one human body to another, something like electricity, by contact between the two bodies, through the medium of the nerves. They talked about the spirits of the dead, how they were organized matter but not the same as resurrected beings because they weren't solid. They talked about the second coming and the physical and chemical changes that would happen in the earth's surface. They talked about the Three Nephites, and Lorin at last got to tell about meeting one of them the summer before he had started college, which she didn't think was as interesting as he did, which hurt his feelings a little.

The Three Nephites were three of the twelve disciples selected by Jesus during his New World ministry, who had asked to remain alive until the second coming. They had survived the ravages of centuries and still walked the earth today, old men but not enfeebled, healing the sick, warning the unwary, and disappearing into the mists of legend as soon as they had performed whatever act they had been summoned for. They had been seen by one of Columbus's sailors during the second voyage, on a coastal island near Cuba. They had been seen in Colonial Massachusetts, helping villagers stave off an Indian attack. They were seen, though rarely together, by families with sick children who were miraculously made well after a visit by a white-haired stranger who had eaten at the family's table and afterward disappeared, leaving the food he had eaten untouched on the plate; by missionaries who had seen a white-haired stranger disperse a hostile crowd that had been about to tar and feather them; by down-and-out men who had had wads of greenbacks pressed into their hands in dark alleys by white-haired strangers who had vanished without waiting to be thanked. They came and went enigmatically, and consistently were reported as having white hair, which reminded you that they were still mortal, though the aging process had been slowed to a crawl. At least some of the recorded sightings of angels could have been sightings of one of the Three Nephites instead. She found old men boring.

They described the nature of the three degrees of glory, the telestial, terrestrial, and celestial kingdoms, as far as they were understood, and explained that marriage and the family unit existed only in the celestial kingdom, and that only those marriages that had been sanctified in the temple carried over into the celestial kingdom. Alice wanted to know if that meant everybody stayed horny in the other two kingdoms. Lorin wondered that too. They explained the doctrine of eternal progression. They had covered the ban on liquor, tobacco, and stimulants like caffeine a long time ago, but now mentioned the importance of modesty in dress, chastity outside marriage, morality in daily life. She attended the investigators' class at the branch, not taking Richard with her, and eventually the thing was accomplished.

On a bright spring afternoon she descended, dressed in spotless white lounging pajamas, into the local YMCA swimming pool, various elders and authorities like the district president scattered through the bleachers to watch, where Lorin, also in white, his heart pounding, stood with her, the cold oily water up to his hips and shriveling his groin, held her left hand in his left hand, raised his right arm, said the baptismal prayer, and gently eased her under the water while she held her nose with one hand and clutched at his wrist with the other. His right hand at her back, he brought her upright again, her face shiny, her hair streaming water, her white lounging pajamas clinging to her fragile body, said "Congratulations" into her ear and helped her up out of the pool, where two lady missionaries waited with a large towel and went with her as she padded off, wet feet slapping, to the locker room. When she was gone he was able to breathe again.

The next morning, Sunday, Lorin, Sorenson, and two other elders confirmed her at the testimony meeting in the local branch. Richard watched from the front row as the eight hands were laid on her head. They all bowed their heads and Sorenson said the confirmation prayer. When it was over she looked up at them all, each in turn, grinning.

———

To keep from thinking about the erection he had started to get when Alice clutched his wrist in the swimming pool, he considered how you might portray the act of translating the Book of Mormon without making it look funny. He did this several times a week.

Joseph Smith had used the downstairs living room of David Whitmer's family's farmhouse. Lorin imagined the heavy furniture pushed against a wall, the curtains drawn over the windows, the door from the hallway closed to keep foot traffic away. David had let him drive a nail into the doorpost and another into the wall across the room, though he did not think his family was going to like that. They had tied a rope to each nail and draped a blanket across it, cutting the room in half at eye level except where the rope sagged in the middle.

He imagined himself as Joseph sitting on a kitchen chair beside the blanket with a black felt hat upside down in his lap and a small table with the plates on it within easy reach. He also imagined himself as Oliver Cowdery facing the other direction on the other side of the blanket. What he had in mind was a kind of double self-portrait, something like what Noel used to do but not exactly. The gold plates were battered at the corners and badly scratched and grooved because they had been buried for hundreds of years and had been carried around a lot before that. The rings that bound them together in an irregular stack were twisted and bent, so that turning a plate over required both hands to jockey the margins without pulling the holes larger, since the metal was thin and soft. Little streams of dirt ran out onto the table whenever he turned a plate, and dried insects, leaves, and even twigs with desiccated buds turned up every few plates.

The Oliver Lorin cleared his throat on the other side of the blanket. The Joseph Lorin looked around to make sure the farm children hadn't crept back in to see what they were doing and then bent over, putting his face in the hat and drawing the sides close to his cheekbones with one hand and, as far as he could, his knees, to cut out what light was left in the room. With his other hand he felt for the plate that was open on the table and laid his palm across it, feeling the burr along the edges of the characters with his fingertips. Sweat trickled down through his hair and onto his thumb inside the hat. It was dark inside the hat, and stuffy, and smelled of someone else's head.

The stone in the bottom of the hat glowed faintly, brightening or fading as he moved his hand one way or the other across the plate. When he had it right the glow, though still soft, was bright enough that he was able to see the shiny sides of his nose and the oily stains on the inside of the crown. With patience he could make out the figure at the center of the glow—a numeral 3 connected to a fishbowl with four upright candles, each with a dot under it—with the word "accomplish" printed in square letters beneath the figure.

"Accomplish," he said.

"What?" said the Oliver Lorin from the other side of the blanket.

The Joseph Lorin took his face out of the hat and said "Accomplish," and waited until he heard the scrattle of the other Lorin's quill before he bent over again. He hated having to repeat things. The next character swam left into the glow as he moved his hand to the right. It resembled a corkscrew with a sharp elbow.

"Design," he called out.

"Divine?" asked the Oliver Lorin, who was always pleased when the text used religious words. There were already more passages of secular narration than he was comfortable with.

"Design," said the Joseph Lorin, raising his voice.

The Oliver Lorin made the little humming sound in his throat as his pen scrattled that meant his feelings had been hurt, and the Joseph Lorin resolved to speak less sharply next time.

"Kishkumen," he said, reading from the next figure. He hadn't seen that one before. Evidently a proper name.

"Spell it?" asked the Oliver Lorin.

It was a long process, and it created syntactic monsters. They had been at it for several weeks already, discovering migrations, apostasies, battles, and assassinations, but there was an immense quantity still on the table. Lorin kept the plates covered with a bedspread when he was not using them, and kept the two translucent stones wrapped in a pair of silk handkerchiefs in his bottom drawer except to take one or the other out to begin a working day. He tended to alternate them, some days using the Urim, other days the Thummim, though he was not fastidious about it, and in fact could not tell them apart very well. On some days neither of them seemed to work. This normally followed a night during which he had masturbated. He would put his face into the hat and the stone would lie there inert, without a flicker, no matter that he moved his hand onto every inch of the plate's textured surface. Other times the glow would be there but it would be dim and yellow and the figure would be too grainy to make out, and one terrible time he saw only a pair of wild eyes staring back at him from the polished lambent stones.

——

There was an unexpected coda. Early on in their visits to the Klings, it had become clear to Lorin and Sorenson that Richard was not having any. Whatever his honest impatience with the doctrines and mysteries heating up his home and brought there by these two dark-suited strangers who had penetrated it, it was clear that he had found a weapon in being able to chuckle at his wife's enthusiasms. It was, Lorin suspected, the only psychological edge the poor devil had on her. Lorin did not mind writing him off; in fact he took a certain pleasure in talking about things he knew Richard would, on principle, not believe. Richard was short and slight, and looked too young to own a house. He worked in the escrow department of a bank in Ann Arbor and his father had cosigned the note enabling them to arrange a conventional mortgage since he did not qualify for a GI one. He had recently graduated from college with a degree in marketing and a minor in intellectual traditions, and had been married to Alice not much more than a year. He had no hobbies but was thinking of taking up photography and setting up his own darkroom in the garage because he wanted to take pictures of his wife naked. (All this information came out later, of course.) He played chess with Sorenson sometimes, slowly and deliberately, frowning between moves and then moving decisively with the smile of someone whose strategy will become apparent later on, and always lost. He thought of himself as serious, and they little knew how closely he had listened to the discussion of the Great Apostasy.

After Alice's baptism Lorin and Sorenson were frequently invited to their house for dinner. They saw her at church regularly, of course, looking as happy as a child who had just been given a room full of someone else's toys. The other members of the branch made her feel welcome, and when she clicked on high heels down the hallway to the main room just before Sunday school or the evening sacrament meeting, Lorin's pulse raced; if he happened to catch her eye as she stepped past people's feet on her way to an unoccupied folding chair during the preliminary music (played by Sister Heinmiller, now recovered), he waved his fingers in greeting and she waved hers back, covering her mouth with her free gloved hand. Sometimes he and one of the other missionaries would chat with her after the meeting, and it was usually then that she would invite him and Sorenson to dinner. "If you can stand Richard," she always added.

Richard was a pain in the ass, both during dinner and afterward. He made a great ceremony of offering wine to the elders and to Alice when they were seated at the breakfast bar eating mashed potatoes and fried chicken, and drinking it himself when they all three declined, sniffing the bouquet, sipping, rolling it on the back of his tongue, playing with the stem of his glass. Lorin burned to tell him he hated wine, but that would sound like protesting too much. Accordingly he talked mostly to Alice and let Sorenson do what he could to keep Richard from going to hell in his own way. He learned a great deal about Alice this way, and was slow in discovering just how far things had already gone with Richard.

"Are you guys trying to tell me Jesus Christ is who they mean by God in the Old Testament but not the New Testament?" he said.

"Sure," said Sorenson. "Who was he praying to in the Garden of Gethsemane? Himself?"

Richard sat up. "I think I can give you a nonanthropomorphic answer to that."

Or: "What do you mean the thief wasn't necessarily saved? Jesus Christ said he'd see him in Paradise. Have you read Saint Augustine?"

"That's a misunderstanding about what Paradise is," said Sorenson, who had not read Saint Augustine. "Everybody goes to Paradise. I'll explain it again."

Or: "What about races? If somebody's born Oriental does that mean he was Oriental in the pre-existence? What if one parent is an Oriental and the other one isn't?"

"That's a good question," smiled Sorenson.

Or: "How do you get off calling yourselves mainstream Christians when you say every man can become a god? If that isn't polytheism I don't know what you'd call it."

"Nobody ever said we were mainstream Christians," said Sorenson. "But polytheism really means many gods governing a single world. Our doctrine teaches that one God created the universe but there are infinite universes. That's plurality, not polytheism. Anyway, remember the Hebrew word 'Elohim' is plural."

The end of it was that a couple of months later, on the Saturday afternoon before a fast-Sunday meeting, Richard descended the white steps into the YMCA swimming pool, wearing white pajamas and still with a furrowed brow, and Sorenson raised a hand over his head and baptized him; and the next day the same circle of elders, Lorin included, laid hands on his head and confirmed him a member of the church while Alice watched, thrilled, from the front row. Afterward he stood up and turned, and shook

hands with all four elders, Lorin included, and returned to the
seat next to his wife, his lower lip stuck out thoughtfully.

## 16

During the course of many Sunday-afternoon dinners Alice
had managed to tell Lorin—and Sorenson, when he could be
sprung from Richard—one or two pertinent things about herself.
She told him, for instance, about her aversion to flies. She could
not stand flies. "I mean if I even know there's one in the same
room with me I feel my face start to get all hot," she said. "I'm
always afraid it's going to land on me, and all I can think of is
I want to kill it. I don't like to kill things, but God, show me a
fly and I'll go out of my mind. I mean really, I'm a different
person."

"Spiders are okay?" asked Lorin.

"I hate spiders but I usually don't kill them. You know, unless they're on the bedroom wall or something. Usually I make
them crawl onto a piece of paper and then I take them outside
and shake them into the flowers. No, it's just flies mostly. If one
ever lands on me I have to go take a bath before I feel clean again.
All I can think about is where they've been."

"One landed on the rim of the milk pitcher once and she
poured the milk down the sink," Richard said. He was talking
to Sorenson in the living room about the difference between sal-
vation and exaltation, but couldn't help overhearing Alice and
Lorin in the kitchen.

"Richie thought that was dumb," she said. "But I wasn't
about to drink anything that came out of that pitcher after that.
You don't know what was on its feet. All I could think was it
might have dropped a speck into the milk. It still makes me sick
to think about it."

Another time she told him about turning all the pictures in
her bedroom to the wall when she was a child. "It was crazy,"
she said. "I felt like they were all looking at me, and I didn't want

to be looked at. Especially when I was getting undressed to go to bed. There was this one especially of two kids in a rowboat and they've lost their paddle. One of them is looking at it floating away and the other one is trying to make the dog stop eating all the sandwiches. There was one of my dad and some other men wearing straw hats and carnations, I think it was after the war. There weren't too many, actually, and some of them weren't even of people. They were castles and things, with a few people wandering around under trees. But they really freaked me. I turned them face to the wall every night before I got undressed and turned them back every morning before my mother came in and saw them. I don't think she ever saw them turned wrong.''

One Sunday afternoon he was helping her with the dishes while Sorenson and Richard argued in the living room, this time about apostolic succession, and she began telling him, rapidly and in a low voice, about the strange thing that had happened to her, her guarded references to which had been burning a hole in his brain for months. He didn't know why she was telling him now. He was a little alarmed, and his first thought was that he should go get Sorenson. The occasion was their honeymoon trip to the Upper Peninsula the year before, ostensibly a time to wander through woods, go boating on crystal lakes, and fish, and watch the sun rise before Richard was to start his new job, but in fact they had rented a cabin and spent most of the two weeks screwing. The experience was relatively new to both of them, and Alice was in a state of great excitement the whole time. There were things she had always wanted to do, and she made Richard let her do them, with the result that Richard was baffled and sometimes uneasy, and more than once he felt he was not taking charge enough.

The cabin was small and dirty. It had a fireplace with grease on the hearth and no screen. It had a wooden table salvaged from a picnic ground, with names and initials carved into it but painted over with a woodsy brown enamel that your arm stuck to if you leaned on it too long. It had a dusty couch and a three-way floor lamp by the window that looked onto the garbage cans. The forest and the lake were visible only from the front door, which had been nailed shut to keep it on its hinges. The bed was lumpy, the rugs were worn through and stained with food and dried bait. The kitchenette had a refrigerator that leaked into a funnel that someone had drilled a hole for in the floor, and a gas stove, only one of whose four burners worked. The walls were painted brown, and the owner had hung pictures of bears and otters and a baying elk. A narrow shelf above the bed held greasy paperback novels.

Alice loved the cabin, and Richard thought it was a healthy thing to live in the woods for a couple of weeks. People in the other cabins came and went past the window, wearing their woolen plaid shirts or their hats pricked through with fishhooks, but the newlyweds stayed mostly indoors. When they went out it was during everyone else's dinner hour, and it was usually a fast run to the woods, where Alice would pull off all her clothes, put her tennis shoes back on, and run off among the trees, calling to Richard to catch her. ("You don't mind my telling you all this, do you?" she asked. Lorin said of course not, and wiped the plate he was holding with great care. It was already too late to go get Sorenson.) Richard was worried that someone was going to leave the pathway and come tramping among the trees and surprise them, so when he had reluctantly stumbled after her and forced her to the ground where she lay giggling, he was not always capable of going on from there. Anyway, it was cold in the woods without your clothes on, so they generally stayed inside the cabin to play.

Lorin already knew, from her pre-baptismal interview, about the brief, happy sex life she and Richard had enjoyed before their marriage, and also, despite his lack of any charm that Lorin could see, that for all the way she talked to him in front of other people, she was very fond of Richard. They were both from the midwest, though from different states, had met at college in Kalamazoo where they both had belonged to the Young Democrats Club, had visited both sets of parents during one vacation or another, had decided that it wasn't necessary to go to bed to prove they loved each other, and had gone to bed the first weekend Alice's roommate was out of the house. She found him thoughtful, kind, and in his own way brilliant.

During their two weeks in the cabin in the woods she also found him tractable in all the right ways, and herself capable of wild, extended erotic flights that she carefully guided Richard into accomplishing for her, and which she got to be so good at that she could hang on the edge of an incipient orgasm for hours, gathering energies volt by volt, before coming with a violence that made Richard very pleased with himself. And one afternoon a remarkable thing happened.

The day was grey and cold, a fog rising from the lake, the garbage can lids shiny with moisture outside the window. A fire popped and crackled through a pile of spongy logs in the fireplace; thin music floated out of the transistor radio on the table. They had been playing since lunch, and Richard now lay on his back on the bed with Alice kneeling over his face, a knee on either side of his ears. Her head was thrown back and her eyes were closed and she listened to the intermittent lapping sound that came from below, urging him to do it faster when he faltered or stopped, excitement rushing like ecstatic water bugs over her body, when all at once she realized she was seeing the transistor radio on the table behind her. She was also seeing the table. Glimmering off at a distant edge of something was the picture of the baying elk, throwing off firelight from its glass. The stone fireplace swam into focus. Exactly what she was seeing these things with was not clear, but she neither stopped to consider nor opened her eyes. Richard was for the moment irrelevant, though in the next instant she saw foam on his tongue and his hairy knees pedalling furiously behind her and the white knuckles of both hands doing something indecent to himself. It was this last thing, in fact, that sent her into peals of laughter and pushed her over the edge. When that happened she saw everything: the bedpost on either side of her, the soiled pillow in front, the clock on the bench, its hands pointed at twenty to three, the grey window with the nose streaks from a neighboring dog, the pile of newspapers in the corner, the fishing pole with the tangled line leaned against the coat rack by the door, the glint off a nail head in the door. When it was over and she lay curled up with her knees across Richard's stomach he wanted to know what had been so goddamn funny and she told him.

"You didn't see that," he said.

"Want to bet?"

He didn't know whether to be embarrassed or suspicious, but when she went on to elaborate the other things he could not help but feel spooky.

"Come on," he said.

"I really did, Richie. It was only for a second, but it was all there. I saw the clock and everything."

"I mean how could you see them when you weren't even looking at them?" he said. "Be realistic."

"I don't *know* how!" she said. "You know how when you look at a window or something and then shut your eyes you see it like a negative, only in all kinds of different colors? It just sort of floats there in the black? It was like that except it wasn't a negative, and I was seeing them all over my body. I mean they were all their real colors and everything. And they weren't exactly floating. I mean they were just there, like I'm looking at them right now. But I *saw* them, Richard."

"Maybe you were fantasizing," he suggested.

"What kind of a stupid thing is that? You think I fantasize about clocks and radios?"

"No, I mean you already knew what those things looked like, and all I mean is maybe they all started running through your head at once."

"They did not run through my head and I was not thinking about them. I can't help it. I saw them."

Richard had found his defense at last. "Sure," he said, and leaned back on the pillow, grinning.

"You give me a pain in the ass!" she said.

Lorin realized he had been drying the same meat platter for a long time. His legs felt sweaty and his wool trousers itched more than usual.

"You say it's only happened once?"

"Yeah. Sometimes I think it's going to again, if you know what I mean, but it never really does. I start to pick up flashes but they never come. That doesn't happen very often anyway. But when you told me that time about Joseph Smith seeing through the ends of his fingers it blew me away."

"It didn't scare you or anything when it happened?"

"No, I loved it. I wish I'd do it again."

"Alice," said Richard, coming in from the living room with Sorenson. He had caught her last few lines on the way in.

"I tell Richie we don't try often enough," she said, and beamed.

Sorenson was pink again. Lorin felt drained.

———

Lorin's creeping malaise had been getting worse, and its progress had coincided, he had noticed, with his gathering familiarity with Alice. It persisted through the weeks of indoctrination, underwent a momentous spasm at the time of her baptism, worsened during the weeks leading to Richard's follow-through, and by the time the catastrophe struck was making him wonder if he ought to tell Sorenson his suspicions about Sister Heinmiller's devil. The morning of the day they talked about Kolob, for instance, had begun with a terrible incident. The alarm clock had gone off as usual while the sky outside was still grey and the room was lined with shadows, and Lorin had reached out as usual with his eyes closed to shut it off and his hand had come down on another hand that was already on it. The clock was on Lorin's side of the room in the first place because Sorenson could not be trusted with it. In his sleep Sorenson had been known to rise and tamper with clocks—push in the alarm release, even set the hour back—so the clock had fallen to Lorin's custodianship. Lorin set the clock at night, positioned it on the table next to the lamp so that he could reach it in the morning and shut it off as quickly as possible, because it sounded like a dentist's drill boring into his mastoid. On this morning he did as he had always done, coming out of an unhappy dream to do it, and his palm and fingers, expecting only the hard cold edge of the electric Seth Thomas, had come down instead on the back of another hand; a hand, moreover, that did not move after he had touched it. It was not his companion's hand. As he lay there, his eyes still closed, he knew he was hearing Sorenson in the bathroom, and that the penetrating buzz that still vibrated his nerves was not the alarm clock at all but Sorenson's electric shaver.

He could of course have opened his eyes, but for several reasons he didn't want to. For one thing, as long as they were closed he could prolong the chance that he was still dreaming, though he knew perfectly well that the dream he had been having had not contained a hand on his alarm clock. It had been about himself and his first companion, Elder Cobb, driving through the night in Lorin's green Pontiac, which was packed full of wet paintings. They were trying to get back to an investigator whom they had left on the beach tied under the seats of an overturned rowboat with the tide creeping in. It had only just occurred to them that they had forgotten he was there, but the closer they approached the more the sandy beach became a housing development crisscrossed by freeways along which millions of headlights bobbed. For another thing he was not sure what level of reality he was willing to confront. If he were to open his eyes and discover the hand was connected to some fanged horror, some livid creature of the night world with warts on its eyelids, that would be one thing. But suppose it was not one of those things. Suppose he opened his eyes and saw something ordinary sitting there, a sweet old man, say, whom he had never seen before in his life, smiling placidly at the walls. Suppose it were someone he knew to be dead. The hand seemed to be male. That is, it was hard and bony, with a coat of crinkly hair beneath which he could feel veins and tendons. It did not move or otherwise respond to the pressure of Lorin's hand, and there was no give to the skin.

Feeling sick, Lorin lifted his hand off, pulled it back beneath the covers, and turned onto his side, his back to the alarm clock, pulling the blankets over his head to keep his neck from being watched, and thought about his dream. He could not recover it, but he padded through countless dim corridors trying to find Elder Cobb, who had kept the keys to his Pontiac and all the paintings inside it, but he couldn't remember Elder Cobb's face, and the two or three people he passed stood with their backs to him, facing the grey walls. Presently he was aware of the strain of keeping the corridors present and full of people and concluded he was faking everything. Besides, Sorenson had come out of the bathroom and was nudging him on the shoulder. He was also aware that Sorenson had been talking to him for some time, cordially at first, then cautiously, then timidly. "The john's all yours, Elder." (Pause.) "Probably time to get up now, Elder, so we can hit the old streets." (Pause.) "We're running kind of late, Elder. Maybe you should get up now."

"Eat shit, Mother Superior," Lorin said from beneath the blankets. It was his first and only outburst at Sorenson, and he was instantly sorry.

A few days after this, an odd thing happened with Sorenson. They came home early from tracting because they were due at a meeting with their district president that evening and Lorin wanted to bathe and change clothes first. While in the close company of his companion all day, walking door to door, sitting in the front seat of the car, sharing an elevator, Lorin had by degrees become aware, especially since lunch, that one of them smelled bad. It was a peculiar odor, something like burning garbage, and when he first noticed it he had thought that was what it was—they were working a seedy neighborhood, they had been turned away by a man in his undershirt who had sat reading a tabloid on his front porch—but it was still there when they were in an air-conditioned delicatessen eating corned-beef sandwiches, and still later when they visited a high-rise office building to keep an appointment with a CPA whose wife had not wanted them to come to the house again. No one said anything, but Lorin was positive the rejections that day were unusually brisk. He was quite sure, in the case of a woman who at first had welcomed them into her living room and good-naturedly dismissed them when she discovered they were not asking if she knew someone named Norman Church (because it so happened she did)—he was quite sure that her nostrils twitched when, chuckling with the elders over her mistake, she showed them the door.

The close proximity of his companion made discrimination difficult. When you broke wind in an elevator you knew who was at fault and you kept your eyes straight ahead or glared at the person next to you, but Lorin could not be absolutely sure until late in the afternoon which of them was the offender in this case. And it was difficult to ask someone with whom you were not on first-name terms if he had perhaps omitted to change his temple garments. Sorenson in any case said nothing all afternoon to suggest he was even aware of the odor, and it was not until he excused himself and went to the men's room while they were stopped for gas and Lorin found himself momentarily left in his own company that Lorin knew who the culprit was. Mortified, he suggested, when Sorenson returned, that they might knock off early; he was feeling a little gamey, he explained; he was not nice to be near, ha ha. Sorenson had been a good sport all day, not said anything, but it would be a favor to everyone if Lorin could just grab a quick bath before their meeting. The district president wouldn't have to open all his windows and risk freezing everyone, ha ha.

"Oh, that," said Sorenson, and smiled.

Back in their room Lorin went into the bathroom and closed the door. He didn't know if Sorenson knew that devils were said to have a peculiarly offensive odor and he didn't want to alarm him if it wasn't anything. He took off all his clothes, sniffing at the underarms of his jacket and shirt, the crotch of his trousers, both shoes, his socks, which he turned inside out after checking the exterior, and finally his baggy temple garments themselves. There were sweat smells under the pervasive odor of burning garbage, but no more than the usual sweat smells generated by a day of chronic anxiety, and quite distinct from the garbage smell. He ran the tub full of water and climbed in, lathering his armpits and various crevices, scrubbing wildly at the soles of his feet, even giving himself a second shampoo. Climbing out, he sang loudly as he dried off with his blue threadbare towel that was still damp from his bath in the morning, and watched the soap-thickened water drain out of the tub, leaving only a pleasant dampness in the air. The smell of burning garbage was perhaps a little fainter in the damp air.

He put on a fresh pair of garments and padded back into the bedroom, still singing to keep his spirits up and to prevent conversation. He found a clean shirt, clean socks; put on a fresh tie; selected his second suit from the closet and climbed into it; sat on the bed, still singing, to pull on a different pair of shoes and tie them. Only then did he glance up at his companion. Sorenson had been puttering around the small writing table they shared, re-reading a letter from his girl friend, and he chanced to turn his head just as Lorin looked up, and their eyes happened to meet. The odd thing happened then. Sorenson's face went white as Lorin watched. His eyebrows drew up into twin circumflex accents, and deep lines suddenly formed in his forehead. The irises of both eyes stood out like black varnished buttons against snow, and did not move or change focus but continued to stare directly into Lorin's eyes. His nostrils flared as though invisible fishhooks were pulling them apart. He looked blue around the mouth and his gums were dark. Lorin turned to look behind him, to see what Sorenson could have seen, what severed arm on the bedside table, what eyeball floating in the water glass, but there was nothing remarkable—his crushed pillow, a twisted necktie on the bedspread—and when he looked back at his companion again, Sorenson was putting his letter away and gathering up his black plastic notebook and three-in-one scripture.

"You feel all right?" asked Lorin, wondering what it would feel like to see a devil peer out of a friend's eyes. Sorenson nodded, and snapped his attache case shut and opened the door. Lorin noticed, however, as they went out, that his companion's hair was wet around the ears and that his shirt collar where it showed over the collar of his jacket was wilted and that he had left sweat marks on the switch plate as he tried twice to turn off the light before finally getting it.

———

About the second or third week of nursing Alice through the Book of Mormon, a new problem commenced to plague him. He was reading in bed late one night, actually about one in the morning, trying to ignore Sorenson's asthmatic snorting on the other side of the room, and feeling the first reassuring signs that he was going to be able to sleep tonight—his head had begun to go numb, and the sentences of the paragraph he was reading made no sense, and he would go back to re-read it and find he had invented all the sentences past the first one—he was gradually drifting off to sleep when he heard someone say, "Poke the cow's eye with a tail," and suddenly froze in his descent. The sentence had been crisply and clearly articulated, the voice thin but unquestionably human, and he had heard it inside his head. He waited to hear more, but that was all there was. It embarrassed him to do it, but he got up and looked under the bed. He crossed the room and listened to the steam radiator under the window. He went into the bathroom, climbed into the tub, and pressed his ear against the drain. Back in the bedroom, he considered the bedside lamp with its erratic flickering bulb and its bent wire harp holding its cracked shade, but after listening closely to the lamp for a minute or two, all the time hoping Sorenson would not wake up, he gave it up and crawled back into bed, knowing that his first impression was correct. He slept unevenly, and the next day tried not to think about it.

That day a belligerent Negro followed them down a residential street shouting obscenities at them, and a mailman stepped out of his truck in the middle of a block and asked them why they didn't take all their wives and go back where they came from. Lorin couldn't think of a fast reply in either case, nor was he very articulate during the rest of the day of knocking on doors and speaking to the suspicious people who opened them and didn't like what they saw standing on the front steps.

Nothing happened that night or the one after, but the one after that, as he was drifting off again between the sentences in his book, he felt his brain relax its grip and suddenly heard, "We do ask that you take too much of this." This time he gently placed his book face-down on the table next to the clock, reached up and pulled the chain on the lamp, crushed the pillow under the back of his neck and stared hard at the spangle of corpuscles that floated between himself and the ceiling. The voice was female this time. It was pleasant to listen to, but it faded in and out as he tipped his head this way or that, and he couldn't make out the words past that first sentence. The next night it was a male voice again. "Our manic season covered three fists of the cloth," it said, and not another word followed, for all his twisting around in an effort to fine-tune.

Nothing more for several nights, and then it happened again late on a Sunday night following a freak late-season snowstorm, on account of which they had turned up the heat in their bedroom when they had come home from sacrament meeting so that the air was thick and sybaritic. Lorin was nearly asleep, lying with his clothes on top of the bed, and suddenly got a heavy dose. "Actually as many as a new bride," it said. It had said something before that but he hadn't caught it in time. "And very lovely things. In fact they are too lovely for the space of an hour." Lorin opened one eye and watched the back of Sorenson's neck for a while as Sorenson, wearing only his garments, sat at the table reading his Bible. It felt very private. Lorin closed the eye and listened for more, but no more came. But much later the same night—he was undressed and in bed by then—he awoke to hear, "As she grew older, the roses in her cheek coalesced into the pimples on her chin."

It went on for several weeks, well past the discussion of angels and into the chemical properties of spirit matter. It was rarely more than a sentence or two, and usually only a phrase or part of a phrase. It was not the same voice every time, but neither was it, as he had thought at first, an indeterminate and constantly changing assortment of voices. He seemed to recognize the same three or four voices recurring in no particular sequence, with possibly a fifth; at least two of them seemed to be female, and one of these, he was startled to realize one night, sounded very much like his mother. There was a touch of something familiar about one of the male voices too, but he couldn't place it. It was not his father. Where they were coming from was as deep a mystery as what they could mean. There was no question about their nature. They were not thoughts, they involved no contraction of his cognitive muscles. He was hearing them, as surely as he was hearing Sorenson's asthmatic snoring or the scuttle of mice in the walls, but not through his ears. The voices were intracranial, but he could not guess by what means they got there.

At times he felt as though he were helplessly eavesdropping on someone else's conversation, but this illusion was shattered when he heard his own name pronounced by one of them one night when he was nearly asleep. His eyes snapped open and he felt sweat form in the small of his back. Unfortunately he missed the rest of the sentence in his confusion, but a few nights later, easing around the brown edge of sleep, he heard it again, one of the female voices, sounding impatient. "Lorin, do you have to have cups in the Ovaltine?" It happened again the next night: "Lorin, did you get the camber from the mezzanine?" The next few occasions were eavesdropping again, and then nothing at all for a few days, during which the discussion with the Klings had proceeded to Third Nephi in the Book of Mormon; and then, just as he was ready to believe the series was past, he received a frontal assault: "Lorin, the girl is emotional, and I'd rather she took salad than otherwise."

This was a new direction. For the first time the message, however oblique, could be said to have an applicability. The girl was undoubtedly Alice, and though he would not himself have characterized her as emotional, and though he could not make out if he were being warned or encouraged, it was a relief to have some rationale at last. On their next visit to the Klings, Lorin arranged to let Sorenson do most of the talking while he watched Alice to see if she did or said anything he would call emotional. This was hard to do since she had chosen to sit this time on the same side of the room as Lorin, with Richard sitting in her usual place, picking at his ear, so it was impossible to look at her without turning completely on the couch, which was conspicuous.

He might have saved himself the trouble anyway, because she was subdued and even a little sulky that night, and said practically nothing, answering Sorenson's programmed questions with a shrug or a "Why not?" She said something bitchy to her husband once when he had asked a civil question, but for the most part she remained silent to the end of the discussion. She offered no resistance, however, when Sorenson, consulting his pocket calendar, set an evening for their next visit. "Probably having her period," Lorin said as they drove home.

"Probably," Sorenson said. His girl friend in Dallas was that way at those times.

The voices went on, but they began to overlap with another symptom. This one was harder to define, but he was very clear about the occasion of its onset. One Sunday evening Lorin and Sorenson left the house and went out to Sorenson's car to go pick up an investigator and her husband whom they had been accompanying to sacrament meeting for the last couple of weeks. When they got to the car, which was parked under a crude kind of shelter built onto the family's garage, Lorin noticed he had forgotten his instant-preparation book. While Sorenson warmed up the car he went back to get it. Passing through the living room he nodded at the two teenage children and the father who were watching television and looked up at him in surprise. "Just me again," said Lorin. He hurried down the hallway to the back bedroom, put his hand on the knob, and froze there. For one brief, insane moment he had never seen this door or its knob before in his life; he had never been in this hallway before. He had no idea who those people in the living room were or what he was doing in their house. It seemed somehow odd and unaccountable that someone named Sorenson was outside waiting for him in a car while he, Lorin, stood here in this hallway with his hand on a doorknob. And he understood, finally, that he was afraid to turn the knob and open the door because he knew if he did he was going to see himself sitting at the writing table, looking up irritably to see who had just come in. He tasted something nasty in the back of his mouth. He took his hand from the knob and backed along the hallway, watching the knob carefully to see if it turned, until he reached the living room, at which point he turned around and walked past the family as calmly as he could, saying goodbye again, and then went out to the car.

"Find it?" Sorenson asked.

"No. If the branch president asks me to speak pretend you're me."

Unlike the voices, which, though irregular, came only when he was starting the decline toward sleep and thus belonged within a certain spectrum of consciousness when his resistance was softened, this new sensation, though less frequent—it was to happen no more than a dozen times—was likely to strike any time. He could be cheerful and normal one minute, frying eggs on the hot plate and regaling his companion with UCLA anecdotes, and the next minute, without warning, he could not look at Sorenson because Sorenson was sitting next to the window, and Lorin would not be able to avoid the sight of himself standing outside the window peering in, his nose and palms white against the glass. Once, in the middle of the day, he could not bring himself to go into the bathroom because he would encounter himself sitting on the toilet. Another time he invented an excuse not to go out to the car to help Sorenson bring in the groceries, because he would have to pass by the open garage to get to it, and he knew who was standing just inside the garage, waiting to step out.

Still another time—this was shortly after Alice's baptism—he was shaving and noticed the movements of his reflection in the mirror over the wash basin were slightly out of sync with his own. He continued for a time, as though he hadn't noticed, and suddenly stopped short. There was the barest hesitation, the tiniest perceptible lag in the pause made by his reflection. He set down his razor, placed a hand on either side of the wash basin, and leaned toward the mirror, his nose only inches away, and stared until he was able to make it out, the smallest trace of a shit-eating smile surrounded by the streaky lather on the face that looked back at him. He picked up his razor, watching closely as the reflection did too, and finished shaving, taking satisfaction in shearing through the head of a small pimple beside his adam's apple and watching the reflection bleed.

# 17

*I*t was not easy to do something imprudent. One of the rules of the mission field was that you and your companion did not let each other out of sight for one hour out of the twenty-four. With companions less personable than Sorenson this rule could, of course, lead to horrors, and even Sorenson had proved now and then a mild irritant. But Lorin was resigned to living out his second year as he had lived out his first, keeping close quarters with a series of companions some of whom he would not like, and he would not consciously have sought his undoing if the devil had not stepped in and poisoned the fish sandwich Sorenson ate one night at an A&W while Lorin, who hated tartar sauce, ate an overcooked double burger and survived.

Far into the night Lorin sat reading at the bedside of his stricken companion, who lay moaning and twisting and who periodically bolted from under the covers and made for the bathroom, slamming the door. A series of terrible sounds issued out to Lorin, who watched helplessly as Sorenson, his face white and clammy, emerged and crawled back into bed to moan and twist some more. Toward morning the sounds of all the flushing summoned Mrs. Green, who came to their room in bathrobe and hair curlers and ordered Lorin to the living room to try to catch an hour or so of sleep on the couch while she took his place at Sorenson's bedside, equipped with a bottle of Kaopectate and a large spoon.

Lorin slept fitfully, wakened several times by the sound of the teenage children coming and going and asking their father why he was there on the couch and where was Mom and so forth, but he managed to drift into an approximate sleep until the house was silent again, everyone having left for work or school, at which point he got up to see what was what. Mrs. Green was in the kitchen drinking coffee and doing the crossword puzzle while a cigarette burned in the ashtray by her saucer. Lorin thanked her for spelling him and went back to the bedroom to find both beds neatly made and his companion gone. He hurried back to the kitchen and stood for a moment by the breakfast table, watching her make an erasure and lightly pencil in an alternative.

"Um," he said.

They had taken Sorenson, it seemed, to the hospital. She was surprised at his surprise. "Don't you remember?" she said. "We even talked about it."

He didn't remember, but of course it was possible. The conversation would have been shuffled into the series of dreams he had had on the couch and been forgotten with them. He got the name of the hospital, and after shaving and dressing drove Sorenson's car to the hospital and found his companion, weak and exhausted, in a room whose other occupant pretended to read an old copy of Field and Stream.

"I see they've put you in the hospital," Lorin said, his eyes darting nervously up and down the length of the bed, stopping at the tray full of plastic bottles at the head, flicking a glance at the vase of flowers on the table beside the neighboring bed, returning to poor Sorenson, who lay motionless, his mouth half open, his eyes barely slits. His hands lay folded loosely on the blanket that was pulled up to his chest. Without his glasses his face looked concave.

"I can see I should have brought you here myself," Lorin said. "Last night," he added.

Sorenson moaned, and closed his eyes the rest of the way.

"I mean, we both thought it would pass," Lorin said. "A little stomach upset. Neither of us thought it was anything like food poisoning. I guess the joke was on us, ha ha."

Sorenson's mouth closed and he swallowed.

"It was certainly nice of Mrs. Green to haul you down here for me while I was racked out on the couch. I've already thanked her, of course."

Lorin became aware that the man in the next bed was paying close attention to the conversation. He sat down in the cold white metal chair closest to Sorenson's head, to insure privacy. "Anything you'd like me to tell her, just say the word and I'll pass it on," he added.

Sorenson took a deep breath, let it out slowly, groaned once and swallowed again.

"Feeling any better?" Lorin asked.

Sorenson's head moved slightly. It might have been a nod. Lorin noticed that his upper lip, beside the wings of his nostrils, had a greenish tinge.

"Well, you just stay here and get well, old buddy," he said. "I'll take care of everything." He stood up, patted his companion's cold wrist. "I'll be in tomorrow to check on you again. Don't worry about a thing."

Without glancing at the neighboring patient, and feeling all knees and elbows, he walked out of the room, down the long corridor to the elevators, descended to the ground floor where he stepped out, bumped into a large white pot containing gravel and a dead locust sapling, headed for the hospital coffee shop where he drank three cups of coffee, his first such indulgence in over a year. His hand shook while he was finding change to pay the cashier; in the parking lot his knees felt like bedsprings. He sat in Sorenson's car for a long time before starting it, his forehead pressed against the steering wheel, listening to the pulsebeat in his ears.

There were certain things you did as a matter of course when your companion got sick. Lorin was going to have to phone his district leader and report the situation. He would be relieved of the burden of tracting for the duration, but he would be taken along to various meetings with the district leader and his companion. He would be given dinner appointments with various members of the local branch. He would be fussed over and asked periodically how Elder Sorenson was doing. He would be told that his first duty was to hang in there and get his companion well. The other elders would josh him about poisoning his companion to get out of going tracting. He would make some pleasantry about breaking his companion's leg next. All this would be set in motion as soon as he made that phone call.

He got lost once or twice because of the system of one-way streets in the downtown area, and an accident on the belt route blocked two lanes for nearly an hour, but it was still only a little past noon when he pulled up in front of the squat white bungalow with the privet hedge bordering the lawn. He rehearsed openers as he rang the bell, because she would be surprised to see him there by himself.

There was no answer. His good angel told him to fly. His good angel told him that the neighbors in all the houses across the street had stopped what they were doing to watch him through the curtains. He shifted his attache case to his right hand and looked at his watch. He set the case down and took his small black appointment book out of his inside coat pocket and consulted a page for the benefit of the neighbors. Then, looking puzzled for the benefit of the neighbors, he picked up his attache case and went around the side of the house, through the staggered row of arbor vitae that marked the lot line, his shoes going squish in the recently-sprinkled ground, and found her, in levis and a sweatshirt, kneeling over a wooden tray of small blue flowers next to a rectangle of soil cut into the lawn. She had a trowel in her hand. Lorin cleared his throat and she started.

"You scared the life out of me."

"I rang the bell," he said. "I didn't think you were home."

"I can't hear it when I'm out here. This is the first day it hasn't been too muddy to do anything in the yard. I've never planted flowers before and I don't know if it's too early in the season or what."

Lorin didn't know either. "They're nice, though," he said, looking at them, whatever they were.

She got up and brushed the mud and debris from her knees. She looked past him at the corner of the house. "I didn't expect to see you two here today," she said. "Where's your friend?"

Lorin told her and she put a hand to her mouth. "I thought you'd want to know," he said.

"That's hideous," she said, her grin under control.

Lorin nodded.

"What about you?" she asked. "I mean what do you do now, while you're waiting for him and everything?"

"It probably won't be very long, actually," he said. "Probably not more than a day or two. I'll probably have to help Elder Beyer. He's the district leader. Something."

They were standing on a grand-piano-shaped slab of concrete that a former owner of the house had poured for a back porch. The porch had gotten no farther than the pouring and hardening. It dropped off abruptly, forming a sharp edge. Dead crabgrass clung to the edges. Lorin looked at the wedge of mud where she had scraped the sole of her tennis shoes and suddenly realized he was passing his attache case back and forth from one hand to the other and that his palms were slick.

"Have to be chaperoned, huh?" she said.

"It wouldn't do to be turned loose on the streets," he said.

"I guess I'm so used to seeing you with somebody that it's a little strange to see you by yourself."

"It does feel odd," he said. "I may go home and hide in bed."

"I wonder if Richard and I should go visit him in the hospital," she said.

"I don't think he'd know you were there. He hardly knew I was. He'd probably appreciate it."

She brushed off a flat coin of mud from her pant leg with the edge of the trowel.

"Of course he might be better when you got there," he added.

"Maybe we should wait," she said.

"That might be better," he agreed.

That left them horribly with nothing else to say. She looked for some place to put the trowel, and finally tossed it into the wooden tray next to a small square of soil containing two bright flowers. She wiped her palms on the seat of her pants and looked up at him.

"I guess you wouldn't want to come in for a few minutes before you have to go find your chaperon?"

He looked at his watch and listened to the blood pound in his head. "I could only stay for a minute," he said.

In the living room she motioned him to sit down on the couch, and then looked over her shoulder down at the seat of her pants. "I'm too dirty to sit down in these. Let me go put on something else." She disappeared down the hall to the bedroom and was gone long enough to set his pulse fluttering, but when she returned it was in nothing to get excited about after all. She had found an old shirt of Richard's and a clean pair of new jeans that had not shrunk to fit her yet and made her look thin.

"Can I get you anything?" she said. "Have you had lunch yet?"

"Actually I had something at the hospital," he said, remembering the three cups of coffee that still had his nerves vibrating.

She smiled uncertainly. "Well. I guess I'll just sit down then." She sat down on the chair she had sat in the first night he had seen her. She removed her rubber sandals, pulling the thong carefully from between the first and second toe of each foot, spreading her toes, and drew her legs up under her, sank down again, a hand on either arm of the chair, and only then looked at him. "I feel stupid wearing these things and they hurt my toes, but all my shoes are muddy."

He laughed politely.

"I started reading the Doctrine and Covenants," she said after a moment. "I started the other day. I haven't got very far."

"How do you like it so far?"

"It's kind of hard to get into. You know what I mean?"

"Not many members have read the whole thing," he said.

"I can see why."

"I probably shouldn't tell you that," he added. He had a vague, distasteful sense that he was saying all the wrong things.

"I don't mean it's boring or anything," she said quickly. "I just mean, you know, it's all broken up and talking about a lot of different things. I liked the one where he predicts the Civil

War. I don't know. I skip around sometimes."

"Most people don't read it from beginning to end," Lorin said, so she would feel better.

"Richard is," she said. "He's amazing. He sits down right there, where you are, before the news comes on at night, and he reads the thing straight through like he was reading a novel or something. He keeps a pencil and a note pad on the couch next to him, and he writes himself little notes. Sometimes he starts talking to me about prophetic impulses and what happens to your head when you're having a prophetic impulse. He's so funny. I tell him, Richie, it's *okay*, you don't have to *convince* me."

"How is he doing, incidentally?" Lorin asked. "His job I mean."

"I don't know. Okay, I guess. He doesn't tell me much. He quit escrow because one of the men in operations told him it was a dead end, so now they've got him over in loans. He's in some kind of training program. He has to go to Detroit every other day practically. He went in today, for instance. I don't really know what he does."

"He doesn't tell you much?" Lorin said, sitting on both hands.

"I think he's mad at me or something," she said. "He gets like that. His nose gets all bent out of shape because I did something or said something that I don't even remember what it was. One minute he's all over me and the next minute he doesn't talk to me for two weeks."

"I'm sorry," said Lorin. "Is it something we can maybe help with? Or the branch president? Maybe you could talk about it."

She hunched her shoulders. "He'll get over it. I'm not saying it's a hundred percent his fault. I mean I can be a pain in the ass too."

"Hard to imagine," said Lorin, who as a matter of fact could imagine it very well. His face felt hot.

She smiled, putting her hand over her mouth.

"You're really nice, you know that?" she said. "I mean both you guys. I'm not saying anything against the other elders, but I'm glad we got you two instead of Zaret, for instance."

"Zaret's a good man," Lorin said, feeling the need to close ranks.

"God, that giggle of his would drive me up a wall. I don't mean I wouldn't have joined the church if it would have been him instead of you, but I really like you two. That doesn't embarrass you or anything, does it? Sorenson especially. He's a cute little guy."

Hating his companion with a murderous hatred, Lorin said,

"His girl friend in Dallas writes him ten-page letters every week. He's told me all about her. She sounds a little crazy, actually."

"I guess I don't know very much about either one of you personally," she said, looking at him thoughtfully. "I mean, obviously you're not married, but are you engaged or anything?"

"You mean me or us?"

"Well, both of you I guess."

"Sorenson isn't exactly engaged, but there's a sort of understanding. It's that way with a lot of missionaries."

"How about you?"

He smiled, he hoped, bleakly. "There was a girl about a year ago, but that's over now." He wasn't sure if he meant Yvonne or Gloriana.

"That's too bad," she said, sitting forward. "Was it serious?"

"Reasonably," he said.

"I guess I'd expect that," she said, sitting back.

"Why?" asked Lorin, pleased.

"I don't know. I think you're just someone that wouldn't get involved with somebody unless it was serious. I mean you wouldn't go into it just to mess around."

"I didn't," he admitted.

"I don't mean to be nosey or anything," she said, "but what happened? I mean, how come it broke up?"

"It's a long story."

"That's okay, don't tell me anything you don't want to tell me." She waved a hand to stop him in case he was going to. "I was just wondering, you know. About missionaries and going through the temple and everything."

Lorin felt as though he were on the edge of a confidence. "Did we sleep together, do you mean?"

"Yeah," she said.

He hesitated, wondering if he would be more interesting if he said yes or no, or left it ambiguous. While he looked confused she did not stop grinning.

"Um," he said.

"I know that's a dumb question," she said. "I was just wondering. You don't have to tell me."

"It's not that," he said.

"It's okay," she said. "You know everything about Richie and me. If you don't want to tell me anything about you, it's not like I was going to pull it out of you. I know you're being a missionary."

"As a matter of fact," Lorin began.

"Anyway I guess you couldn't have gone through the temple if you had, could you? I mean don't they make you wait a year or something like that, and if this was just a year ago . . .''

"Well, there is a kind of probationary period, but . . .''

"Then you did,'' she said.

"Well, I'd been kind of inactive for the last few years,'' he said. His collar was damp and he felt revolting.

"What was she like? I'll bet she was gorgeous.''

"She was attractive,'' he said.

"Don't talk about it if it's too painful. What's she doing now?''

"I don't know.''

"You haven't kept in touch or anything.''

"No.''

She sank back in her chair. "This is the most I've known about you since I've known you.''

"I hope it doesn't ruin our friendship,'' he said.

"No. I like it.''

While they stared at each other across the small, empty, quiet room, he reflected that they did not have any names to call each other by. Whether she had ever addressed him as Elder Hood in the beginning he could not remember, but it would jar him to hear her call him that now, or at any time since her baptism, and he knew he had not been jarred that way. Likewise—such was the coerciveness of habit—it would have felt like a dangerous familiarity if she had called him Lorin. He could not think of anything else she might have called him in the meantime; she must, then, have never addressed him by name at all during all the past months. For his part he was damned, he decided, if he was going to call her Sister Kling now, but he was fearful of the alternative. While his trip over here alone was not in the strict sense innocent, he was by no means sure what exactly he had expected to do. His heartbeat had not steadied itself since he had left Sorenson in the hospital, but that didn't necessarily mean he was going to do something drastic. He had once seen a dog straining at a leash and barking murderously at an enemy until the leash had slipped, whereupon the dog had turned and slunk off, its tail between its legs, glancing back fearfully at the enemy. Being suddenly laid open to a choice you never expected to have to make took your breath away and made small spots of light bash around in front of your eyes. It would help define things, he suspected, if they had something they could call each other.

"Did I tell you Richard was in Detroit?'' she asked artlessly.

"I think you mentioned it. Yes.''

"So here we are talking about our sex lives and neither one of us with a chaperon.'' She doubled up her knees and wrapped her arms around them. "Does that mean you'd better go?''

"Probably."

"Listen, would you just stop playing a role long enough to tell me what you're thinking?"

"I'm not," he said. "I'm really like this."

"Sure. And I'm just a happy homemaker in the suburbs who likes to mess around in the garden."

"I am," he insisted. "I don't mean this is the only thing I am, I mean I've done a lot of other things too, but I'm not putting on an act. That doesn't necessarily mean I like it. I just do it." He sat up straight. "People are always a little more complicated than the surface shows," he said.

"I don't know how complicated I am, but I know I get bored out of my skull being a happy homemaker in the suburbs." She was staring between her raised knees at a point halfway between herself and Lorin.

Lorin felt unsettled. A confusion of roles had thrust itself on him. "Maybe I shouldn't ask," he said, "but were you ever planning to have children? I mean that can give you a direction to take."

"You're right. You shouldn't ask."

"I'm sorry."

"Anyway, it's too late to worry about planning. I think I'm pregnant."

"That isn't necessarily a bad thing," he said uncertainly.

"But no, I wasn't planning to, if you want to know," she said. "I think my damn diaphragm slipped, or I got it in crooked or something."

Casting for something to say, Lorin asked, "What does your husband think about it?" He didn't have a name to call him by either.

"I haven't told him yet. I'm still not positive. He'll probably think he's Mr. Super Virile. He's the one that wanted them. I know he talks big about how you don't have to have children just because you're married, but I'd have been pregnant six times a year if it had been left up to him. You know what I feel like? I feel trapped."

"You shouldn't have to feel that way," Lorin said.

"It's not that I don't like kids, it's just that I don't like the idea of just staying home and keeping house in the suburbs. I mean, if you think that's what I'm like then I've been playing a role pretty good."

She was close to tears. Now he would have to comfort her, Lorin thought. He stood up, the blood roaring in his ears, and went over and put a hand on her shoulder.

"What's that for?" she said, looking at it.

"Try to take it easy," he said.

"God, now he's going to be a missionary again. Look, I don't need the big missionary fatherly advice or you to tell me how understanding you are. You'll probably start telling me about being a mother in Zion. That's all I need."

"Not really," Lorin said. "I mean, that's not what I was going to say."

"Richard's already started telling me how my testimony isn't as strong as his because it doesn't have a strong intellectual base or some shit like that. I feel like telling him to take his testimony and shove it. The branch president will probably start on me next." To his astonishment she put her hand on top of his where it still rested, clammy, on her shoulder. "I haven't got anything of my own," she said, furious tears in her eyes. "I can't even be a Mormon without him deciding he has to be one too so he can tell me I'm doing it wrong. It's like that all the time. He either laughs at me or he follows me around like a puppy. What the hell does he know about it anyway?" Her hand had moved up and was clutching Lorin's wrist. Her fingers were small, thin, and tight. "I know more about it than he does, and I don't need you to give me the sister in Zion number."

She had drawn her legs under her, and now suddenly stood up on the chair, her arms around his neck, crying into his collar. Lorin tentatively patted the small of her back with his left hand, her shoulder blade with his right. He felt the room tip sideways when he kissed her, but it was just that she had put all her weight on one foot, bending the other leg at the knee, and the foot had slipped between the cushion and the arm of the chair. Flashes of Sorenson safe in his hospital bed came to him. He remembered salient details of his cathedral painting that had hung in the Blue Couch, and suddenly knew how he would redo them now if he had the chance. Going down the hallway to the bedroom, feeling her small hand in his, he heard the furnace kick on behind the louvered doors on his left, and it struck him for the first time that the house had no basement, which explained why the washer and dryer were in the kitchen. The house he had shared with Yvonne had had a washing machine in the basement, but no dryer; a clothesline had run from the screened porch out to an apricot tree in the back yard, but it was so long that its unsupported middle hung a bare four feet from the ground when it was loaded, so their clothes had frequently picked up a coating of grit along one edge. He wondered if Gloriana did her own laundry or sent it out.

Their clothes lay in piles on both sides of the bed, his dark suit, now showing wear, in three pieces across the room, one leg of the trousers pulled inside out; his black shoes and her new jeans lying together beside the magazine rack, his shirt and tie coiled up with her white cotton underpants in the seat of the rocking chair. His temple garments provided the only hesitation, both because they were hard things to get out of in a hurry and because she wanted to look at them, for she had never seen anything like them before in her life.

---

That night they came for him. He was standing in a broad, flat plain that was cut by lines that stretched off into the distance, meeting at a point on the horizon to the right of folded snow-capped mountains. Clouds with flat bottoms floated overhead, drifting north toward the vanishing point, moving faster and becoming elongated the closer they moved, rushing with a terrifying speed as they progressed, and finally disappearing into a point in the air over the convergence of the lines. The sky was full of flying things. As he turned, someone stepped behind a tree. He would have to be very careful. Picking his way through piles of broken rubble, he passed under an archway and found himself in a courtyard. A long shadow extended across the ground from behind a white pillar. As he watched, it began to move, its shoulders rising and falling, and it grew longer. In another moment whatever was casting it would come out from behind the pillar. He pushed open the door behind him and passed a table with a cage on top of it, in which something grinned at him through hair. Running now, he reached the top of the stairs and looked left and right. Someone had been there just ahead of him; he could feel the particles of the air rocking gently. He followed a white hopping thing that kept a uniform distance from him down the corridor. It hopped awkwardly, as though crippled, pausing at times and then making fitful little jumps and then a large one, bouncing off the wall and falling back to the floor again. He could not get close enough to see what it was, but just then the bishop's round bald head swung down from the ceiling on a rope. It stopped in front of him and said, "Eeee. Lorin," and scuttled off on tiny legs. They were fitting a small black bag for him in one of the rooms at the end of the hall, but if he walked quietly past the door they might not hear him. If they did, he would say he had just seen the bishop. He sat down at the desk and began filling out his weekly report, accounting for one hundred sixty-eight hours since last week, wondering why he hadn't done it before. He didn't look up when they passed him, carrying the bag; he was trying to keep his figures straight without letting them see he was having trouble making the column total up correctly.

He knew they were standing behind him, holding the bag, but he would act as though nothing were wrong. He would continue to write his report while they stood there. They put the bag over him and drew the string. He would fudge the hours somehow.

———

He went to a florist the next day and took a bunch of nasturtiums to Sorenson's room. That pleased the man in the next bed, who was recovering from a second hernia operation. Sorenson was alarmingly better. The flowers touched him; the gesture was meant to be facetious, and that was what he liked about it. He expected to be discharged tomorrow. Could Lorin come by before noon to take him home? Of course, said Lorin, stricken. Before noon, on the dot. With engine running and wheels spinning. They'd be back on the tracting beat before you could say barf. Elder Sorenson ready for that, hey? Sorenson smiled through pain. He thought they might squeeze another day or two of convalescence at home out of this thing. That would be a terrible shame, Lorin said. The man in the next bed said Elder Sorenson had been working on him already, so don't expect him to be out of commission too long. He was afraid of that, Lorin said. He fished a Joseph Smith tract out of his attache case while they were all chuckling—Sorenson had been rushed off without his, of course—and gave it to the man and left for his appointment with the district leader which was not until three o'clock but he didn't mention that.

He got lost again trying to avoid his mistakes of yesterday while negotiating downtown traffic, but found the subdivision he wanted at last. He parked his companion's car on a different street this time and walked along a chain-link fence, rounding the corner just in time to face a surly terrier that circled slowly behind him, the fur along its back standing up, and darted at his achilles tendon while he fanned the air with his attache case all the way to Alice's door. She was shaking with laughter by the time she answered his ring, having seen the whole dance from the front window. "I'm sorry," she said. "You looked so wild out there in a black suit and everything, swinging at a dog."

"I was just trying to get the little shithead in range," he said, not liking her very much.

"I'm sorry," she said again, quietly.

They fell into a mad embrace just inside the door. He set his attache case down so quickly it rocked and tipped onto its side.

"Hey, did we really do it?" she asked, pressing the side of her face against his chest.

"I think we did," he said.

"Richie wondered how come I was in such a good mood last night," she said. "I had to tell him you'd come over because I had to tell him about Sorenson. I had to make up a good reason because I was pretty bitchy yesterday morning when he left."

"What did you tell him?"

"I don't know. Something stupid."

"Listen," he said, "I have an appointment with the district leader at three."

"What you're trying to say is you can't stay long, is that it?"

"What I mean is, if I'm late he's going to want to know why."

"Tell him you were out tracting or something. Knocking on doors. Kicking dogs."

"You're not supposed to go tracting alone."

"What are you supposed to be doing?"

"I went to see Sorenson at the hospital. I mean I really did. Then I just drove around for a while."

"Tell him you got lost."

"I could do that," he said.

She pulled her head away from his chest and looked up at him. "But you don't like that."

"He might think it sounded funny. I mean I had all day to get there."

"Why don't you just say you don't want to today, okay?"

"No, I don't mean that. I just thought we might talk about it a little. I don't mind admitting it's shaken me up a little."

"Sure it has," she said. "It's something you weren't supposed to do. How do you think I feel? Listen, you don't think this is something I do every day, do you?"

By this time they were sitting on the couch, Alice with her head nestled against his chest and her knees in his lap. He had an arm wrapped awkwardly around her, and because she was virtually on top of him, had no place to put his hand except on her ass. "All right, talk about it," she said. "Go ahead. Talk."

"It isn't that easy," he said. "For one thing, I don't think you understand why I'm upset."

"Oh God," she said, pulling her skirt down over her knees. "I'll bet we have to go through the missionary bit once a day."

"It happens to be true," he said. "I'm not saying I like it. I'm just saying I happen to believe it."

"So do I," she said. "No, I really do. Listen, I don't have any trouble with the gold plates and the angels and stuff. But you're only human, for God's sake. Can't you believe it and still be normal?"

"That doesn't define the issue correctly," he said. "I'm not saying we won't do it any more. I'm just saying we need to understand exactly what it means."

"Do that some more," she said.

"I mean I feel like I've just jumped off a roof," he said. "I haven't been feeling well for the last few months anyway, and this isn't helping any."

"Up a little higher," she said.

"In fact I've been feeling rotten," he said. "Like I had cancer or something."

He was a half hour late getting to Elder Beyer's apartment, and he was exquisitely conscious of the odors he was carrying and hoped the district leader would not recognize them. The district leader was, incidentally, displeased at his lateness, and had had to telephone the family they were scheduled to visit to say they would be late. Lorin had never much liked Elder Beyer anyway. And the next day Sorenson was home.

———

It got difficult after that. For the first day or two Sorenson was still too weak to resume tracting, and Lorin was all solicitude and helpfulness. While his companion sat propped up in bed looking pinker but still ghastly, Lorin tidied the writing table, polished the windows, scoured the bathtub and wash basin, borrowed Mrs. Green's vacuum and bunged out the corners and under the beds, pressed Sorenson's brown suit for him, rummaged for all the dirty laundry he could find, towels, pillow cases, sheets, shirts, socks, temple garments, handkerchiefs, the bath mat, both tablecloths, all three dishtowels, the curtains from both windows, stuffed them all into three large canvas bags and set off to find a laundromat that would not be as crowded as their usual one always seemed to be, as he didn't want to leave his ailing companion alone longer than he had to.

"What are you going to do when he's all well and out of bed?" Alice asked as they lay naked and goosefleshed on her bed in the pink bedroom that he found a little embarrassing. The washing machine churned in the kitchen, and he could hear little ticks through the hum of the dryer from shirt buttons hitting against the glass. Her freckles continued down to her shoulders and then, except for a random constellation here and there, she was white. She was also thin. Her upper arms showed the dips and curves of tendon and muscle, lacking padding. Her breasts were small and widely separated, a washboard of ribs showing between them. Her pelvic bones stood out. Her knees had a larger circumference than the part of her thighs directly above them. "I don't know," he said. "I'm going to have to do some fast thinking." He had gotten lost again and was worried about the time.

On Saturday the district leader and his companion, Elder Holt, came over to see how Sorenson was getting along, and commended Lorin for being a good nurse. Lorin was, he couldn't help it, pleased. On Sunday Sorenson felt strong enough to go to church. Lorin sat with him on a back row and avoided eye contact with Alice, who sat several chairs away on the row ahead of them and kept glancing back at them behind Richard's head. In the foyer after Sunday school the Klings joined the crowd that gathered around Lorin and his stricken companion to ask how Elder Sorenson was getting along. Lorin seized the chance to wander apart with her, casually, and stand in a corner beside the fire extinguisher, as though they were chatting about temple recommends, because the branch president had begun interviewing them for a temple preparation class. Plans were still hazy, but there was some thought that they might be able to use Richard's vacation, which would come late in the summer, to drive to Utah and have their marriage solemnized in either the Salt Lake or Logan or Manti temple.

"I guess I've got to invite the two of you over for dinner," she said. "It'll be awful."

"Sister Milburn has already invited us," he said.

"When will I see you again?" she asked.

"I think he's going to want to go tracting tomorrow. I'll try to call you."

"But when do I *see* you again?"

"I've been going out of my mind trying to think," he said. "I can't think of anything that won't look funny."

"Richard is going to Detroit again."

"When?"

"I don't know. Monday or Tuesday."

Richard, looking paltry and vulnerable, came over and joined them after shaking hands with Sorenson.

"Brother Kling," said Lorin affably, extending his hand.

"I just wanted to thank you for coming over the other day to tell us about Elder Sorenson," Richard said. "I guess he's had a pretty rough time."

"I thought the two of you might want to know," Lorin said. Forewarned was forearmed, else he would have fallen down on the floor and confessed everything.

"I just invited them over for dinner, Richie," she said, straightening his collar where it had crept out over his lapel. "But Sarah Milburn got there first."

"I want to discuss the Book of Abraham with you sometime," Richard said. That was the book translated by Joseph Smith from papyri found buried with an Egyptian mummy and around which an aura of mystery still hovered. Richard was frowning, but

Lorin knew that to be a signal that he had been doing serious thinking on a philosophical point.

"If you hurry you can invite us over one evening during the week," Lorin said, trying to be jocular.

"I'm going to be in Detroit most nights this week, so we'd better wait till next Sunday. Did I tell you I'm in the training program for loan officers at the head office?"

"No," said Lorin, trying hard to look surprised and interested. "Tell me about it." He couldn't remember if he was supposed to have known that, and he couldn't make out what the expression on Alice's face was trying to tell him as he listened to Richard.

———

Fortunately Sorenson became enervated quickly the next day, and they had to quit around noon and go home. By two in the afternoon, at his wits' end thinking of an errand he might run that would plausibly occupy two hours and leave him sweaty—there was scarcely a shred of dirty laundry in the room and they still had milk and eggs in the refrigerator—Lorin hit on a ploy. He sat on his own bed, in full sight of his companion, a pillow propping his back, and started re-reading that day's quantum of scripture. He closed the book and got up and sat down at the table to add something to his instant-preparation book. He went into the bathroom to examine a small red pimple under his eye. He wandered back into the bedroom, stood before the window and looked out for a long time. He sat down on the wooden chair and propped his feet on the radiator. He cleaned an ear thoroughly with the end of his little finger. He sighed. He got up and looked for a book to read that wasn't doctrine.

Finally Sorenson spoke up. "It's a shame to keep you tied down just because I'm sick."

"Just beware of tartar sauce from now on," Lorin said. Sorenson did not, however, go on from there, so after a while Lorin cleared his throat. "Would it look terribly bad, do you think," he said, "if I went and took a walk around the neighborhood or something, just to clear the pores, you know? Go for a little drive, something like that? Cabin fever, ha ha."

Sorenson looked unhappy.

"I could even pick you up a new bottle of Kaopectate," Lorin added slyly.

"You're making me feel like a burden," Sorenson said.

"I just feel like doing something physical," Lorin said. "You don't need a nurse any more, so I'm just spinning my wheels."

"We're not supposed to be out of each other's sight is the

only thing," said Sorenson. "I know how you feel."

"You should have seen me while you were in the hospital. I was watching you from the closet like a hawk."

"Maybe we can go out again," Sorenson said. "I've rested long enough maybe."

"I don't know," Lorin said, looking at him in alarm. "You look pretty green to me. I'd hate for you to pass out on somebody's doorstep."

"Yes, but I hate keeping you cooped up like this." Sorenson stood up and groped for his shirt, which he had thrown onto the foot of the bed when he had lain down.

"Good Lord, don't make yourself sick on my account. I'll stay, I'll stay."

"I guess it's not such a good idea after all," said Sorenson. He sank back onto the bed and closed his eyes.

Lorin bustled around the bed, fluffed Sorenson's pillow. He went into the bathroom and brought back a glass of water. "Here we go, old chum. Down the hatch." Sorenson drank a couple of sips, took his glasses off and laid them on the table next to the bed and rubbed a hand over his eyes.

"I've got a headache like you wouldn't believe, Elder," he said. "And I'm afraid to take aspirin for fear I'll barf everything. Go ahead and go out. I just want to lie here."

"I can't do that," Lorin said. "Just leave you here when you're this sick. Are you sure?"

"I'll be all right," Sorenson mumbled. "Just lie here. Not move."

"I won't be gone long. You sure now?"

Sorenson had flung an arm over his eyes. He nodded.

"Well, if you're sure," Lorin said.

He stopped at a filling station with an outside phone and called her. She sounded depressed.

"It's all right," she said. "I know you had a hard time getting away. But I've been sitting around the house all day afraid to leave because the phone would ring when I wasn't here. You didn't even ask me yesterday if it would be convenient or anything."

"I'm sorry. Can I still come over?"

"Sure. Why not?"

Feeling miserable, he drove through town, found what he thought was the right exit from the tangle of one-way streets in the business section, passed through a strange neighborhood of elegant white clapboard houses with deep, rich lawns, rounded a curve in the road, and saw to his horror he was headed for the narrow bridge that would put him on the wrong side of the river.

A string of cars had gathered behind him. He pressed on, and took the first turnoff he came to on the other side of the river. It was a narrow asphalt road that wound through an experimental farm operated by the state college, and wound further from the river, over gentle hills and fields in which rows of something green and scraggly grew on uniform stakes. He swung onto a dirt road that seemed to lead him back toward the river, but presently it ended at a concrete pylon over which the freeway ran. It was nearly four o'clock when he parked down the street from her house, in the other direction from where the terrier had met him, and walked the thousand yards to her door and rang the bell. She looked at him reproachfully when she opened the door.

"I got lost," he said.

"It's all right," she said, stepping aside to let him in.

They sat on the couch and put their arms around each other. She looked sullen but let him kiss her. "You're mad at me," he said. "It wasn't my fault."

"I know. I'll get over it. It's just that I've been thinking what it's going to be like, that I only get to see you when Sorenson lets you. I mean that really turns me off."

"I'll think of something."

"I mean what am I supposed to do? Call him to see if he can spare you? I've got better things to do than sit around the house waiting for the phone to ring just in case you managed to leave the room while he wasn't looking."

"I know it isn't fair," he said.

"Besides, pretty soon I'm going to start looking pregnant, and then you won't even want to see me."

"Don't be silly," he said uncertainly.

"You're going to be gone by the time I have the little bundle of joy anyway," she said. "You'll be back home probably seeing your old girl friend and I'll be here with Richard and the bundle of joy."

He pulled his head back to look at her. Her eyes were filling with tears.

"Don't look at me," she said, wiping her eyes with the back of a fist. "I'll be okay in a minute. I've just got to not think about it."

"I like to look at you."

She laughed hoarsely. "Who's being silly now? God, I'm such a bawl baby." She jumped up and went into the kitchen. He heard her pulling kleenexes out of the box and blowing her nose. In a minute she came back. Her nose was red. She stood over him and held out her hand. "Okay. I've had my tantrum.

If you can stand going to bed with me, I promise to be very good."

He wondered about the time and whether her husband had indeed gone to Detroit today, but now that the storm had tentatively ended he was afraid to bring it up. They sat on the edge of the bed and he let her undress him, at least down to his garments, and he had to stand up and take those off himself.

"God, those are ugly," she said. "Richie and I are really going to have to wear those things when we do the temple thing?"

"Theoretically," he said.

She stood up and faced him while he unbuttoned her blouse and unhooked her bra. "What a thing to find when you take somebody's clothes off," she said. She raised her arms so he could slip her skirt over her head. He knelt to slide her underpants down and she put a hand on his shoulder to steady herself while she stepped out of them. "Now aren't those much nicer?"

"Much nicer," he said as they lay down.

"Don't try to humor me," she said.

He could not help being distracted by doubts, at the same time he was aware she was going out of her way to make things right. He kept hearing sounds in the other rooms, and car doors kept slamming outside. She stroked him gently with the back of a fingernail. Something creaked inside the closet. She whispered something in his ear that he didn't quite catch, and then drew back, her hand over her mouth. She curled up into a ball, giggling, and then suddenly threw herself on top of him, forcing him onto his back. She kissed him rapidly down the length of his chest and stomach, pausing to bite him gently before continuing down one leg while he stared at the ceiling and listened to the crunch of feet on the unpaved road out front. She was all darting knees and elbows. She rolled onto her stomach and said, "Forget it. I changed my mind." He felt his face go numb as she turned toward him on her side and gently drew a small bony foot up between his legs. The bed extended behind him into a long, sloping hill dense with scumbled white marigolds. She was busy with the palms of both hands. The light over the hill turned a pale apricot, and he watched a speck in the remote bowl of the sky making shallow looping circles. He smelled crushed blades of grass; sprigs fell into his hair and tickled behind his ears. That interested him, though he was not sure he could afford the lapse in attention necessary for private impressions. She would not hold still, that was the other problem. It was hard to gather impressions into an integrated unit when they kept coming at you all over your body as well as from the closet and from the neighborhood outside the window. Still, he was aware that he had sunk deeper into the grass and that the looping speck in the sky was closer. Presently the ground opened under his head, and that was all right too. Grass stood on either side of the gap, waving gently as the wind brushed it. He felt himself slowly tip backward as it widened under him, and soon he was upside down, hanging by the heels and rocking from side to side with the wind. The other bank had fallen away, and he watched the sun rise toward the mountains that hung upside down in the distance, and birds drifted by on their backs.

She had settled down now and was breathing in jerks. A motorcycle went by outside. His heels came loose, and through the back of his head he saw the face of the cliff sweep past him, studded with flat rocks bearing writing. He spun for a long time, his arms and legs spread wide, watching the patchwork of fields below him get smaller. The speck was in a different part of the sky now, flapping like a live dishrag. Its circular loops had degenerated into erratic and frenzied zigzags. He tried to keep a constant distance from it, but this meant falling past objects so rapidly that he couldn't tell what they were. He also could not tell which direction he was falling, or if he were still upside down. He opened his eyes to look at Alice, but she had floated away against the ceiling; her body had become attenuated and he could see specks on the sheetrock through it, and a single strand of dusty cobweb that undulated as a breeze from the window caught it. He closed his eyes again. He was upside down. He swung past the heads of a room full of people who looked up and pointed to him. He swung back and they had become animals, that leaped and snarled at him, and climbed over each other in the effort to reach him. He felt her teeth on him again and opened his eyes. The room was full of people bending over to watch. They crowded around the bed, the ones in back craning to see past the heads of the ones in front. She looked at him in surprise as he pulled away. He closed his eyes again. She stretched out beside him and placed him between her legs, rubbing him back and forth. The soles of his feet burned. He was standing on her front step facing her through the storm door, whose glass had been replaced by a screen, against which she was making him rub himself raw while she pressed into him through the wire mesh. Her eyes glittered. Her mouth was opened wide and she kept making sounds like "Ah? Ah? Ah?" as she moved her hips from side to side. He did not know how close the flapping thing was to him and he was afraid to look around for fear he would lose the momentum that was about to hurl him over the edge.

Unfortunately, Richard was home by then. They heard him moving around in the living room. She pushed away from Lorin and dropped to her hands and knees beside the bed. Her face was white. She groped for the closest thing on the floor—it was one of Lorin's socks—and held it to her chest while she looked frantically around for something else. Lorin lunged for his pants, knowing he could never struggle into his temple garments fast enough. Alice paid no attention to him, other than to grab at the leg of his trousers as it went past her and let go when he didn't release it. Lorin thought badly of her for not keeping better track of her husband's schedule. He also disliked her for thinking only of herself at a time like this. Mere seconds had passed, but those mere seconds were enough to tell them that Richard was not going to come down to the bedroom. Kneeling there on the floor next to each other, random clothes pressed against different parts of their bodies, they heard him go into the kitchen and open the refrigerator. There was a clinking of dishes against milk bottles, and then the refrigerator door closed. A drawer opened and they heard him rummaging among the silverware. They stared at each other as they heard him go back to the living room and sink into the couch. A newspaper rattled, and a spoon clicked against something hard. Suddenly she dropped the sock and hurled herself at Lorin, burying her head under his chin and holding him tightly to her body. Startled, he put his arms around her.

"He's got to have heard us," he whispered.

"Of course he heard us," she whispered back.

"What are we going to do?" he asked.

"God, I don't know. He's waiting for us to come out."

They stood up quickly and began dressing, Lorin struggling into his temple garments and then buttoning his shirt in all the wrong holes while Alice moved swiftly with a quiet, stricken purposefulness. He tied his shoes, put on his suit jacket and stuffed the tie into the pocket. Then, because there was nothing else to do, they left the bedroom, closing the door behind them, and walked down the short hallway to the living room, Lorin in front, Alice a few steps behind. Thus it was Lorin who was just in time to see Richard's back disappearing through the door to the garage and the door close behind him. Alice stepped from behind Lorin and stared at the empty couch with the dish of half-eaten butterscotch pudding on the coffee table in front of it. Lorin pointed to the door. They heard the garage door swing up and a scramble of feet on the concrete floor, and then they heard the door to the Volkswagen open and slam shut. The engine started. Through the window they saw Richard back out the driveway, glancing at the window only once, just before he pulled into the street. The expression on his face was tormented, but Lorin couldn't tell if he was able to see them through the glass.

"Where's he going?" asked Lorin.

"Probably to his parents'," she said. She stood a long time in front of the window, looking in the direction Richard had driven. Lorin watched her. Then she said, "He won't even believe the baby is his now." She turned around and faced Lorin. There were tears on her face, but she was trying to smile. "Hey, I don't want to say go, but go."

"I can't leave you to face this alone," said Lorin.

"I don't want to talk about it, okay?" she said. "Just go."

"Listen, if it will help I'll talk to him."

"I'm going to be sick to my stomach," she said. "Just go. He doesn't need you to talk to him." She did look ill. Her hand was over her mouth and her eyes were small and hot. Lorin raised his hand to touch her shoulder, but she turned and ran down the hall to the bathroom and slammed the door. He followed her as far as he could and stood outside the door listening to her vomit. He timidly knocked when she sounded through. "Can I call you tomorrow?" he asked.

"Yes. God. Anything. Just go away."

"Are you sure you'll be all right?"

"Yes. Yes." He wished he could see what she looked like when she said yes, because her tone told him nothing.

"I'll call you tomorrow, then," he said. "Alice?" he said. It was the first time he had called her Alice. It sounded odd. "If there's any trouble, call me. I don't care what time it is."

She didn't answer, and he picked up his attache case where he had left it by the coffee table and let himself out the front door. For the benefit of the neighbors he glanced at his watch and reached for his appointment book in his inside coat pocket, only then remembering that he wore no tie and his shirt buttons were in the wrong holes. He walked to his car, keeping his back straight and his step resolute, knowing the pit of his stomach had rotted through and was leaving the air foul behind him. He got lost getting home, and when he arrived Sorenson was sitting at the writing table, his hands in his lap. He was staring at Lorin. The wings of his nose were white, and he was white around the lips. Lorin had forgotten for the moment that his companion had been ill. It was a lot to burden a sick man with.

# 18

Knowing you had let everyone down made you conscious
of how much you liked your little back room with its own john
and hot plate and writing table and soft blue walls and the companion who couldn't quite look at you for a couple of days while
he came and went without you. You studied the colors of your
suit coats hanging in the open closet next to his suit coats and
you noticed the way the light shifted in the room after three
o'clock. You heard your mother's voice in your ear as twilight
collected around the elm outside your window and deepened the
corners of your room. It said "Oh Lorin," as if she had just found
the ashes of the stories she had read to you when you were little.
When the telephone rang you knew it was someone who was
going to tell you she had just died, and you were relieved that
it was only Richard.

Richard's voice was pitched a perfect fifth higher than usual.
"I just want to tell you, Elder Hood, that you are a malicious person, a hypocrite, and a coward. I don't hate you, because you
can't help what you are. I feel sorry for Elder Sorenson because
he has to live with you. I don't want to say anything else but
I just wanted you to know what I thought of you, and I think
you are so little of a person that I don't even feel threatened by
you." He hung up. He had been reading from notes, Lorin
decided.

———

Lorin was pretty sure that when all this was over he'd do
a painting of Joseph Smith in bib overalls and with cowshit on
his boots digging through the mud for the gold plates. He'd probably take liberties.

Lying on his bed waiting for the phone to ring, he imagined
climbing down into the declivity he'd seen in his mind's eye when

Moroni was telling him where the plates were and what he was and wasn't supposed to do with them. He imagined the soft ground and the heels of his gum boots cutting into the slope. He could smell crushed grass and he didn't mind that the seat of his pants grew heavy with caked mud because he was a hayseed kid and didn't know any better. He found the half-buried boulder with its crust of orange lichen and set to work with the trowel he had stolen from his mother's potting shed. It was a small tool for a large job, and the afternoon was well advanced before he had undercut the boulder enough to loosen it and had dug a trench deep enough to tip it back without the risk of its getting away from him and rolling down the hill.

The hole he had exposed on dislodging the boulder smelled of damp mold. It had been cut in a rough rectangle, and flat rocks had been lodged against the walls to keep them from crumbling in, but only three of them were still upright, the fourth having been pushed partly over by the weight of shifting earth. The plates lay on a flat rock under the shadow of the tilting wall, and the breastplate, badly rusted, lay on what looked like a coil of decomposing leather strips off to one side. The floor was littered with dead sowbugs, their dried shells nearly transparent. A red millipede scuttled frantically in circles and disappeared into the crack where two of the rock walls joined imperfectly.

The hole was deep enough that you couldn't reach the plates or the fragment of armor from the edge. You had to climb down into it. Lorin wasn't supposed to take them out of the hole until he had permission, but he thought he should probably check to make sure they were all right. He would roll the boulder back over the hole in a minute, and fill in his trench, and scatter dead leaves over the freshly turned earth and probably no one would pay too much attention to the way the ground looked even if they did come by. He lay on his stomach, his arms dangling into the hole and his chin resting on the edge, and tried to make out the scratches on the top plate. He wouldn't be able to read them without the stones, which he guessed were the two transparent eggs lying half-buried in the leather next to the breastplate, but he thought he might be able to tell if he were looking at them upside down. Unfortunately the markings were too faint, at that distance and in that light, for him even to be certain whether they were organized in lines or in columns, or whether the fine webwork of reticulations he thought he could see across the surface of the metal were merely a crust formed by natural oxidation. Meanings lay hidden under those marks, in any case, and he was going to decipher them. He would be withdrawn and preoccupied while he was doing it. Alice couldn't expect him to spend all of his time with her while he was doing it.

He started to get up, intending to push the boulder back onto the hole and tidy up where he had dug around it, when he was grabbed from behind and his face was pushed into the loose dirt piled next to his trench. He had a confused sense of a pale spidery light moving across the clods of earth, and then a knee dug into his back, forcing the breath out of him. His wrist was seized in a grip like a steel claw and pulled up sharply behind him. The sudden pain made him draw in his breath, which he could not do very deeply because of the pressure on his back, which was just as well, since he had aspirated a small quantity of loose soil as it was. He had scarcely a moment to collect his thoughts before a hand gripped him by the hair and began to thump his head against the ridge of soil. Lorin had avoided fights all his life because he was skinny, and the one or two fights he had been unable to avoid had ended by embarrassing him. He had never understood the distinction between skinny and wiry except that wiry people were never embarrassed in fights and skinny people always were. Wiry people could even take their shirts off and not be laughed at.

The pounding of his head against the ground was making his brain go silly. He would have been happy to give up, but he was not sure he had that privilege. He wished he had not heard the pop in his elbow, because he knew he was going to worry about tissue damage. He was already wondering how he would explain a torn ligament to his father, who would ascribe it to malingering, when the hammerlock was released and he felt himself picked up by the shirt collar and the seat of his overalls, which gave him a stab of pain as the seam pulled tight across his crotch, and shaken like a dust mop. He remembered to keep his mouth closed so his teeth would not chip against each other, and when the loose white sleeve of the robe snapped like a towel in front of his face once he quickly shut both eyes. The splotches of colored light swimming against his eyelids alarmed him because he was afraid something had shaken loose during the pounding of his head against the ground, and he dreaded that when he opened his eyes he would see curtains of blood starting to run down, coating the retina. He opened them carefully and was grateful to see the hole he had uncovered and the boulder at the edge of it, the grassy edge of the hill he had climbed, the distant valley below him, where brown pastures were studded by clean white farm buildings, and a distant windmill grinding slowly in the wind, all vibrating at an angle but clean and distinct.

When he was flung back onto the ground and felt his ribs kicked repeatedly it was pleasing to think he had something to be grateful for. He had not suffered brain damage or optic damage, and though the small of his back was crushed by being sat on, and though one of his heels was pressed into his buttock by having the opposite ankle pulled across it like a figure 4, and though he received an intermittent fist in his back and had his face pushed into the ground between blows, the ground at least was grassy here, and the smell of crushed clover was sweet.

He had resigned himself to wrestling all night, but it was over by the time the clouds smoked red in the west. His elbows were scraped raw and the knees of his overalls were in shreds when he was left alone, sitting on an anvil-shaped rock with his head in his hands. He limped home through early-evening shadows, after turning the boulder back into place to hide the plates and scattering leaves over where he had dug. He had his mother's trowel in his pocket, and he would restore it without her seeing him do it. He had lost, but it had not been a fair fight.

---

He woke in the middle of the night and remembered his Nephite. He wished he hadn't told Alice the story. That only reinforced it and he wanted it to go away.

He remembered looking up from a fit of coughing and seeing a little old man gliding behind a lathe in a distant corner of the shop. It was the summer before he started college. It was one in the morning, with a hot wind smelling of brine off the Great Salt Lake. The shop was out near the airport. He hated his job. He dropped his broom and went over to see who it was, and found his man crouching on the floor behind the lathe. That was his mistake. He should never have gone over.

"Can I help you?" he asked.

"That's an ugly cough you got there," the man said.

"What?"

"I been listening to you."

The man fumbled with the ends of his string tie. He didn't look like any of the draftsmen Lorin knew.

"Are you from the front office?" Lorin asked. "I'm the night custodian."

"I suppose you got it working here," the man said.

"What?"

"Your cough. You got it working here."

"It's just a cold. Actually it may be bronchitis."

"I don't guess the dust out here is doing it any good," the man said. "Metal filings and all."

"I have the key to the stockroom if you need to get in."

"Don't smoke, do you?" the man asked.

"Excuse me, but you aren't with the front office or anything, are you?"

"Get them worried about a lawsuit. If you smoked they'd just say don't blame us, he's killing himself."

Something about the man made Lorin nervous. His hair crawled in wild curls all over his head, and his chin trembled. He looked like a transient, but a transient couldn't have unlocked the cyclone gate to the grounds.

"You probably eat meat," the man said.

"What?"

"Worst thing in the world for you. You probably eat eggs too."

"Listen, I'm supposed to ask people if they're supposed to be out here."

"Those things cause degenerative diseases. Cancer. Tuberculosis. I'm afraid to ask if you drink milk."

"I'm only here for the summer. I don't have much authorization. I should probably get this swept out." He picked up his broom and began to sweep, hoping the man would disappear from his peripheral vision.

"Sprouts," the man said.

"What?"

"Leafy vegetables. Fruit. Weeds are good too, but you can't find anything that hasn't been sprayed. Dandelion, purslane, nettle, chickweed, plantain. They're all good, but that spray they use will kill you."

The man's shadow moved away and Lorin looked up, but he was only dragging a wooden crate over to sit on.

"Food is a trap for solar vibrations," the man said.

"I think I'm supposed to call my supervisor," Lorin said.

"Some people don't need much food. They get all the nutrients they need from the sun. I hardly eat at all, for instance."

Lorin swept and swept.

"I have two good bowel movements a day, too," the man said.

"I'm pretty sure I'm supposed to call in every hour," Lorin said, inventing frantically, but the man had gotten up and was already limping toward the stockroom. Lorin held up his key to ask if he needed it, but the next instant the man had opened the door and disappeared inside.

Moths fluttered in from the night sky over the open loading dock. Crickets chirped in the weeds along the invisible chain-link fence. A red light winked on a hill somewhere in the distance.

Lorin swept a few waves of dirt into a ridge and waited. Finally he went over, unlocked the door, and, still carrying his broom, stepped inside. He looked under the shipping clerk's desk, then wandered up and down the aisles of screws, bolts, hubs, flanges, and chains. He inspected all the crates containing electric motors, and crushed a black widow spider that ran out of one. He looked under the workbench on which the shipping clerk packaged parts. He looked up at the I-beams near the ceiling, feeling foolish. He looked at the calendar with the girl holding an oil can between her breasts. He walked backwards toward the door, fumbled behind him for the knob, opened it and closed it carefully after he was back in the shop.

He wondered, lying on his sweaty pillow and listening to the telephone getting ready to ring, if he were being punished for disliking a Nephite when he met one.

———

He dreamed he was sitting in an underground room in the temple. The walls were white but dirty, the paint having chipped in places, and there were finger marks and scuff marks from heels all over it; plaster dust lay in the corners. A white curtain hung down one wall. Folding chairs lined the other walls, several of them occupied by people he knew. Sorenson, for instance, sat in one across the room from him, talking to a girl Lorin assumed was the bitchy girl friend from Dallas, except that she did not look like the picture he had seen. A few chairs away he saw Dave Chalmers seated between Sally McCormick and Karen Moellner, three friends from his ward when he had been in high school. Dave was leaning back, his fingers laced behind his head, an ankle crossed comfortably over a knee, his jacket open. He wore a narrow black knit tie. The two girls were leaning forward, talking to each other across him. Larry Peterson, who had been his priests' quorum advisor, was standing by the blackboard, leaning a hand on the chalk tray, the other hand on his hip, the skirt of his jacket pulled back. He was listening to a discussion between Elder Zaret and Gloriana, who had recently joined the church. Lorin couldn't hear what they were talking about through the quiet buzz of voices in the room, but Larry had a patient smile on his face as he waited for them to finish. Other people were wandering aimlessly around the room. They were all waiting for something, but he didn't know what. He wondered what was behind the white curtain on the wall. When anyone walked close to it, it moved slightly, as though the air around it were disturbed. His curiosity pricked, he got up and went over to see.

As he approached it the curtain began to stir, and presently a low, terrible wind came up from behind it. The curtain billowed and flapped. He saw an opening behind it, evidently a tunnel broken directly out of the wall and lined with rock, as though the room had been built against the side of the mountain. He stepped back and the wind died down. The curtain floated back down, gently brushing the floor. He looked around at the others, but in order not to embarrass him they were pretending they hadn't noticed. In fact they were not paying any attention to him at all. He realized that soon each of his friends was going to enter the tunnel and go away, and he would not be allowed to go with them.

His feelings hurt, he started to go back to his chair when a young man about his own age stepped in front of him. "You're Lorin, aren't you?" he said.

"Yes."

The young man looked expectantly at him for a long time, then smiled. "You don't remember me, do you?"

Lorin looked at him closely. The man was nondescript enough: narrow face, puffy eyes, light brown hair parted on the left. Not as tall as Lorin, but perhaps a little heavier. Neatly dressed in coat and tie, with a handkerchief in the breast pocket of his coat.

"I guess I don't," said Lorin. "I'm sorry."

The man looked as though he thought that was funny. "Think about it a minute," he said.

"Yes, I'm trying to."

"I'll give you a hint. Remember the peas from the neighbor's Victory garden and how you dropped one in the hedge?"

"Yes." Lorin felt his scalp creep.

The man watched him for a flicker of recognition. "Still can't remember?"

"No."

"Okay. How about this one. You bought your first suit with money from your paper route. You were thirteen and in eighth grade and you were in love with a girl named Nina. The suit itched like crazy and you had to wear your pajama bottoms under it."

Lorin looked with all the strength of his eyes and his recollection at the man, but could not place him. "I give up. Who are you?"

"No. Think about it a minute. Your mother's name is Grace and your father's name is Charles. He hates being called Charley or Chuck. Getting warm?"

Lorin shook his head. He was trying to think, but his brain was not working right. The man was obviously enjoying this. "In sixth grade you slugged a Mexican kid who was out on third base but said he wasn't."

"No. That wasn't me," said Lorin.

"Sure it was," the man said, grinning.

"I don't know who you are," said Lorin.

"I'll tell you in a minute if you haven't guessed. Once when you were trying to do algebra, the light over your desk went out. You twisted the bulb to see if it was just a loose connection, and the overhead light in the room went out. You got up to see if someone had flipped the switch behind the door, and the light on the table by your bed went out. You thought the house was haunted. Guessed yet?"

Lorin didn't remember that. "No," he said. "I wish you'd tell me."

"I will in a minute," said the man. But everyone else had gone into the tunnel behind the curtain now, and the men were removing the folding chairs and pushing the blackboard out on its casters, and then the room was empty.

# 19

*S*orenson was a prince about the whole thing. His initial chagrin, disappointment, and distaste for his unlucky companion
over, he went out of his way to be kind. Though still weak himself, he cooked breakfast the morning of the day Lorin was to
be excommunicated, while Lorin lay in bed staring at the shadows
creeping across the ceiling. "A little toast with those eggs, Elder?"
he asked, as Lorin picked at the stew of an omelet on the plate
that rested on his chest. Getting no answer, he said, "I can add
some canned peaches to the mess," and waited, expectantly,
holding the can and an opener up where Lorin could see them.
Lorin did not, however, look at them. "Can I get you anything
else at all, Elder?" Sorenson asked. Lorin thought about shaking his head, but couldn't seem to get around to it. If he rested
for a while he could do it.

"Would you like me to press your pants?" Sorenson asked
a few minutes later. Lorin didn't answer, so he did, giving the
left leg a secondary crease to the right of the original one. "I guess
that's been done better," he said, holding the pants up near the
window to examine his job. He glanced at Lorin. It was difficult
being normal around someone who was in big trouble if he died
tomorrow. "Buck up, Elder," he said. "We've been companions
a long time, I know you pretty well. You'll get back in the church
before you can even turn around. I think I know you well enough
to say that."

Except for an attack of diarrhea that sent him running to the
bathroom, Lorin spent the rest of the morning lying in bed staring at the same point in the ceiling, until he grew tired of it and
turned on his side to stare at a rope of dust between the edge
of the carpet and the molding where the floor met the wall. He
wondered what particles had gone into that elongated clump,

what were its elements, what bound them together. Hair, he decided, was basic. The nondescript grey substance could be anything, clothing fibers, collapsed spider webs, dead skin cells, but strands of hair were probably what made the various particles cohere. The various things that went into dust didn't look like dust when they were in their original settings, but they looked like nothing else when they consolidated in ropes or lumps like this one. Powdered bodies of insects, maybe.

He was still thinking about it when it was time to dress and go out to the car. Mrs. Green was running the vacuum cleaner as they passed through the living room. She shut it off long enough to smile and say, "Getting a late start today, guys. You're taking it pretty easy since you got sick." Sorenson slowed down to say something about bankers' hours, and Lorin stumbled into him, stepping on the heel of Sorenson's shoe, which came off. "Sorry," Lorin mumbled. "Don't worry," said Sorenson, hopping on one foot while he pulled the shoe back on. Mrs. Green beamed and started her vacuum up again.

During the first part of the long drive, along the Interstate past townships, drive-in theaters, shopping malls, white barns in rich loamy fields, clusters of mailboxes at junctions where dirt roads branched off from the rutted frontage road below them, and clouds piled in the sky larger than mountains, Sorenson didn't try to make conversation. They stopped for lunch in a coffee shop that was part of a red-brick tourist information center in a bosky dell beside a river just off the Interstate, heavily shadowed by giant elms. Lorin ordered beer with his fish sandwich, and Sorenson avoided looking at the frosted stein with the foamy crown. When they resumed the drive Lorin was suffering from heartburn, and Sorenson knew better than to try to make conversation while that was going on, even in normal times. Accordingly they allowed the cornfields and tract homes to pass unremarked, though ordinarily they had always had something smart to say to each other about tracts and cornfields.

The silence, which made Sorenson fidgety, was actually still water through which Lorin's thoughts ran like busy fish. Sitting there in the front seat of the car next to his worried companion, the wind slipping through the slightly opened window and sending a cold line of air down the length of his face, Lorin was thinking about elevators. He had always dreaded being caught in an elevator between floors, especially in a building late at night when there was no one to hear you if you pushed the alarm button. He reflected that you could probably escape by climbing through the roof of the car. He wasn't sure what you did then, standing on top of the car in a dark shaft surrounded by cables and pulleys, but at least it was possible to get out of the car between floors; he was pretty sure of that. That made him feel better. Then he thought about different places you could hide if you were hitchhiking in the desert and wanted to play a prank on someone who picked you up. You could point to a clear horizon and say there was a dust storm coming, and then when the person who had picked you up looked out the window trying to figure out what you were talking about, you could quietly open the door on your side of the car, drop to the ground, and roll under the car, being careful that you didn't lie in the path of one of the tires. Or there were juniper bushes you could roll behind. For that matter, the desert out near Fish Springs was pocked with holes and declivities, some of them filled with rusty beer cans. There were lots of places. If a wind blew, he wouldn't necessarily hear you open the door. Desert winds could be noisy.

Lorin rolled his window down a little more. The wind whipping over the glass made conversation impossible; he wanted to be alone with his thoughts a while longer. One of the things he intended to ask Sorenson before this was over was about the brain's electrical field, because he had always wondered about that. Cats' fur flashed when you stroked it in a dark room, and he wanted to know if it was theoretically possible to elicit a charge from someone's brain, say, if enough hands were moving around on her head and creating friction.

There was one last thing—they were starting to pass factories now, and that made him think of it. If you were an elderly crank and you wanted to worry a serious person, a way of doing it would be to palm a key to the stockroom where he worked at night in some factory, say, and walk on in as if you owned the place, and then hide behind the door when he came in to find out where you were. You could stand there behind him, quiet as a shadow, when he came in to look for you, and follow him up and down aisles full of machine parts, peer with him around corners, bend with him to inspect the space under the workbench. If you felt like it you could go home with him, hiding in the back seat of his car, stay with him all his life, sit with him while he slept, put a hand on his alarm clock so he would feel it when he woke up. There were any number of things you could do if you wanted.

It was after two o'clock when they reached the gritty metropolis, and close to three by the time they had made the necessary cloverleafs and found their way to the mission headquarters in a large new building with broad panes of glass and a northern exposure. It resembled a Howard Johnson's and occupied a tract of land purchased by the church only a few years before, located on the edge of a new development that was to include a computer-industry complex and research park. The mission president was a young man scarcely into his forties, slender and boyish, with a worried, toothy smile as he came out and shook hands with Lorin, and ushered him into the conference room. "Nice to see you again, Elder Hood," he said. He had been a one-term Democratic congressman from Utah, defeated in his bid for the Senate by an avuncular Salt Lake attorney who had condescended to him during televised debates, and against whom he had struck the voters as an ambitious pup. Swallowing his defeat, he had accepted the church's call to serve as mission president for three years in the Great Lakes mission. He was now beginning his third year, and for all Lorin knew to the contrary would shortly resume his political life and wing through to the presidency this time.

Lorin felt President Olsen's friendly hand at his back urging him, his knees like spaghetti, into the council room, where several men in dark suits sat in red leather chairs around the long conference table. His own branch president was one of them. He looked at Lorin and then let his eyes wander just past his shoulder. The carpet felt deep and soft under his feet, and for a moment Lorin wished he could have the sensation of feeling it without his shoes. "If you'll just sit up there at that end of the table, Elder Hood," the mission president said, pointing. "And Elder Sorenson, if you'll go sit with him—that's right, just pull that other chair out, ycu can put that stack of papers on the table—we can get started. Where's Elder Warnick?"

"He had a phone call," one of the men said. "He said he'd be back in a minute."

"Well, we can go ahead," said the mission president, looking at his watch. There was a moment of shuffling as the men stood and pulled their chairs out and knelt on the carpet around the table, their elbows on the chair seats. Lorin found himself forehead to forehead with the mission president's first counselor, Elder Judson, who kept his eyes closed to avoid looking at him while President Olsen gave the opening prayer. They returned to their chairs. Lorin heard a lot of throat-clearing. "I'm afraid, brethren," President Olsen said, his expression somber, his forehead wrinkled, "that it's a pretty ugly case." He was shuffling through a sheaf of papers in a manila folder, but couldn't seem to find the one he was looking for. He dipped into his attache case that lay open on the floor beside him.

Lorin meantime looked nervously at the men at the table, some of whom met his eye and smiled grimly. Most of them did not. He wished Sorenson would put an arm around his shoulder again just once, the way he had done right after they had sat down. He was too confused to be sure how many men were at the table, but there seemed to be at least a dozen. Elder Warnick came in, apologizing for the phone call, and sat down the table to Lorin's right, nodding once to him. A couple of men sat together in a row of red leather chairs, with arms, that lined the panelled wall next to the door. Another man stood at the side of the table, leaning between two of the seated men while he adjusted the tape recorder on the table.

"Maybe you could read the charges now, Elder Rowbotham," the mission president said. "I'd like to ask you to listen closely to this, Elder Hood, to make sure there isn't anything inaccurate. Go ahead, Carl."

Elder Rowbotham pulled his glasses out of his breast pocket, put them on, and looked up and down the length of the sheet of paper in front of him. "Well," he said, "the charge is adultery." The word made everyone nervous. There was a brief moment of quiet throat-clearing and shifting around in chairs. Elder Rowbotham looked up once and then resumed reading, speaking through the fingers of the hand covering his mouth. "According to the charges, Elder Hood is charged with going to the home of a Brother and Sister Kling while his companion was in the hospital—that's Richard Kling and his wife Alice Kling, both as I understand it recent members of the church—while his companion was sick in the hospital with what I understand was food poisoning and other implications, and on that day when her husband was away Elder Hood is alleged to have committed sexual intercourse with Sister Kling." Rowbotham shifted uncomfortably, removed his glasses and put them back on. Lorin sat with his elbows on the table, his upper lip pressed against his clasped fists, staring at the slowly winding reels of the tape recorder. He glanced up as Rowbotham paused and saw the mission president looking at him with hurt eyes. One of the men to his left was examining a thumbnail. Another was looking out the window. The others sat with bowed heads and open eyes, listening.

"It's further alleged," said Elder Rowbotham into his palm, "that the next day, his companion still in the hospital, Elder Hood returned to the home of Brother and Sister Kling and committed the act of sexual relations again. And it's further alleged that the following day, after his companion was back home from the hospital, that Elder Hood left his companion during the day on the pretext of doing laundry, drove his companion's car to the Kling home, and had a sexual relationship with the aforementioned Sister Kling again." Rowbotham coughed, and Lorin looked up. Elder Warnick's forehead was shiny. The mission president had slumped down in his chair, his elbows resting on its arms, and was pressing his own clenched hands against his upper lip. His gaze fell just short of Lorin.

"The following Monday," Rowbotham continued, "upon returning to his own residence with his companion after spending the morning tracting, his companion still being ill from his spell of food poisoning, Elder Hood left his companion alone and returned to Brother and Sister Kling's home, and there had a further act of adultery, and it was at this time that the young lady's husband, that is Brother Kling, came home and the act was discovered." Rowbotham removed his glasses and set them on the table. He tapped the edge of his sheaf of papers on the table to straighten them and laid them down.

The mission president stared at the tape recorder during a long silence. Finally he said, "Those are the charges, Elder Hood. You've heard them read and had a chance to consider them. Let me ask you. Are they true?"

Lorin cleared his throat. "Basically," he said.

The mission president raised himself in his chair and frowned. "I'm not sure I understand, Elder. What do you mean by basically?"

"I mean yes, I did do those things."

"Well, but you seem to hesitate. Was there some ambiguity about what happened that you think might help your case or that we ought to know about?"

"Not really."

The mission president lifted his hands. "All right, let me ask it. Did you actually penetrate the girl?"

"Yes. Except for the last time."

"Well, that seems simple enough, Elder Hood. That seems to me to constitute an act of adultery. I mean what is there to split hairs about? This is all we're asking. Are the charges as you heard them true?"

"Yes," said Lorin. "Except for the last time."

"Fine. That's all we're asking."

"I'd like to ask a question," said one of the men to Lorin's left. "Before you actually did this, I mean the first time, did you feel any hesitation or reluctance, and afterward did you feel as though maybe you wished you hadn't done it?"

"That's actually two questions, George," said the mission president. "I'd like Elder Hood to take the first one first, if that's all right. Did you have any hesitation or reluctance about doing this, Elder?"

"Yes, I think I definitely did."

"Could you describe this feeling?"

"Well, it was a little like looking over the edge of a tall building and wondering if you're really going to jump."

"What did you go up to the top of this building for?" asked one of the men on the other side of the table.

"I don't know, actually. I mean I didn't go there with the idea that I was actually going to do it."

"But you're not really describing a feeling of reluctance, Elder Hood," said the mission president. "I'd really like to know what was going on in your mind that day. I mean did you think there were going to be extenuating circumstances that would make it all right, or what?"

"No."

"Well—" The mission president made a helpless gesture. "Then what happened? We're just trying to find out what happened and why. What led up to it? What was the breaking point? I don't think there's anybody in this room who doesn't know what a sexual urge is. We just want to know what overcame this reluctance you say you had. If she met you at the door with her clothes off, all right, say so."

"I think it may have been when she put her hand on top of my hand," said Lorin.

"What?"

"She was crying, and I put my hand on her shoulder, just, you know, to comfort her. And she reached up and put her hand on top of my hand. Then she sort of moved up and put her fingers around my wrist." He heard someone swallow.

"What was she crying about?" asked one of the men sitting beside the door.

"Not about that. She was just feeling bad about being pregnant and being stuck at home from now on and having to be a housewife."

The mission president looked revolted. "So we've gotten from a hand on the wrist into bed with somebody's pregnant wife. I suspect we've left out one or two steps in between. Why don't you tell us about them?"

"Well, it's a little hard to describe. I mean we sort of looked at each other, and I'm afraid I kissed her. And the next thing was we were walking down the hall to the bedroom. I can't remember exactly the order of things."

"Whose idea was it to walk down the hall to the bedroom? Yours or hers?"

"I don't think either of us actually said anything. I mean I don't think there was a verbal suggestion or anything like that."

"All right. Who led the way down the hall?"

"Actually, as nearly as I can remember, she did. But of course it was her house."

"All right," said the mission president, rubbing his temples. "What happened next?"

He told them what happened next. The clerk got up at one point and leaned over Elder Osborne's shoulder to peer at the needle on the tape recorder. He turned the knob a quarter-turn to the right and sat down again. The sun went behind a heavy summer cumulus and Lorin felt the chill in his bones. Elder Johnson interrupted once, and Lorin had to repeat the part about her wanting to look at his garments. The afternoon crept on. He told them about taking the flowers to Sorenson and leaving the tract with the man in the next bed, about the terrier and about how he had tried to suggest to Alice that they talk about it a little before just rushing into it a second time. That he had told her flatly that he believed the Gospel was true—not to be sanctimonious, but just so they would know where they stood, that he wasn't doing this lightly.

"Excuse me, Elder Hood. What did she say to that?"

"She said she believed it too, but she was only human. Something like that. Or maybe she said we both were human."

He told them about being late for his appointment with the district leader, and that he had felt sick and shabby the whole evening at the home of the investigating family Elder Beyer had taken him to. (Elder Beyer sat shaking his head in disbelief as the tape recorder turned and groaned on the table in front of him.) He described the conversation with Alice in the foyer of the church, and his ambivalent feelings when he learned that Richard was going to be safely out of town.

"Why ambivalent, Elder?" asked a tall man with a thin mustache, who sat on the other side of Sorenson. Lorin had to lean over the table to see him.

"Well, I'm not sure I really wanted to do it, with Elder Sorenson home sick and everything. But I wasn't sure how to get out of it now. It was something I couldn't explain to her."

"You were having second thoughts."

"Yes, I definitely was."

"Would you call them the first stages of repentance?" asked one of the men assigned to take his side.

"I don't know if you can call it repentance if I went ahead and did it again anyway," said Lorin. They might like him a little better, he thought, if he took their side.

"Do you feel like you were maybe being coerced this last time?"

Lorin thought for a minute. "No, I don't think so. Not very much anyway."

"I'm sorry, Elder, I couldn't quite hear you."

"I said, I'm afraid I didn't need very much coercion."

"I suppose you'd better tell us about it."

"There isn't much to tell, actually. She was crying again."

"Excuse me," said one of Lorin's advocates. "Does it seem to anybody else that the young lady does a lot of that?"

"I was thinking the same thing," said Elder Warnick.

The clerk had gotten up and was adjusting dials again.

"She doesn't cry all that much," Lorin said, afraid he had left a wrong impression. "This was only the second time I've seen her do it, I think."

"Still, do you think you might have been pressured just a little by her crying, Elder Hood? I'm trying to get both sides of the picture."

"Maybe just a little," Lorin said.

"I think we can stipulate that Elder Hood had ample encouragement," the mission president said. "Let's move on. What happened?"

Lorin did his very best to give an account of the last meeting that would be objective, clear, and comprehensible. He did not mention the swarm of associations that went with it, because they had been subjective. At the end of it there was a long pause while the tape recorder ground slowly on. Then someone said, "She picked up a sock?"

"She was just trying to cover herself," said Lorin. "It was just a reflex. She panicked."

"I don't get it," said one of the men who hadn't spoken before. He was heated and red-faced. "There were only two men in the house, and she'd already been in bed with both of them. What was she trying to hide?"

"No, I think I can understand that, John," said Elder Warnick. "She was scared and behaved irrationally. What I'd like to know is what Elder Hood and the young lady felt toward each other."

"Felt?" asked Lorin.

"You know. Was this whole thing just physical excitement, sensuality, did you fall in love with each other, or what? I'd really like to know."

"I think we may have been in love with each other," said Lorin.

"Elder Hood had baptized Sister Kling himself," said his branch president, speaking for the first time. "That wasn't mentioned, and I don't know if everyone here knew that or not."

The mission president looked around. Several of the men nodded their heads.

"This may not be the appropriate time to say this," the branch president went on, "but I think it's worth putting on record that much as I lament what Elder Hood has done, and I lament it as much as anybody in this room, if not more—I admit I was bitterly shocked when I learned about it—I have to add that as president of the branch Elder Hood has been assigned to for the last few months, I've come to know and like him very much. He and Elder Sorenson have worked closely with me many times, not only with investigators but with members of the branch. I've been consistently impressed by their testimonies, their hard work, their dedication, not to mention their long hours. I think Elder Hood has made a terrible, painful mistake, I don't want to gloss over that. But it needs to be said that up until that mistake took place he was, from all the indications I've had, and I've had a good many in the short time I've known him, a good missionary, a serious and responsible representative of the church, and except for that mistake one of the finest young men it's been my privilege to work with."

Several men nodded, and there were grunts of approval on both sides of the table. Lorin felt his eyes mist up. "I want to second everything President Dyer said," Sorenson said. Lorin was startled to hear his companion's voice. "I don't know if everyone knew this, but Elder Hood refused his mission call the first time because he felt he wasn't ready and accepted the call later even though he was older than most missionaries. Most missionaries probably wouldn't have accepted the call at his age. He's been an absolutely tremendous companion, and I just want to say that even though I'm his senior companion, Elder Hood has always been like an older brother to me."

The room was silent. Lorin wanted to look at his companion because Sorenson's voice had been thick with emotion, but he was afraid they would both cry if they made eye contact.

It was nearly over. The mood of the room had softened since the branch president's testimonial. They asked Lorin to repeat the part about her hand on his wrist, since that had seemed to be the turning point, and the part about stroking her knees while she was crying the second day. There were a few more questions, and then everyone had run out of things to say. The tape recorder whirred on, slowly. The mission president shuffled together the documents in front of him and tapped their edges into alignment on the table top. "All right, Elder Hood, if you'd like to just take a seat out there in the auditorium, we'll call for you in a few minutes." The bright but worried smile with which he had greeted Lorin was gone, and he now looked serious and even unfriendly. Lorin stood up and nearly fell when he found his knees didn't work, but Sorenson caught him, with an arm around his shoulders. With his companion's help Lorin stumbled out from between his chair and the table, nodded to the two or three men in the room who looked at him at all, and walked to the door. He had never felt disliked by so many people in a single room before. Sorenson opened the door for him and followed him out. Together they walked across the carpeted lobby to the small auditorium where visitors were given slide shows on Jesus among the Nephites—no show was going on at present—and sat down on two of the velvet seats in the back row.

"I guess this is it, old buddy," said Lorin finally.

"Don't let it eat you up," said Sorenson. "You'll get back in. Don't worry."

"It's times like this I wish I weren't basically a serious person," said Lorin.

"I know what you mean."

"For what it's worth, Sorenson, I just want you to know that you're the only companion I've had that didn't give me a pain in the ass."

"I feel the same way," Sorenson said. After a second he said, "About you, I mean."

"I'm sorry this had to embarrass you too," Lorin said.

Sorenson sniffed once, patted Lorin on the arm, and pulled out a handkerchief. He peeled off his glasses and wiped under his eyes. Then he wiped the lower rims of his glasses and put them back on.

What seemed a long time later, Lorin saw a shadow fall across the doorway to the auditorium and Elder Warnick leaned in to tell him he could come back to the council room. Lorin followed Warnick back across the lobby, avoiding the eye of the receptionist behind the desk, Sorenson following him. Back in the council room Lorin's branch president, his watery blue eyes paler and redder-rimmed than before, pulled the chair out for him, and Lorin sat down again, Sorenson sitting next to him. The next part was brisk and ugly. In a few words the mission president explained to Lorin that he and his two counselors had spent several difficult minutes on their knees in his office. He (Lorin) was to understand that a matter like this was one of the heaviest burdens a mission president could have, and that though he (President Olsen) had had to face it twice before, it had not gotten any easier. Personally he liked Elder Hood and was sure all the brethren present liked him and thought well of him; he had every reason to believe Elder Hood's testimony was strong; but that fact, laudable as it was, made Elder Hood's offense all the greater and indeed all the more inexplicable. And so on. Before many more minutes had passed, Lorin had ceased to be a Mormon. The business over, everyone got up from the table; a few of the men shook hands with Lorin, whose palms were sweaty, and filed out of the room.

Sorenson waited in the conference room while Lorin followed the mission president into his office where he was given his instructions for returning home, meeting with his bishop who had of course been notified, as well as the president of his home stake, then facing the members of his home ward with a confession of what he had done, and the gradual process of reinstatement. It would take time, it would not be easy, no one could do it for him and no one ever said it wouldn't be humiliating; punishment was always humiliating. But President Olsen suspected Elder Hood—he'd still call him that—had the guts to do it, and the patience, and the desire, or he—President Olsen—was no judge of a man. Lorin thanked him and returned, hollow-eyed, to Sorenson in the conference room.

———

Alice was excommunicated too, of course, in a separate ceremony, her husband sitting ghastly pale at her side, dark half-moons under both eyes. He had resolved to stand by her and help her fight her way back into the church. She thought the whole ceremony was pretty heavy and she didn't at all like having her body talked about at a conference table in front of a tape recorder. She cried through most of it. Lorin did not see her again.

Three days after his own excommunication he was driven to the airport by the district president and two strong elders, neither of them Sorenson, who had been reassigned a new junior companion and was back on the streets tracting again, still a little shaky. Left to himself, Lorin was quite sure he would have fled to Canada or joined the army or sneaked onto a Greyhound bus going any direction but home. But the district president and Elders Boynton and Fitzpatrick stayed close to him, carrying his suitcases and garment bags for him, all the way from the multi-tiered parking lot, to the ticket desk, up the escalators and down the long concourse to the gate, stood with him while he was issued his boarding pass, waited with him in the queue behind the sliding glass door until it opened. They shook hands with him and he was swept away down the long accordion-pleated funnel into the plane, where the girl in the bright green dress with yellow piping took his boarding pass and scowled at him. Later he watched the vineyard of his labors collapse below him into squares, patches, wrinkles, and finally wisps of thready wet gauze.

———

His mother and father met him at the airport in Salt Lake. Both had haggard faces. His mother threw her arms around him and wept into his ear. His father's hand shook when he reached to take Lorin's attache case to help him carry it. His mother had to sit down while he and his father waited at the baggage-claim carousel. None of them had said a word yet. Out of the corner of his eye Lorin saw an old friend from high school who looked blankly at him and went on past, without a flicker of recognition. His mother's shoulders were heaving, and suddenly he realized his father had been talking to him. It was something about Lorin's younger brother, who was working that night, so couldn't come with them. His sisters were both out on dates; no point in making this a bigger deal for them than it had to be. They'd talk about it in the next few days. His mother was taking it pretty hard. No point in hashing through it tonight. Walking to the loading curb in company with an insolent skycap who wheeled a dolly, Lorin noticed his father now had a pronounced stoop, his mother a brave erectness. He pulled out a pistol and shot himself behind the ear. He helped the skycap load his bags into the back of his father's station wagon. He opened a clasp knife and slit through veins and cartilage in his wrist and died on the curb before his mother's weeping face and his father's heavy shaking of the head and the skycap's sullen stare; and devils crept out of the storm sewer and drew a bag over his head and body and pulled it shut, tying the string in difficult knots.

# 20

He did not go to the bishop for a post-mortem. He did not go to church the following Sunday and confess publicly. He did not even stay long under his father's roof in the pink clapboard house near Thirty-third South and Highland. Two days after his return he rose, did not shave, dressed in his levis and fatigue shirt that had been left hanging at the back of his—now Stephen's—closet, found and assembled his easel, his cases of paints and brushes (the tubes split and hardened in the interval), twenty or thirty canvases which he removed from their stretchers and rolled up, loaded everything into the back of his green Pontiac, which to his brother's chagrin he repossessed on the spot, and that same afternoon, the car belching smoke from its tailpipe, after telling his parents he would have to work it out on his own hook and having their stricken faces pressed into his memory to haunt him forever, set off for California.

His state of mind was still unclear, he decided during the long familiar drive across the trackless wastes of southern Utah, Nevada, California's Mojave, most of it under the panoply of hard winking stars in the cold desert night (he drove without stopping, except for gas and rest rooms, and a hamburger in St. George and another, at dawn, in Fontana), but he thought he detected small seeds of resentment starting to twitch, turn over, and sprout inside him. It was hard to remember, in the rubble his life had just become, that he was still only days away from the first warm embrace with Alice. But other things firmly connected his present with his past, and it was these things that needed careful thinking through.

The unidentifiable creeping malaise, for instance, that he had become aware of those long months ago, had remained with him, but had crept further rather than retreated since his excommuni-

cation. His very bones felt thin and mealy. Touching his fingertips to the pulse in his wrist or his temples made him ill in the
same way that running his hand over the stump of a leg would
make him ill. Worms had continued to crawl along the nerve endings the length of his legs each night, and more and more often
the voices had murmured their inscrutable messages inside his
head as he faded into sleep at night. Very few nights had passed,
before or since his excommunication, in which his dreams had
not contained this sequence, or a variant:

He is walking through the grounds of a deserted carnival at
night. There are three men with him, and though he can't see
their faces, they seem to be directing where he should go. At the
end of a long boardwalk they enter a tent, on whose walls hang
a phrenologist's diagram of a human head in profile and enlarge-
ments of pictures he recognizes as taken from the Tarot deck.
Bleachers are set up against the walls, but at a greater distance
than the interior of the tent seems able to contain. People in dark
suits with hats pulled over their faces are sitting at random intervals on the benches. On an upturned apple box in the middle
of the floor stands a man, pale and naked, with an enormous erection. Lorin has never in his life seen another man's erection, so
he is not sure of the visual source of this part of the dream. The
man is lean and muscular, with short-cropped hair, standing at
parade rest, his feet slightly spread, his hands clasped loosely
behind him, his chin up, his expression serene, his eyes fixed
on some point above the doorway to the tent, his penis red and
heroic, his balls tightly packed. One of Lorin's guides points to
a small doorway behind one of the bleachers, and presently an
old woman in a leather jacket comes in through it, carrying an
axe. She nods to the people in the bleachers, who don't notice
her, and then walks up to the man on the apple box, pretends
to be surprised at his massive arousal. She says, ''I knew it,''
and raises the axe. Lorin does not care to watch this part, so he
wanders over to look at the phrenology exhibit; but as he does,
an enormous white asparagus stalk flips past him, end over end,
and is swallowed by a duck he has not noticed before, sitting in
a cage on the table. He looks back and sees the man, white as
polished bone, on a black pedestal, holding a baby with one hand
and a bunch of grapes high in the air with the other. His eyes
are blank and his white hair is curly. His balls hang easily below
the tragic chip left by the axe. The people leaving the bleachers
are now unmasked and appear to be young girls; one by one they
go past and stroke the statue's scrotum until the marble is black
and shiny.

Versions of this dream had contained hands from which all the fingers had been removed and whose palms itched uncontrollably, a full bladder that he could not empty because someone was always standing by the urinal watching him. He resented these dreams, he decided by the time he had left the San Bernardino Freeway and negotiated the tricky interchange that put him on the Hollywood Freeway, just as he resented the persistence of the gnawing sense in his viscera that something was wrong with him, because they seemed to penalize him for being a serious person. He had returned to Los Angeles, he decided as he drove past a salmon-pink building on Sunset Boulevard that had once been Ciro's and was now called Le Crazy Horse, to regain perspective. You defined yourself by entering your past. You healed yourself by returning to the places where you had been happy.

---

For the first few days he drove up and down the winding coastal highway, as far north as Ventura and as far south as El Segundo, east and west along Sunset and along winding canyons. Not until he had steeled himself by driving past the bungalow across from the cemetery (now needing paint worse than ever, a dirty white pickup parked in the driveway), and past the Blue Couch (now a thrift shop with a used-clothing rack and a bird cage in front), did he feel ready to confront the past directly. He had slept in his car in state beach parking lots and eaten unwholesomely at drive-ins, and had not taken a bath since leaving Salt Lake. His face, unshaven for a week, looked like an armpit when he saw it in the rear-view mirror. He was down to ten dollars, and his Chevron credit card had expired while he was on his mission. There was nothing for it but to fight for survival.

He drove to the university one afternoon, paid to park in one of the visitors' lots, and avoiding the art building walked to the old union building to look up an address in the student directory. He felt a small stab when he couldn't find her there, but then he remembered Floyd's last name and felt another small stab when this time he found her. She no longer had the same address, and was now listed as a graduate student in biology. There was no answer when he dialed her number from a pay phone. To while away the time, he leafed through the directory looking for names of his enemies. Noel was not listed, neither was Pavel. Harry was there; Harry would never change. Simon was there, but listed as a speech pathology major. Shannon was not there. He leafed toward the W's to look up Yvonne but faltered before he got there. He dialed again, got no answer. The street name was unfamiliar. He found a street map at the information desk and looked it up over a cup of coffee in the union, surrounded by noisy students he had never seen before. The street was in Santa Monica, close to Rand. He called an hour later, and this time she was there.

"Gloriana?" he said. His voice was unexpectedly high.

"Yes."

"Hi. This is Lorin." There was no sound from the other end. "Hood," he added.

"Good Lord, so it is."

"Hi. Listen, I'm just back in town, and I wondered if maybe I could drop by and say hello or something, if you weren't doing anything."

Dead silence followed. He tried to think what her reaction was during the silence. "Gloriana?" he said finally.

"Yes," she said. "I'm still here. I'm being a little nonplussed." He thought he detected a suppressed laugh in her voice.

"Listen, I need to apologize for disappearing so suddenly last year. It's a long story."

"I'll bet it is," she agreed.

"But I don't want to talk about it over the phone. Especially if you're busy. But I'd like to drop by and say hello some afternoon soon, like maybe tonight. It's a pretty interesting story."

"I have to fix dinner pretty soon," she said.

"I didn't realize it was that late," he said. "Listen, I can grab a bite somewhere and come on over whenever it's convenient. I'm calling from campus."

"I guess it'll be all right," she said. "You won't be able to stay long."

"No problem," he said. "I can just grab a bite somewhere."

"Come over about eight, I guess," she said. "I'll arrange to be at a good stopping point then."

"That will be great," he said. "Listen, you don't happen to know where a good place is to grab a bite, do you? I've been gone so long I've forgotten what's good."

She thought for a second and suggested one or two places, among them the Village Delicatessen. He thanked her. She told him her address, which he already knew, and described the best way to get there. She was punishing him, he decided.

"Listen, this is none of my business," he said, "but I was just wondering, I couldn't find you under your own name so I looked under Hopkins and found you there. I guess you're married now."

"Oh yes."

"I wasn't trying to pry or anything. I was just wondering if I was going to be disturbing anything."

"My goodness no," she said.

She could have left the my goodness unsaid, he thought.

He had a pastrami sandwich at the Village Delicatessen and watched very carefully as the sweaty cashier made out his change, then drove the streets for a couple of hours, finally making his way to her address, which turned out to be a white frame house with a pepper tree in the front yard. It was still daylight, though barely so. A short flight of concrete steps with a black iron rail led up to the front door. He rang the bell, feeling the absence of his attache case a strange sensation. He hadn't rung anyone's bell since the last day he had gone tracting. He heard muffled footsteps and the door opened. She no longer wore bangs; her hair was longer now, and parted in the middle. She had lost weight. He hadn't noticed her cheekbones before; now he did. She wore no lipstick or eyeliner; she had always worn both before.

"Good God," she said, staring at him.

# 21

*H*e had to admit he was not pleased with the way Gloriana had turned out. Lying there on the floor of the basement in his sleeping bag, his hands laced under his head, he watched the moonlight creep across the spines of the books that lined one wall and counted the things about her he hadn't liked. For one thing, she had acted as though his visit were an inconvenience. He could tell her something about inconvenient visits. She hadn't even introduced him to Floyd, who had remained somewhere else in the house while they were talking. From time to time Lorin had heard doors opening and closing and footsteps creaking floors at various distances from where he had sat on the couch. Once he had heard water running in the kitchen, but there was apparently an access to the kitchen that didn't take you through the living room where you would have to be polite. For another thing she appeared to be cultivating a trendy look, which didn't suit her. Her face had looked better when it was round and topped by bangs. It looked washed-out and angular now without makeup, and parting her hair in the middle so that it framed her face like an inverted V seemed an affectation. So did wearing her hair long and straight. For another thing, she was not very interested in hearing about his mission, and was only politely amused at the part about Alice. For another thing she seemed to take herself more seriously than she needed to. When she told him what she was doing in graduate school, what her plans were, when she was going to finish and what she was going to do afterward she didn't look at him directly. She talked with her chin tilted up and looked past him as though contemplating the next day's problem and how she was going to approach and solve it. Finally he hadn't liked the way she had avoided the question of where he was going to sleep tonight. He'd had to bring it up himself. He was also a little put off by the expression on her face when she had gotten up to go see if Floyd minded if he crashed in the basement for one night. He had his own sleeping bag, he'd explained. That was good, she had said. There wasn't a spare bed. He hadn't exactly expected her to make a joke about his sleeping between them, but he could remember a time when she would have. He had listened intently to try to pick up words or phrases in the distant buzz of conversation, but he couldn't. He wasn't even sure what room it was coming from. She had come out eventually and informed him it was all right, and he had thanked her and asked her to extend his thanks to Floyd too, but he suspected the irony was lost on her.

All this had been settled by nine o'clock, and it was apparent that if he had not been staying here this would have been the appropriate time to leave. She needed to put in a couple more hours of studying, she had said. Lorin had not given her the chance to drop the hint twice. He was feeling pretty hammered himself, he had said. He guessed he would just grab his sleeping bag out of the car and go on downstairs and stay out of everyone's way. Go to sleep early. Big day tomorrow.

Lying there on the cold concrete floor in the dark next to the pingpong table on which he had laid out his toothbrush and comb for tomorrow, he listened to the creak of footsteps overhead for a couple of hours, and doors opening and closing, and occasional muffled voices, and thought about what he was in fact going to do tomorrow. He started to masturbate once but stopped when it occurred to him there was a chance her behavior had been staged in case Floyd was listening through a wall and that she might come down to the basement after Floyd had gone to bed— he remembered they kept different hours—and tell him all was forgiven. While he waited he returned to his plans. He was aware that the full impact of being excommunicated hadn't hit him yet. It was similar, he suspected, to the delayed realization that you had lost a leg or worse. The first thing, of course, was to find a job. He would find a job tomorrow and a place to live temporarily, so as not to spend one more night than he had to crowding Floyd's pingpong table. He would even invite Gloriana over once or twice, if she thought she could spare the time, before he told her it was obviously all over. Most of all he needed a place with plenty of light where he could set up his easel. He had a lot of lost ground to make up, and he was anxious to see what had happened to his intuitive processes while he had been giving his technique a rest. He would be more careful in selecting his friends this time too. He had no idea where Noel was, or Yvonne, and he had no intention of finding out. He was almost sorry that he knew Simon and Harry were still around and that he might run into them, though he had no intention of getting close to the UCLA campus. He would hold off making friends until he had a better idea of what he was going to do with a redefined life. You did not resume continuity by pretending that nothing had broken. You resumed it by acknowledging disaster and then picking up what pieces remained and going on without the pieces that were lost. If you did it with dignity no one would snicker as they saw you walk away. You survived humiliation by becoming stronger than your enemies.

He was a little irritated that Gloriana hadn't come downstairs even to say goodnight. He had not heard footsteps for some time, and squinting at the faint green glow of his watch he made out that it was nearly midnight. He would not, he decided, give her the satisfaction of masturbating while she was sleeping comfortably overhead with someone in a warm room. He would lie there and plan his moves until he fell asleep. The two flattened squares of moonlight had moved from the bookcase to the place where the wall and ceiling met, and he fixed his eyes on them and conjured a sun-filled beachfront apartment with a sunken living room containing soft leather chairs and a grand piano, and his easel bearing a monumental canvas on which luminous flowers pulsed against a spectral background, and a naked girl who looked like Alice sat huddled in a corner of the dark leather couch waiting for him to be through. It was a line of thought that made him happy, and he continued it until small white things crept down the wall on tiny feet that looked like nipples, and then he went to sleep.

———

He came upstairs the next morning after he had heard Floyd leave and found her eating a grapefruit. A newspaper was propped in front of her against a milk carton.

"Good morning," he said. He felt unbathed.

She looked up. "Hi. What can I fix you?"

"Listen, don't go to any trouble or anything. I know this is inconvenient. Just if you have any coffee or anything."

"Just let me finish my grapefruit."

He sat down across from her because he felt stupid standing there. Sitting down at the table didn't feel quite right either. It was as though he expected to be waited on. He said, "Oh," as though he'd forgotten something, and excused himself and went back downstairs. He straightened the net on the pingpong table and examined the two ten-speed bikes that stood propped in a corner. The green one was slightly smaller than the gold one. He twiddled the knobs on an old cathedral-shaped radio that rested on a dusty table that was littered with wires and screwdrivers and a curved needle-nosed pliers. He scanned the books in the case by the stairs and even took one out and opened it. It had something to do with calculus but he couldn't tell if that meant it was hers or Floyd's. He put it back, glanced at his watch, and went upstairs. She was at the sink rinsing off her hands. A crumpled grapefruit rind lay on the counter next to the sink.

"I'll make you a waffle," she said. "Do you want coffee?"

"If you have some already made. Don't go to any trouble." Actually he was feeling the onset of his caffeine-free headache—something he was liable to since returning from his mission—and hoped very much that she would make some.

"Boiling water isn't any trouble. You don't mind instant, I hope." She held up a jar of Folger's, and his ears suddenly roared.

"No, no. Two percent is fine," he said.

"What?"

"Instant, I mean. I'm still not awake."

"How did you sleep last night? Was it too cold?" She spooned coffee crystals into a fragile-looking cup with a scrolled handle.

"No, it was fine. I have a warm bag." He kept watching her to see if she would look at him, either to smile or to warn him with unblinking eyes that he was not funny.

"You get your choice," she said, pulling a package out of the freezer. "Blueberry or honey nut." She held one in either hand and looked past him out the window.

"Blueberry, I think. Unless that's your last one."

She ripped the package open and dropped a pair of frozen waffles into the toaster, then went to the cupboard to get him down a plate. She was wearing a short denim skirt and white tennis shoes that squeaked on the linoleum when she turned. She had to stand on her tiptoes to reach the plate down, and he watched the backs of her knees as long as it was polite. He pretended to read the paper while she came and went behind him, getting out the butter and a bottle of syrup, pouring the water into his cup, rattling in the silverware drawer for a knife and fork for him.

"I'll poach you a couple of eggs too," she said, putting the plate of toasted waffles and the coffee in front of him.

"Thank you," he said. He thought he had protested enough. He hated poached eggs but he couldn't tell her that.

"It's none of my business," she said from the stove, "but what are you going to do?"

"Actually, I haven't decided yet. I need to get back into painting as soon as I can. I let that slide while I was on my mission."

"I mean before that," she said. "I mean like today, as soon
as you eat these eggs and disappear."

He had wanted to take a shower first, but he wasn't sure it
was the right time to ask.

"I was going to start looking for a job today," he said. The
waffle seemed to have stuck in his throat.

"The reason I ask is Floyd wasn't exactly thrilled to have you
here last night."

"I can certainly understand that," he said. "And of course
I don't want to make things awkward."

"Floyd happens to be a very introverted person," she said.
"It makes him uncomfortable to have someone in the house. It
violates his privacy."

Lorin nodded and put another forkful of waffle in his mouth
and drank his coffee and hoped she would pour him another cup.
"I'll be out of his way as soon as I can brush my teeth," he said.
"I'm feeling pretty gamey but it shouldn't take too long to do
that." He looked up to see if that had made her angry and was
startled to see her studying his face.

"You kind of gave me a shock last night when I opened the
door and saw you," she said.

"If you'd been living out of a car for a week you'd look pretty
bad yourself."

"Have you been sick or something? I mean your eyes look
bad."

He had been afraid somebody would notice. "I'm all right.
Just a little out of touch."

"What kind of job are you going to look for?"

"I'm not in a position to be very picky. Anything I can get,
I guess."

"I hope you find one," she said. She lifted the lid of the
poacher to see if his eggs were done.

"I can always sell my blood," he said.

"Not if you still have ulcers," she said. It pleased him that
she remembered.

"Listen, I hate to impose on you any more, but I wonder if
I could use your shower."

She scooped the eggs onto his plate, into a puddle of syrup.
"I'll get you a towel," she said.

Before noon he had gone to three restaurants, two bookstores,
a pipe shop, and a clothing store, and had been told no six times

and maybe once (one of the restaurants). That wasn't a bad ratio when you were out tracting. He stopped for lunch at a Denny's on Sepulveda and afterward found his way to the office and left another application. To reward himself he drove to the beach to digest his club sandwich and potato salad with the sound of breakers in his ears. He sat for an hour on an iron bench in a grassy enclosure on a bluff with the ocean at his back, next to the statue of St. Monica, while a bum in a soiled undershirt slept in the shade of a palm tree a few yards away. He watched the uniformed doorman pace back and forth chain-smoking under the canopy of the hotel across the street and tried to remember if you tipped doormen as you were going in or coming out.

He had seen the last of Gloriana. She had not made the smallest gesture toward suggesting he stay another night at their house in the event employers didn't fall out of the trees to give him a job that day. She hadn't asked him where he was going to stay that night either. He had stayed in the shower longer than he had intended, but she hadn't come into the bathroom to talk to him through the curtain while the room filled with steam, nor afterward while he was chastely wrapped in a towel standing in front of a cloudy mirror shaving—he would grow his beard back after he had a job, he decided—nor had she come downstairs to watch while he put on one of his missionary suits and thus transformed himself into something she had never seen, nor while he rolled up his sleeping bag and packed his toothbrush and deodorant back into his overnight case, and she hadn't gone with him when he carried everything out to his car. He had gone back to the house one last time to thank her and say goodbye and had found her already curled up in a corner of the couch with books and papers spread out next to her and across the coffee table. She had looked up and said good luck, and then he had driven away. It was a strange way to have seen the last of someone you used to be naked with.

He shifted on his bench and watched a game of volleyball down on the beach for a while, then watched the breakers roll in. It was a cool day—a light wind rattled the palm fronds over his head—and there weren't many people down there. The few he could see seemed to be mothers with small children, or elderly men, or long-haired people huddled in clusters playing bongo drums. He wondered what Alice was doing now, and glanced at his watch to see what time it would be in Ypsilanti. He was sorry he had made things difficult for her, and thought he might write her a letter sometime. He found himself hoping she hadn't lost her testimony because of him. He wondered if she and

Richard had made love yet or if he had ruined that too. The glance at his watch had told him he was putting off the afternoon's confrontations. He saw the doorman disappear around a corner with someone's dog on a leash, and decided he would try the hotels next.

By three in the afternoon he had gone to five of the big ones along Wilshire between Santa Monica and Beverly Hills, and suspected he had made a fool of himself. He was fairly selective in the kind of job he applied for—he would not be a doorman because people sneered at you from across the street, but he wouldn't mind being, say, a desk clerk. In his navy-blue suit he even looked a little like a desk clerk, he thought. One of the hotels had a gift shop, a brokerage office, a clothing store, and an airline ticket office in the lobby, so he steeled himself and went to each of them too, though he hadn't been sure what to say he was applying for in the brokerage office. It was a torture going to each of these places, but you didn't spend eighteen months selling a religion to strangers without learning something about getting past things that traumatized you. The applications he had been filling out all day had been exercises in ingenuity as well. His experience at the Blue Couch, of course, could be described different ways. Sometimes he had been a small businessman and sometimes a fry cook and sometimes a bookkeeper. Other times he had waited tables or run a small art gallery. His mission was a little trickier. In most cases he described it hazily as volunteer work, hoping it would be confused with the Peace Corps or something. Where he thought it would do no harm, he let a sectarian note creep in and leave the impression that he had done his time at the barricades as a young minister for an unidentified church, working with underprivileged people somewhere in the midwest.

At ten to five he found a phone on a corner next to a liquor store and called Gloriana to tell her he had given her address and telephone number as his own, since he didn't have either one of his own yet, and to ask if he'd gotten any calls from his morning applications.

"I've been gone most of the day," she said. She didn't sound happy.

"I should have asked you if it was all right," he said. "I didn't even think about it till I had to fill out my first application. I didn't use you as a reference."

She didn't answer, and just then a truck roared past the corner where he was standing.

"Sorry, I didn't hear you," he shouted into the phone. "This is a very noisy intersection."

"No, I didn't say anything."

There was another long silence, except for the traffic noises. She was making it hard for him to behave normally. "I hit quite a few places today," he said finally, putting a finger in his unoccupied ear. "A couple of them said they'd get in touch. I'll hit a few more tomorrow. I'm pretty sure to get something in a day or two. Then if anybody calls after that, you can say you never heard of me, ha ha."

She said something he didn't catch.

"Sorry, I missed that," he said.

"I said it was all right."

"Thanks," he said. "Listen, I really appreciate this, Gloriana. I'm going to grab a bite somewhere now, and then find a place to sleep in the car where I won't get mugged, and then maybe I can give you a call around noon tomorrow to see if anyone's phoned. Will you be home then?"

"I don't know. No, actually, I wasn't going to be."

"Well, I can try you later. When would be a good time?"

"Lorin, it doesn't matter. I'm going to be gone all day so I won't be here if you do get any calls."

"I hadn't thought of that," he said. Actually it had been the first thing he had thought of. "What time will you be leaving in the morning? I can give you a call then just in case anybody has called first thing in the morning. Sometimes they do that."

"I don't know. All right, call me at nine. No, nine-thirty. After that I won't be here. Why can't you wait and call me the next day?"

"Will you be home the next day?"

"I don't know. Yes."

"That's what I'll do then. But let me give you a ring tomorrow anyway just in case." She didn't answer. "I'll just go grab a bite somewhere now," he said. "Then look for a place to park." He listened while a bearded man with tattoos on his biceps got out of a cab and went into the liquor store. "Then I'll talk to you in the morning." He didn't hang up.

"Lorin, Floyd doesn't want you here," she said after a while.

"That didn't bother you before."

"I don't want to talk about it."

———

He slept that night on the back porch of a beach house whose front step was littered with a week's folded newspapers, and had troubled dreams in which burglars came to the door and saw the newspapers and went around and around the house looking for him, once nearly stepping on his head. In the morning he trudged half a mile down the beach to the nearest restroom, which had spray-painted names on the walls and smelled of urine and dead fish. He stood under a cold rope of water from the only shower that worked, in a concrete enclosure that made him worry about athlete's foot, and afterwards shaved at a filthy sink that had no mirror and no hot water. He put on his same navy-blue suit and walked barefoot through the sand back to his car, holding his shoes and socks so they didn't fill up and ignoring the stares of some hairy young people standing around an orange tent on the beach as he walked past them. He had eaten a double-burger last night, and he was down to three dollars and some change, and he was nearly out of gas. He ate breakfast in a coffee shop on the pier and watched cars and pedestrians and motorcycles pass back and forth dimly in the glass that covered the pastry shelves behind the counter. He drank a third cup of coffee while watching the time, and at nine-fifteen he went to the pay phone next to the newspaper racks. No, no one had called, she said. She was on her way out of the house right now. Probably wouldn't be back till evening. Call her tomorrow. She sounded distracted.

"Um," he said.

"What?"

"Listen, I hate to ask this, but I phoned my parents this morning and they're sending me a check in the mail. I've kind of gone through all the cash I brought with me. I'm reimbursing them of course, as soon as one of those jobs comes through." There was a cold silence on the other end. He wished she wouldn't do that. "I gave them your address to send the check to me. Was that all right?"

"Yes." She definitely sounded sullen.

"The other thing I wanted to ask you," he went on, not able to breathe very well, "and I know this is an imposition, feel free to say no, but what it is, I don't think I'd make a very good impression on employers looking like I'd slept in the car, in fact I look pretty seedy right now, in fact I look like how you saw me the other night, and I wondered if it would be okay and everything, I mean my credit cards have all expired and restaurants don't like out-of-state checks, if I sort of camped out at your place for another night or two, maybe picked up a couple of meals while I'm at it, I'll take you both out to dinner as soon as that check comes from my parents, but actually Floyd wouldn't necessarily have to know I was even there, I thought about what you said, I could come over after he was in bed and kind of hang out in the basement. How does that sound?"

His voice was tight by the time he'd finished, and through the roaring in his ears he finally heard her say "Shit." He was pretty sure he had never heard her say that before.

"If you can't see your way to do it, don't feel pressured or anything, Gloriana," he said. "I mean I'll understand. A no is as good as a yes. I *expect* you to say no."

"Lorin, I've got to go. I'll think about it."

"Listen, that's great. I'll skip lunch today and just keep pounding pavements so as not to lose any time and give you a call this evening. I don't suppose you necessarily want company for dinner or anything."

"Lorin, I said I'd think about it. That's all I can tell you right now. I'm late. Call me tonight."

"There's one other thing I wanted to ask you," he said, trying to get it in before she hung up. "Does Floyd know about us? Because if he does I certainly understand why you'd want to say no."

She hung up without answering, and he knew he would go through the day wondering if she had heard him or not. He didn't actually want to call his parents. He had caused them enough grief already, and they had their hands full with his brother, and he didn't want to put in an appearance, even by telephone, until he had something good to report. He had a few shreds of decency left. He would call them if she said no.

———

By mid-afternoon he was feeling light-headed and irritable from lack of food, as well as rumpled and sweaty, and he had been perfunctory and even flip on the last couple of applications he had filled out—one at a drugstore in Westwood Village, the other at the bank across the street. He had never worked in a bank, and it was the only job he had applied for today for which he could not somehow fudge his past and claim prior experience. He had not thought about trying banks, but he had drifted back toward the university that afternoon, his tank nearly dry, and had begun hitting shops in the Village, and the bank was in the way so he hit the bank too. When he had to account for the last year and a half he wrote "Mission for LDS Church." Under "Reason for Leaving," he wrote "Excommunicated." It gave him a rush of pleasure to do something reckless.

He left his car parked in the multi-level structure at Bullock's, counting on his out-of-state license plates to make it impossible for the police department to find him when he ignored the ticket he was going to get, and walked up to campus to try the university's personnel office. He thought of ways he could be reckless there. He could apply for the job of chancellor. He could apply for a job as a male model in the art department and surprise anyone he used to know who was still around. Actually he was hoping to run into somebody he used to know who would offer to buy him a hamburger. He passed several students on the quad outside the administration building who were on the verge of looking familiar, but then they would move and become strangers with strange faces. He filled out various forms in the personnel office, including a loyalty oath, and left them with the secretary, and then went to the counselling office on the third floor to see if Marty McBride still worked there as receptionist and might feel like buying him a hamburger after work. An unpleasant woman in her forties with lavender highlights in her hair sat behind the desk where Lorin had used to sign in. She had never heard of Marty McBride. He wondered if his old counselor, Dr. Palmer, were in by any chance. He would have to make an appointment, she said. Lorin tried to look thoughtful, as though combing through his own schedule for a free hour. He thought he had better come back another time, he said at last. She nodded and flipped the appointment book closed. Actually, he had not been able to think how to ask Dr. Palmer to buy him a hamburger, and he was not sure Dr. Palmer would remember him anyway.

Back out on the grassy quadrangle in front of Schoenberg Hall he thought about going over to the art building for the sake of touching old bases, smelling the familiar smells of linseed oil and turpentine, that sort of thing, and seeing if someone like Harry, say, were still around and would buy him a hamburger. But then he decided he would look conspicuous dressed the way he was, and he dreaded the thought of brushing against a wall or door-jamb that had wet oil paint on it and damaging his suit. He went to the union building instead and read a copy of the Daily Bruin until four-thirty. He had developed a headache and was in the mood to be ugly if anyone spoke to him. Students came and went, and the smell of food coming out of the cafeteria made him ill. Finally he decided to take the chance that she might be home. He went to one of the phones in the lobby and sorted through his remaining change for a dime and dialed carefully so that he did not, in his shakiness, get the wrong number and lose the dime. He also hoped he did not get Floyd. There was no answer, but he had no place to go, so he sat in a deep leather chair across the lobby and stared at the row of phone booths for fifteen minutes, and then tried again. There was still no answer, and he returned, tight-jawed, to his leather chair to wait her out.

By six o'clock he had tried four times, and had formulated the sentence he was going to hit her with when she finally did answer. It was still light outside; he would give her until sundown. He left his chair in the lobby long enough to go to the cafeteria, where he rummaged a handful of sugar packets from one of the plastic bins by the cash register, and returned to his chair, feeling the salivary glands under his ears open and sing from the layer of sugar that was dissolving down his tongue. By seven he had called her five more times and had gone back for more sugar. He would not be rude after all, he decided. When she answered he would sound concerned, as though he had been afraid something had happened. He was getting a stomach ache, and he was certain that the same people were passing through the lobby over and over again to look at him. He propped his elbows on the arms of the leather chair and put his fingertips together, resting his thumbs on the bridge of his nose, and closed his eyes. Angels crept out of the phone booths and stood around the lobby, pretending they weren't watching him, and talked about him in low voices. By eight o'clock he suspected he was going to be sick. If she answered now he was going to tell her to forget he'd ever called, he'd manage without her help, thanks anyway. He tried to dilute his stomach ache by drinking water from the fountain next to the restrooms, and tried the number three more times, at five-minute intervals, and the third time, just shy of eight-thirty, there was a click after the second ring, and a swollen pause between the click and the voice, during which he died a thousand deaths. A man's voice said, "Hello."

"Is Gloriana there?" His own voice was strange in his ears.

"No. You want to leave a message?"

"I guess not. It's not important or anything. Maybe I can call her tomorrow if that's apt to be convenient for her all the same thanks."

"Whatever," said the voice. There was a click, and Lorin was left holding a dead black bone to his ear, sticky with palm prints.

He ran out of gas while he was still several blocks from her house and had to push the car to a curb. He wrote the name of the street and the number of the house he was in front of on the back of the ticket he had gotten in the Bullock's lot and walked the rest of the way in the dark, carrying his sleeping bag and his overnight case. He was worried about leaving all his possessions on display under a streetlight, but the important ones at least were locked in the trunk—his suitcases and portfolio and box of letters. The garment bag with his two other suits and a tweed sport jacket hung from a hook in the back seat—there was no room for it in the trunk and he would have had to wad it—and the back seat and floor were packed tight with his rolled-up canvases and his paint case and collapsed easel. It was too dark to get a good look at the neighborhood, but he didn't like the uncut grass he saw on several lawns, or the broken glass on the sidewalk.

It was nearly ten o'clock when he found the house. Peering through the garage window he saw there was only one car, something low-slung with lights from the neighbors' back porch glittering off it, so she hadn't come home yet. He left his sleeping bag and overnight case on the retaining wall between the garage and the house so she would see them as she pulled in, in case he missed her. He walked slowly along the sidewalk toward the end of the block until he decided he had gone far enough—he didn't want to get out of range in case she came home and got into the house before he could run back—and then walked the other way, passing the house with its lit front window-curtain, and continued several doors to the south, until a curve in the street put him out of range again, and turned around. The pains in his stomach felt like blunt knives and if a mugger jumped out of a hedge at him now he would collapse and surrender everything. He worried that neighbors were watching him from their bedroom windows. Each time a car went by he felt a surge of hope that it was Gloriana and a horrible certainty that it was going to pull over to the curb and policemen were going to climb out with their pistols drawn and tell him to stop where he was, please, and take three steps forward with his arms out.

By the time a pair of headlights turned from the street and bounced up the driveway he was sitting on the bottom step of the porch, leaning against the iron rail. The light in the living room had been out for some time, and he had concluded that Floyd must have gone to bed, but if he had come out and challenged him Lorin would not have moved from his spot. He would have remained there, his arms locked around his shins, his head resting on his knees while they picked him up and tipped him into the back of a police car and beat him with hoses at the station house. She got out and ran over to him. Her white tennis shoes flashed in the moonlight.

"What are you doing here?"

"Starving to death. Why?" He kept watching her tennis shoes.

"Lorin, you're going to get me in trouble."

"I'm sorry," he said. "I haven't eaten all day. I hope you don't think I like doing this."

She stood over him for nearly a minute while he stared at her knees. They were nicely silhouetted against the grey moon-washed driveway behind her.

"Lorin, if I brought you a sandwich could you stay in your car again tonight?"

"I ran out of gas about a mile from here," he said.

"I'll make you a sandwich. Wait right here."

She was back out in a few minutes. He heard the door click shut behind her. "Thank God Floyd's asleep. I was afraid he'd

hear me and I don't know how I would have explained this."
Something white floated in front of his eyes and he took it.

"Thank you," he said after his second bite. It was chicken salad.

"Don't gobble," she said. "It'll tie your stomach in knots."
The sandwich was gone in six bites. He counted them. "Lorin," she said.

"What."

"If I lent you some money could you put gas in your car and go somewhere?"

He felt his penis shrivel. He had been afraid it would. "I can't ask you to do that," he said.

She went back into the house and came out a moment later carrying her purse. "I haven't got much here," she said, rummaging inside while Lorin looked out at the street. A small dog was walking across a patch of lighted asphalt. He could hear its toenails. "Could you get by on ten dollars?"

"Yes." He watched the dog jump onto the curb and sniff at a tuft of grass, then lift its leg. He became aware that Gloriana was holding something in front of him. To his peripheral vision it seemed to be the size and shape of a stick of gum. He took it and stood up. "Thank you," he said. It was folded in fourths and stiff. He put it in his left trouser pocket. The dog darted up a driveway and disappeared. It had been square and shaggy, probably a Scotty. Lorin wondered if it lived there or was going to leave its pile in a stranger's back yard. He took his suitcase off the retaining wall and balanced his sleeping bag on a shoulder and walked around Gloriana's car, smelling the hot engine. He heard her say "I'm sorry, Lorin," just as he stepped into the street. The shadows were deeper on the sidewalk on the other side of the street because there were more trees there, as well as a tall hedge lining the driveway where the Scotty had gone. He hoped it wouldn't come trotting back out and start barking just as he got to the other side. He hated yappy little dogs. He wondered whether Gloriana was going to put her car away before she went back in the house or just leave it out all night. It was probably a safe neighborhood. She could probably just leave it out.

───

He slept that night in his car, which he parked off a canyon road in a debris-filled cul-de-sac where a model home was under construction. It was late by the time he found the place and he slept badly and dreamed of bones floating in water, drifting into random patterns as invisible currents cut beneath the surface and gradually dissipated. A femur nudged a translucent scapula before making a three-quarter turn to click against an entire rib cage that drifted past. Some ribs were missing, like the teeth of a comb; the remaining ones hung like fingers and gradually disappeared toward the ends where the murk blurred them. Someone's pelvis bobbed against a lily pad, and further away he saw the horseshoe of a lower jaw darting from side to side. The mystery cleared when he could make out that a dozen or so grey fish, carp possibly, were nibbling at it on different sides, scouring it for crumbs of flesh, or snails, or algae. When he woke up and peered through the palmprints of dust on his windshield the first thing he saw was a construction worker pissing against his front left tire and grinning at him. Three or four others were standing by a pile of lumber under the trees, watching. Still holding the army blanket closed around his chest, he reached over and groped for his shirt on the back seat while the construction worker shook himself dry and zipped up. Lorin buttoned his shirt and struggled into his pants, and still barefoot started his car and drove down the canyon while the unfinished house and the construction workers vanished in a billow of smoke and flame through which bloody arms and legs spun from the grenade he had coolly tossed over his shoulder on the way past.

Over breakfast in a motel coffee shop he felt panic lick at his heart. He watched the Mexican busboy wipe the end of the counter and reflected that even if he got a job today he was going to need lunch in a few hours. It was also time to have a room to sleep in, with walls and a door. He placed the collect call as soon as he was sure his father would be at the office. It mortified him to do it, and he lied as little as possible, explaining that his job didn't start until next week but he wanted to get out from underfoot today if possible, he was staying with friends and they'd been grand about it but he hated to mooch, you know how it is, wear out your welcome, ha ha. He was too old to be doing this, he thought when he picked up the cashier's check in the afternoon and ran to cash it before the banks closed. He ate fish and chips at a place he used to go with Yvonne, near the Basket Bazaar, and thought about ways to return Gloriana's ten dollars that would soil them.

That evening he moved his things into a furnished room at the top of an old house near the beach in Santa Monica with scalloped siding and a ruined tennis court where the tenants parked their cars among the weeds that grew up through cracks in the cement. He had found it late in the afternoon, advertised by a sign in a window with a telephone number. The landlord told him he could pay rent by the week. The bed tried to swallow him when he lay on it to ease his headache, and the walls smelled of boiled cabbage. He was wakened twice by crashes outside his door and the pounding of feet on the uncarpeted stairs leading up from the front vestibule. His army blanket didn't cover his feet. He wished she could see him now.

# 22

You felt better having your own address, even if it was a hole. It annoyed him that he would still have to use Gloriana's phone number, because it meant he would have to keep calling her until something turned up. He didn't want to give her that satisfaction sooner than he had to, so he let her stew for a few days while he took the lay of the land and made himself at home. The room was as depressing in the daylight as he had thought it would be. The walls were brown and spotted with mildew. A single light bulb hung on a cord from the ceiling with a blue ruffled shade clipped onto it. Sitting on the bed, feeling the springs relax under him like rubber bands, he could see through his curtainless window onto a balcony belonging to the house next door. The railing looked unsafe, the wood soft and rotted where the bolts pinned it to the deck. Through the uprights he could see a half dozen pots of what he guessed was cannabis standing in orderly rows. A girl came out to water them each morning, but she never looked his way. His other furniture was modest, a table and a chair, both of which were sticky with other people's germs until he had worked them over with a can of Borax he'd found in the bathroom across the hall and an old T-shirt he wasn't going to wear any more. A second window, with a seat built under it, gave onto the street, and through this one he hoped to salvage enough daylight to paint by as soon as he had unpacked his easel and paint case, which he was going to do as soon as he had a job. Whoever lived downstairs didn't like him and had pounded on the ceiling with a broom handle the first night when he had paced his room before going to bed, so he made a point after that of being in his stocking feet when he was home. There was no closet; he hung his suits on a steam pipe that ran up the wall from the radiator under his window seat and along the ceiling until it pierced the lath and plaster and disappeared into the attic, and kept his other clothes in cardboard boxes which he could shove under the table where they wouldn't be in the way when he wanted to pace.

He had gotten his first glimpse of a fellow-tenant the morning after moving in, when he had looked into the communal refrigerator that stood around the corner from his room. The sound of the refrigerator door opening seemed to trigger a rattle of bolts in the door of the room just opposite. Lorin turned to see a fat young man with sweat on his lip peering at him across a door chain.

"Just checking to see how much room there was," he explained.

"That's my yogurt on the bottom shelf," the fat man said and closed the door.

Lorin felt insulted, and considered eating one of them—there were at least ten cartons there, lemon, plain, black raspberry, peach—and returning the empty carton to the bottom shelf, but he didn't, and a week went by before he saw his neighbor again. In daylight the man looked pathological. He was leaving the small dirty neighborhood grocery store down the block, carrying a large brown shopping bag and waving his free arm back and forth like a flipper as he walked, breathing hard. He didn't seem to recognize Lorin, who hurried on past so they wouldn't have to nod. He wasn't sure who lived in the room to the left of his at the top of the stairs. No sounds ever seemed to come from that side, but once when he was leaving early he caught a glimpse through the half-open door of a puffy white face watching him.

In a frenzy of inventiveness he applied at an insurance office, an advertising agency, an import shop, a computer firm, a furniture and appliance store, even one or two places he didn't understand the business of. Between these forays he came back, shaking with hunger, to his room where he ate tuna fish out of a can with a plastic fork and lay on his bed with an arm across his eyes and imagined himself bloated and dead when the landlord came to find why he hadn't taped the envelope with the rent money to his door. He gave Gloriana five days and then phoned her from the grocery store, intending to tell her he forgave her, but before he could get to that she told him he had gotten a call. He wasn't surprised. He was beginning to understand that his life was ordered by patterns.

"He called Monday," she said. "I didn't know how to get hold of you so I told him you were out of town but would be back pretty soon. I hope it's still open. Why didn't you call me like you said?"

It was too complicated to explain. He wrote down the information, thanked her, and drove at once to the Village to present himself. He would tell her later that he forgave her. He tried not to be surprised that the call had come from the bank, where he had gone on whim one afternoon because he happened to be in front of it, but in fact he was. The mystery was cleared when he sat in front of Mr. Acton's desk in New Accounts and at one point in the interview Mr. Acton leaned back, beaming genially, and put his hands behind his head and his suit jacket fell open and Lorin saw the unmistakable outline of temple garments. The scooped-out neck was obvious, and he could even make out the right-angle stitch marks over the nipples. He waited patiently for the interview to come to the part about the mission and excommunication, and felt like a hundredth sheep facing an indulgent shepherd, but to his surprise it didn't come up. It was some minutes into Mr. Acton's affable description of the lunch room upstairs, the benefits program, vacations, the hours and the softball team before Lorin realized he had a job. He was to come in on Monday and would work with Miss Corning on the teller line for a few days before going to the head office downtown for a week of teller school. Lorin tried not to blink, since that would show he had not been paying attention. Mr. Acton offered his hand across the desk. Lorin took it, half expecting to feel the patriarchal grip, thanked him and went out, his head reeling. He called Gloriana's number immediately, from a phone in the drugstore across the street, but there was no answer. He felt as though he needed to be congratulated by someone and thought about ordering a coke at the lunch counter so he could at least tell the waitress. Instead he went home and re-stretched one of his old canvases, and by the time it was dark outside and he had to flip on the overhead light, he had painted the worst daub he had ever done in his life. It covered three-fifths of the painting of a girl with a guitar that was underneath, and it looked like an omelet splattered against a window. That was all right. He had just been fooling around. He was out of practice, was all. Some of his tubes were hard and cracked too.

He ate a cold TV dinner and went to bed numb with fear.

On Monday he reported to Mr. Acton, who did not seem as friendly as he had seemed at the interview and who introduced him immediately to Dave Archibald, who ran operations, who in turn introduced him to Mary, Maxine, Maida, Janet, Gerald, Joe, Larry, Kathleen, Marcia, Sylvia, and, back in the vault, Fred and Jose. There were others, and he promptly forgot them all.

Judy. Toby. He would not be there long enough to have them become part of his life, but he would be polite. Kit, Josie. Another Larry. They were all different ages, but the men were mostly young. John was middle-aged and British, and worked in safe deposits downstairs. Lorin wondered what his deficiency was that he should have a tacky job like this one at his age. Peter was pale and had red hair and sad basset-eyes and was in love with Rosemarie who was vacuous and divorced. He learned that during coffee break from Margaret, who worked in escrow and had everyone's number.

He spent the day on a tall stool at the elbow of Mary Corning, who was in her fifties and had grey hair coiled in a bun held in place by a wicked Spanish comb. She wore a red sheath dress and glasses shaped like half-moons that she peered at you over the tops of. She told Lorin she was an old maid. She also called him sweetheart, which she also called most of her customers. She smote the checks and deposit slips that came across her window with her teller stamp and date stamp as though she were making short work of them and kept asking Lorin if he understood what he was seeing. He let himself be taken to lunch by a Duane somebody, whom Dave Archibald put onto him. Duane was about Lorin's age but short and wore slicked-down hair and a Cornell tie tack. He was in the officer-training program, moving from branch to branch, learning operations here, loans there, escrow somewhere else. Duane lost interest in him by the time they had gotten to the Hamburger Hamlet—on the way Lorin explained he was here only temporarily and had no plans to stay with the bank, which he afterward thought was saying more than he needed to—and they spent the lunch hour mostly looking past each other and wishing it were time to go back to work.

In the afternoon he resumed his place at Mary's side. He watched her take deposits, cash checks, turn to the telephone beside her window to call bookkeeping and ask to have a hold put on the account for the amount she was about to give the customer standing in front of her, who, Lorin noticed, pretended not to be paying attention. He learned about less-cash transactions and courtesy endorsements, and what a teller-exchange was, and which ledger you consulted to find out how much interest a customer had lost because a bookkeeper had posted a deposit incorrectly. When the bank closed its doors at three, he followed her to an adding machine and watched her balance her cash and become irritated when she was over by a capricious figure—$3.78 or something like that—and eventually had to have one of the vault tellers come out and find the error for her.

After drinking coffee with Willard Pirtle, who had just graduated from UCLA in psychology and who invited him to come with him and his wife to the Unitarian church sometime, he filed cancelled checks until five and then went to his car where he had parked it in a dirt lot that he had used when he was a student and was surprised to find still there, and drove home. He found something to eat and afterward wrapped himself up in a blanket and sat on a pillow in the corner of his room on the floor where he couldn't be seen through either window and closed his eyes while his ancestors began to gather over his head to talk about him.

———

He spent the second week of his new life in Downtown Los Angeles, where he felt as though a lid had closed over him and he would never be seen again. A tiny doll-like woman named Cassie, who had a pixy haircut and enormous eyes, and her two assistants put Lorin and twelve other people, most of them young men in the officer-training program, through hypothetical problems, which they acted out through model teller windows on casters, where someone with an account in another branch wanted to cash a check at your window or someone with insufficient funds was trying to pull a fast one with a second endorsement and how did you stop him or someone tried to make a deposit in an account not his own and what did you do. He was reimbursed thirteen cents a mile to make the drive and was panhandled twice on Flower Street.

The following Monday he was given his own teller stamp, his own cash drawer, his own window. His stomach was in knots all day, and when he balanced his cash after the bank closed he was short by fifty dollars. When he was neither arrested nor fired he felt better, but he knew that Mr. Acton was revising his opinion of him and would watch, from a distance, saying nothing, until the devil stepped in and took another fifty dollars. On Tuesday the devil decided to let him dangle a little longer; his cash balanced perfectly, and Janet asked him if he could give her a ride home. Janet was twenty years old, divorced, had a one-year-old, and wore stockings that had runs all over them. At first Lorin had thought she just snagged a new pair each day, but then he realized she had no other kind. On Wednesday he felt badly done by when a large woman with pink hair and expensive gloves presented him with a check drawn on the Sunset branch in Pacific Palisades and he said he would have to clear it with his supervisor and she called over Mr. McCaffrey from the officers' platform who told him in the hearing of all the other tellers on the line that Mrs. Snyder had a savings account in the Westchester branch that would curl his toes so please cash her check like a good boy. On Thursday he looked up in the middle of the afternoon when someone cleared his throat and was frightened to see himself standing at his window, facing him, looking bored and irritable with pale blue eyes and a brown beard. He looked down at the check that the other Lorin had slid across the counter like a holdup note and realized that it was only Floyd, who had grown a beard since the last and only time they had met. Floyd seemed not to recognize him. He cashed Floyd's check and counted out the bills on the counter without directly looking at him again, and said as little as possible so that his voice would not give him away. He felt shaky the rest of the day.

On Friday he decided that Janet had been watching him all week when she thought he wasn't looking. She was the only attractive girl in the place, except for Maida down the lobby in statements, and Maida actually looked too much like a candy doll. He thought he might start trying to be interesting in front of Janet next week, even though her tastes ran to roller derbies and drive-ins, because he was tired of being horny. An affair with somebody who worked the same place you did might be awkward, but it wouldn't have to be a big affair.

That night he looked at the daub he had left to rot on his easel and went to a movie to put it out of his mind. He had never gone to a movie by himself in his life. Coming out he thought he recognized Pavel in the line of people waiting for the next show. He tried to remember if Pavel was one of the people he was going to avoid, but their eyes had met, so he walked over and extended his hand.

"Hello Pavel," he said.

"I'm not Pavel," said Pavel.

Lorin looked closely and his blood froze.

"Call him Paul," the man behind him in line said.

"I used to be Pavel," said Pavel, fingering the medallion on his chest.

Lorin looked at the man behind him and then back at Pavel, who had lost interest and was watching a girl in high-heeled boots get out of a car. The car pulled away and she walked past the ticket window into the lobby.

"What happened?" he asked the man.

"He's not deaf."

"I'm sorry."

Pavel turned around. "Can I have a cigarette, Morton?" The man lit one and handed it to him.

"Do you remember me, Pavel? Paul? I'm Lorin."

Pavel studied him, then turned to his companion. "What did he say?"

"He said his name is Warren and he wonders if you remember him."

"Yeah. I remember Warren." He flicked the ash off his cigarette and touched the end to a coarse black hair on the back of his hand. The hair shriveled and the man grabbed his wrist.

"I'm going to take it away from you."

"I won't do it any more," Pavel said.

Lorin had seen the round white puckers like candle wax and an angry welt that was seeping. "I guess you're his brother," he said.

"You can probably take off now without breaking anybody's heart." The brother wore thick rimless glasses and his beard was shorter than Pavel's, and flecked with white.

"I'm sorry," Lorin said. "It's just that I'm an old friend of his, I don't know if you ever knew about the Blue Couch, actually we were friends at UCLA, it was a coffee house a little close to here, and I've been away for a couple of years, and he's the first one I've seen since I've been back, actually he's the second, and I was naturally concerned."

He was aware that Pavel was listening to him. So were the other people in line.

Morton took off his glasses and put them in his pocket. Then he smiled. He reached out and patted Lorin's cheek. "Fuck off, Warren," he said, smiling.

Lorin backed away, feeling the muscles in his cheek twitch. "I'm sorry," he said.

He drove to the beach and walked barefoot on cold sand for an hour until he felt better, and then drove home. He climbed the stairs to his room, hearing groans in the walls on either side of the staircase and an enigmatic shuffle behind the door where he had seen the puffy face. He stayed awake hearing sounds of furniture being moved around downstairs and tried to remember what movie he had gone to. He thought about Sorenson and his horny girl friend. He wondered if being horny for a long time was bad for your health.

———

In the morning he remembered Gloriana's ten dollars and walked down to the grocery store on the corner. There was a heavy smog alert, and the sunlight had a gassy lavender glow to it. He waited until the black woman wearing a turban was through with the phone outside the doorway and called Gloriana's number. It was Saturday; someone ought to be home. Floyd answered, but it was no more than he expected.

"Hi, I wonder if Gloriana is there," Lorin said. He felt as though he were holding his voice between two fingers.

"No. You want to leave a message?"

Lorin thought about mentioning the ten dollars but decided that since he forgave her there was no point in stirring the waters. "Do you know what time she'll be back?"

"No. Who is this? Mark?"

"Actually no. My name is Lorin Hood, but you probably don't remember me, it was a long time ago."

"Who?"

"I guess just tell her Lorin called. It isn't anything important. I'll try her later."

"You want me to have her call you?"

"Actually I'm going to be away from the phone for a while. I'll just try her later." He was about to hang up and creep away when he suddenly had a thought. "I'm calling from the university," he said. "She isn't up here by any chance, is she?"

"She's supposed to be. You tried her lab?"

His heart pounded at this rush of information. "I couldn't get an answer," he said. "Maybe I misdialed." He picked up a gum wrapper from the floor of the booth and rattled it next to the mouthpiece. "Let's see. Is her number—wait a minute, I can't read my own writing any more, ha ha."

Floyd gave him a number. He sounded bored. Lorin asked him to repeat it while he frantically scrawled it on the wall of the phone booth. "That's what I thought I called, all right. Well, I'll just try again, ha ha. Thanks very much."

"She was probably down the hall in the john."

"I never thought of that. Maybe I'd better give her a few minutes." He hung up quickly. He had been afraid he was going to giggle insanely and give himself away.

After copying the number from the wall of the booth onto the back of the creased and worn parking ticket he still carried in his wallet he dialed it and waited for whatever would come. A male voice answered. He was always getting those.

"Is Gloriana there?" he asked politely.

"Just a minute." He heard the white noise over the receiver turn pinkish brown and a muffled voice said, "Anybody seen what's her name?" Lorin imagined a large barn-like laboratory with dirty sinks smelling of formaldehyde, and caged rats perched on benches and racks of test tubes on top of a stained white refrigerator and three or four graduate assistants in white lab coats sitting around eating sandwiches and drinking coffee, their fingers yellow with acid. He heard mutters of conversation through someone's palm, and then the sound turned white again.

"I guess she's not here. Who's this? Mark?"

"Actually I just wanted to return something and I couldn't reach her at home. Do you know if she's planning on coming in?"

"Sure don't." Lorin thought he detected a smirk in the voice.

"Maybe I can just come by and leave it on her desk. Which building are you in?" He felt the thrill of closing in.

The student gave him the name of the building—Lorin had never heard of it but would find a campus map somewhere—and the room number, and added, "If it's edible I wouldn't leave it here. She'll never see it." Lorin heard a rude guffaw in the distance. He thanked his informant and hung up. He wondered what he ought to do. Make a sandwich, perhaps, and drive up to the university and stake out her building. Hide in the men's room until he heard her footsteps going by in the hallway, if he could remember what they sounded like, and then pop out as if by accident. Wait in the laboratory with her colleagues and see her try to explain him to them when she came in, if she ever did. In the end he bought a sack of corn chips and went back to his room to eat them in bed, because he wanted to think about something.

It had occurred to him that his bones had been speaking to him for some time and he had not been listening because he did not like what they were saying. It was time now to lie down quietly and pay attention. He carried his easel with its daubed canvas to the center of the room and undressed and got back into bed. Slouching with a pillow at his back and a towel draped across his chest to catch crumbs, he munched on the corn chips and thought things he had never thought before. He looked at the burnished omelet streaked by white with green flecks in it where it rested foreshortened and shiny on his easel with the light from the street window touching it, and he realized that he disliked painting. He ate another corn chip and wondered why he had never noticed that before. The thing he was looking at right now, with the late morning sun glazing it, had given him no pleasure the afternoon he had painted it, even though he had painted it in a fit of euphoria. He worked a mash of corn chips out of a molar with his tongue and thought further. The brush strokes on the girl's face and arms, where the omelet didn't cover them, and the glint of highlight from the fire on the surface of her guitar were clearly visible across the room, and he remembered the care with which he had put them there and the strain of wishing he didn't have to. The painting under his daub had taken him a week to do, he remembered. He had not enjoyed the visual experience of seeing substance collect in the particles that got brushed in day by day, nor the surprise when dimensions opened unexpectedly as the result of overlays that gave rejected shapes a new context. He had not even enjoyed the kinetic sensation of feeling the smooth glide of a brush across a dry surface suddenly become raspy as its load of paint ran out.

He thought further. The still-life he had done in Yvonne's house had been a misery from the hour he had begun gathering its parts to the moment he had stuffed it, still wet and unfinished, into his loaded car and driven out of her life. His handful of canvases that had hung in the Blue Couch, among them the study of Yvonne that had drawn Gloriana's attention, were testaments to hours spent swallowing back the yellow froth that boiled up from his stomach. In the dark chambers of his heart he knew he had been relieved to see his nude decomposing in Simon's bathtub, where no one would see it again and know he had done it. He could not think of one picture he had created in joy.

He could feel his heart beating. He was eating corn chips faster, and presently his fingers touched only the oily inside surface of the empty package. He wiped them on the towel and wadded the bag and sat up on the edge of the bed. His feet smeared patterns in the dust on the floor as he moved them back and forth in his agitation. His sketchbooks, reams of paper with his marks on them, had been compendiums of toil performed through pain and hatred. The yards of canvas he had covered with still-lifes, landscapes, figures, faces, stone buildings, apricot sunsets, had mocked him as he had covered them and they mocked him now, the ones that had survived, rolled up and stuffed into a corner under his table for beetles to crawl into and die. He stood up and walked to the window that faced the street and looked down. The iron fence that enclosed the weed-filled yard was still there. The concrete steps leading down to the sidewalk had not reversed themselves. Grass still grew from the same crack in the sidewalk. Cars swept past on Ocean Park in both directions, slowing as they approached the crest of the hill in front of the house and then gathering speed as they descended away from each other. He went back to his bed and sat there a minute, then got up and went to the window again, then to the window overlooking the balcony with the cannabis, if that was what it was, then back and forth the length of his room several times. He was swollen, and that bothered him, but more importantly something inside his head was beginning to race out of control, and he knew he had to keep moving or a revelation of some kind was going to burst open an important vessel.

He pulled on some clothes and went out, feeling the sidewalk tip as he walked the six downhill blocks to the beach, forcing him to veer sharply to keep from falling. He stopped once to steady himself against a bus stop bench and then went on, carefully, his arms extended at either side for balance. He was conscious several times of the sound of pounding feet coming up behind him on the sidewalk and thundering past him on both sides, though there was never anyone there. The used clothing store on the corner across from the beach was closed, but he glanced into the window as he went by and saw his head pass through a birdcage that hung in a stand beside a broken leather chair. Across the street he took off his shoes and felt the sand burn his feet as he climbed a dune and side-slipped down the other side, narrowly missing a blanket on which a brown girl lay on her stomach while her boy friend nuzzled her back. They looked up at him and Lorin stumbled past pretending he hadn't seen them. The beach was crowded, despite the smog, and he seemed to be the only one on it wearing street clothes. He was vaguely aware that this made him conspicuous, but it was too late to think of that now; it was like dreaming you had gone to work naked and only noticed it halfway through the day, by which time you had to tough it out. He passed people on towels and blankets who stared at him through their dark glasses. Down by an outcropping of rocks where the sand flattened out some small children were chasing seagulls into the surf and running back as the line of foam snaked up the shining sand behind them. He had to watch his feet because they followed the tilt of the ground, which changed every few steps, and if he didn't keep control they were going to carry him across somebody's blanket, but the sand kept swallowing them and he couldn't always see where they were. He passed a girl in a lavender bikini spreading zinc oxide on her mouth and squinting into a compact. She didn't look up, and he felt himself getting smaller in her mirror as he left her behind. His face felt hot, and he guessed he must look distracted. He tried to look as though he had an urgent appointment and wasn't sure he could make it, and even glanced once at his watch, but it was dense with ants crawling under the crystal. His fatigue shirt had turned dark where it clung to his ribs, and he felt sweat run down the inside of his arms. He knew that as soon as he got to the pier he was going to turn around and stumble back the way he had come, and the same people were going to stare at him again and wonder what was wrong with him. He was keeping pace, at least, with the revelation careening around in his head, and as long as he did it would not break through and dump him in a heap over the shaft of somebody's beach umbrella while he floated off to one side to watch the crowd gather.

His legs were quivering by the time he reached the stairs that scaled the bluff to the pier, and sand had climbed under his levis and was itching the backs of his knees. On an impulse he climbed the stairs instead of turning around and going back. He would not be a spectacle if he could help it. He could hear the mechanical band in the carousel playing "Eleanor Rigby" and when he reached the top of the stairs he sat down on the curb in front of the carousel and put his shoes on. The carousel was nearly empty, and riderless painted horses rose and fell as though they were swimming. He stood up and began walking down the pier, rapidly, keeping to the left-hand sidewalk and counting the cars that passed him in both directions, cancelling each other out. The other pedestrians were mostly wearing street clothes, so he didn't feel as conspicuous, though one or two people turned to look at him as he hurried by, so something about him still looked odd. He tried to count the weaving masts of the sailboats moored on both sides of the pier, but he couldn't be sure he hadn't counted some of them twice, so he stopped. He passed the harbormaster's office and the bait and tackle shop and the lobster house. A man with a green dragon on his chest sat in the doorway of the tattoo parlor and watched him go by. He passed the restrooms, which occupied a platform that hung out over the water, and noticed the silver backs of swarming trash fish in the water directly below. Something startled the fish and they flitted off for an instant, exposing a skeleton floating just under the surface. The water boiled under it and he looked away, and then the fish were back. The street ended in a turnaround, and he descended a flight of wet iron steps and came out where people stood fishing from the lower platform. Tackle boxes lay open on the deck and pieces of fish seeped blood onto the slippery planking. He stopped, eaten by curiosity, behind three men who were leaning over the rail.

"Catching anything?" he asked. He had always wanted to do that.

The man on the end turned to look at him and then turned back. His face had been on upside down, so the smile that had split his forehead under his dirty felt hat with the hooks stuck in it was actually a frown, and the white undulating caterpillar of a beard in which two marbles had rolled was really a pair of eyebrows. Lorin gripped the stair rail and climbed back up, feeling a little more control over his balance. He began walking back the way he had come, but on the opposite sidewalk, since the one he had come down on was now squirming with eels. The soles of his feet felt blistered inside his tennis shoes, and between the heat and the violet smog he was developing a headache, but that was all right; it meant his head was still behaving normally.

The sidewalk broke open in front of him and he stared suddenly down into the black pilings of the pier with their scab of barnacles and the thrashing black water that rocked them back and forth, but he was too quick to be caught by surprise and darted around the thrusting beak of the split before it broke the pier in two. He was nearly hit by a car that was creeping toward the turnaround, and thumped its hood with the heel of his hand and said "Nice job!" to the driver, whose face through the windshield was a mass of worm trails. He felt a little ill, but ocean smells always did that to him, and besides he hadn't eaten yet, except for the corn chips. He walked faster, passing a middle-aged couple with a yellow poodle on a leash, trying to keep his elbows from jabbing the air. He remembered a newsreel he had seen as a kid showing grown men in a walking race. Their elbows had jabbed the air and their pelvises had jerked back and forth in the effort to extend their strides and still keep one foot on the ground at all times. They had looked grotesque and self-important, and he didn't want to look like that. None of them had been trying to keep the lid on something that was going to shred their brains if they slowed down, but it wasn't necessary to look like a fool while you kept control.

By the time he passed the carousel he realized he should have stopped and eaten something—a bowl of clam chowder perhaps—at the lobster house, but he decided not to go back. His head was in pain from hunger, but there was a lightness to his body that he didn't want to coarsen. The air itself was shining as he crossed Ocean Avenue and walked as fast as he could past the civic auditorium and up a side street that turned into a dingy residential neighborhood within a block, and if he could take enough of it into his lungs he would float. The neighborhood was filled with peeling frame houses that had outside staircases with mailboxes hung in a row beneath them next to the electric meters. A green ambulance turned the corner behind him and slowly passed him with its right front tire flaccid as a bag of porridge, going flup flup flup against the pavement. A bare ass stared at him from the rear window and remained there, smiling, until the ambulance slowly sank below the brow of the next hill, shimmering in the heat waves that rose from the asphalt until it winked out. He cut across to Ocean Park along a street lined with dense spruce trees and garbage cans crushed in a row along the curb. He couldn't bear the pace any longer and broke into a run up the hill to his own building, and climbed the stairs to his own room, and fumbled the key at his lock. His head was pounding but was otherwise dormant at last.

On the other side of the door, he knew, he would find himself lying naked on his bed, a crushed bag of corn chips on the floor beside him and his hands locked across his chest. He would be bloated and pale. He would have a bemused smile on his cold lips because he would be in a place no man had seen and come back from. He was a long time getting the key into the lock because his shoulders kept shaking and he couldn't aim it, and then, once it was in place, he couldn't get it to turn. But that was all right. He had kept control. He put his head against the door to steady himself. He could take his time. It would turn sooner or later.

———

He watched himself as a thirteen-year-old in period costume come out the door and peer around the corner of the porch to make sure his father had gone off to the north forty or wherever it was and his mother had not come out the kitchen door to head him off. Then he watched himself creep down the wooden steps with their curls of green paint, cross the yard and push open the wagon-wheel gate and follow the dirt path up past the stock dam, and then he joined himself. He was looking for a quiet place to pray for a revelation.

He crawled through a break in the barbed-wire fence and walked along a shady road, his boots heavy with dung and cold mud, to the edge of the woods belonging to a neighbor who had spread stories about his family. He scanned the hills in the distance and the rock-strewn pasture beyond the road he had walked along, then ducked under a branch and entered the woods.

He imagined a spring setting. The trees were spindly and just coming into leaf, like the aspens up Mill Creek Canyon, and there were still patches of dirty snow on the ground, and soft spots where his feet sank under a paste of leaf mold. The sunlight was thin, the warmth in the air tentative. He reached a clearing where dead stumps hulked through a foam of pale lavender wildflowers, looked around to make sure no one had crept through the woods behind him and knelt down in the wet grass.

He wasn't sure how you did this. He tried various positions, and discovered that if you sank down until your heels pressed into your butt and kept your eyes closed and contracted every muscle as hard as you could, you felt as if you were getting somewhere. He imagined muscles like rope standing out on his brain and one of his front teeth felt ready to snap. A clutter of lights swam against his eyelids and pulsed sympathetically with the stabs of pain in his back. A mild euphoria seemed to settle into his bones. He fancied he was sinking slowly past his heart and lungs into unknown corridors where the light was a dusky rose and the air was warm and damp. Pictures of ancestors hung on the walls above him, pulsing with blood. He was about to go deeper when something unpleasant happened.

At first it felt like ice crystals forming at the back of his brain. His head went numb and a bruise of lights coalesced in either eye, wild splotches of color through which tiny people ran, waving their arms. His elbows pressed into his body until he thought his ribs would pop, and air was forced from his lungs. He realized he was crushing his chest with his knees. He tried to touch his face with his hands, but they were shaking too violently and he couldn't bring them any closer. His head was pulled down between his shoulders. He couldn't draw a breath but a sharp fetid odor rose from his body and penetrated his nostrils, making his sinuses ache. Sharp stones cut his back. That was what made him realize he wasn't on his knees any longer. Behind the aura in each eye the daylight was turning brown. A rush of childhood memories coursed through his brain—a week spent sick in bed drinking large mugs of fenugreek tea, an unkind word to his mother when he was eight, a prank for which his father had swatted him when he was eleven, stealing peas from a neighbor's garden when he was five. A certain serenity stole into his knowledge of approaching death. Pain would end, life drew to a close, duties not performed would be given to someone else, days would pass without him and flowers would ripen on his grave and his friends would think of him now and then and admit they had always liked him.

He could even savor his disorientation a little. Trees floated at various angles around him, with a tender green haze around their branches and twigs. Through the murk that the daylight had become he could see, at some ambiguous distance, a long white tube of light dipping into the branches, making brittle silhouettes, and drawing back up. He could see it was moving closer, feeling its way among branches. It moved left and right, stopping once or twice until it hovered the width of a hand over the tallest stalks of columbine, and then came toward him again. Trees that were bathed in it suddenly warped and shimmied and then became invisible behind it. As it came closer Lorin could see that the edges were not sharply defined after all but were a haze of particles in frantic motion. It came directly at him with appalling speed, and his last thought as he felt his pants turn warm was that no one but himself knew that death was a tube of light from another dimension that sucked you from the earth. He heard the squeal of a terrified pig in a remote part of his brain, and then the light moved onto him. He was aware that a white noise in his ears that he hadn't noticed before had suddenly stopped, isolating the squeal, which reached a crescendo and dropped a minor second and gradually faded. At the same instant the pressure on his chest lifted, and his elbows dropped to the ground.

The murk had been scoured from the air. He lay there feeling his chest rise and fall. Out of the corner of his eye he saw that the grass he lay in looked like white flamelets, moving slightly, as though the light had set up a small wind. On his left the dead stump stood bleached, ringed with flowers that had small spectral petals. Directly above him two men in white robes stood looking at him. Bark had been peeled from the dead stump and lay in rags among the wildflowers. The rags were bleached out too, and looked like strips of fat. The remarkable thing about the two men was that they looked alike, but one was older. Lorin had peered into the rippled mirror that hung over the wash bucket outside the kitchen door and speculated which of his own features were likely to mutate, given age and ripening and decline, into his father's features. He actually favored his mother's side of the family, the pale eyes, the thin nose, the long bony face and heavy lip, but now and then, taking himself by surprise, he had caught a flash of something belligerent and tainted in the face that looked back at him that he had seen in his father's face. It was barely traceable, lurking behind the pale eyes or at the corners of the mouth, and it was always gone the next instant.

The older man pointed to the younger one and said something about a son or the sun. Lorin wondered if he was going to mention any of this when he got home. They were talking about abominations and false prophets, and Lorin reflected that he could no longer feel the pains in his back and sides, in fact could not feel his back and sides at all, or his feet or hands. He suspected this meant your kinesthetic responses shut off during visions. It meant your nerve endings picked up other signals, your senses fine-tuned to other frequencies. It explained why, now that he thought about it, he was not hearing the chirp of birds or the buzz and click of insects or for that matter the rustling made by the wind in the white flamelets beside his ears. All he could hear was the mild voice of the younger man explaining dreadful things to him, and he worried that he wasn't going to remember them all. He strained to listen very closely, but there were no muscles you could flex to hear better. The most he was able to do was cause a roaring in both ears, and that created interference. Still, he enjoyed watching the shadows ripple across the robes of both men as the wind gently caught the folds. He experienced a mild pang as the younger man's voice began to fade out, and presently he was aware of colors separating into unstable bands around them both, and he saw the claw of a dead branch through the face and chest of the older man.

He lay for a long time staring at a webwork of twigs in early leaf against a cold blue sky before trying to get up, and when at last he did his knees buckled under him. He crawled to the nearest sapling and pulled himself upright, but his muscles had gone soft. He made his way home, groping for branches and fenceposts, crawling when there was nothing along the roadside to reach for, and finally crept up the steps to the small farmhouse kitchen, omitting to glance at the mirror that flashed white at him as he went past. He opened the door and limped past his frightened mother who followed him into the living room, wringing her hands in her apron and asking him if he were sick as he leaned his forehead against the fireplace mantel. He told her he was all right, just leave him alone. He would be fine in a minute.

He became aware, while breathing between his teeth, that a clean pink daylight was starting to soften the walls of the room, and early-morning sounds of cars and people coughing came up from the street. And then he knew it had been daylight all along. He heard a frantic scrattle of a key at his lock and opened his eyes in time to see himself stumble through the doorway into the room, holding his head and moaning. He was ready for the interruption but wondered where he had been.

# 23

Lorin studied the eggshell forehead, unable to shake the impression that it was translucent and would break through if he pressed a thumb against it. The eyelids, distorted through the glasses, had been sealed with a dark glue. The mouth was set in a hard line, and the corners turned down. He suspected the corners were his fault. They had dressed his father in a white temple suit and had placed one hand across the other on top of his diaphragm. Lorin bent close to make sure the nails were blue at the cuticles, because a small part of him clung to the suspicion that it was all a mistake.

"Have you touched him yet?" his mother asked.

He rested his fingertips on the back of his father's hand. It was like touching a dry frog. Someone bumped him from behind, and he used the opportunity to return his hand to his pocket and finger his keys.

"Scuse me, Lorin," the man behind him said, patting him on the arm. It was Hal Kratzer, his old deacons' quorum advisor, looking ruddy and uncomfortable. They had all looked uncomfortable at seeing him in church, but so far no one had said anything.

"Nice to see you, Hal," Lorin said, shaking his hand but trying not to touch the back of it with his fingertips. "Glad you could come."

"Listen, I wouldn't miss this one," Hal said. He looked down at the fragile face with its oversize glasses. "That guy," he said. "You know what I mean?" Tears stood out in his eyes when he looked back at Lorin. Lorin nodded, and shook hands again.

"How are you doing, Grace?"

"I'm doing all right, I guess," said Lorin's mother. "I'm hanging in there."

"Atta girl."

"You know that poster?" she said. "The kids sent me a poster, I don't know when it was, last year maybe. It shows a cat, or I guess it was just a kitten, something anyway, hanging onto a branch."

"I guess I don't, Grace."

"Maybe we ought to move," Lorin suggested. "We're kind of in the way here." Several people had stepped around them, trying to see into the casket. He recognized Herb Clawson, who had been ward clerk at the time of Lorin's excommunication. "Hi, Herb," he said as they shook hands. "Glad you could come."

"It's been a while," said Herb, gripping him by the shoulder. "When did you get into town?"

"Flew in Monday. Stephen got in last night. He's around here somewhere."

"That *was* Stephen I saw. I thought he looked familiar. Listen, your dad looks great."

"Thanks. They did a good job."

"Those guys are real artists, you know?"

"The poster says 'Hang in there, Baby,' " Lorin's mother said. "That's what I'm doing, I'm hanging in there, baby."

"That's the stuff, Grace," Hal said.

Lorin stepped back out of the way, nearly knocking over a basket of flowers shaped like a peacock's tail. More people had come by and were waiting to say something to his mother. A young woman in a purple maternity smock glanced in the casket and looked away.

"You're still in L.A., right?" Herb asked.

"Yes. I'm working at a bank in Westwood Village, if you know where that is." He wished Stephen or one of the girls would take his mother into the chapel and make her sit down.

"Oh sure, out by the temple. Do you ever run into Bob Gordon? He's still out there, I think."

"I don't know what they sent it to me for. It wasn't because of anything that happened, I mean no one had died. I guess they just wanted me to know they were thinking about me. They wanted me to hang in there, baby. So that's what I'm doing. I'm hanging in there, baby."

Hal was beginning to look bored. Lorin reached for his mother's arm. "I haven't run into Bob, no. If I do I'll tell him hello for you. Thanks, Herb. Why don't we go sit down, Mom?"

"No, wait, he's in West Covina. I saw his dad the other day, and he said West Covina."

"I'll tell him hello. Thanks, Herb." He put an arm around his mother's shoulders and led her to the row of folding chairs that lined the wall beside the casket. "Let's just sit here till it's time to go in," he said, looking around the room for Katy or Sonia.

"That Hal Kratzer is the nicest man," his mother said.

"Yes." Lorin spotted Jeff Cummings and his daughter across the room talking to some people by the table where a girl in a white dress was handing out programs. Margaret Cummings had been a tall girl two or three years older than Lorin, with big feet and bony knees, and he had been in love with her when he was nine. She looked rangy and homely now. He wondered if she had ever gotten married.

"You remember my son Lorin, don't you, Alicebeth?" his mother said. Lorin stood up to shake hands and a woman with breasts like pillows presented her cheek, which he kissed, smelling powder.

"How wonderful that you could be here, Lorin," she said.

"It's my father," he said, feeling stupid.

"Grace, isn't it a comfort to have your children with you now?"

Lorin looked wildly around the room for a sibling. The room was full of people who looked familiar but whom he couldn't name. He did remember Alicebeth as a large woman with a shiny face who sang "The Holy City" in sacrament meetings when he was a deacon while her husband accompanied her at the piano. He wasn't sure he would recognize her husband now. More people had gathered in front of the casket and others stood in groups around the carpeted floor, talking quietly. Some looked at their watches. Banks of flowers stood at either end of the casket, and through the doorway to the chapel he could see more flowers in pots and urns and baskets arranged in front of the sacrament table. It was a hot afternoon; both entrances had been propped open, and the traffic noises from Highland Drive made him feel trapped in the heat. He realized he wanted to punch somebody.

"Mother, look what just came." Lorin looked up and saw Katy holding a long box containing blue and gold carnations, with a filigree of sweet williams and forget-me-nots wrapped around the stems like fishnet. "Lynn Ballou wired them. He was too sick to come himself but he sent these. Isn't that sweet?"

Lorin was touched. Lynn was his father's oldest friend, and was rotting away with cancer of something or other in California. His mother took the box from Katy and burst into tears. Lorin put an arm around her. "It's okay," he said. He wasn't sure what he meant.

Katy dropped to her knees and adjusted the box on her mother's lap. Her eyes ran and she was smiling. The skin around her nostrils was wet and pink. "Wasn't that nice, Mother?"

"Lynn should have been dead himself by now," his mother said to Hilda Jorgenson. Lorin scarcely recognized Hilda. Her head shook, and loose grey skin hung in folds under her jawbone.

"Hi, Hilda," he said.

"How are you holding up, Lorrie?" his sister asked, talking low to blend with the general murmur.

"I'm okay. Where's Stephen?"

"I think he was having a nicky fit. It's almost time to start. Want me to spell you?"

"Yeah. I won't be long."

He helped her up—Katy was pregnant and had a hard time changing positions—and settled her in his chair.

"I'll be right back."

His mother looked alarmed. "Where are you going?"

"It's okay, Mother, he's not going away."

"Have you touched him yet?" she called after him.

Lorin made for the door to the parking lot, shaking hands as he went with strangers who had familiar faces. He stood at the top of the concrete steps blinking at the hot asphalt and the mortuary hearse parked at the bottom with its back doors open and its gleaming red interior looking like a hot throat. He fought an urge to step back into the viewing room and look to make sure nothing in the casket had moved. He walked through the parking lot, checking behind all the cars and finding nothing but a couple of small neighborhood kids playing in the weeds by the fence.

"Does your mother know you're here?" he asked.

The little boy looked up. "Yes." He had dried mucus all over his lip.

"She sent us," the little girl said.

"Stay away from the cars," Lorin said. "You'll get run over."

He left the parking lot and walked down the winding narrow road that led off Highland. There were no sidewalks here, and the houses with their asbestos siding were small and sat close to the road on cramped lots separated by pyracantha hedges and low fences. The traffic sounds from Thirty-third South were a constant presence in the air, like flies, but the neighborhood pleased him, tucked away out of sight. He had always liked the narrow little streets and the heavy cottonwood trees whose roots had buckled the asphalt. As a kid he had sometimes walked with his father to a neighbor's house to buy eggs, which he got to pick warm out of the coop while the neighbor held the hen. The street ended behind a frame bungalow in whose front yard an orange school bus was parked. Three hairy young men, one of them wearing a fringed vest over a bare torso, and a girl in a granny dress sat on the front step and watched him go by. He climbed through the fence and entered the school ground, passing the lunch pergola and the tetherball pole. He found his brother standing under an elm tree looking at the monkey bars. Stephen's back was to him, and his hair hung in a tangle over the collar of his blazer. He was wearing grey bell-bottom pants, and if he had gotten mud on the cuffs climbing through the fence Lorin was going to kill him.

"It's time to start," Lorin said.

"Show me where you hit that Mexican kid who was out on third base," Stephen said. His stringy beard needed clipping. Lorin had forgotten to tell him to clip it this morning.

"I don't know where anything is any more," Lorin said. "I think it was over there where the bike racks are now. When they tore down the old building and built the new one they moved things around."

Stephen dropped his cigarette stub to the ground and stepped on it. "I was trying to remember if these are the same monkey bars I cracked my head on. They look too new."

"Don't leave that for one of the kids to pick up tomorrow," Lorin said. "Put it in your pocket. No, these are new even since Katy's time. You know what used to be here? I just remembered. This wasn't asphalt here. It was fenced off and had grass, and the school kept goats in it."

Stephen put the flattened stub in the pocket of his blazer and brushed the smear of ash off the flap. "I don't remember goats."

"We got to feed them out of a bottle. They were some kind of science project. I don't remember what happened to them. I think they died."

They passed the rings and Stephen took one and swung it on its chain. "What science? You got to watch them rut or something?"

"You know what those things look like?" Lorin said. They looked back at the circle of rings hanging from their chains. The one Stephen had grabbed still swung back and forth. "They look like gallows."

"Cute," Stephen said.

Lorin held the loose board while Stephen climbed through the fence, and then climbed through himself, snagging a thread of his jacket on a splinter.

"How are things back at the ward?" Stephen asked. He gave a thumbs-up sign to the porch full of hippies. "Sorry I left. I couldn't take any more for a while."

"You might have stuck around to give Mother a little moral support. She's not in very good shape."

"Don't be pissed. I just wanted to be out of there till they shut the box."

"It wasn't easy for the rest of us either, but we managed okay," said Lorin.

"Get off my ass, Lorrie, okay? I said I was sorry." He picked up a handful of loose pebbles where the paving had broken and tossed them, one at a time, at a wooden post holding a mailbox. "I'll even sit with her during the funeral and hold her gnarly little hand if you'll hold the other one." He flung the remaining pebbles at a trash barrel full of hedge clippings. "Christ, did you *see* him? How can she stand to look at him?"

"She likes looking at him, and she wants everybody else to too," Lorin said.

"To too," Stephen said, grinning.

"She even wanted me to touch him," Lorin said, remembering the dry frog.

Stephen's grin faded. "Jesus. Did you, Lorrie?"

"Yes. And that's what you're going to do if they haven't put the lid down yet. And she's going to see you do it."

"Wrong," said Stephen.

"It's not so bad. You'll see. It just feels funny."

"Not this kid," said Stephen.

"Come on. It'll make her happy."

As they crossed the road to the parking lot he heard organ music coming from the chapel.

"They've started already. Come on."

They ran up the steps to the viewing room, which was still full of people, though they had begun to file through the doorway to the chapel. His mother was staring into the open casket, with Sonia next to her holding her arm.

"Come on, Stephen, just do it. You'll be glad you did."

"Lorrie, forget it. I mean it. I can't even look at that thing."

Lorin had laid his hand on his brother's back and was escorting him through the crowd. "It'll be okay, Stephen, I'll stay with you. Hi, Miriam." A short woman with a beehive hairdo had just stepped over and patted him on the arm. She pressed a handkerchief across her mouth. Lorin stumbled as his brother suddenly stopped.

"Oh my God," said Stephen.

Lorin looked and saw his mother bending over the open casket. All he could see of his father was the last exposed button on his shirt and the pair of crossed hands. He tried to remember which one had been on top before. The men from the mortuary were starting to look busy. One of them moved a spray of flowers from the end of the viewing table so that the other two could have room to work. "Don't close it yet," Lorin called.

His sister turned. "Hurry," she said.

One of the men was gently lifting his father's head and another was fitting a white temple bonnet onto it. He tied the straps under the chin. Lorin's mother looked at her two sons as though she was not sure who they were. The resistance Lorin felt in his brother's back was making him impatient. "Come on. You can't not do it now that you're here," he said into Stephen's ear.

"I'll look at him. That's all I'll do. She can see me do that."

"You're going to lay your hot little paw on him," Lorin said.

Katy came in from the chapel. "Come on, you guys, they're waiting for us." Her husband was behind her, an apple-cheeked youngster with short sandy hair, who would always look as though he were just back from his mission. Lorin stepped to the side of the casket and put an arm around his mother. She was running her hands across his father's face and arms and chest. She made quick, darting little movements. Lorin felt the muscles in his brother's back go hard.

"I think they want to close it," Sonia said.

"That's all right, Sister Hood," one of the men said. "We'll just wait till you're ready."

"I don't think I'll ever be ready," Lorin's mother said. She had taken her hands off her husband's chest and stood looking down at his face. Lorin watched Stephen's hands whiten across the knuckles where they rested on the edge of the satin lining. He knew he would have to act. Still with an arm around his mother, he reached in and patted his father's rigid hand just below the wrist. He tried to touch as much of the coat sleeve as possible.

"Okay, Pop, R.I.P.," he said.

He kept his hand there and watched Stephen's hand let go of the edge of the casket. He had never noticed before, but the web between Stephen's thumb and finger had a row of pink scars like tiny buttons. He wondered how long Stephen had had those. The hand shook as it touched down on his father's hand and closed its fingers around it, making his father's hand move. Lorin let go and stepped back, reaching into his pocket to feel for his keys, and then Stephen let go. Lorin kept an arm around his mother and nodded to the director. The three men moved to the front of the casket and lowered the lid. He saw a shadow swallow up his father's face and then only a gleaming white lid with convoluted brass ornaments. His mother sobbed. Lorin took his hand from his pocket and made a fist and gently punched his brother's shoulder. Stephen's face, in profile, was splotched. Sweat trickled down his face, catching on hairs.

During the service Lorin tried to imagine his father in the celestial kingdom. It was hard to concentrate because his mother kept making chirping noises in her throat. She was sitting between him and Stephen. He hoped no one outside the family was hearing them. They were on the front row of the chapel, and she was flanked by her children; Katy sat next to Lorin, with her husband beside her, and Sonia sat on the other side of Stephen. Stephen was twisting a program, and Lorin felt like reaching behind his mother and jabbing him in the shoulder. The eulogy had been given by Carl Winn, an old friend from his father's high-school days, and a man and a woman from the mortuary were singing "In the Garden." Katy was snuffling into a handkerchief. He put a hand on her knee and squeezed, and she smiled. He folded his arms and closed his eyes and tried again, and eventually a waxed, rouged figure in a white suit came into focus, sitting stiffly in a chair in a room that swam with colored lights. The eyes were open and covered with a glaze, and were magnified by the oversize spectacles. His father stared at the backs of people, Lorin included, in the chapel through a scrim that resembled a dusty spider web torn in places, letting lights flit through like fireflies. A door opened in the wall and an elderly man with a thatch of white hair stepped down and turned to help a stout, white-haired woman climb through. She wore opaque stockings and breathed heavily as she straightened her skirt. The two of them stood over the chair and looked at Lorin's father. Dead, isn't he, said the woman. Looks like it, said the man. He touched Lorin's father's shoulder and the body tipped and fell out of the chair.

That was not satisfactory, and Lorin let it fade. "In the Garden" was over and the next speaker—it was Bill Thornbury, one of his father's business associates—was telling a story about Charles refusing a drink once at a professional convention and as a result getting the prize account or something like that. Lorin hoped there would be more stories like that. They would do his mother good. Katy had given him an appalling report on their mother when she had picked him up at the airport. The elders had come over and given his mother a blessing with consecrated oil; and ten minutes later she couldn't remember they had done it and asked why they were there and why didn't they give her a blessing. Later in the same day Sonia had found her sitting in the station wagon in the garage with her hands folded in her lap. The doors were locked and Sonia had had to beat on the window. Her mother had rolled it down then and said, "Where is

Charles and why do I feel so bad?'' Lorin himself had found her
talking to his father's picture in the study yesterday, and not just
talking but evidently listening too, because there were pauses in
her monologue, and then she would say something in the tone
she used when she was contradicting you. He had been on the
point of turning and quietly leaving, but she had looked up. ''Just
seeing how you were,'' he said. ''I'm talking to your father's picture,'' she said, irritated. ''I'll come back later,'' he said. At least
she had known it was a picture. He ventured a glance at her now,
while Thornbury was telling the story about how Charles took
a wrong turnoff on a dirt road once while driving back from an
oil field in Nevada years ago and had found himself at three in
the morning hopelessly lost, with two smashed headlights, somewhere deep in the Wah Wah Mountains. Lorin knew she had
heard that story a hundred times, and he noticed she was smiling as she listened to Bill tell it again. The point of the story was
the spiritual experience his father had when he entered the mouth
of an old mine drift to pray, and since that part always made Lorin uncomfortable—in fact it gave him the creeps—he tuned out
and decided to try one more time.

Resuming was difficult. Vapors flitted back and forth behind
a grainy transparency and gradually hardened into the old couple
moving around the room tidying up. His father still lay on the
floor, his nose flattened sideways and his arms flung out. The
old man gripped him under the arms and hefted him to his knees
and then his feet, where he stood tottering. The old woman fitted
his glasses back onto his face and straightened his collar. Get him
looking nice, she said. That's what we'll do.

The gist of the story was that Lorin's father, in the mine drift,
had felt a strong presence of something that loved him, and he
had gotten up from his knees and strode out of the cavity in the
hillside with a confident step, able to see every rock in his way,
every piece of broken timber over which he might have fallen,
even though it was three o'clock in the morning and there was
no moon, made his way through sagebrush and juniper to his
car, though he had wandered from it a long way, and had driven
away, unerringly selecting the correct dirt road that was indistin-
guishable from every other dirt road, knowing precisely at which
point to drive over an embankment into the dry riverbed and how
far along in which direction to follow the bed before climbing the
other side and confronting another bewildering maze of rutted
trails, of which he would select the right one, his rods and cones
reproportioned miraculously, his sense of choice touched by divine hands in the dark; and Lorin was glad when it was over,
and the woman from the mortuary sang the Twenty-third Psalm,

which Alicebeth, he suspected, would have been happy to sing if she had been asked.

He caught up to them in the dark corridor, his father stumbling between them as they guided him around brooms and buckets and old typewriters. They stopped at a doorway covered by an iron lattice. The old man pressed a button and the floor vibrated. When the car had settled into place they got on and leaned his father in a corner where he stared at the lighted numbers above the door as the elevator shuddered and began to move. Hope we don't stop between floors, said the old woman. The old man grunted. They ascended slowly while the last speaker, Rex Evans, the elders' quorum president, stood up and walked to the pulpit, buttoning his coat. Lorin glanced at his mother. She looked interested. Stephen was sitting with his elbows on his knees and his head between his hands. He ran his fingers through his long hair as though looking for something to pull. Rex, it seemed, was just going to read some things that Charles had liked. He cleared his throat and took his glasses out of his breast pocket.

The elevator stopped and they helped Lorin's father out and led him, each holding an arm, down a long hallway whose carpet was worn to the threads and coming up along the wall, exposing ridges of dirt. They passed doors whose knobs had fallen off and whose windows were dark. Some doors stood open and Lorin could see desks and chairs piled into corners next to windows which gave onto air shafts with broken windows on the other side. Fingermarks blotted the gold leaf on the walls, and initials had been carved into doorjambs. They passed a sullen angel sitting in a doorway, his white robe open to his navel and stained yellow around the buttonholes. He watched them go by but didn't move. They entered a large parlor where a dozen old people sat in wooden chairs against a wall. Two or three stared at them as they came in. A shriveled lady with a ribbon around her neck put a hand to her mouth and tittered. They led him to a crone in a wheelchair. Kiss your grandma, son, the old man said. She's been waiting to see you since I can't remember when. Lorin's father's eyes, their whites the color of saffron, flicked left and right. His mouth curled at the corners and a drool escaped as he bent to kiss the thin hair through which her pink little scalp flaked. Her dentures clicked in pleasure and she waggled her fingers, straining against the straps on her wrists. Here's your grandpa, the old woman said. They stood him upright and turned him around. A skinny old man with pants too big at the waist stared up at him. You got my peepstone? he asked. Lorin's father reeled backward and fell over a cart containing a stack of clean towels and a bedpan. Lost my damn peepstone, the old gentleman said. A burly angel in a lab coat led him away, and the old couple helped Lorin's father to his feet again and restored his glasses to his face. Time to meet the rest of them, the old man said. Sweeten up now, the old woman said.

Through the closing hymn, Lorin watched his father led from chair to chair to meet palsied ancestors who stared at their laps or grinned at remote memories. When he had met them all the old couple led him to a balcony and propped him carefully in a webbed lawn chair. Don't touch the rail now, the old man said. It's loose and you'll fall. They left him and went inside, leaving the door ajar in case he fell anyway. Lorin and Stephen and Katy's husband joined the other pallbearers—a cousin and his two sons—in carrying the casket down the steps to the hearse. It felt as heavy as a piano, and Lorin watched his brother's back. Stephen had done very well. During the short drive to the cemetery and along the winding roads between spruce trees and sycamores inside the gates, Lorin kept an eye on his father sitting in the lawn chair. His arms hung down and his head was tipped back. Through the thick glasses, the yellow eyes stared out over a landscape of broken spires and roofs that had fallen in and winding roads that had buckled away from the sides of mountains, and huge mansions whose walls had slid into heaps of rubble exposing empty corridors down which tiny dark figures flitted, keeping to the shadows. There was the barest movement of the eyes in their pink bath as they watched pale things that flew in the murk that deepened out of the canyons.

At the gravesite, the pallbearers hefted the casket onto the suspended bands over the hole and stepped back. Lorin took his brother aside while the others were gathering around the grave.

"Thanks, little brother," he said, and put a hand on Stephen's arm.

Stephen flung the hand off. "Don't ever try that shit with me again," he said. His face was white.

Lorin went and found his mother and the girls. The four of them stood together while Katy's husband dedicated the grave. The women's heads were bowed. Lorin kept an arm around his mother and looked around at the crowd gathered behind them and on the other side of the hole. It was a long prayer. Lorin could see Stephen at the edge of the crowd, ashen-faced and sullen, smoking cigarettes and grinding them into the grass with his heel. Later, as they all returned to the cars, Stephen walked at some distance from the rest of them, and during the drive home Lorin kept looking at him but Stephen wouldn't meet his eye.

"I hate to leave him there," his mother said.

"You know he's okay, Mother," Sonia said.

———

At the house afterward, while the relatives and friends ate the meat loaf and casseroles and jello salads and rolls and carrot sticks and radishes brought in large baskets by the ward Relief Society, the two of them went out to the back yard with the pint of scotch Lorin had brought with him in his suitcase. They sat on their heels side by side, hidden by the garage, leaning against the white clapboard wall and took turns with the bottle while Lorin told Stephen what he thought of him for being the disrespectful, callous, thoughtless, and unfeeling little shit he had turned out to be. Lorin was very disappointed in his brother. He had been for years.

# 24

$L$orin crawled out of bed and felt his way on his hands and knees across the floor to where his alarm clock buzzed, and shut it off. He sat for a few minutes with his back against the wall, holding his head with one hand until the nausea went away, and with the other cradling his penis so it didn't touch the floor. The room swam with gauzy wings. In a few minutes he got up and plugged in the popcorn popper he had filled with water the night before and shook instant coffee from a jar into his mug. The mug was brown from not having been washed, and he could feel a crust on the rim with his thumb. While he waited for his water to heat he groped in the cardboard box under the table for his spiral drawing pad and his jar of pencils, which he carried back to bed, and then he went to pour his coffee. The water was only tepid but he didn't want to wait. The light in the room was the color of cold chrome. He reset his alarm clock for two hours hence and turned it to the wall so he wouldn't be able to see it getting close to the time it would buzz again, and then returned to the bed and opened his pad to the first clean page.

Kneeling over it, feeling the lumps of twisted blanket under his shins, his face close to the paper so he could make out what he was doing without turning on the overhead light, he began to draw lines. He had been drawing lines for a week, ever since he discovered he had begun cheating, and he thought he was beginning to see improvement. When your intuitions were behaving you could let them go for a while and concentrate on your technique. That brought tone back to your motor nerves and refreshed your spirit. Today's lines, for instance, were already more supple and various than yesterday's lines. Yesterday he had begun to coax contrasting thicknesses out of his pencil's tip by a careful adjustment of thumb pressure and the angle of his wrist, without slowing or speeding the movement of his hand across the page, and today he was able to take that flexibility for granted while he drew lines that would do other things as well. He watched as a line materialized in the track of his pencil that resembled a python that had swallowed a pig, and then abruptly—the extension of the line also changed the scale of the thing it resembled—an earthworm with its seven pulpy hearts, and then a distant horizon with clots of forest at uneven intervals. It was a small accomplishment, he was prepared to admit that, and that was why it was better not to have friends. You had to explain things to friends. That had been his problem before. He had felt that every moment had to justify itself. Today's lines were richer than yesterday's lines, and it was better knowing that no one had seen yesterday's lines and gone away thinking they were the best you could do. He covered his page with lines and turned to the next page, feeling the impress of lines from the page he had just covered on the surface of the clean white one. Lines could be invisible and tactile, and drawing visible lines across a surface already scored with the other kind deepened the mystery of intersecting surfaces.

He didn't draw the same kinds of lines every day. Today for instance he drew long lines, that thickened as they reached the end and then attenuated and ended vaporously. Yesterday he had drawn short lines that had one hard edge and one soft one that feathered off into the pores of the paper. The day before yesterday he had drawn lines that seemed to emerge from the paper rather than track across it, and implied their own continuity under the skin of the paper. Wavy lines were something he hadn't learned to be comfortable with yet. He had devoted a couple of days to wavy lines but had dropped them when he found them trying to conform to the shape of an object, because his purpose for now was to draw lines that had their own integrity, into which objects would have to work their own way. He would return to wavy lines later. Wavy lines had another problem. They seemed to suggest movement, and until he could create the illusion of movement within the nerves of a static line, he would not take the easy way out.

As the light in the room increased he was able to work with his face a little farther from his pad, and eventually to kneel upright, which relieved him, because he had felt like a toad in the earlier position and had developed a cramp in his elbow. He could hear cars beginning to go past, and knew that soon his alarm clock would go off again and he would have to eat something and dress and go to work. He raised up once to ease his back and realized he had gone hard. He paused long enough to pour another cup of coffee, knowing he was going to regret it later in the morning, and went around the room straightening books on the table and sorting through neckties draped over their hanger until he was normal again, and then returned to the bed.

He turned to the next page, determined to do as much as he could before he had to leave, and already preparing his plans for tomorrow's lines. Tomorrow maybe he'd use a brush and ink again. It was important to alternate your media, because they determined the character of your line and the whole way you went about producing it. Soft pencils left a track that turned to mush across the paper and it was tempting to let them do all the work for you, so from time to time you worked with hard pencils, number threes or harder, that had no forgiveness to them and forced you to create the illusion of nuance when in fact there was none. He liked charcoal too. Charcoal left a dusty residue like a soiled ghost on either side of the line you were drawing. Ball-point pens didn't give you back anything, they felt inert in your hand, but you sometimes found they had left an interesting line that degenerated into gaps and hyphens and then dropped an ugly clot of black paste to harden on the page. Fountain pens made your whole arm feel unstable as you drew, and that was exciting, like being just on the edge of control all the time. Lettering pens with India ink and a variety of nibs gave you a hearty succulent line that flexed and bullied its way across the page and seeped through, leaving a porous replica of itself on the next page. Brushes loaded with ink or watercolor made a wobbly, clownish line or a line of apparent ease and suppleness, depending on something as small as whether you woke up happy or frightened. It embarrassed him how much he was looking forward to the lines he was going to draw tomorrow and the next day. Beginning the day after that, perhaps, he would let his lines touch, and would see what that produced. He would cause a dense line to intersect with a wispy, attenuated one. He would draw one with a downy back and let it rub against a crisp thin cursive one, and allow the point of contact to absorb and radiate the charge from the rest of the blank page. He would place two lines at an oblique angle to each other, not touching but straining to touch, their system of tensions creating an energy in the white space between them and a void in the white space outside. He would cause substance to well up and enter his lines and the implied surfaces between them, and have come from nowhere, and be there even if nobody was looking at them.

He turned to the last page he would be able to fill. The room was an opalescent pearl-grey now, with stripes of white sunlight cutting across the wall, and he knew he was nearly out of working time. He filled the new page with short, eyelash-shaped lines, drawn upward rather than downward, precisely because it opposed his hand's natural inclinations, and working outward from a point just below the center of the page because his impulse had been to begin at the top and far right and work toward the center. He heard his alarm clock make the sound it always made just before it went off, and dropped his pencil and lunged across the room to stop it before it did. This was the same small white square electric Seth Thomas—now with a cracked casing—he had used on his mission and which had given him a nasty surprise one morning when he had reached to shut it off without looking. He always plugged it into a wall on the other side of any room he slept in now, so that however deeply he might be sleeping when it buzzed he would have time to see it before he got there to shut it off. You couldn't stop them from touching your things, if that was what they were going to do, but you didn't have to blunder into them in the dark.

He ate a bowl of granola sitting cross-legged on his bed in the corner, holding the bowl close to his chin so he wouldn't drip milk into the hair on his stomach. He had outgrown his squalid but comfortable little room, and as soon as he got his next raise he intended to move. The walls were covered with drawings he had torn from sketchbooks and thumbtacked there to study where his lines had gone soft, and he would need more walls. The drawings contained the germ of a hundred studies, more than he could work out on canvas in a year. He sometimes got a prickly feeling on the soles of his feet when he studied them, because he was not sure why he should have been able to do them. They had been culled from the thousands of sketches he had made in the pre-dawn hours over several months, and he had made them without a model. The result was unsettling. The faces, for one thing, had a look of specificity to them, as though he had known their owners intimately. Tacked to the wall over his bed were sheets of paper covered with thin faces, warped and disturbed faces, faces with beaky noses and warts under the eyes, faces whose mouths had irregular teeth and smirking corners. There were faces of young women in heat, of boys with nasty habits, of crones who had no food in their cupboards. There were faces of men who were successful but had cheated. There were patriarchal men with kindly smiles but whose breath you knew smelled of dirty cheese. He had never achieved this level of verisimilitude working from a model. There were faces of gnomes and sorcerers too, and faces of men that distended themselves into faces of animals. The curve of a cheekbone, the pulpy firmness of a lower lip, the droop of skin under one eye came from

BONES

238

no place in particular that he could identify; it was as though they inhabited the paper he drew on and he had only located the parts and drawn them out like string.

But there were things besides faces. On the wall across from him there were whole bodies, for instance, and these surprised him more than the faces, because bodies had proportions and articulations that were not static, but changed with each change in gesture, and you always risked getting the further arm or leg out of perspective with the nearer one if you worked without a model. But he didn't. There were dancing women in feathery gowns; there were men holding pieces of furniture or climbing murky staircases. There were drawings of creatures that had no names. Some were concealed in dark interiors, their presence merely suggested by highlights made with a putty eraser.

He put his face into the bowl, glad that no one could see him, and licked up the last of the milk and the few clots of granola he had missed with his spoon. He carried the spoon and bowl across the hall into the bathroom with him and rinsed them out before he got into the tub. While soaping out his pores he reflected that it was a good day when you had done your lines and hit the traffic patterns right and got to work on time, had your clearings run and your checks filed in time to drink coffee upstairs before the bank opened. Those few precious stolen minutes— provided no one came over to talk to you—allowed you to assimilate what you had learned from the lines you had done this morning and to project what things they had made you capable of that you weren't capable of yesterday. Routine was a virtue. You could measure progress against routine—this day six months ago I was here, eight months ago there. That he disliked his job was irrelevant; he had always disliked his job. What was important was that no one paid attention to him and that he got a small raise every few months—his missionary suits were beginning to wear out—and that painting by artificial light sometimes created striking color combinations because you always over-corrected for yellow and didn't know by how much until you saw it in the morning.

By the time he heard the rap on the door he was drying his chest and the bathroom was filled with sunlight from the window over the tub. He looked at his ghostly image in the steamed-over mirror and saw the nimbus where his eyes should be. Before the end of the day his bones would feel alive too. He wrapped his towel around his waist and picked up his spoon and bowl and razor from the wash basin and walked out past a small huddled creature in a bathrobe, with a face like cottage cheese, and heard the bathroom door slam before he had gotten his own door open. Inside his room he rummaged in another box and found clean underwear—he had not worn temple garments for a couple of years, and still felt incomplete without them—and two socks that looked alike and put them on. He selected a pale blue shirt from a hanger on the steam pipe, and while buttoning it watched the woman on the balcony of the adjacent house lower a cat to the ground in a bucket. He debated whether to wear his tweed jacket and his grey flannel pants or a suit, and if a suit whether his brown one or his navy one or his black one. He went to the window where the light was better and held up a foot to look at it. The sock seemed to be navy rather than black. He stepped into his navy-blue trousers, shuddering slightly at the familiar feel of wool next to the skin. Knotting his tie in front of the bubbly mirror propped against a stack of books on the table, he avoided his eyes and concentrated on the number of times he had wrapped the long end around the short one. Then he untied it and did it again, feeling the sweat start to run down his legs. As a last thing, he carried his shoes to the window and examined them. He licked his thumb and rubbed out a smudge on the toe of one, then pulled them on and tightened the buckles. He filled his pockets with the litter of items on his table—keys, change, comb, wallet—slipped his watch on, then his jacket, and then went out the door, locking it, and went down the stairs to his car, mindful that they tampered with your sketchbooks in your absence.

———

Yvonne came into the bank one day, and he hid behind a pillar in statements until she was gone. That afternoon he clawed through the signature-card file, knowing he would not find her there, at least not under her own last name, because he would have seen it before now, somewhere, on something. He hated himself for not having stepped out in his suit and tie, nodded to her, and then passed on with a puzzled frown. He regretted not having watched to see what she was doing at Maxine's window. That would have told him at least whether she had an account there, and he would have spent patient weeks watching for her signature with its distinctive slovenly handwriting and her first name to turn up and scald him across the eyes. After work he offered to buy Maxine a drink at Mario's in order to sift her in case she happened to remember the woman with the wicker handbag crusted over with shells who had come to her window just before lunch—sometimes a customer would say something to make you remember her—but he had never offered to buy Maxine a drink before, and she made some excuse, looking at him with worried eyes. It was all right. He had better things to do than inquire after ghosts. He had been startled, was all.

This was on the same day that street people had barricaded the sidewalk in front of Lew Ritter's in the Village, using oil drums stuffed with old clothes and set on fire. It was also the same day Janet had asked to be transferred to the Pasadena branch—he was sorry about that, he liked Janet—and that he learned Sam Bandera, one of his old teachers at UCLA, had died. He found that out from a copy of the Daily Bruin that one of the part-time tellers had left in the coffee room. The copy was a couple of days old, and he reflected, eating his tuna sandwich, that Sam would be cold and buried by now. Sam wouldn't have remembered him, but Lorin nevertheless felt a sense of loss. It was also the day he had hit all the signals wrong coming in from Santa Monica and consequently reached his usual parking lot too late to find a space and had been forced to use the multi-level lot at Bullock's, which made him late and guaranteed him an expensive ticket, and forced him into a different traffic pattern when he left to go home. A lane was blocked, and he had to turn right on Westwood Boulevard, which carried him into the university campus, which was overflowing with cars going the opposite direction. There was no turning around while the rush was on, and he didn't want to continue on through campus and join the logjam at the Sunset exit, so he pulled into a lot by the gymnasiums—it was after hours, so he could park free—and got out and sat on a bench to wait. He felt conspicuous in his grey suit, but it was nearly dusk, and presently he wouldn't be noticeable. He reflected that he had experienced two links with his past on the same day and had handled himself very well, except for the small embarrassment with Maxine. It was just as well that Maxine had declined, because she would have asked questions out of politeness and he would have had to rake up old fires, which would have interfered with the work he wanted to do that night.

Evening smells drifted across the stream of cars that now had their headlights on, and it was pleasant to remember that most of his enemies were still young. He was able to distinguish the eucalyptus and ocean smells, and from somewhere the sweet odor of cut grass, and the inexplicable smell of fried meat, and the smell of pink light off a cloud bank in the west; and then something horrible happened. He had been watching a girl in a miniskirt cross the lawn at the bottom of the brick steps at the distant end of the lower quad, where the turf sloped down into a wide shallow bowl. She was heading toward the women's gym and for the moment was alone on the dark grass. She had a book bag slung over a shoulder and was barefoot, and her hair kept blowing into her face. She was too far away for Lorin to see her face reliably, or even to know if the pleasant lust he felt at the sight of her quick bare thighs was justified, but he liked watching the way she enjoyed her own visibility, alone, blue and yellow against a landscape of black pine trees and brick steps and serpentine concrete paths flanked with lamp poles whose globes were starting to flicker on. As he watched, her head came off and floated gently behind her, the long hair still fluttering, until the appalling torso had taken a few steps out of range, and then it dropped to the grass and rolled into a low spot behind one of the concrete benches. One of her legs had dropped out of the skirt and lay thrashing on the ground, while the other one, no longer able to carry the body in the normal way, bent at the knee once and took a weak little hop, and suddenly one arm dropped off at the elbow, and the fingers scattered from the hand like seeds. The torso wrenched apart at the line marked by the belt of her skirt, and while the skirt itself flapped off toward the trees the pelvis toppled from the leg that held it up and bounced away like a furry soccer ball. Her thorax, with its remaining arm and the stub of another, hung motionless while the wind ripped the blouse from it, and then splintered into ribs and dropped to the grass, spread too far apart to come together again. Two bent little old men came out from under the apron of low branches on the spruce trees and hobbled over. One of them carried a short spade and began digging a hole in the lawn while the other one limped back and forth picking up the arm and head, a leg, a handful of phalanges, and dropped them in the hole. They pushed the dirt back into place and adjusted the turf, and then, after peering into the gathering darkness in every direction, they bent low and embraced each other around the shoulders, their foreheads and noses together, and danced a fast jig on the spot where they had dug, and ran off into the trees again, holding the spade between them. He waited a while longer, until the line of cars had loosened and thinned out, and then went back to his Volkswagen and drove home to his secret life.

———

It was an unimportant gallery on Crenshaw, and he had to share it with two other painters, and his first name had been misspelled on the mailed invitations, but it was his first exhibition, and it lasted for a week. Lorin drove down every night that week after work, and looked at the guest book to see if anyone he knew had come in, and then strolled up and down pretending to be a patron, looking at the suspended canvases on all the walls, his arms folded across his chest, leaning forward here, stepping back there, his heart pounding. There were never any familiar names in the guest book, and he never saw anyone he knew in the gallery. There were never more than three or four people there at a time, either, but they seemed to be a different three or four each night, and that pleased him. He listened to as many conversations as he could without appearing rude, but he could do that without much trouble because even very quiet voices carried in an uncarpeted gallery that didn't have many people in it.

He liked to be fair, so he always strolled first past Brad Smith's collection. They were pleasant, he enjoyed looking at them. Brad did crowded cityscapes full of colored lights reflected off wet streets. His buildings and cars and shiny pedestrians had a gnarled, carbuncly look to them, an effect that Lorin knew he could never do himself, but he was content to let Brad Smith be the one who did them. He would always spend a few minutes after that looking at Susan Fellows's collection. Susan did smooth desert landscapes like tanned leather, that had dunes rippling toward you out of a middle distance and things like oblong flat mirrors suspended in the sky like windows. They were pleasant too. Susan and Brad both did pleasant work. Then he strolled past his own collection, fearful each time that he would not like it as well, but he always did.

He always began with the pea pod. The pea pod was hung in an inconvenient place—if someone was at the drinking fountain you had to wait till he was through, and by that time you might have lost interest—but the light was good. The pod itself gaped open like spread labia, a resemblance that had startled him when he overheard a couple talking in front of it. Looking at it through new eyes after they had gone on to the dead angel painting, he had to admit he had inadvertently painted a green cunt, shining and wet, crowded with peas, many more than a normal pod would contain. The peas themselves were of various densities. Some were solid and rough, with irregular bumps and knobs like asteroids, others were hard and smooth like pool balls, still others were shimmery and indistinct, and occupied the same spaces with the solid ones, overlapping like a double exposure. It had been an experiment in mixing modes of reality—how many peas from how many planes of existence could cohabit in the same canvas, much less the same pod?—and he had made it an experiment in simultaneous perspectives as well. Some of the peas, the solid as well as the vaporous ones, loomed swollen as though seen under a magnifying glass; others, some of them clearly closer to the viewer because they eclipsed bigger ones, were small and shriveled, as though seen through the wrong end of a telescope from the top of a hedge.

The nasty little creature who had shaken his bed and scuttled away hung in a recess between two of the double self-portraits. He always studied it with conflicting feelings. He had painted it conscious that he could not be certain whether he was working from original recall or redacting the drawing he had made immediately afterward. It was grotesque enough, though scarcely traceable against the pattern of the carpet it scuttled across, and partly masked by the waving bedclothes, but he could not, if someone asked him to, lay his hand on his heart and swear confidently that a secondary dimension of artifice had not crept in between himself and the object he was attempting to connect to. He had used a tangled construct of coat hangers as his model, supplemented by strips of torn sheet and a skein of blue yarn. The creature in the garden—it hung over the desk with the visitors' book—had proved almost insuperable, and every time he looked at it he took pleasure in remembering the process of approaching, being deflected from, and ultimately solving a difficult problem. He had tried several studies of it, in soft pencil, in crowquill on green paper, in charcoal, in watercolor, but it always seemed to turn out either a tall insect or a Martian in a helmet. Finally he had noticed that in each successive study the flowers and leaves and boysenberries in the garden took over more and more, crowding even the pivotal hollyhock, and so he had let it go its own way. The finished canvas crawled with ripening vegetation—swollen roses, succulent geraniums, a splatter of sweet williams and forget-me-nots, intricate difficult leaf systems —behind which the creature itself was invisible. He nevertheless had titled it "The Creature in the Garden," and enjoyed seeing that title in capital letters on the small card fixed to the wall next to it; and he enjoyed overhearing people ask each other where the hell it was and not telling them, even though he knew.

There were five or six other paintings of his in the exhibit; they were at least a year old and he had included them only because he felt the numbers were necessary. He had had to look carefully through the accretion of his paintings of that year to find five or six that wouldn't embarrass him, and he was not displeased with these. They were essentially exercises but they had a certain meretricious charm—a potted fern in a porcelain bucket, a fluted vase with long strands of ivy dripping out of it, that sort of thing. In fact it was one of these—a small canvas showing an old-fashioned bathtub standing free in a room without walls, only bare timbers, at the top of a flight of wooden stairs—that had actually sold. He had walked in one evening and seen the tag taped to the bottom of the frame, and had gone immediately back to the office, his heart pounding, to ask George or Shirley for details. The buyer was no one he had heard of, and a part of him felt sick at the thought that he would never see that bathtub and those exposed beams and that staircase again. It had been an exercise in displaced still-life. The bathtub was the short, deep kind you used to find in old houses in rural Utah, that had brass taps and a blue beehive stamped into the porcelain. He had found it in the window of a plumbing and heating store in Inglewood one Sunday afternoon and had stood there drawing it carefully into his spiral pad while people passed him on the sidewalk, some of them stopping to look over his shoulder, which had driven him wild. The wooden stairs were the basement stairs in Gloriana's house, which he had drawn a long time before and kept, never knowing when he might use them; the room without walls was from the ground floor of a house on Pico that was being demolished to make room for a real-estate office; he had gotten there with his pad the last day the shell was standing, and had drawn furiously, while the wreckers had given him a bad time, standing in front of him striking silly poses and telling him to draw them if he was such a hot-shit drawer. The apricot-colored sky behind the bathtub had come from the last evening he had spent in his parents' back yard after his father's funeral and before flying back to Los Angeles. He had made a quick watercolor sketch of it while the relatives had come and gone in the yard and the house and his brother had watched him. He had not worried too much about the shape of the clouds or the slit across the surface caused by the telephone wires or the grotesque hieroglyphs of birds against the clouds; he had just concentrated on catching the saturation of the orange and pink as nearly as he could, and committing it to memory. He had put all these together in the small oil study and had been surprised at how well the parts had seized onto each other and cohered.

He made a point of coming back, the last night of his exhibit, to see what the owner of his painting looked like when he came to pick it up. It proved to be a pleasant elderly man in a black overcoat and pointed brown Italian shoes, who told Lorin, when Shirley introduced them, how pleased he was to meet him and how impressed he had been with his exhibition last year in Laguna Beach. Lorin had never been to Laguna Beach, much less had an exhibition there, but he did not want to embarrass the old gentleman, so he smiled vaguely past his shoulder and offered his hand one last time. He did feel he owed an explanation to Shirley, whom he could feel looking at him, but that could wait.